COSMIC FORCES:

THE PANDORANS

THE PANDORANS:

BOOK TWO

THE PANDORA INHERITANCE

or
☾ Amethyst Pyne
and the
Higgledy-Piggledy Mess ☽

THE PANDORA INHERITANCE

ALEX JAMES

COSMIC FORCES

THE PANDORANS
Book One: The Pandora Sequence
Book Two: The Pandora Inheritance
Book Three: The Omega Sequence
Book Four: The Pandora Arcana
Book Five: The Sirens Sequence
Book Six: The Daughters of Pandora
Book Seven: The Lucifer Sequence

AMAZON SEVEN
Book One: Mission Queen
Book Two: Impulse Attractor
Book Three: Queen Renegade
Book Four: Intergalactic Ingenue
Book Five: Princess Executor

THE CHRONICLES OF THE TERRAGUARD
Book One: Maker of Rules
Book Two: Valley of Death
Book Three: Ship of Fools

SAGA OF THE URBAN SORCERERS
Book One: The Summoning of Barker Moon
Book Two: The Reckoning of Emerald Tarragon
Book Three: The Shaping of Cheryl Equinox

DARK STREETS
Book One: Agents of Fear
Book Two: Avatars of Wrath

Also:
Venus IA

Author's Note

A big thanks to all the people who contacted me to say they enjoyed "The Pandora Sequence."

Given that it did seem to suggest a larger universe to explore, I have taken that path.

However, the strange and circuitous circumstances of how this and the subsequent novels in "The Pandorans" series came to be ended up forming a fairly mystically intriguing story in themselves.

Suffice to say that (as with "The Pandora Sequence") once the decision was made to keep writing about The Pandorans, things did indeed "get weirder".

Once again, have a read, see what happens.

Alex James
September 2019

The Pandorans
Book Two: The Pandora Inheritance

Cover Design and Illustration by Lily McDonnell

Book production by Ingram Spark.

Paperback Edition 3.0
(some typographical corrections, several extended scenes)

February 2020

This book is dedicated to the memory and works of

Alan Watts

"

You

are

an aperture

through which the universe

is looking at

and exploring

itself.

"

PAST IS PROLOGUE

Mitch sat on the couch in Pan's apartment.

It was almost empty now, just a few boxes and the couch to go.

He was trying to write on a small white pad, without much success.

There was a white flash in the room before him and he spoke without looking up.

'Been wondering when you'd turn up.'

'Hi, Dad.'

'Too late to help with the moving.'

'You have telekinesis and gaps. What more help do you want?'

'Just teasing, sweetheart.'

'What are you writing?'

Mitch shrugged. 'Nothing.'

He extended the pad to Amethyst.

She shrugged. 'What do you want me to do with this? It's been so long I've probably forgotten how!'

She accepted the pad and pen nevertheless.

'I want you to make a list for me.'

'A list?'

'Just a short one. I want you to write down the names of the six people you trust most in the world.' Mitch smiled. 'Okay?'

THE PANDORA INHERITANCE

PART ONE

TALLER

CHAPTER 1

Amy thought for a second.

She had come here for something else, something specific, but now she had this to contend with.

'I hijacked your thoughts, didn't I sweetie?'

'Kind of.'

She found herself caught off-guard at how much she loved her silly old Dad these days.

'It's okay.'

She quickly scribbled down the six names, at the same time wondering how long it had actually been since she had used a real pen and paper to create a message, then put the pad and pen back on the desk. 'Huh.'

'What, sweetie?'

'I'd forgotten how elegant it is, to do that. That's a nice pen.'

Mitch smiled. Amy's heart swelled when she saw the deep affection her father had for her. 'What brings you by, Ames?'

'I just wanted to say…' Amy shrugged. '…I mean; I wanted to let you know…'

'You're okay?'

'Yeah. Not that. Well, kind of that.'

'You're *kind of* okay?'

Amy spat it out. 'Dad, I think things are going to get weird.'

'Weird?'

'Yep.'

'How weird?'

'Just, *weird*. I mean, this time around, I think things are gonna get *really weird*.'

'You just went from vanilla weird to *really weird* in under three seconds.'

'Okay. I did, didn't I?' She looked absently around the almost-empty apartment. 'Anyway, I just thought I should swing by, and give you the heads-up on that. This time, the weirdness is coming back, weirder than before.'

'You said 'this time' again.'

'I did, didn't I?' Amy shrugged, smiling sheepishly.

Mitch stood from the couch. She could tell that he was surprised. She wall taller now, almost as tall as him, she realised, and her father was fairly tall. She was wearing boots though, with thick soles. Her Dad reached out and toucher her hair, just brushing the side of her temple, pushing a loose lock back over her ear.

'I like your hair back like that.'

'Mum doesn't.'

He made a face. 'You've seen your Mum?'

She laughed. 'No. I came straight here. Just; the last time. She likes it down. Sexy.'

'She said that?'

'No, but, you know. What she's like. What she wants me to be like.'

Her father huffed, but smiled sympathetically. 'Your mother and I do not agree on many things, but sometimes I do understand her.' He nodded. 'Your hair tied back like this; it makes you look… mature?'

'*Old?*'

'No!' Mitch laughed. 'Like a serious young woman. You know what your mother is like when it comes to…'

'Vanity?'

'I was going to say aging.'

'That is seriously not a word you can use within earshot of mother.' Suddenly she threw herself into her father's arms and hugged him as tightly as she could. 'She always tries to manage me. If only she knew what I was really doing.'

She let go, and stood back again. Her father had tears in his eyes, and now so did she; then he put both hands on her shoulders and looked her right in her eyes.

'You can never tell her, sweetie.' His steely blue irises looked extremely fatherly. 'All this business with the Pandora Sequence, the astral plane, the Anunnaki; it has to stay our secret – only the people who went through it together can know.'

Amy nodded. 'I know, but something's really starting up again, Dad. Something – soon.'

Mitch sighed and let her go.

'Well…'

Then he looked around and scratched his head.

'…I guess that was bound to happen, sooner or later. Things have a way of doing that, don't they?'

'Yep.' Amy nodded, putting her hands on her hips and looking around absently as well. 'They sure do.'

'Weird, huh?'

'Yep.'

'Like things weren't weird enough last time?'

Amy shrugged.

She'd been thinking about this one.

'Well, if you think about it Dad, I mean; you're in your early forties. You made it through your teens, and university, and now you've been a proper adult for like, what? Twenty plus years, right? And in the space of those years, your life has had ups and downs, like everyone, but apart from the odd brush with Uncle Pan, and some minor celebrity, it was all pretty normal; a fairly normal, middle to upper-middle existence, up until he got himself shot. In fact, even in a normal life, it is pretty normal to have a friend who's a bit 'out-there', who drops in and out over the years, right?'

'Until that friend gets shot, and put in a coma?' Mitch was looking slightly bemused. 'One supposes…?'

Amy rolled her eyes and pushed on. 'So, the one *truly weird* thing that has happened to you was not so long ago. And granted; I mean it truly was a *huge, huge, blow-out bag of weird*, right there, no denying that, but, like; it is, in fact, only about… one percent? Of your whole life? Right? One percent of your whole life that has actually been really, truly, star-gate trees, reptilian overlords, 'my drama teacher is the devil', I prevented a million-plus deaths by talking to ancient-cosmic-influencers weird. Right?'

Mitch held his breath.

'Well... when you put it that way.'

Mitch couldn't help but admit.

'...okay, I suppose you do have a point. Or, a perspective there, at least...'

'Well, whereas, my life, or, okay, from *my perspective*, I mean; I didn't even get through my teens before "The Big Weird" hit. I mean, I'm not even twenty-one yet, right? At least, I don't think I am. You can kind of lose track, on the astral plane.'

'Time certainly works differently there, as we well know. Speaking of which, we should really do the protoc –'

'Exactly! And like, this big, weird wave we all caught, that is really just *base-line normal* for me; that is a wave I am still surfing, and which I will probably keep surfing, and it will roll right on through, as far as I can see, with me still on it; as far as *we all can see*, right? For all of us who took The Pandora Sequence? Really, it'll just roll on, right to the end, right? But for me, Pandora is... well, it's just... me. Just – normal me. Do you see?'

Mitch laughed, delighted.

'So, for my eldest daughter, weird is – "just life"? That's what you're telling your poor old middle-aged father?'

'It is.' She laughed back, perhaps not quite as delightedly.

There was no doubt however that Mitch Pyne had really changed now, she saw. So entirely-much for the better, so much more than the version she had known, and avoided, throughout the her late-teens, before this last, weird year had brought them back together.

'So, yeah. Perspective-wise, weird is really all I know. Weird isn't even my new normal. It just is. Or if you like, isn't. Weird, that is. Weird is my vanilla.'

'Point taken.' Mitch nodded. 'Do me a flavour...'

'Uhhh...'

'...and just rip the paper off the pad there, and fold it up and hand it to me, will you?'

Amy smiled as she obeyed, feeling she like had made her point. 'What is this?' She kidded her Dad. 'A magic trick?' She handed the folded paper to her father.

Mitch looked around, his eyes searching the remaining boxes. Pan's old gothic-style apartment seemed huge now everything had been cleared out, including the giant black bookshelves. All that remained were two piles of three boxes by the door, and two piles of two boxes beside each other on the couch, leaving just one empty seat. Amy knew that was where his father had sat to watch TV and binge-drink every night during last year, twenty-eleven, his bad year. That spot was where he had been sitting, thinking, and remembering, just then when she had popped in.

She wondered what he had been thinking about.

'Come out to the balcony with me. I want to show you something.'

CHAPTER 2

They walked across the empty room. The hiss of Mitch pushing the sliding door echoed through the apartment, then the sound of the city was there, along with the cold, and the odd, seldom-photographed view of the Sydney Harbour Bridge; the one you never saw on postcards, or from phone pics online, because it was only possible from the top floors of this old gothic apartment block, looking out between two skyscrapers, over a slightly less-tall heritage listed building.

'Wow. I forgot…'

Amy was momentarily awestruck.

She stared out at the Harbour Bridge for a while, doing her best to ignore the cold, realising that once the boxes and the couch were gone, she might not ever see this view ever again.

'…the world is filled with weird and beautiful angles, tucked away, where nobody knows.'

She stared on for another half a minute with her father beside her.

'Nobody really knows this place exists, do they?'

'There's about a dozen buildings like this left in the Sydney CBD. Owned by old families, and rich people. Some are swish hotels, but there are always floors like this that are private apartments. I hear Wyatt Styger's son uses the penthouse of the one with the gothic landings, a few blocks over, as an art studio. Rio DeVora has a couple, I think, that she rents out as offices; but now we have this one, and it has the best view.'

'We?'

'Well, the company. Olivera and Everco. Long story, legal labyrinth, but we have it. I think Everett wants to keep it here for Pan, so that when he wakes up out of that weird black Sirian coffin, he will always have a place. But we can't keep all his stuff here, all those occult books and anthropological artefacts. It's too powerful to have all in one place.'

'It helped him find you. It started all this.'

Mitch shrugged. 'Well, there's that I suppose.' He smiled at her. 'It's heritage listed; they all are. It might be looking right down Pitt Street, but it's just completely off the table for developers, so to speak. So now it's ours, and the city gets to keep it.'

Amy nodded and looked around at the big empty room, with its art deco cornices and chequered monochrome tiles, dark-wood fittings and gothic parlour alcove. 'The company. Olivera and Everco. Heather and Mitch?'

'Yeah. Makes you an heiress, you know.'

'Not sure I like that title.'

Again, Mitch shrugged. 'So, the company; so-called Lever. What about it?'

Amy could tell that her father liked the name about as much as she did, but she let it go. Instead, she frowned and tried to work out the view. 'Where the heck is the entrance to this building anyway? I don't think I've ever come in through the front door!'

'You get to the apartments through a back entrance. Tucked away, down one of those odd diagonal public laneways. Alcove and buzzer.' Mitch stared out. 'I won't miss this place, to be honest. Hardly been back here at all. Always creeped the hell out of me.'

'That'll all be gone, without all Pan's anthropological occult stuff here.'

She chuckled and he glanced at her sheepishly.

'So, how weird are we talking this time sweetie? If this is just – vanilla weird, so far?'

Amy nodded to herself. 'Well, remember how you were living here, and drinking and smoking too much, and you saw Uncle Pan's ghost, only it wasn't his ghost it was his astral body, and then Heather rescued you and introduced you to her Uncle Bo, and it turned out that it was all connected to Uncle Pan's experiments with the human genome and expanded consciousness down in Peru, and Aunt Saph was being influenced by an alien? And it all added up to there being other civilizations much older than ours in other dimensions, and how we all took a potion that gave us superpowers in a mansion owned by a billionaire who was being held hostage by Satan until Yelina the Earth Goddess destroyed it, and then I started a civil war on the astral plane between the Anunnaki reptilian clans, and you and Heather went right up to the top level of the cosmos and asked the Elohim to save everyone in Los Angeles from an earthquake that would have killed a million people and triggered the apocalypse, or something really like it?'

'Kind of hard to forget, sweetie.'

'Weirder than that.'

'Oh.' Mitch nodded. 'Okay.'

CHAPTER 3

Amy nodded to herself.

He seemed to take that pretty well.

She looked around at the balcony patio. The balcony table and chairs were still there, along with another very positive sign as to Mitch Pyne's growth; there were no empty wine bottles along the balcony edge, no beer cartons filled with empties, no overflowing ashtrays, or even stale mugs of half-finished coffee. Not as there had been, in abundance, the last time she had been here.

Mitch had really cleaned up, literally and figuratively. However, she did take particular note of two things; a line of drink cans along the back wall, and a small, plain cardboard box on the table. Written on the top were the words:

CALL ME

Mitch reached down and handed it up to her.

Amy smiled gratefully. 'What's this? A prezzie? A smartphone?' She snapped the top of the box open. 'Oh, I think I've seen the idea of these coming through, on the aastral plane…!'

Mitch shrugged. 'We think we might be able to break into the market.'

The packaging might have been plain, but as she slid the phone out, the design itself was anything but.

She gasped. 'It's totally transparent!'

'Yep.'

'And it's light as a feather!'

'Yep.'

'And you feel like… you can't drop it.'

'Yep.'

'Like it… just casually wants to help and protect you!'

'Yep.'

'How soon, Dad…?'

'A year or two, three. Maybe longer before we can retro-engineer the tech. But we'll get there. That one works, it's yours, but it's chockers full of Pleiadean tech. It charges continually from the wi-fi grid, bonds to your biorhythms, and becomes an extension of yourself. Nobody else can use it, it won't share anything you don't want, and you can do a complete online take-down on anything you regret posting.'

'Nobody's going to let this just…'

'We know. It's just a sample for us, for now. We know it can be made by Pleiadeans, but now we have to figure out how to make our own Earthen ones.'

'Earthen?'

'Their words. Earthen tech, for Earthlings, seems to be their chosen phraseology. So, go ahead and use it, and let us know how it goes.'

'Wow.'

'Texts and calls and data and all that will be routed through Everett's second hand Pleiadean ship, from anywhere on the planet, so they'll be untraceable.'

She gave him a massive hug.

'Thanks Dad!'

'It's all Bo, really. Him and his people, reverse engineering that Pleiadean tech. He says not a lot of it works in third density, but it's more the signposts it delivers. And he gets to zip all-over the world in an invisible flying hotel while he works the rest out.'

Amy put the phone in her jacket's breast pocket.

'And, Dad, that vanilla weirdness I spoke of? I have a feeling that it might extend, pretty soon. Right now, in fact, into… Cherry weirdness?'

Her father rolled his eyes, turned around, leaned down and took two of the cans from the row along the wall behind him.

As he straightened again he extended one to her.

'Don't tell Heather. It's my sacred stash.'

'She's getting you off sugar?'

'She thinks. Try it.'

'Oh!' Amy assessed the can. 'It looked just like…'

'We've just copied their branding style until we figure it out.'

'We?'

'Just try it.'

Amy cracked the can and sipped.

'Oh, wow.'

'I've been having a go at getting back to the style of fizzy lolly water we had when we were kids. Before they made it toxic and addictive.'

'This is definitely addictive!'

Mitch cracked his and sipped as well. 'Didn't say I'd succeeded. But, it's good to have people around who can work on the important things!'

Amy gulped a bit more as she turned to the view again, and studied the small building directly in front, which stood two floors lower. It had to be what they called 'turn of the century', although since that phrase had been coined, the turn of the subsequent century had passed. Turn of the *last* century now, she supposed it was required to say. Still, it would have been a big, impressive building in its early-twentieth-century time, with five floors of red-brown brick covering half a quarter block. The building's roof framed the lower edge of this view of the Harbour Bridge. It was an old, triangular-gabled, red-tiled roof, with wide gutters and deep-red wood-carved and plaster veneers. That would have to be heritage listed as well; people would be living and working in these old nineteen-hundreds, twenties and thirties apartments for centuries to come, with their chilly spaces, clunky plumbing, but holding rare and worthy aspects. It was a nice thought.

She calculated that if that one was five, then this one was seven floors up. She could still easily see cars and cabs and trucks and buses pretty clearly, moving in streams, along with the people up and down along the ten different footpaths of the five-point intersection on the corner of the building to their left. The people were hurrying across the walk lights there, jay-walking up and down further along. Traffic was starting to back up further with each light change.

Then she recognised something. A familiar store. She had never quite put it together that it was Pitt Street, the street itself, that separated the two skyscrapers, which allowed the special view, as much as anything did. But, then, of course it was; with the view right down to the Harbour.

'Speaking of weirder, Dad; the view looks weirder tonight.'

'Yeah, that.' He grinned. 'Can you see it? Sometimes at twilight with the neon of the city just starting to come through, I think I can see the edge of it over the Harbour, beside the Bridge.'

She stared, then pointed.

'Is that him?'

'I think so.'

'Yes, I can see the edge. Just. At least, I can see there's a shimmering edge of *something* there, in the sky.'

'Sometimes it looks like there's more than one. Circling slowly around.'

'Keeping an eye on us? I think I've seen a few Pleiadean ships pass through my part of the astral; at least, parts of them pass through. They're big discs, with decks, and windows around the sides. Practical but beautiful, and they can vanish; change density in a second.'

They sipped their sodas.

'What are you going to call this?'

Mitch hummed. 'Fizzy Lolly Water?'

She giggled. 'Fizzy Lolly Water. FizzyLollyWater.'

'Fizz-Loll-Woz.'

'*fizzylollywater.*'

'FzzLzzWzz.'

'fzlw.'

'Wizz.'

They started laughing and didn't stop for a few minutes.

It was probably the best time she'd had with her father in three years.

CHAPTER 4

Still, it was getting colder and darker by the minute.

'You want to go see him, don't you?'

'I want us both to go see him. I thought we could have dinner first?'

'We can have dinner up there, if you like?'

'Would he mind? Would you mind?'

'No. I think that's why you came, isn't it? To debrief us?'

Amy smiled and gave him a shrug that economically indicated that she had come here to see him – and whatever else worked.

'Okay. We've got time though. We can hang here a bit longer.'

The wind, which had essentially left them alone until then, suddenly blew up and made them both shiver. Almost unconsciously, they hugged the balcony a little more, and leaned over a bit. On the streets below, down at the intersection, rush hour was kicking in. She watched her father assess, scan around, up and down.

'You're right sweetie… it does feel weirder than 'normal weird', somehow.' He sounded like he meant it. 'Oh, and we really need to do astral protocol…'

Amy muttered to herself. 'It's never just one thing, is it?'

'What's that sweetie?'

'The more you look into things – nothing's ever just one thing. It's always a combo.'

'A combo?'

'A combination of factors that need to come together, and be balanced, like an equation, for anything to work.'

Mitch nodded to himself in approval; Amy sensed that he'd found a poetry in that which appealed to him. 'The more complicated the task, the more balance required.' He hummed to himself. 'I always thought movies were a bit like that. Any story really. The characters, their actions, their fates; what intervenes and what they overcome. If the equation is balanced, all those things add up to the feeling the storytellers what you to have at the end – to understand the equation, to comprehend the experience, to feel its purpose and get its point.'

Amy glanced back through the door, to the lone sofa within. It looked warmer in there of course, but she wasn't the kind of person who went inside before she had properly taken in a view, just because it was getting cold.

'Did you have those kinds of deep thoughts sitting in there for a year?'

Mitch guffawed. 'Hardly. But, since I came back here, and I've sat there again? Sure. You gotta come full circle before you realise it's not a circle, it's a spiral. Ascending, descending; you've gotta come back to where you left to see how far you've come.'

She let him have that.

Below, the pedestrians were interweaving through their own streams. You could see the pattern of things up here, Amy thought; the ebbing and flowing of cars at the lights as they stopped, dammed up, then were released; the lights, the turn lights, the sparkling formal dance of the city traffic. Weaving their way down the black and grey and faded footpaths, moving through and against and with each other, the pedestrians were the same; they reached the walk lights, they stopped, little crowds built-up, then they were released. Amy gained a slight, further insight then; with rush hour, the people heading toward the train station had the flow advantage. There were more of them moving there, a greater collective force; they would achieve their directive first.

She looked back down at the five point intersection.

'They say this city is a grid... but that's deceptive. It's a fan that spans out from the docks. It has lanes and alleys and weird bends that lead to mystical five-point intersections, like that one down there, to buildings where psychonaut science-sorcerers can keep a magical occult library for years, with nobody knowing. This city is a higgledy-piggledy mess.'

Mitch looked across at her, startled, almost offended. He had lived here his whole life, just about.

'Ahem! It's old, it's organic; it's early twentieth, with the late-middle zig-zagging through and early twenty-first pushing its feelers up regardless…' Mitch shrugged. 'Isn't that what your generation is into? Authentic, organic, artisan integrity? This city is a two hundred year old monument to the Industrial Age.'

'Yes, Dad. Exactly. It's a higgledy-piggledy mess built on a sacred site that puts up a nice veneer.'

He huffed, then uttered, sulkily. 'New York and London are much worse…'

'Yeah. I only mention it because there are three different people looking up at us from two different pedestrian corners. Look.'

You could make out individual people from up here as well, even determine their general demeanour, colour scheme and body language. But the way all three had stopped, and were looking up…

That was odd.

Amy caught movement, closer, and looked back across to the gable roof. On the top floor, beneath the old gutters, through a dirty window in a darkened room, there was a man looking out at them; up and across. Amy scowled. He was right there, not that far, just across the street really so far as distance went; but with the height and the separate buildings, he might as well have been peering out at them from another dimension. He might also have been pleasuring himself with a leering grin.

These things were often hard to tell.

'Yeah…' Amy spoke softly, her consciousness suddenly yanked right back to where she'd begun. '…the astral protocol. How long do I think I've been gone versus; how long have I actually been gone? I'd say it was about four weeks since I last dropped in? Maybe five weeks? We've been busy since. Enough to catch some attention. But I think I've slept... I lost count, but – maybe thirty times? Long days, but...'

She looked over to her Dad. He was looking at the three pedestrians. They'd caught his eye.

'...Dad, is it still twenty-thirteen? I think it was February last time I was here on the Earth Plane, so it should be March something...?'

Then she heard what she'd said.

It was cold out here, and cloudy.

The city was starting to get dark at rush hour.

In Sydney, March meant early-Autumn, sunshine and warmth.

Not this.

Then her Dad was looking at her.

A bit bewildered, a little sad.

'Oh, sweetie, this is why Everett wanted to put protocols in place to begin with. Yes, it's still twenty-fourteen. But it's a Friday night, in bleak midwinter; July fifteenth! You haven't been in the astral five weeks this time; you've been there five *months*.'

CHAPTER 5

Thys blinked like a cartoon character.

'Five? Months…?'

Wow.

It wasn't the first time she'd lost track.

Days usually.

Sometimes weeks.

But this, five months out; this was a big jump.

Sure, time worked differently there, everyone said it; days were inconsistent lengths, sleep was more powerful.

'That's okay.'

It had to be; she heard it in her voice.

'Now that you say it… I think? I think; that works out…? I dunno; maybe, about right? Anyway; it feels okay. Doesn't feel… out of whack, you know?'

Mitch was relieved. 'I guess. I'm trying to remember how it felt from my side, the last time it happened to me. It's been a while.'

They both looked down again at the people at the lights.

The three pedestrians were still staring up, all three, no mistaking, right at them.

'You need to come through the astral more often, Dad. There are things I need to show you. There are still things I need to tell you, today – about the weirdness on the way.'

Mitch cut her off.

'Look, further east; two hipster-backpackers.'

Indeed, there were now two other people staring up at them from down the street. Now from the other side of the intersection. Amy could never remember the name of the intersecting street, but it was one of five that intersected around a very curious statue.

That too, she had always intended to check out, to properly assess - to sanse and make sure.

'Are these people anything to do with the impending weirdness, sweetie?'

Amy wasn't sure what to say.

Underneath, they were just ordinary people, really.

Wandering-minded ordinaries.

'Kind of.'

These sorts of people, just the normal folk on the street, had not idea they were supposed to protect their minds.

Wouldn't know where to start.

Never remembered, never even knew, when they had been hijacked by piggybackers.

'Given that I am part of it, and you are in it too, and they are clearly observing us. You learn to spot them from a distance.'

Maybe it was getting serious.

Amy looked back down and reassessed.

Of the three who'd paused at the lights, without responding to the changes for three cycles now, two were businessmen, neatly dressed in dark suits and white shirts, while the other was a younger man sporting a very well-manicured look that Amy would immediately associate with an estate agent.

They were all just staring up; those three and the new couple. Tanned young backpackers across the way, holding hands as though frozen into the gesture just as the Anunnaki had tapped into them.

As Amy observed, another stopped beside them, as people sometimes did. They tried to follow their line of sight, but couldn't see anything. They exchanged glances and moved on, shrugging. Street performance, people getting high, mental instability.

Or just something they couldn't see?

Who knew; time was ticking away.

There was, after all, no apparently remarkable spectacle for them to see and join in with observing, and there was, indeed, a kind of mental imbalance on display, and indeed, once more, something only the immobilized bunch could see.

'It's never just one thing...' Amy uttered.

'What's that sweetie?'

'They shouldn't be doing that.'

'Who?'

'The Draco.'

'You're sure it's them? Maybe they just found out there's a weird millionaire hanging around up here today? People are taking in interest you know. People do.'

Amy shook her head disapprovingly. 'They piggyback. They project into the minds of people with no protection.'

'Well; there are lots of them, Amy. We put out the information we can, but...'

But Amy was deep into it now.

'People on auto-pilot, just daydreaming. People with no conviction as to the path or purpose of their lives. People with no idea that there is anything more to consciousness; just the lower-chakra impulses passing for a life. Food and shelter and reproduction and distraction; blinkers on, roaming about, slaves to time, wide open, easy to hack. Anunnaki culture encourages that.' Amy nodded to herself, her jaw clenching. 'But also stress, and anxiety, and weariness, and depression...'

'I know, Ames. An exhausted active mind is just as good as a vacant and uninspired one.'

'It's simply low-level astral projection for them, Dad; don't even need a starcophagus. Just focus; just basic meditation technique. Just...' Amy threw up her hands. '...a psychic piggyback! An easy surf!'

'You mentioned this last time, Ames. You were upset about it then, too. You said that the Anunnaki don't need CCTV. To then CCTV is just... tired people. Bored people.'

'And worse...' Amy uttered as she looked up and down the street again.

Her father knew that the game.

But he lived here.

Lived with it. He could process and cope.

She didn't really live here any more.

And it was always a shock to come back and see...

This.

Now the vehicles, the people, the signs, the windows, the doors, everything; all suddenly seemed to be very much in deep collective the shadow of the surrounding skyscrapers.

Amy could suddenly see, conversely very clearly in the newly formed darkness, how all the metal in the window frames down below on street level were tarnished, how all the promotional posters on the city walls were faded and scraped and tattered, and how all the plastic signs that would light up with neon at night were cracked and dirty. She could see huge swathes of grime and mould, just behind and beneath everything. She could see, in the shadow of whatever sudden cloud that had formed between the buildings, how the pedestrians looked so tired as they walked, how they pushed themselves so wearily as they marched along; heads down, shoulders hunched with short and angry stomps.

All the patches of many stages of repair along the footpath seemed to make it a rough and uneven path, a path that remained static in a constant state of disrepair, used too consistently to be anything other than patched to minumum satisfaction.

A well-put-together business woman in high heels tripped but collected herself, but somehow she carried the perceived embarrasment forward with her; a man with a briefcase accidentally bumped shoulders with another man, one with an anger spike and the other one startled, both moving on without confrontation but without anything to do with the stored, sharp emotion they now carried; a man looking at a lotto ticket as though it were his last hope as an attractive woman watching a noticeably younger woman pass by felt irrationally less attractive, and seeing the lotto ticket thought maybe she too should try her luck, knowing it was hopeless, that youth was always in the past.

Amy could see and sense these things, but only in passing.

And there was nothing she could do.

Sansing, she had started naming it.

When you saw, and sensed simultaneously.

Mitch spoke, low.

She knew that he could sanse it too.

'They usually just watch me. I see them. Peering out from behind someone else's eyes. Frozen still, staring. I just treat them like another version of the government Alphabet Soup; like the Anunnaki Secret Service; the A.S.S. – I call them the ASS!'

Amy shook her head, but still smiled. 'Dad jokes about our clandestine alien oppressors? Really?'

Mitch made a face; *gotta laugh, right?*

Amy smiled. It made them seem less scary she supposed.

'ASS is way too broad in several ways, Dad. It's like saying "The Human Secret Service". Those guys are what you'd call the Draco Secret Service; the admin side of them anyway. So that would be the DSS. Sorry it's not as silly, but if it helps, it is just one aspect of one clan. The largest of the clans that likes the humans the least, probably.'

'They're mad with you, Ames?'

'Me, yes. You, not especially. There's nothing they can do about what happened with us all, not now. The Pandora Sequence is part of the dye now; it's part of the astral planetary atmosphere and ecosystem. They adjust and carry on, it's what they do. But they keep watch.'

'It's what all life does, I suppose. Adjust and carry on.'

'Until it doesn't. The Cold War is still very powerful idea in the astral. It's almost status quo. Lots of people I know; we try and keep it that way. But it's hard.'

'So…?' Now Mitch was concerned. 'They're more mad with you than they are with me? In particular?'

'Yes. But, I want to show you, and Uncle Bo, and the others. I need advice, but –'

'Everett keeps talking about these sorcerers he hired.'

'What?'

'He hired some sorcerers. From Adelaide, apparently.'

'Adelaide?' Amy had never been there. 'Sorcerers?'

'More than one path to the well, apparently sweetie. I haven't been to see him myself for a few weeks. From what he told me, they are different from us, but they aren't *too different* from us, and what we can do, if you see what I mean? They just seem to have been born switched on, into the energies we work with; but especially with the energies of the planet, of Earth.'

This was news.

'Okay.'

'They did some sort of job for Everett, at The Rocks. But I can sort of feel what you're thinking.'

'You can?'

'Not the words, but; do you ever get that? I get it quite often; a sense of what someone's thoughts are adding up to?'

'I don't know. Maybe.'

'Anyway; these sorcerers told Everett that there are creatures; demons and angels, that have expanded perspective, expanded consciousness, and for them, it's like – they can see all these people, like we can from up here, but they can also read their spirits, their chakras, their auras, or whatever term you want to use for the expanded energy systems around our bodies, from a perspective like we can see from up here.'

'You mean, these sorcerers think the aliens we call Elohim and the Nephilim are actual demons and angels?'

Mitch looked at her strangely. 'Aren't they?'

She let out a long sigh as she spoke. 'I suppose.'

'But look; apparently, these other ones, they aren't necessarily just mistaken 'expanded consciousness aliens' from 'a way-advanced civilization'. These ones are something else again.'

Amy smiled wryly. 'What would that make them? ECA-WACs?'

They both paused and considered before they simultaneously shook their heads.

'We'll come up with something else...' Mitch whispered.

She nodded tightly back. 'Err... yah!'

'I did think; maybe we should ask them. But then; people hve been asking them hings for millennia, haven't they?'

Amy made a face. 'But - these others; they're from the Earth? From here, our planet?'

'Yeah. Something like that. The way it was described to me is; they are part of the planet – this is third density, the astral is fourth, but they come from second density, from a place called the Inner Earth Realm.'

Amy pulled her neck in a bit. '...very D&D...'

'Hey!'

'Not that there's anything wrong with that!'

'Well, apparently it's all based on something real. Or at least, another realm of conscious existence where the cosmic manifestation of that kind of land, that kind of realm, can actually exist.'

'Seriously?'

'...well, we know that our guys, the ones we know; the Sirians and Pleiadeans and what have you, can kind of – reach down, and push.'

'Push?'

'Well, maybe not *push*. But you know. Maybe push sometimes. Maybe other times more like... shuffle?' Mitch looked down into the street. 'See that guy at the lights, in red and blue? Let's just for a second ignore that he's navigating an extremely complex world he had no hand in creating, and has no hope of controlling, as he clutches almost randomly with fragile realisations in desperate attempts to comprehend a culture filled with terrifying internal conflicts and bewildering contradictions.'

'Ignore – how?'

'Let's not be glib now sweetie.'

Amy sighed. 'But I like glib.'

'And glib likes you. But, just for the purpose of this illustration, okay? So, what if our red-blue guy is just wandering about, longing for a lady who's red-green? He thinks that's what he wants. That would make him happy. Cultural conditioning has him telling himself that a red-green woman is his heart's desire. But because we can see his stuff, his aura and his chakras and his longings and desires, we know that his longing is a false and destructive desire, it's negative conditioning. Because together, they're both going to be more red, but with blue and green mixing between them. What's that? Blood red and ocean blue. Their passion for each other will eventually drown them.'

Amy huffed.

'I'm just painting a picture sweetie.'

'I know Dad. I get it. But – the Sirians and Pleiadeans can see that, right? They understand how complex and nuanced those colours, those forces, *actually are?*'

'That's what I'm getting to. So, what our friend needs, we know, because we can see his aura and stuff, in order for him to be happy, or productive, or to seek out his dharma or fix his karma, or at least get to a place where he can see what he has to do to fix them, or, in the very least, a place where there is a sign to the place where he can see that there is a way; is to avoid the thing he desires.'

'Snap him out of his negative cultural programming.'

'And sometimes all that takes is to shift your obsession and see something else. From a particular angle, say, that suddenly has great appeal. And suddenly, our guy is gob-smacked by red-yellow lady. Still the red he likes in a lady, but suddenly, yeah; the yellow. He gets it. They can still have big red-red passion, and they make their own green. Together.'

Amy huffed again.

'Okay. So... what's the green?'

'The green?'

'The green they make together. A baby? Love? Do they open a B&B? The heart chakra's supposed to be green isn't it?'

'I don't know, these are just thoughts! The important thing is – they make it together.'

'Oh. I thought the important thing was that they made green and not blue.'

Mitch wondered. 'Maybe it is. Maybe that too.'

Amy let out a long green-blue huff. 'Okay, Dad. I can accept that the gist of some kind of point is actually around about, somewhere within that analogy. Or is it a metaphor?'

Mitch shrugged. 'Ask the Pleiadeans.'

'Sirians if it's grammar.'

'Look, the point is sweetie; that's all it takes for people, usually. At least, to get going. Some people have no interest in all the greater forces in their lives. They dress it up, but in the end they just want a solid match; someone who will take them though.'

She smiled. It sounded nice really.

'So, down here, we see our red-blue guy, who's lonely. He's heading this way – and he's walking past red-green lady, very sexy from his point of view, full of desire for her, and it's driving him nuts. But one day, he's going to ask a girl like that out, and one day, one of the ones who says yes is going to actually like him, and that's going to be great for him, and them... you know. Physically.'

'Uh. Dad, please...'

'But being terrific in bed together will drive them both into a deep emotional blue funk, becasue, in the end, they don't actually like each other that much. In the end, all they have is fighting, and make-up sex, and when the passion wears off, all there is, is the fighting. Like it was with your mother.'

'...Dad...!'

'...sorry, Ames...' Mitch rolled his eyes. '...but; you know what I mean...'

Sadly, she did. Exactly. She'd seen it happen between them.

'Now; we could, if we wanted, send whispers into his ear, and push him in the right direction. Give him what he needs, and actually wants, if he thinks about it, and what will take him as close to being happy as he can currently be in this life.'

'...which we can see, because we're advanced aliens, and we're up here. With...?'

She looked at him and they he shrugged.

They both knew.

'...better technology, basically. Nano and bio and quantum and – whatever comes after that. As a result of that tech. Whatever it turns a culture into after...' He swiped casually down Pitt Street. '...whatever it does with all this.'

Amy looked over the skyline.

She had seen the edges of that, from where she had been all these months.

'From where we look, with our heightened view and colour palette of wisdom, and find our man a red-yellow lady. Someone with whom he's compatible, who's maybe headed the other way. So; their paths won't cross.'

'Oh no!'

'Ah, but – we have the technology.'

'We do?'

'And we can whisper in their ear from up here!'

'We do?'

'Sure can! Because we have our kaleidoscopic map of cosmic colours and auras, and we are wise enough to deploy it with good will, and because we want the best possible outcome for everybody with a noble intent. So we whisper in his ear; go to the zoo. We whisper in her ear; go see the lions!' He whisper-hissed. *'Wear something yellow!'*

'Really, Dad?' She laughed. 'What, and they meet at the zoo, at the lion cage, and fall in love?'

'Yeah. Something like that. Then they even have a story, right?'

Amy smiled. 'So, from up here we use... what? Pleiadean, Sirian... all the way up to Orion tech or Elohim consciousness to achieve this? What's that got to do with the these whispers? These underground sorcerers?'

Mitch rolled his eyes.

Amy shrugged.

'Well, imagine if you don't need the tech. Imagine if that's just... what you do. If you're already a creature of this Earth, part of the planet and interweaved with humanity. You see these things as a panther sees the jungle, as a bee detects pollen; like we smell a good restaurant on our way to work, and book a table for dinner! Think about it. These Inner Earth entities; coming and going, just like the aliens do, but from somewhere else *here*. Not out there. Here. From The Earth. They can influence us with psychic impulses, appear in temporary embodiments, or in mystical... mist! All that stuff we've had our own stories about, for all those centuries. Doesn't this sound more... human? More earthy? More like the folk tales we used to have, before the aliens?'

'So, what? You're really saying all that's real too?'

'Everett says it was Yelina who put him on to the sorcerers.'

'You mean, that's what she's here for? To show us The Inner, as well as The Outer?'

Mitch smiled.

Amy knew this look from her Dad; he thought he had her.

'Okay, okay hold that thought. But now imagine you're thirty floors up, and your consciousness is not just looking down from here, on the...?'

'Seventh floor.'

'...right, the seventh floor. Imagine you're an exec, on the thirtieth floor? And you have powerful psychic abilities, linked to the core of the planet, the Inner Earth, and, in its way, that's just as good as any Pleiadean or Sirian tech. You can zoom in and zoom out of people's thoughts and emotions; you're like a modern sorcerer. And instead of seeing just basic red and blue and yellow and green, like we were saying, you do actually see all the colours and combinations; the full kaleidoscope of human karma and dharma, and human now and human reality and human potential, just like the aliens do. You see the human colour palette, each person's aura and energy grid like a Monet or a Picasso; an Escher or a Dali. They could add or subtract, boon or bane him, mix his life with someone else's and turn him rose or turquoise or scarlet or aquamarine...' He looked over at his daughter, again, suddenly emotional, realised. '...Amethyst or Jade!'

He grinned, and Amy smiled.

'How is she, Dad?'

Mitch shrugged. 'She wants to work the heiress thing, and her mother wants to let her.'

'Oh.'

'You should go see her.'

'Yeah, I know. But, we always get too drunk. I might need to give her some space.'

They were silent again for a second.

'Okay, next chance I get!' Amy cracked. 'We'll go out for lunch.'

'Good girl. She loves you, you know, your little sister; more than you can imagine.'

'Uhhh...' Amy let out a short, deep breath. 'Okay, I know. I love her too.'

Mitch was grinning now.

Amy shook her head. 'So, keep going. These Inner Earth entities understand all the complex potentials of the primal human drives; our hearts, our desires, our spirits and our souls. Just like the higher consciousness... EVA-WACs do.'

'Is that going to catch on?'

'I don't think so.'

'Just checking.'

'But what you're saying is, here on the seventh floor we just have to make stuff up, take best guesses. But meanwhile the aliens in the high rises and the fairies in the deep forests see us and read us better than we can ever see and read ourselves? When does humanity ever catch a break in this cosmic scenario?'

Mitch smiled but shook his head. 'Okay, so; one; the advanced aliens are all caught up in the balance of things – in ascension, in the creation of a progressive spiritual reality that is good for all the universe. That's what they want for us, right? These Inner Earth equivalents – they're forces of nature. Think about the Old Gods. Zeus, banging everything he wanted. Not giving a toss that it was driving his wife bananas. Doesn't that sound more like...?' He looked back down as the swarming, ebbing and flowing world of traffic. '...people? But you're right, aren't you? The Sirians and Pleiadeans, they see themselves as above all that; they want to lead us away, to be above all that too. These guys, the Earth entities, they just want us to fight and fuck and have fun; or have fun with us.'

'Like – Tricksters? Or, The Fates?'

'Like the genuine Old Gods of myth and legend, like the Bad Old Devil Himself, and the white bearded Sky God; Big Daddy Lightning and Thunder, and Old Cave Momma Earth; stories around a warm fire. Old Testament! Wrath of God type stuff!'

They had a giggle.

'And two; these forces of nature, they were made here, with us, on Earth. They know us, they're part of us – they've 'come up' with us, from the soil, in the sunshine and the rain and the deserts and snow, the forests and mountains; they're in our cities, because they were in the towns, and in the villages before that. They are still in another dimension, but closer somehow.'

'Closer.'

'These sorcerers say they're more real to us, more relevant, than the aliens in some ways; and totally sentient. Their own wars, their own agendas. But they're real, the Old Ones. Real as lava or hurricanes or childbirth or dementia.'

'And Yelina…?'

'Think about how Yelina opened that hole under the tree behind Oliver's mansion – we didn't vanish, did we? *We walked into the Earth.* I felt it, under my shoes. You did too. It was cold, and damp, and you could smell the soil and sense the life; the burrows and snakes and earthworms and insects and bugs down there. That's close to us. It's not vanishing into a gap of light. It's closer than –'

'But that's just like me!'

'Huh?'

'Like – when I went into the astral plane around Earth, the astral field there was – was mine! Ours, as humans, but – mine! It was like, this is part of me, of my field, too. That's why… look,

Dad, we need to get the others, I need to show you something.'

'Okay, okay; but let me just make my point.'

'Which is?'

'Everett…'

Mitch let his name hang a second or two.

'..and, Yelina.'

Amy shrugged. 'What about them?'

Mitch turned and pointed out, down Pitt and to the left.

'See the white one? The modern-looking one? It's one of the tallest, at the edge of the city but right on the Harbour, almost. New and modern and beautiful.'

'That's him?'

'Everett is there, with Yelina; one of those beings the sorcerers warned us about. Up there, on the fortieth floor. And he has a Pleiadean ship.'

CHAPTER 6

'But…' Amy wasn't sure of his point. '…we *like* Everett, right? And you mean, *literally,* on the fortieth floor. Not the fortieth… actually, what do you mean?'

Mitch shrugged. She could see; he didn't really enjoy where his thoughts had taken him.

'I dunno. But; I thought I should say something. To you.'

'To me?'

'Just in case.'

'Just in case of what?'

'Well; what you just said. I've seen how powerful you are up there in the astral. You're so strong! And you're already much wiser than I was at your age.'

What was he saying?

'Look. Forget I said anything, sweetie. There's a film premiere tonight. Eight o'clock on the red carpet. Do you think you could come along?'

'Film premiere?'

'Olivera Studios are still pumping out their slate of terrible dystopian fantasies; but this is one of their 'smaller movies'. One that none of their sociopathic executives had anything to do with.'

'Jeez. Who lct that happen?'

Mitch smiled, tightly. 'This guy had a vision and… well if you ever meet him you'll see. It was in the can before Kyvza and Don Eissley took over the entertainment division, but they shelved it after a hack edit and a few bad test screenings. However; I have used my retired film critic powers and influence…'

'You own the company now…'

'Exactly; to nudge them into giving it a limited release.' Mitch shrugged. 'And now, here we are.'

'Where are we... exactly?'

Mitch grinned. 'Now, it's an Oscar contender! With real grassroots buzz! Can you believe it?'

'What's it called?'

'Have you heard of Adison Achilleos?'

'Adison...?'

'His other films are amazing but he always seems to be five years between drinks.'

'I feel like I should. What are they called?'

'He made *Little Pink* in two-thousand-four, then *In The Room* in twenty-oh-nine.'

'I feel like I *should* know them. I think, maybe...?'

Jeez, it was hard to remember. There were so many films that were actually being made these days, let alone how many were dreamed up, all around her, all day and night, and all in betweens, in the land in the clouds where she lived right now.

'So, what's this new one called?'

'*Umbrella Stand.*'

'What's it about?'

'Apparently, it's –'

'Actually, don't tell me. I hate spoilers.'

'So you'll come? Catch up with Heather?'

'Okay.' Amy let out a long, shallow breath. Now she saw it. 'I don't suppose I have to get back to my Astral Queendom straight away.'

'And we can spend a bit more time together!'

'I suppose we can. But wait; I mean, a premiere?'

'They're nothing. I've been to plenty.'

'Dad! I'll need an outfit?'

'That's how I can tell you're here on business.'

'How –' Amy looked down at herself; at what she had worn, back from the astral, without thinking. 'Oh.'

'That's cool and all, but you can't wear it on the red carpet.'

She could, she thought rebelliously, and she probably would, if nobody stopped her.

'I guess not.'

She looked back down at the Draco; they were still watching.

'Amy; are you sure we're not in danger? Are you sure *you're* not in danger?'

Amy shook her head. 'They won't attack. They won't risk it.'

'Risk it?'

'Like I said, I've kind of...' Amy shrugged. But it wasn't to brush it off; it was more like... it just was what it was. 'I've made an impression. It's complicated. But they have rules, sacred rules, and one of those rules is that they aren't allowed to attack non-Anunnaki possessed humans in third density; not openly.'

'Lots of people broke a lot of rules – last time.'

Amy stared down again at the Draco piggybackers, then shivered. 'I think I've seen enough of the street life this evening. Let's get back inside.'

This time, Amy slid the balcony door open for her father. He bowed shortly and entered, but as she re-entered, Amy took one last look down at the intersection.

The two business guys were looking around, scratching their heads, as though having lost their train of thought. Uphill, the backpackers were walking away, still hand in hand, chatting away, but with a kind of puzzled air, like they couldn't quite remember what they'd just been talking about. The estate agent was nowhere in sight.

'Higgledy-piggledy piggybacks...' Amy muttered under her breath, shaking her head. 'God-damn Draco Anunnaki.'

She entered the apartment, but out of the corner of her eye she saw, and tried to ignore, the sixth piggyback, in the window reflection, still watching them from inside the old building across the street.

Smiling.

CHAPTER 7

Once back inside, Mitch had caught sight of another open box, just out of sight beside his old favourite-spot on the couch.

'Ah! Right there! Hiding in plain sight!'

Still holding her fizzy lolly water with one hand, Amy hissed and clicked the sliding-door to a hard close behind her, immediately feeling warmer. Then she saw that, as her father crossed the living room, he was making a broad, deliberate gesture with his free hand, drawing his fist slowly closed in the air. Corresponding to his gesture, the rediscovered box was sliding, swirling slightly, straight toward him across the floor.

'Wow, Dad!'

'Getting better at this!'

When he and the box met in the middle, he squatted and reached in, removing a hardcover book with a purple cover. Then he took from his pocket the folded list of names that Amy had given him earlier, and slipped that between some middle pages, swapping out another sheet of paper from the same place.

Then he returned the purple book to the box.

When he folded the cardboard back down, Amy saw his handwriting in black marker on one of the flaps.

MITCH – KEEPERS – (NOT FOR STORAGE)

For some reason, all the packing and emptiness suddenly made her feel sad. Mitch smiled, awkwardly.

She saw that he wasn't mad with her for having an ulterior motive for her visit.

Instead, this was her father's worried smile.

Not really a smile at all.

But that was okay.

'Everything's changing…' Amy told him.

He put a brave face on it. 'Same as it ever was, sweetie.'

'Shall we just… pop up, over there now then?'

Mitch smiled. 'We've started to call it gapping. Moving through the dimensional gaps. "Gapping".'

'Really?'

'Don't like it?'

Amy shrugged. 'I'm sure it will catch on. That seeing and sensing at the same time, I'm calling that sansing.'

Mitch picked up his oversized black overcoat, the one Bo Everett had given him many months ago now, before everything had really kicked off, and threw it on. It looked almost like a monk's habit, and it had always suited him… but oddly, maybe not so much any more.

'Naming things divides the oneness of the universal consciousness even more; but it's how we navigate our way through reality and back to the oneness of universal consciousness. Can't remember who said that but it's a good one.'

She made a face and gulped more soda.

It was pretty good.

'Don't like that one either?'

'No. It's just… some people have known all sorts of things, about what we know now, about reality, for thousands of years. And what difference has that made to those poor wage slaves trudging along through the valleys of the skyscrapers down there?'

Mitch shrugged and gave her his best fatherly, reassuring smile. 'They forged the path for us to follow, sweetie. And led us to what we know now. And now it's up to us to forge on again, taking what they learned and we've learned, and encouraging others to follow us.'

She made another face.

'And so on, I suppose?'

And took another gulp of soda.

'Oh, and also Ames, speaking of learning to navigate…? There's another thing we've discovered.'

'We?'

'Me and Heather.'

'Oh.'

'You see, we can't just be gapping across the world, city to city, or even just across town, willy-nilly anymore. Since people know who we are now, and Heather is – well; Heather is Heather...'

He took a breath, sighed it out, paused, then told it to her straight.

'...look, sweetie, the fact is, we're a good-looking family with money. We've come out of nowhere; we're new, and people want to know all about us. People want to know *everything* about us, apparently, and "us" includes "you".'

'People?'

'People want to know where you are, some of them. Ordinary people, the Alphabet Soups, the tax department; but really, more so, just – the *people*.'

'But... what people?'

'Well; people on the internet, mostly.'

'The internet?'

'Apparently this internet thing is really taking off, and there's something called "social media" now. Everybody wants to show everybody else what they're doing. It's fast and easy and growing by the day. The more fascinating you can make yourself seem to everybody else, the bigger your... I think they call it "online presence" becomes.'

'Oh.'

'Oh what?'

'Well, I guess I thought that if I stayed away I would escape all that.'

'So you know?'

She heard herself sigh again. She was sighing a lot. Sighing, huffing. She was, technically, still a teenager, she supposed.

Or, wait; was she twenty now?

She didn't...

Wait... hadn't there been some kind of party, not so ong ago...?

(Oh my God I am twenty now do not think about that *do not*

make it real!)

She was almost... twenty one!

It seemed like nothing, back in the astral, but being here again, all of a sudden, it seemed like...

It was making her snippish.

'Dad, of course I know. There are new Anunnaki temples to new media deities appearing allover the Dracopolis like... gopher infestations! Giant gophers with collagen lips and fake tans and breast implants and homemade sex-videos they pretend that they don't want anyone to see, but really they want bloody *everyone* to see!'

She was squirming, and her Dad could see.

The idea, that world; it clearly did not appeal to her in the slightest. Then her father smiled, and gave her an outrageous Irish accent.

'Well sweetie, you'll just have to go back and kill all the gophers on the astral plane!'

She knew the response of course; it was something special they shared, one of the first great, silly American comedies he had even shown her, and she threw back an equally outrageous slacker voice.

'Correct me if I'm wrong Dad, but if I kill all the golfers on the astral plane, they'll lock me up and throw away the key!'

They both laughed again, hard and stupid with each other, and then she gave him a little hug. They'd always had that; and he always knew how to use it to make her feel better.

'Look, I know it's... changing everything. Opening things up. Everett says its influence is only getting bigger, sweetie. He says it's only going to make the conservatives more fearful, and the progressives more emboldened. Which in exchange will make the progressives more afraid and the conservatives more emboldened.'

'All in ways we haven't seen yet...?'

'Presumably. Everett has some kind of ability to gauge potential futures with that ship. He says that in five or six years, by twenty-

twenty, social media is going to be – a monster. It's going to make and break careers, get people killed, get people saved, get people thrown out and even get people elected, sweetie. Uncontrollable. But the fact remains – people are endlessly fascinated by people who seem elusive. And you…'

'I am elusive.' Amy nodded to herself. 'I'll give myself that.'

'At least, it's starting to seem that way. There's a suggestion online that you're an *actual recluse*, you see…' Mitch grimaced. 'And people want to know why. They love the drama.'

'Ah. And what better way to attract attention, and create drama, than by announcing you don't want any.'

Mitch shrugged. 'I'm sorry, sweetie. The Anunnaki gave us the bait, and we have devoured it. People with struggling lives and no mental space who read dumb webpages and lying newspapers and go to made-up celebrity news websites want to know what we do with our lives. It embarrassing and ridiculous, but it's…'

'Awful!'

'And escalating.'

'*Why?*'

'Well, like I said, it's just the way it's set up. It's just one of the things that's allowed to run rampant, hurting people. One of the things I assume you… are trying to… do something about?'

'Oh right.' Amy nodded. 'Of course. Yes.'

He placed a gentle hand on her arm.

'I'm so sorry, Ames. Like it's not enough we have the Anunnaki watching, and the dimensionals dropping by every – '

'Dimensionals?'

'The Pleiadeans might be helping with the ship, but they are still monitoring our behaviour. How we handle the new responsibilities. The Sirians and Orions as well, not to mention the…' He pointed up and twirled his finger around. 'Angel-aliens and space-demons and ECA-WACs such….' Then he pointed down and twirled his finger again. '…whatever they really are.'

'Dimensionals? That's a word now too?'

Mitch spread his arms helplessly. 'I can have my own words!'

'Okay, okay!' Amy chuckled. 'At least it's better than *Lever.*'

'Don't mention that to your Uncle Bo, okay? He and Oliver Hines paid a lot of people *a lot of money* to test that name and tell them it worked.'

She rolled her eyes, and they both made a face, but her father could see it as well; that was the least of her worries.

'Something's still bugging you.'

'Listen, Dad, the weirdness I was talking about…?'

'Something to do with the increased Anunnaki surveillance out there?'

'I think so.' She took a long sip of the soda. 'And, this time…'

'This time what? Not just Cherry weirdness? Watermelon weirdness too? I'll run out of your favourite flavours!'

'Dad, the weirdness that's coming; it might be because of something… that I might do.'

'Something you *might do?*'

'Umm; yeah.'

'Ames, you have that look on your face. The same as when you used to come to me and tell me that Jade *might be* getting cross soon.'

He also sipped, meaningfully.

'I do?'

She took another too-long sip, slurping slowly with wide eyes over the top of the can.

'And Ames, whenever you used to do that, it would always turn out that it was not because of something you *might do* to her, or one of her dolls, or one of her outfits, or even one of her boys, but something you *had done*, already, and that was what *would* make her cross. You recalling any of this?'

She gulped the can again, then hiccupped from too much fizz.

'Huh.' Mitch looked at her with a raised eyebrow. 'You're going to tell us about all this – right?'

'I'm going to – try. To – show you.'

Mitch lowered the eyebrow raised his soda can.

'Oh well. You're a clever girl, you know what you're doing, and

I'm sure it will all turn out for the best! Cheers, daughter.'

Her relief was audible. 'Thanks, father.'

They clunked cans.

'Come on, Everett's a busy man; don't want to keep him waiting.'

'Waiting?'

'Oh, he knows you're here. That Pleiadean ship keeps track of everything.'

'Everything?'

'Well, everything Earthly, or "Earthen", so far as I know.'

'Ummm…' Amy tapped the side of her can. 'Shouldn't we… leave these here? If Heather finds out?'

Mitch twitched his nose. 'Quite the contrary!'

He led her back outside, onto the balcony. It was still freezing cold. Mitch leaned down and snatched up another soda can from his sacred stash.

Amy giggled. 'Bad Dad!'

'Uncle Bo likes his soda, sweetie.'

He then unfolded the sheet of paper that he'd swapped out from the purple book and slid it onto the balcony floor, keeping it in place against the wind with the toe of his black sneaker as he stood. Amy recognised the symbol; it was the 'totally human' sigil that Oliver Hines had created, supposedly divorced of all Anunnaki design and unconscious training symbolism; the intended symbol for Lever.

'Allow me?'

Mitch held out his hand and she took it as he looked down at the symbol, then up again, and out, through the skyscrapers and over the red-gabled heritage building, down Pitt Street to the Bridge, to the shimmering edge of Bo Everett's second hand Pleiadean flying saucer, hovering over Sydney Harbour.

Amy understood; the symbol, plus line-of-sight.

Up from the paper sprang a sharp sliver of white lightning, reaching a good meter above their heads.

Her father pushed the paper through the gap with his foot,

then glanced at the last Draco, still watching them from the window across the way. She was not at all surprised, realising that he had also noticed the extra surveillance.

'Fuck 'em.' He grinned. 'Let 'em see.'

Amy smiled, feeling quite cheeky.

Then they stepped through the gap and were gone.

CHAPTER 8

'I've learned the hard way, when you come and go from the astral, you don't necessarily think about clothes…'

Amy stepped into and enormous office space, surrounded by glass.

She stared around, for a moment awestruck.

'Apologies to Uncle Pan…' She turned to her father, pointing sharply in the other direction. 'But – that – is a view of Sydney Harbour.'

They were looking down, flanked by two other skyscrapers, at a nevertheless essentially unobscured view of Circular Quay, much higher than the Harbour Bridge, which stretched away to the left, with the Opera House and inner coastal suburbs spanning to their right.

'But wait – this isn't a Pleiadean ship. Is it?'

'A slight detour, my dear young lady! But you see; between Oliver Hines and myself, we had leased almost a fifth of the building and didn't even know it.'

Amy was startled to hear Everett's voice behind her as she completing a full circle, but of course, they had all taken The Pandora Sequence; they could all "gap" now.

Then, there he was; tall and red-haired, unshaven, Robert Redford's face on Conan O'Brien's body, with Liam Neeson's gruffness, and, even though he had given most of his original fortune away to Mitch and Heather, still more money than Richard Branson.

Bo Everett, with his arms wide-open in greeting.

'How stunning to see you again, Amethyst Pyne!'

Amy opened her arms in turn.

'Uncle *Bo*?'

The questioning inflection was in regard to his clean, light-cream, three-peice suit. He lightly brushed his chest with one hand, while striding toward her with the other extended. She accepted and shook, knowing that both the grip and hold would be expertly judged and perfectly timed.

'You like?'

She looked him in the eyes as he smiled. He had not changed for the worse, either. Not this man; a human so legendarily self-possessed that no Anunnaki could penetrate his psyche, no matter how much they would like to see what was within, and piggyback a while.

'Wow, you look great Uncle Bo!'

'As do you, dear child. You were saying? In the astral you don't worry about clothes? How embarrassing, were we to ever bump into each other up there!'

Mitch growled as he handed Everett the can of soda.

'Now, now, Uncle Bo...'

Amy smiled back at the man who had once been a giant to her, but now seemed ever so slightly... yes, she was taller.

'Dad, Uncle Bo knows full well that if it were on the cards for us to bump into each other, he would know all about it by now. And so would Yelina, no doubt.'

Everett laughed uproariously. 'How true my dear, how definitely true!'

'Of course,' Amy smiled slyly. '...what I meant was; the ordinary sleepers are all kinds of naked out there on the astral plane anyway, psychologically. Clothes sort of morph in and out on astral bodies; they're sort of props, even for me. When you see it, you'll realise that, a lot of the time, people forget they have bodies, and they're just sort of gaseous, and shiny-glowing, until they need to act something out with another astral body, and then they just manifest the props they need.'

'Like clothes?'

'Whatever they need.'

'Fascinating.' Everett folded his arms and nodded. 'You know,

Pynes, I must visit the dream realms more often.'

Clearly, it sounded ghastly to him, and he possessed no such intent whatsoever, and he smiled in such a way that was charming, yet still let them know that. Then he turned back to the view.

'When this building was first erected, not so long ago in the grand scheme of things, Everco leased five floors, and kept leasing them even though there was no real reason other than the prestige of it. Then we forgot.'

'You mean; you forgot...'

Mitch grinned.

Everett shrugged. 'Almost the same thing. However! People kept doing things here, for us. A skeleton crew. They could have been doing those things anywhere; it's becoming so that we can all be doing all of our things at home now, really, and talking to each other on screens, like normal people. But this building was designed to try and return the social aspect to the workplace, to the high-rise; to the city, one supposes. Open plan floors designed to maximise the panoramic vistas. To contain art and good food and places to meet up. The Pleiadeans like that kind of thing, and our Pleiadean contact likes it especially, it seems.'

'Is that still Eya? The one who stood up for us?'

'Yes, and her husband Iba. I think he's her husband. There's another contact as well, her name is Uki. This was her command. From what I can gather, Uki is a kind of career explorer. Planet to planet, in and out, just the facts, recorded and stored away for someone else to worry about. However, when things started happening here on Earth – when me and Pan and you, Mitch, started happening, she became stuck here, in a way, with Eya and Iba, who were the cultural experts. She wanted to leave, they wanted to remain. They prevented the Orion Renegades killing you and Heather at Pan's wake, and were apparently fighting about the repercussions when The Dark Force used Uki's ship as part of its sinister leapfrog, down from the Cosmic Abyss through the astral plane, to maintain his hold on Hines – and make a play for you.'

Everett looked down, over his nose, at Mitch.

'An effort in which he, or "it", thankfully did not succeed.'

Mitch simply nodded; clearly he still didn't like to ponder on it.

'In the aftermath, as you know, Uki believed the ship to be essentially beyond repair, so far as any extent of undertaking that a Pleiadean of her standing is prepared to mount, you understand.'

'How damaged was it?'

Everett shook his head, a little nonplussed. 'To be frank, I'm still not really sure. Too much for them, nothing to us. From what I can tell, it's... tired. Shocked, wounded perhaps, maybe even scarred; but not ruined.'

Amy smiled. 'It's recovering?'

Everett nodded and smiled back, somewhat tightly. 'It is recovering, yes. Hanging about, resting.' Then he smiled more openly, as though he had only just then convinced himself of the truth of this. 'Taking in the sights! Yes. That's why it's here, I believe. When the so-called ruined ship was bequeathed to my own care, it was Eya who suggested that I park her over the Harbour, and work everything else out from there. And so, that's where it is. Out there. And yet, somehow, the ship is also here. It's out there, and in here, in this building.'

'Wow!' Amy was astonished, wide-eyed as she finished her soda with a few echoing slurps.

'Wow indeed, Miss Pyne. I have come in some mornings and the view from this very floor is different. It's the view from out there – the view the ship would have, projected here. Like it is showing me what it sees from out there.'

'It wants you to know...?' Amy wondered.

Everett remined tight-lipped.

'And what about... after?' Mitch enquired. 'Say, you... nurse it back to full health? Do you think it will want to leave?'

'Uki will honour her promise, as I'm assured that Pleiadeans always do. In any regard, I suspect being nursed back to full health by a human, even a Pandoran human, still counts as overt local contamination. And so, dear Pynes, here we are, and here it is!'

'But…'Mitch strolled a little, sipping, looking around.'…what will the owners of the building say? If the ship…?' He spluttered briefly. 'Wait; what is the ship, exactly?'

'Well, in regard to what the owners of the building will say, we shall see, shan't we? I believe that will depend very much who the owners of this building are, after I am through with my plans. Pending permission, of course.'

'Bo, you have permission to do whatever you want, you know that, don't even ask.' Mitch waved his hand absently, then froze a second. 'Wait – what for exactly?'

'Hah!' Everett seemed to be enjoying this. 'I intend to use what influence we have here, Mitchell, and I still have at large, to my advantage, to my niece's and to my eventual, one assumes, step-nephew's advantage. It seemed – sensibly intuitive? Given that, upon first arriving with Eya, in asking the ship if there was anywhere it liked, it came here, to this building. And given what has occurred below floors?'

'Below floors?' Amy frowned.

'Synchronicity kicked in, when events revealed that after the merger we seemed to have a lot of property leased here, and now I am negotiating on behalf of Lever to buy it.'

'Buy it? The floors or… you mean the whole building, don't you?'

'Why not? Or, at least, to purchase a controlling interest in it? Enough for a sign maybe? What do you think, Amy?'

'I…' She shrugged. 'I think you should just do whatever you do, Uncle Bo, to make the ship work. It's what you told them you would do, it's what you always do; you make things happen.'

Bo smiled; that appeared to have been a very good answer.

'As I was saying, we managed to consolidate all the lease agreements, and make a further investment. The result is that Lever now occupies the top seven floors, and has put in an offer to secure the future of what we hope to be the Lever Building.'

'The Lever Building…' Amy uttered.

Then something occurred to her.

'But – wait. We were 'gapping' to the ship, weren't we? This isn't actually the Pleiadean ship, inside the building – is it? You haven't folded the third and fifth dimensions into each other over the Circular Quay skyline *just yet*, have you Uncle Bo?'

'Yes and no; who's to say? But; mostly no, at least for now. Although I suspect that the ship will probably map this building and…who knows? Connect?'

'That's why you feel we should have the control over what's in it; and who comes and goes?'

'Indeed, Miss Pyne, indeed! The ship of course remains out there for now, over the Harbour, but it seems to already serve as a hub at times like these; I am not at all convinced that, being a multidimensional, or trans-dimensional craft, that part of it has not already infiltrated this floor.' Everett grinned. 'It does tend to anticipate my haunts; but it has not done so formally, nor permanently, dear Amy. Not, as I said – *just yet.*'

Amy laughed. 'And this is really – that building?' Amy made a full circle turn once again. 'The big, modern-design, open-plan one? The *huge deal?*'

It was – she could tell by the view.

The space was genuinely enormous – white and silver and glass and marble, at least two hundred square feet, with a number of spiral staircases and pillars that centrally divided an elliptical floor plan, ready to be customised to their specifications.

'Nice start, isn't it?' Everett guzzled some soda. 'Oh! And the penthouse rooms are delightful! We have a permanent reservation on the best one. You must come and stay!'

'Absolutely!' Amy nodded. She shivered, still smiling. 'But it's cold up here in the clouds.'

'Yes; well...'

Everett set his soft drink down in the middle of the completely vacant floor. It looked like an installation piece; a comment on the commercial retail bubble or something. Then he looked around with his balled fists pressed casually but purposefully into the deep pockets of his cream trousers.

'...we don't actually have a full staff yet, exactly, but for the skeleton crew; a few eager beavers and sniffer pups; and the developers on the floor below.'

'Developers? You mentioned something before..?'

'Yes, yes; we left them to their own devices. But still, hardly worth heating all these floors up here as well. I met you up here for secrecy; the rest will come. The people will come...' He smiled. 'We don't even need to build it; and they are already coming!'

She leaned down to look at the corresponding Lever logo on the floor, beside her Dad's piece of paper, then picked the paper up.

'Corresponding symbols allow us to gap.' She nodded. 'And Hines' secret bunker?'

'Still there.'

'Uh huh.'

Everett moved to stand beside her, staring out at Circular Quay below. 'I hear you have some secrets of your own?'

She looked sideways at him. 'Which I've come to share with you.'

He rounded his jaw a little. 'Uh huh.'

Mitch stepped up to admire the view as well, on her other side, but was a lot more conciliatory as to her personal space.

'The last few times you've come directly back Amy...' Everett's voice had a slight growl to it. '...you've been dressed very casually. This time, however...?'

'I came in my Ymira uniform.' She looked down at it again, then at the two men. 'Yes.'

'Does this have anything to do with these... secrets you wish to share?'

She looked from one to the other, both staring at her.

Then she huffed.

'Honestly, you're like my two gay Dads who've caught me sneaking home at five in the morning in leather gear!'

Their eyes bulged.

'Look; Xylata wanted us to have new uniforms. She wanted us to make a visual statement. Like this Lever symbol; like nothing they've ever used before.'

'They?' Everett demanded.

'The Ymira. The Anunnaki we've allied with.'

'Well, they're very stylish.' Mitch grinned, helpfully. 'Gay Dads notwithstanding!'

Everett was silent.

'It's fairly sci-fi, right?' Amy seemed slightly embarrassed still. 'But, it seems like we can't get away from that. Pop culture is in our DNA now. It's certainly all through the astral plane.' She looked down again at the upper arms and breast plates. 'The stripes and insignias didn't seem quite *so pink* when I was there…'

'Very striking…' Everett conceded softly. '…against the black.'

'Very – pink.' Amy kept staring down at herself. 'Theirs are lime stripes.'

'Theirs? These Ymira you've mentioned?'

'Yeah; Ymira. Xylata's clan. You remember, right? I'm kind of…' Amy shrugged. 'I'm kind of their CEO now. They're my brand, my company.'

'Is that so?'

'It's a whole thing, Uncle Bo! It's happening! You need to come with me and see it!'

He didn't seem convinced.

Her shoulders slumped.

'Green for reptilians, pink for…' Amy groaned. 'Oh no! I'm the only human so far; they made it pink for humans!'

'Oh dear…' Mitch uttered. '…although I suppose it is a very Anunnaki kind of decision. You shouldn't be too surprised.'

'Well, that's just another thing that needs changing.' She shook her head a little, suddenly amused by her own bemusement. 'I don't know why it does surprise me. I think it's more that I didn't pick it up.'

Everett hummed, almost growling.

'What colour, I wonder, would represent all of humanity?'

'Well I guess we'll all just have to work it out!' Amy gave a huge shrug, and let out a big sigh. '…look; we can handle all that when we get there, okay? I can tell you the whole story.'

'When we get there?' Everett sounded doubtful. 'Where is – there?'

'She has something to show us, Bo.' Mitch sounded very assertive. 'Out there, where she works. We need to listen to her and respect that she's made a formal request of us. We're going, okay?'

Amy was so pleased he'd said that.

She looked at Mitch.

She could see her own eyes in his; the shape, the angles of skin, the things that projected a person's character. In time, even her smiles-lines would emerge the same as his. She liked that.

She turned back to her uncle, her honorary uncle, she supposed.

'Please, Uncle Bo. You need to come with me, both of you. You need to see something.' She looked to Everett. 'I need advice. From my people. From my friends.'

Everett's face was like stone as he turned from her and stared out at the view.

He said nothing.

'Well…' Mitch turned and reached out, once again placing his hands on her upper arms. 'It does look like a very cool cosplay to me. But; a very professional one. And, you're taller, too.'

He stepped back and removed his coat, then held it up like a dresser. She turned around as he helped her into it, catching sight of Everett again as she did. This time, she caught something, a quick trickle of emotion, and understood why he was so still, so impassive.

'What's the material?' Mitch seemed to admire it. 'It's like leather but…?'

'It's very astral. Crocodile print skin. Or it might be real; I haven't got it tested yet to see what it manifests as in third density. All I do know is that the crocodile thing is Xylata's idea of wit.'

Amy completed her full circle, then ruffled herself around in the big coat until it settled.

'That coat fits you better than me, I think… are your shoulders a bit wider, as well…?'

'It's the manifestation energies in the astral…' She padded the shoulders, pulled in the lapels. 'It makes you more – *you*, somehow. And, I think I'm just standing straighter – taller, than I used to.' She smiled, beguilingly. 'I used to have tall girl syndrome.'

Mitch smiled, proudly.

'I remember.'

CHAPTER 9

They silently admired the view a bit longer, with Everett remaining conspicuously quiet.

Finally Mitch spoke up.

'Heather always comes back from the astral plane looking radiant; she says I come back more telegenic. And look at Uncle Bo. The Pleiadean ship seems to have taken years off him!'

She didn't want to look at him again, not just yet.

Mitch could see something was going on with them.

'Very black, very leather, very cool, Amy. The coat really pulls it all together.' Mitch turned to Everett. 'So, Bo – we were the only ones in Pan's old building, and now we're the only ones here. We seem to be okay gapping into empty buildings and not being seen. But we can't do that everywhere, all the time.'

Everett turned to him.

'Go on, Mitchell.'

'Since we – inherited?'

Everett smiled wryly at him.

Mitch continued, smiling back. 'We've discovered a lot of buildings around town that we now own, like Pan's. We've cleared what was left of the tenants in Pan's building; most of them we had to help adjust a bit, being affected by proximity to Pan's labyrinth, so to speak, but they're all doing fine. Might be useful, some of them; psychic and sensitive. You know how these things pull in karmic families. But these others are all enormous apartments in the middle of a major city, in the middle of a real estate boom, and they're all empty; who knows what else there is? I think we should think about something formal.'

'The world is full of nooks and crannies…' Amy smiled. She looked around again. Their current space was hardly that, but she was sure they were there, somewhere behind the big spaces. If not, they would be created, simply by creating something in a space this big; seven floors and counting.

'We need to find more of them. More nooks and crannies. Or create them.' Mitch smiled, echoing his daughter's thoughts. 'I can tell you about that later; I have an idea, but I think I might need someone good with real estate looking into it.'

'I think I see where you're going.' Everett nodded. 'Remind me; I think I have just the person. She might even be around here somewhere.'

Mitch smiled; he'd done well.

Everett turned from the view and looked back down, with Amy.

'Once it's catalogued, Pan's Library will be stored here. It will be protected by the ship, up here, in storage.'

Mitch remembered Amy's slight distress at the idea. 'But it's not because Uncle Pan won't ever get well again, sweetie. Or ever come back again, it's because –'

'Those books up there are dangerous in the wrong hands. I know. Xylata and I have Kyvza's occult... well, they call it an arsenal.' She returned her attention to Everett. 'Who's cataloguing Pan's things, Uncle Bo? We could probably use someone to look at ours as well. Maybe even combine them?'

Everett returned her gaze. He seemed impressed.

'That would be a strong show of faith from your new clan, Miss Pyne.' He looked out again. 'The ship will protect them, Mendoza will archive them. The Pleiadeans and Sirians seem fine with that; I didn't want to argue.'

'Mendoza?' Amy grumbled. 'I'd wondered...'

'Wondered what, Miss Pyne?'

She grumbled louder. 'If we ask for his help, it means that whatever we have, and whoever we lend them to, the Sirians will know all about it. It's enough that the Pleiadeans will know; given you're storing them in this office building.'

Everett nodded.

'True.' Mitch sighed. 'But they're our Pleiadeans, and our Sirians, and they're the only people we trust who can deal with them if anything goes wrong.'

Amy scoffed. 'The same Sirian Goddess who forcefully ascended Mendoza?'

'Misha...' Mitch whispered.

'And don't forget; the Draco were helped by the Sirians with their sixth density security systems. We still don't know who. Those people nearly got you all killed – if it wasn't for Xylata...'

Everett shrugged. 'Misha wants to help. Just like Xylata wants to help. Just like the Ymira – want to help.'

Amy didn't like his tone, but she understood; he hadn't been there, he didn't understand. That was why he, they, had to come. Still, her judgment was in question, and she experienced a little temper spike, and asked a question of him within a tiny tantrum.

'And what about these Adelaidean sorcerers? What were they helping with?'

Everett nodded to himself. Amy sensed; she'd handled it relatively well, considering all of his experience, screwing with and baiting people.

'They asked for one of Pan's books in payment. I gave it to them.'

Amy was shocked. 'You did what?'

'They'll bring it back; or give it back if we need it. It's how the good ones work. But they seemed to think that taking another sorcerer's library wholesale was a somewhat dark thing to do. The tradition there is to attend the wake and wait for the books to choose you.'

Unable to help herself, Amy grinned. 'Ooh, I like that tradition.'

'I thought you might. I imagine your paths will cross, sooner or later, you and these people. They were very interested in the notion of the so-called Karma Forge; but as I suspect your father has explained, they deal exclusively within the realms of Inner Earth, and its impact upon our world of third density – they might not put it that way, of course. They clearly deal sometimes with the astral, but when those realms cross specifically, it is very strange, and nothing I have dealt with personally.'

Amy immediately thought of Yelina. 'What does your wife think?'

Everett raised an eyebrow at her. 'She recommends leaving them to their own devices. She says that, in regard to Earth energies, 'they know what they are doing'. Yelina is one of the only people I would trust when they make that statement about someone I don't fully...' He considered the last world, then let it go, somewhat reluctantly. '...understand.'

That was his power, Amy knew; one of them anyway. To be an alpha male who could admit that; that there were things that he couldn't understand. It was part of the strange equation, the weird combo, that had started all this; his determination to understand Pan.

'I think I've seen them, Uncle Bo. Coming back and forth through the astral. Next time I'll say hello. But, they take strange paths. They seem – tangential to ours, but... wilder? It's not as easy as you think to cross those kinds of astral boundaries, and especially not ones like that. It's like crossing a seasonal river; some places there are bridges; some are old, some are new. Some will withstand the next flood, some will collapse. Some are just long deserts that you have to walk a long way across, and hope it doesn't flash-flood in the middle when you try. And either side, there are worlds within worlds, with portals and gatekeepers to negotiate, and cul-de-sacs and dead-ends and even traps; prisons. To get to where the Inner Earth crosses with our Earth, you'd want a guide.'

Everett raised his other eyebrow at her. 'And you want me to accompany you there?'

Amy sighed. 'Not there, specifically; I haven't even really done that. I just need to show you something – in my astral, in the normal astral. Just – next door. Simple. Here to there. See what I see for a sec, and tell me what you think.'

Everett nodded, his face impassive.

'Amy, Mitch; the sorcerers offered us a warning. It might tie in with what you've just said.'

The enormous white room – white floor, really – seemed extra cold all of a sudden.

'I can feel it. You're going to talk about The Dark Thing, aren't you?' Amy shivered, even in her new black coat. 'Is it all connected somehow?'

Immediately, she felt like a conspiracy theorist.

'As if this isn't all crazy enough already?'

'Yes, yes…' Everett looked around. 'Spaceships and sorcerers.' He smiled at Mitch. 'Crossing the genres, eh Mister Film Critic? A post-modern cinematic device that we old fuddy-duddy classists get very fussy about. It has to be done – just right.'

Mitch shrugged. 'I guess. By the time I started writing professional reviews, Tarantino was well out of the gate.'

'Of course.' Everett grumbled and gazed moodily around the office again, looking to relocate his soda. 'In a way, you know, That Dark Thing is all we have been talking about from the start.'

Everett walked slowly to a small point on the floor in the distance, then plucked his drink up, as though he were a stage magician who'd conjured it back out of thin air. Then he straightened and looked back at Amy.

'But, you know that well enough already.'

'You're freaking me out, Uncle Bo.'

Bo took a gulp of his Fizzy Lolly Water and looked out, past her, at the Harbour. It was almost fully night now; as she turned to match his gaze she noticed that the lights along the ceiling had dimmed up automatically, but the glass did not reflect them back.

Was that 'modern' or 'Pleiadean' or a 'tech-combo'?

She wasn't fussed.

The huge, empty, elliptical design looked like a space ship in itself; although perhaps its vacancy lent it to appear more like a spaceship's hangar?

It didn't matter.

It wouldn't seem haunted much longer.

Everett, and Mitch and Heather too probably, would soon fill it with people, with guests in the penthouse, if they weren't living there themselves.

'The ship likes the building…'

The statement from Everett came suddenly, and sounded as though he were suspicious of it. He started to walk back toward them. Darkness seemed to be falling very quickly.

'Open plan floors and wide social spaces. The view of the Harbour.' He nodded. 'These Pleiadean ships…' He looked back at Amy, as though she should know this already. '…in a way, they are powered by art, by beauty. By an integrity of heart and mind, a purity of intent and a willingness to create. But I think it is unsure of this third density world it has crash-landed into. I think it needs to power-up, to re-enegrise on third density creative energy, third density beauty, third density *culture*, if it's going to stay.'

'That's nice, Uncle Bo.' Amy went and stood beside him, side by side, like allies; like he wanted. 'It has to get to know the places, the people; the nooks and crannies and higgledy-piggledy.'

Everett looked at his can.

'Fizzy Lolly Water. Indeed. Indeed.'

'Me and Heather spent a week or so on the ship, slept there.' Mitch stepped up again as well, folding his arms. 'If you stay with it long enough, it will take you somewhere. Or perhaps, it will go somewhere and you just happen to be along for the ride.'

Everett chuckled, short and deep.

'Where did we end up last time, Mitch? Was is The Blue Lake? Or the MCG?' He too folded his arms at the view. 'The ship flies where it wants, and it will go somewhere if you request a destination; but in the end, it seems to want to stay around here. Around Circular Quay, around Sydney, where Eya said it would like to be. I hit upon the idea of the sorcerers because every now and then it flies over to Adelaide; it found them, and I asked Yelina who they were. They seemed like her sort. It looks for certain types, sometimes; sorcerers, witches, mystics and sages, brings them up and lets them do something to the power systems or the guidance systems, or sometimes just to choose a nice pattern for a guest room. One time it very leisurely circled the Parklands for a few days, then came back here via the Flinders Ranges. Another time it zoomed to Brisbane in a few minutes, and found some Indigenous Elders, and they asked me to come and sleep on the roof with them. In our dreams, we told stories and played music. That lasted a week. Then it took days to come back, grazing around the Great Diving Range, wandering out to the Grampians, the Blue Mountains; but it always comes back here. It went to Melbourne, and sat in the middle of Port Philip Bay for three days; then spent another three hovering over the Royal Exhibition Building.'

'And the MCG…?' Amy smiled.

Everett smiled back. 'It didn't take it long to absorb the coliseums. But here, The Harbour, is where it seems to rest now, absorbing energy. Particularly wherever there was play, and drama, and music; it hovers over places that are long gone. Inside, sometimes, you can see it relive the memory of those places…'

'Inside?'

'I don't think it knew Australia existed; not really. In the short conversations I have had with Uki and Eya, I gather it has spent a lot of time in what we would call The West. That was its mission; that stream of culture, I believe. I'm told it spent a lot of time in New York, and in London. It didn't like Los Angeles, but when it went to Prague, they thought it would never leave. The same with Berlin. It crossed paths with the other ships but I believe that, not long before we came across it, it had been in Peru watching Pan, knowing that he would bring something into Western culture, create a new inroad somehow.'

'You think it was the Pandora Sequence?' Mitch asked, amazed. Then he scoffed at himself and smiled. 'How could it not be…?'

'Uncle Bo; you're saying, it recorded... past performances, somehow? It can – see history?'

'The cityscape and the architecture, they are beautiful, yes.' Everett turned to her and gave her a rare, wry smile. 'But it's what people do in the buildings that matter. It sat over Kings Cross for weeks.'

'Kings Cross? Where the sex shops and strippers are?'

'I seem to remember young Pan having a penchant for the sacred dances…? Everett drifted a few seconds while Amy didn't know where to look. '…but yes. And, no. I confess, I was shocked by the choice of that particular observation point, but it seems the place has been more than its reputation over the years. Australian Vaudeville, The Sebel Townhouse Bar, and in close proximity to many, many theatres; performance and dance centres of – all kinds. Not all of them burlesque of the escalating variety, and of course, The Opera House a cheap cab ride away for most of the time; and so many music hall establishments, in the pockets of history, in between.'

'In between? Your prediction, about social media?' Mitch frowned. 'The ship; something about it, sees through time…?'

'You can hear the acts; the melody, and the dialogue at least, in your dreams, when you sleep up there.'

Mitch put his hands to the side of his head. 'Yes; yes you can, can't you?'

They all stared out. The city itself, the lights on the Bridge and the Opera House seemed to illuminate the city-side of Circular Quay by themselves. They didn't; the whole area was spectacularly well-lit at all times of night, but it did seem that way, poetically.

'There have been times I have been on the ship and looked out, and dreamed… of enormous forces, battling in the sky above the Harbour, for the fate of the world, the future of the human race; circling, swirling, smashing into each other, impacting with the ocean as they fall.'

He sighed, then turned away.

For a moment Mitch and Amethyst Pyne thought they too

could see –

'Howevaah!'

Amy and Mitch jumped, just as they were starting to think they could see the Pleiadean disc as well, right there in all the reflected neon and halogen, in the middle of al the –

'Right here, right now, in this time, in third density, for us; our big ship, my big ship…!' He paused and stared out like a hawk. 'Seems to need *structure!*'

'Structure?' Amy enquired, a little testily.

'Yes! Structure! As well as culture!' He nodded. 'Like an artist needs a stable place to work, you see? Before they can produce art; especially when you're starting from the ground up, like she is! But there is a lot of clearing to do, energetically, before the ship can be whole again, here in Olde Sydneye Towne.'

'Is that why you hired second density energy manipulators?' Amy asked, feeling brave. 'These sorcerers?'

Everett frowned at her, smiling, looking down now it seemed.

'Now you're seeing it. A fellow businessman, he set up his base there, in Adelaide, for a woman he was chasing; we sometimes trade information. After the ship found them and Yelina cleared them, my colleague sent the sorcerer, and some other, as you might say, second density energy manipulators, here as a favour; to repay an old debt. And they did what they could do, to understand what was happening here.'

'So you really do mean; a sorcerer, don't you?' Amy demanded. 'Like Harry Potter, or Gandalf?'

Everett nodded. 'Yes. Although, these were… less Michael Gambon and Maggie Smith, and more – David Lynch and Isabella Rossellini. But… these folk were, indeed, not amorphous fifth or sixth density manipulators of crystalline structures, or plasma patterns. They were humans, like you and me. Separated from the mainstream consciousness by something extraordinary in their genes, but… people. Ordinary, but extraordinary people. People who work with Inner Earth energies; cosmic energies, emotional energies and archetypal forces too – the combination of dimensions on this world are sometimes extreme, but often they bring up interesting people, with interesting abilities; bring out the best in them, if they are lucky.'

Amy nodded to herself. 'So we're not the only forces at work here, then? On Earth?'

Mitch turned from the view now, looking concerned.

'Do we get a chance to meet them?'

'It seems that each of us must walk our own path, Mitchell, and they have been summoned back to their chequerboard city, to walk their own. But what their leader told me was that this. That we should expect more of the darker Earth forces to rise. Many terrible things occurred here – right down there, across The Rocks and beyond – where this city was first initiated, from its earliest days. It took a long time for any kind of true Western culture to emerge here, on this continent, that represents any kind of purchase, any gravity, any gravitas, from which to lodge a position of sustained interest; at least, so far as conscious fifth dimensional energy of any kind would see it – let alone a sentient, flying castle…' He looked curiously at Mitch. 'It really does seem to enjoy the memory of this… Sebel Townhouse Bar…?'

Mitch nodded. 'The reputation was for rock-and-roll debauchery, but artists gathered there, from all over the world – I've heard the legends; some very odd mixes and crossed-paths. For about two decades, it was where anyone who was considered any kind of creative force from overseas stayed, and slept; or at least drank, and smoked and snorted and shot; and copulated with hookers, and each other, in a way only people in the entertainment business can, while they were here. It was the first time entertainers from this country, one of the last frontiers on one of the last borders between Industrial Age and Twenty-First Century Civilizations, could connect with the Greater Western Culture, on an Ongoing Basis…'

'The ship seems to have taken its first great store of energy from there.'

'Jesus…'

Mitch looked out again at the Bay.

'…what *on Earth* must it think of Australia?'

'Indeed! Or the Earth itself?' Everett slapped a hand on his shoulder. 'We shall see, Mitchell. We shall see. This is all just starting. This is all just attraction, magnetism; the forces of cosmic consciousness coming together as incarnated beings, assessing and aligning. There is much yet to learn, much yet to be revealed, before the true patterns begin to emerge. But there is, for now, one important issue remaining…'

'And what's that, Bo?'

CHAPTER 10

'The Dark Force!'

Again, Everett had suddenly raised his voice to a booming timbre, making Mitch jump out of his skin.

'Wuhuh!'

'The Satanic Thing from The Cosmic Abyss…!'

'Don't *do that!*'

Everett cried out. 'It burned a path, all the way down to us, they say…!'

'Jesus!'

'…from the cosmic abyss through Sirian astral space, through the Pleiadean ship, into Hines' private quarters. When it departed, the way remained for you, Mitch, to ascend, to go back to the void, and beyond. To save the human race...'

Everett's eyes bulged.

'...so – they – say.'

'But did we?' Mitch demanded. 'Save us? Ask yourself.'

Amy looked at her father; she knew that this was what he was really concerned about.

Maybe, she thought, *I shouldn't ask him what I was going to ask him? Maybe... they shouldn't see what I want to show them...?*

'Of course we did, Mitch – well, you and Heather did.'

Everett was looking at Mitch as though he'd had a mental lapse. But Amy knew this look; Mitch had been waiting, and he was determined to make his point.

'I know, Bo. I know it seemed that way. Like we all helped. And don't forget Suzie. She threw herself into the abyss with Lucifer to get me and Heather, to get us all out of that thing's… *thrall.* But listen to me…'

Mitch looked back and forth between them.

'...both of you. The Dark Thing, whatever it was, or is... it had been sleeping. For a while. It had me; it told me I was in Limbo forever, with nothing, forever. And I believed it. I felt a terrible despair, that will always be there. That I can always remember.'

'Oh, Dad...'

'It's okay sweetie; I have superpowers and Heather, and a multi-billion-dollar company.' He smiled at her and rolled his eyes. 'It all evens out somewhere; I'll manage.'

She embraced him, hugged him tight.

'But sweetie; you have to listen.'

'Okay Dad.'

'There are times I think, maybe The Dark Thing wasn't thinking too clearly when it decided to – punch down? Maybe it's a True Beast? Like, an Animal Monster? And it just came out of some kind of Abysmal Cosmic Hibernation, because it sensed a morsel too tasty to pass up, and that's all it was? Maybe Hines was bait for people like me, like us – and we got away, just at the last minute, and maybe that's all that happened?'

'So? What's wrong with that.'

'Just one little problem, sweetie; it's clearly completely ridiculous.'

His daughter released him and looked into his eyes, surprised.

'What sweetie? You think it just played out like "a missed opportunity for Old Nick to gobble a midnight snack?" I just... slipped out of the trap? Lucky me?' He sighed. '...I'm sorry, this *Thing;* it just doesn't work like that.'

'Who can say, Mitch?' Everett offered.

'I was there! In the room, Bo!'

'Of course, Mitch.' Everett closed his eyes and opened them slowly. 'According to Hines, and you Mitch, and even a man as grounded as Harding, I think we can all see that the danger...'

'It isn't over.'

Amy stepped back. 'What do you mean?'

'Just listen, sweetie. So this... Dark Being? It's supposed to be a true Demonic Force, right? One of the more Evil Creatures on this side of the Western Galactic Spiral Arm…? Well, you'd think it would have closed the trap door behind it, wouldn't you? Old and wise as it is? Let all those people die in the Terrible Earthquake? That would then have triggered a Global Collapse and ended – Civilization As We Know it? Don't you think?'

'Burned the bridge behind it, you mean?' Amy nodded. 'So we couldn't – what did they call it? Storm Heaven? I have – thought that. I didn't want to contemplate it, but –'

'That's how it works. The evil in the darkness repels us; but sometimes, it has a message for us.'

'A message?'

'Not intentionally, perhaps. But by revealing itself, we can extrapolate from what it reveals. Like anything, we can see how it behaves, and learn. I mean, I'm not… mental, am I? I mean; it doesn't make any sense, does it? The Dark Thing, allowing us all to make the journey, via a path it made itself, to *save that many people?* Does that sound like Satan to you? Great and Evil Lord; Benefactor of the Miracle Quake?'

'I guess…' Amy gulped. '…not…?'

She tried to think.

'…but, maybe it's so old and wise, so bored, it didn't necessarily see a threat coming from a backwater world like this? Or, maybe it doesn't care about the consequences? Maybe – closing a gate behind it, to make sure a million ants don't get away? Make sure all those insects die? Maybe something like that is not even on the radar for a creature that old and half-awake and uncaring?'

She made her offering, even as Mitch held her gaze with steely unlikelihood. But Amy persevered.

'I mean, does an ice fisherman cover his ice hole, after he…?' She trailed off and sighed. 'They do, don't they?' She huffed and swirled her soda can, sipping its emptiness for a last drop of sugar on the rim, and scowling. 'So you think it might all be a trap? That – we all – might be part of it?'

Everett spoke, solemn now, no hint of a joke.

'The sorcerers say, if this is true, that we are fighting for the human race to ascend, then that is not an outcome everyone wants.'

'Well...' Amy scoffed. '...we know that!'

'Regardless, it is known, well known, upon their plane of influence, as it is well known within ours, that demons, and Draco, will not easily relinquish control, that it must be wrested from them to the bitter end...' He looked at Mitch, then refolded his arms, still clutching his soda. They heard the can crunch a little, and his chest seemed bigger.

'Tell her.'

She looked to her father. 'Tell me what?'

'Amy, I didn't meet them, but I'm convinced that these second-density sorcerers are on our side; fighting the same fight. And they say that this Dark Thing, the thing we sometimes refer to as Satan, this Demonic Force; it does not let anyone go. Not without a massive brawl, an angel on your side, or a cunning plan – *or a very good reason of its own*. And let's face it, at that time, I had none of those things...' He managed a weak grin. 'Unless Harding is an angel and he's not telling anybody.'

'Regardless...' Everett agreed. '...The Dark Thing lets *nobody go*; at least, not the way it simply – '

He spread his huge, freckled hands.

' – let Mitch go.'

He double-clicked his fingers.

'Let us all go!'

The click echoed throughout the two hundred square meters.

'And Oliver Hines?' Amy asked, not really wanting to know.

'I have people watching him. But your father and I believe now that The Dark Thing did indeed let him go; but only to shift focus.'

'What?'

'It had to, sweetie.'

'Why?!' Amy felt tears in her eyes.

Mitch sighed, then spoke with a kind of resigned growl.

'Ames. It let us all go. Not just me, not just Hines; everyone who was standing outside that room. All of us; and all of them at the party. I told you, this evening on the balcony; what I believe, what I've seen about the expanded consciousness of aliens, of other beings; ascended beings. Their tech, their reach; the higher up the chain of expanded consciousness you go.'

Amy stared at him. 'And?'

It was clearly something he'd been holding in a while.

'...I am aware, just a fraction, of the field of influence a creature like that could have. I have felt it; how old and powerful it was. It could have devoured the Hines Mansion, devoured all Hollywood, and certainly it could have stopped us; prevented the Miracle Quake, made it the Massacre Quake; devoured or at least *caused and claimed* all of the Two or Three or Five Million Dead, whatever it would have been; the toll as it would have been without the Elohim Intervention. True, Harding broke the contact spell by destroying the sigil on the ceiling, but the Dark Thing; it can see ahead, many variations, for many centuries. Millennia, perhaps.'

Amy and Everett exchanged a glance.

Everett nodded, but was silent.

'I'm not saying it's invincible. I'm not saying there isn't something...' She saw her father search his mind for the flipside. 'Look; we know that beyond that Thing, beyond The Abyss, there are higher beings, like, more of Orion, higher than Orion, and probably again, older and wiser... maybe even God and The Source; but that Thing, it is quite simply a totally manipulative, malevolent force of *pure dark nature*. And it is old, and wise, and clever; and it let us go.'

Everett spoke softly. 'Mitchell, my boy, you can't continue to torture yourself like this...'

Amy looked to him; her Uncle Bo's voice was sadder than she'd ever heard it.

'Look, Bo; if you're on the fortieth floor, with an alien spaceship that could probably... I dunno; put another thirty invisible floors on this building without us even realising we were in them? Show us a path to fame and fortune, if we just take three steps, based on the data it's already collated about talent and celebrity?'

'I suppose...?'

'Well, what could that Thing do, then? One hundred times more expansive and totally evil? Lucifer is lesser than that Thing, but he was able to offer me and Heather total dominion of Earth. Imagine what something that old, and powerful, and smart and psychopathic, and all the time it's had to get better at what it does; what could it do?'

Amy was almost shocked when Everett attempted a response.

'If it is...' Everett began carefully. '...as you say, Mitchell, then it is the demonic, cosmic equivalent of the evolution of... a Megalodon shark; but with the entire galaxy as its ocean?'

'No, Bo. It's a godlike, demonic force; a psychopathic torturer just a couple of notches down from... what I could tell – God Himself. Like I said; it's not invincible; it still has to engage, and play....'

Something in Amy's mind sparked.

'...but whatever Russian Doll Level of Cosmic Cities on the Galactic Planes it's looking down from...?'

Mitch snarled and shook his head.

'...it is a Grand Malefic Chess Master, bent on plunging everything into darkness, playing from a view, *a view it understands and can manipulate,* looking down from the one thousandth floor.'

Mitch shrugged.

'Conservatively.'

Everett hummed deeply to himself, staring back at Mitch, just a second too long for comfort, as though he had not enjoyed the inference to his own perch of power.

Amy nodded.

She saw it now.

'And it made a move, didn't it?'

It seemed that she had decided, as she stared Everett down.

'Didn't it?'

'It seems so, Miss Pyne.'

'You've talked about this before?'

'Heather is also very concerned.'

'And you're not, Uncle Bo?'

'I am; just – not to the extent that it stops me moving forward.'

'Then I'll tell you what I believe. I believe it had Oliver Hines. It had Olivera; it had a foothold, one lazy line attached to him out of who knows how many? A dozen across space-time? A dozen million? And it let that fish go, because it saw my father as a better option. And not just Mitch; it saw what was happening. The whole Pandora Sequence, all the Pandorans, and all the repercussions. Lever versus the Draco. Who knows? And it dropped an atomic load of chaos on us by cracking a pathway, a cascade of cracks, through the dimensions, that will always remain – for whatever purpose that was, for whatever purpose it will have from here. It could have just taken a bite; Hines, Mitch, or made a meal of the party – or a banquet of the Quake. But instead, it made a move; it collided us all together; Inner Earth, Us, Anunnaki, Pleiadeans, Sirians, Elohim, Nephilim, Orions and All Of The Above; within that cascade, top to bottom. And now it's waiting. Waiting to see what chaos the contents of Pandora's Box will unleash upon the world. Because it saw something bigger; bigger than five million deaths in a Hollywood Quake, further down the line – along with all the original evils Pan has unleashed upon the world.'

'And, this is what it saw…?' Mitch looked out at the ship again. 'It made us? And gave us this ship, gave us these powers?'

Amy pulled the black coat closer around her.

'No, it didn't. Maybe it let us keep them; but Pan's mind made that happen. Everett's money. Yours and Heather's bravery; Suzie, Aunt Saph, Aunt Trudy, Cricket, Vance, Father Lance at the church, Yelina at the mansion, Harding and his men, and Xylata at the end, all helping you get to the angels – and then the angels helped us! The Elohim! Misha, Uki, and Obsidian – any one of them could have stopped us, stopped you, at any time. Okay, okay. Maybe this Dark, Evil Thing wants us going for ascension too soon? Huh? We've each heard a bit, I'm sure, about how humanity has tried and fallen, ebbed and flowed, here and there and back again, as many as four or five times before now, right? Heard about how we can't remember it, can't learn from it, can't consciously course-correct, because the Anunnaki created what we now call The Karma Forge? This planet's culture, essentially? So, maybe we destroy ourselves this time, like we almost did every other time before, and this is the reason why? Maybe this has always been the reason why, and it's just a big huge loop? We just have to make sure that this time it doesn't happen! Right?'

They were both looking at her with sympathy, but also with great doubt.

'Right?'

'But…' Mitch seemed stuck on the idea. 'What if this really is the final shot we get, and The Thing just left us alone because we're what fucks it up? Because of what Pan found – and we do? Maybe it's that – going too soon helps the other races make the choice to destroy us? Like half of them want to now anyway, right…? And this Dark Thing – it knew that?'

Everett shrugged. 'Maybe it simply created the path, and left the door open, to create more chaos in general? I'm sure that's what the Nephilim do, when they do; by all accounts this thing isn't even – a personality. It may not even have an agenda; no more than sifting through the flotsam and jetsam and debris of a cosmic tsunami.'

Amy thought; thought hard.

Her Dad had slipped, and was backsliding through his fear.

'Look, guys; maybe it just busted down, went back, and didn't give a shit, about any of it?' Amy snarled again. 'That's what evil does down here! A lot!'

Everett spread his arms and made a face; they might all be right, the shrug seemed to say.

Mitch spoke softly, still looking out, to where the Pleiadean ship was supposedly observing.

'Maybe all of the above, and below. But all information tells us; we need to be ready for attacks on all sides, all quadrants, all dimensions, as these ancient forms of powerful evil make their play to defend their current stranglehold on power.'

Amy nodded, but huffed.

'Look; I agree, I agree; of course I agree! But from my side, all I really know is, things will be better when the Draco have been defeated, and the Anunnaki are gone. That's my focus; these things happen over decades – we each need to stick to our own focus; Uncle Bo, you make the ship better; Dad, you and Heather, run the company; and I'll get rid of the Draco. This is what I have been trying to tell you, ever since I got here, and you need to listen, okay? I need you to come with me, through the astral plane, and I am going to show you how I'm going to do it. Because I can do it; but I need your help. Okay?'

That seemed to shake him out of it.

'Really sweetie?'

'Yes, Dad. Yes!'

I think...

'As you say.' She could practically feel Everett's stress leave his body as he spoke. 'Show me the way!'

She turned to her father, but he was still staring out at the ship.

'It left the hole in the ice. And it's still watching.'

'I know Dad.' Amy sighed. 'We must be cautious.'

Lightning cracked over the Harbour.

'After all...' Everett uttered. '...this is Australia.'

CHAPTER 11

Everett's phone broke the mood after a silent minute or so, as a basic tune went off and he pulled it out from his white breast jacket pocket; it was a Pleiadean hybrid, the same as Amy's.

Amy kissed her father on the cheek.

'It's okay Dad. Wait and see.'

He smiled, tightly, but she could see he was unconvinced.

Everett ended his call after a few brief words.

'I see your father has hooked you up with the latest contraband alien tech? After a while, you can simply will it to work; ingenious! No headphones or even –'

Hers vibrated and she removed it from her jacket; the transparent rectangular screen now showed Everett's contact details, that the date was: July 15th, 2014 : 6.15pm, along with the weather, twelve degrees Celsius, and her name: Amethyst Pyne. However, as soon as she looked at it again, the screen registered her gaze and many other icons began popping up.

'Wha...'

She looked up; Everett seemed to be flicking them over to her, through the air with his fingers.

'Some toys for you to try. Ten years ahead of their time, we believe. Well; maybe five.'

'Oh! These are apps!'

Everett took note. 'We're trying to think of our own name for them.'

'Don't bother Uncle Bo. I might not be in the thick of the astral just yet, but I can see ideas and trends and – icons – come and go; some things just come through and they are; the colour sticks, the theme sticks, the name sticks – people will try different variants, but these are universally called apps, for a long time to come.'

Everett seemed impressed. 'Nice intel, Pyne. You can keep it coming if you like!'

Amy watched as the apps popped up across her screen with a holographic effect; she tried to move them with her finger and found that her finger went inside the plastic, that some of the icons were actually deeper into the screen than others. She held it up sideways to her face, with her finger pressed down and, amazingly, she could not see her finger coming through on the other side. Normal Earth smartphones had just started being able to manage this many apps, but even the expensive ones had not mastered… whatever this was.

'We're thinking of calling it 'quantum positioning'; something funkier than 'Quantum Phones'. We're not sure what the tech does specifically, but clearly it creates a pocket dimension of some sort within the basic frame.'

Amy made a face. 'Clearly!' She shrugged. 'Sorry Uncle Bo, the little time I spent at Uni, I did all creative and creative theory; I only know what this is in terms of sci-fi; but what do the Qantas lawyers think about a Quantaphone?'

Everett grinned. 'My dear Miss Pyne; this is science fiction – our very lives are science fiction now!' The grin increased; he was so excited by it. 'We live in the future!' The grin abruptly dropped. 'And there are still lawyers in the future; and they are still working on it.'

Amy kind of loved him like a real uncle at that moment.

'Don't worry Uncle Bo – I'll come up with something.'

The grin returned, and he spoke a little more mischievously.

'I'm sure you will, Miss Pyne, I'm sure you will!'

Then he was distracted again.

'Ah!' Everett smiled and nodded as his hand went involuntarily to his ear, listening to a call, even though there seemed to be no physical tech attachment there. 'One of my sniffer pups is bringing up your friends...'

'My...?' Amy frowned deeply as she and her father exchanged

a quick glance, which Everett read accurately, and immediately.

There were no friends.

Everett thrust the phone back into his pocket and spoke to someone, into the air, his head slightly inclined.

'Miss Lavé, could you hold, please? We're not quite ready…?' He clenched his teeth, but continued to speak in a pleasant tone. 'I see Miss Lavé. Please hold.'

He turned to Amy.

'Your *friends* are in the lift with Miss Lavé, almost here. Now, to be clear, we can't have anyone hurt. What is your best guess as to who they are?'

'Where's security?' Amy demanded.

Everett spread his hands. 'Nobody knows we're here! I have my most aggressive assistants on the floor beneath with the developers, and Miss Lavé was scouting the lobby. Automated building security must have picked up a name you spoke?'

Mitch snapped out of his malaise and started paying attention.

'Autom…?' That seemed a lot to process. 'A name? Like, Amy?'

'Amy!' Mitch snapped his fingers. 'You said you were CEO of Ymira!'

'I did? I did! Fuck – *I really did!*' Amy thought fast. 'What backup do we have? Where's the big man – Harding?'

'Guarding Heather – she's out shopping!'

'Shopping?'

Mitch moaned. 'Finding you a dress for the premiere!'

Everett seemed to pluck something from the air and fling it at her.

'Real time,' he snapped. 'We're on forty-four.'

Her phone was still in her hand when it vibrated. The screen was displaying a video feed, looking down from a central camera, positioned above the elevator door. She knew instantly what was happening. A counter on the right of the screen was climbing; thirty seven; thirty eight… fifteen seconds; fourteen seconds.

'This tech is too helpful; it's picked up Ymira as my business name, put it on a cleared list, they've turned up and she's let them through as business associates! Gaia, God and Ghost! Either this lady's way too eager to please, or the building software is!'

The assistant, Miss Lavé, front and centre on Amy's screen, was tall, lean, and dressed in a tight but neutral white shirt and black slacks; a textbook-sensible office assistant.

Everett gave his trademark growl. 'Annoying combo of both, I suspect.'

'If they're Ymira, I don't know them.'

Mitch was looking at his own phone. 'They're wearing pink; you said you were the only one.'

'They're wearing Ymira uniforms, which means, if they are not Ymira, which there is no way they could be, according to most other Anunnaki clan customs, that is a breach of military protocols too disgraceful from which to return alive. Which means only one thing.'

'What's that?'

Amy watched the counter.

Forty.

Forty-one.

Almost here.

She looked at Everett, her gaze steely as death.

'Kamikaze Anunnaki.'

CHAPTER 12

'Kamikaze Anunnaki?' Mitch was aghast.

'The two of them will take the entire top off this whole building, Dad.'

'Jesus!'

'Uncle Bo, get on that thing and tell Miss Lavé to run, *run for her life,* as soon as the doors open – run for the man running at her – Dad, you need to run at her, sprint, and as soon as you get to her – gap. Gap anywhere, it's better that she finds out we can gap than she dies.'

'I've ordered silent evac of all staff.' Everett spoke sharply into the air. 'Lavé, listen to me, your life is in danger, the people with you are *terrorists*, they are *loaded* and coming in *hot*; the door opens, you *bolt*; do not think, sprint right toward the man coming at you, do not stop; he is your only hope.'

Amy looked at the screen; if she'd heard, there was no indication. Then Miss Lavé glanced up, cool as a cucumber, right at the camera as the floor hit forty-four; not so much terror in her eyes and furious determination.

The lift dinged.

'Now!'

Lavé could take an order at least. The pink-striped, black crocodile leather uniformed Anunnaki stepped out behind her, somewhat startled by their usher's instant sprint away, but seeming to make a split decision, right on her heel, to chase her.

'They're not chasing her they're getting as close as they can to us!'

Amy looked around, up, right, left, down, looking for – ah, there it was. The living trickle of opal light, of beautiful, crystalline, astral dust.

There was always some, if you knew how, and where to look.
She drew it to her.

'Hu-monster!'

One of the Anunnaki seemed to have a battle cry.

'Die!'

Miss Lavé was fast, and out ahead of them; she was as tall as she had looked from above, with long legs, and a decent sense, it turned out, of self-preservation. She might even have been running in a slightly jagged line, in case anyone behind her took aim. Amy couldn't see Mitch, didn't know where he'd gone, then her father ran right into her, sideways like a blindside football tackle; immediately as they connected there was a bright flash and the pair vanished.

The two Anunnaki were still running right at her.

'That's what Dad got good at; what did you get, Uncle Bo?'

She was moving back, right back toward the window; Everett followed her lead.

'The visuals; dimensions top to bottom; nooks and crannies; and the sight, like our dear friend Sapphire. Good combo for business, for shaping the empire. Physical melees, not so much.'

Blue astral light began to glow from all around the Anunnaki's human bodies as they slowed their run and stopped short of them, still about twenty meters away but way too close in any regard, with no cover at all.

'What are they doing?!' Everett demanded.

Now they were starting to shine, a thin line around them; bright blue like Arctic ice.

'If Anunnaki abruptly exit their human hosts within third density, on Earth, within earth's atmosphere, they die; their core kind of *blows out*.'

'Explodes?'

'You think they ride human bodies for the fun of it?'

'I never...'

'Okay, they do now, a lot of the time, but originally, that's why they developed the body swapping technology – why all the dimensionals did; created the starcophagi, all that.'

'So – this is some kind of ghoulish protest? Like those poor Buddhists who set themselves on fire?'

He started backing up more, and Amy fell further in step.

There could only be a few steps remaining until they back right into the glass behind them.

'No, this is more like a conventional crazy with a fanatical agenda, strapped to a tonne of explosives. Anunnaki blood can remain stable in our atmosphere, so long as they exert a constant, ever-demanding effort of willpower. Remember? Dad and the others said Kyvza was walking around, down in his –'

'*Donotspeakhisname!*' The woman hissed.

Great… a Kyvza fanatic.

Amy had to think.

Right now, she was fucked; they totally had her.

But she couldn't let Everett see that she didn't have a plan.

'How many developers down there?'

'Thirty. Smartest people we have; made the Pleiadean phones.'

Could they get out in time? Who knew?

'Okay…' She kept talking. 'So, if when the Anunnaki die, they're surrounded by – can you see the opal-coloured dust? The third density astral energy?'

'The pixie rainbow dust?'

'The…?'

'Pixie rainbow dust!?'

The fake-Ymira Anunnaki coming toward Everett scoffed; it was shocking to hear, because even though they were standing only twenty meters away, perhaps fifteen by now, as they slowly spread apart, edging up for a pincer engagement, the voice seemed to come from far away, back behind them. As though it had been projected from back down two hundred meters, right from the end of the massive floor, and yet reached them as though the speaker were right there, right up in their face.

'Hear his shattering ignorance!'

Everett shrugged sideways at Amy.

'That's what Yelina calls it… the pixie rainbow dust…?'

'Sure…' Amy shrugged back. 'Nice. Cute.'

'I thought so. I'm not totally hyper-masculine, you know.'

They were almost completely backed up to the window now, feeling the cold radiating onto their backs, not quite shoulder to shoulder.

'Sure, sure. So; if they're surrounded by pixie rainbow dust, if they draw it toward themselves…' Amy sighed. '…I just call it opal, though.'

'Fair enough.'

'They call it chroma; I'm just going to call it opal, okay?'

'Fine with me. But please, do go on to explain how they will destroy the building and kill us all with it…? This – opal?'

'Oh, right!'

The female hissed.

'Fetid fools! Jibber-jabbering over jargon!'

Amy ignored her, but was starting to tremble a bit. 'The more of that opal they can gather, the more the explosion increases – exponentially; and there is a lot in a place like this. Fifth dimensional ships, gapping to and fro…'

'Amy, they have a lot.'

'I can see – Uncle Bo, what else can you see?'

'The ship is weak; it can't do anything. But it is saying a name.'

Amy was still thinking.

Kyvza had a cage, under the Mojave. Xylata had walked around in it naked too, out of her human suit, by all accounts. How had he done that? How had she? There had been no story of him exerting force to maintain physical integrity; in fact, Heather said he had danced around, flopping his willy, giving a performance like a nineties movie villain. But – that was where her mind was going; that room. How else had that story gone? Mendoza had taken them there – there had been a Sirian security system…

Damn. That was a dead end; the whole Mojave vault must have been crafted by Sirian techs, must have been some sort of Faraday Cage for astral power, to draw off the opal dust. And that vault had been filled to the brim, stacked with crates of magical, occult items, items Xylata had used to bargain a strong seat on the Central-Eastern Edge of the Anunnaki Trade Diamond, restoring the Ymira name.

Massively useful then.

Not so much now!

Amy tried to think again.

She took one step toward the female who was leering at her.

'You're betting we stay here while you blow up! That we try and attack you; rather than let innocent people die up here, and when the top of the building falls to the ground? One of you dies killing us, one of you – boom?'

They were really playing it, she saw. Drawing as much from the atmosphere of the building as they could.

'We draw the chroma; so much of it here in the Human-Pleiadean bacterial swamp!'

'I see it…' Everett uttered. 'They're pulling it into themselves; the opal, like a vacuum! I can see it around them, sticking to them like a glittering swarm of bees!'

Amy gulped, tried to keep thinking; they still had her.

If she and Everett gapped, everyone died except them.

If they fought, maybe they would kill one, maybe the explosion wouldn't be quite so bad, but still – the explosion would be massive, and all the shrapnel would have to do would be to kill a few people; or for the debris… the docks below, the ferries. Even on a cold winter's night, out of tourist season, at this time – it would kill thousands, surely.

She tried to pull some in – open… how had Xylata taught her? Not a gap, but a field?

'Where's Mitch!' Everett demanded.

'He won't be able to get back – they have all the opal, there's not enough to generate any kind of – *anything* here! Not even…' She looked at Everett. 'Uncle Bo…we've left it too late, we can't get out!'

CHAPTER 13

Kyvza's vault, she kept thinking about –

Sirian sixth density tech.

Why?

The story her Dad had told her… Mendoza, the Hollywood occultist and glamour-photography 'talent spotter' to the studios, from back in the seventies and eighties, had negotiated the 'crystal gap trap' (as he later called it) and gotten them into Kyvza's vault. She hadn't seen him do it, but she had met him, before and after, in the astral; after he had gained sixth density ascension.

What did he have to do with this?

She looked to Everett and was stunned to see that he was as nervous as she had seen him, which was not a lot; but still – some was enough, and it didn't help.

'So, Amy; one assumes the power within which you have become well-versed comes into play around – *now?*'

And then she realised.

'You say that Pleiadean ship is too weak, but it still functions as a hub?'

'Yes – why?'

She raised the phone again, and shouted at it.

'Mendoza!'

She shouted into it, as far as she could focus, as deep into it as she could stretch her mind.

'Mendoza! Help!'

The two Anunnaki were really shaking now, bright ice-blue. Amy could see the start of an outline of the reptilian Anunnaki heads; the real ones. A smaller, more streamlined female face, and a larger, more fanged, fierce-eyed male. This was really not a good sign of how much time they had left before –

Everett couldn't comprehend. 'They're just letting themselves go? *Just like that?*'

'Worse than that, they're milking it; they're gonna force it, as much opal as they can suck in – God-damn Kamikaze Anunnaki!'

She cried out into the clear crystal interface again.

'Mendoza! Now, Mendoza, now!'

'Why?' Everett demanded of them. 'Why are you doing this!?'

'Ohhhh; fuck; me – *sideways!*'

Amy suddenly realising what she was doing wrong.

'Mendoza!' The cries were still desperate, but somehow, now, very confident. 'Coordinates! *Now* is July Fifteenth, Twenty Fourteen, Forty Fourth Floor, on the Cleverco Building!'

She looked at her phone, at Everett's updates.

'Six Twenty-Three Pee Emm! Now, Mendoza, now!'

The male Anunnaki was about to blow.

She was going to die and this was the fucker who God and Goddess had chosen to take her out; a lesson in hubris and humility.

She took a deep breath and let it out. Any second. She strode toward him, once, twice, and stared him down, right into his bright yellow, bloodshot, insanely determined eyes.

And she spoke into the phone with supreme calm.

'Right now Mendoza, or I die; right here; right now.'

Lightning hit the building.

There was a fierce crunch as the glass window behind them cracked; both Amy and Everett spun around involuntarily as the building's power went out, then emergency power came back on. Visibility was now minimal, barely-half-light, and consequently they could see both their own reflections again, spiked and fractured, and the insane Anunnaki standing behind them, glowing more and more brightly, more lethally and electrically blue.

But they could also see that something had attached itself to the glass outside. There was a slowly-twirling funnel, its wide-open end against the glass, with the thin end reaching back through the rain and into the gathering storm-clouds, like the tip of a twister that had connected to the side of the building, on the glass, right in front of them. Amy hadn't even seen the harsh weather approaching, but it was here now, above the Harbour Bridge, over the skyline of the North Shore; rolling charcoal clouds, filled with bursts of flailing lightning. With a shock of force that jolted them both a primal-step backwards, hail stones pelted into the windows, blasting and smudging the view right before them.

And yet, through it, they could see a man, in the sky, running down a set of spiral stairs. The man was at first incredibly tiny in the distance, but as he descended, he seemed to become larger, as though he were an increasingly magnified image somehow projected into the sky.

Amy glanced back; the Draco was open-mouthed, with his arms upward, drooling and quivering with a full, bright blur halo.

She turned back.

'Mendozaaaah!'

Mendoza was getting closer, and closer, very quickly now, halfway down the stairs, down and around, around and down, his sockless, white-sneakered feet scampering at a speed close to panic, his open left hand causing bright blue electrical sparks as it skimmed and spun down and around the balustrade, until he was right there, life-sized, right in front of them at the base of the spiral staircase.

'Sirian tech…' Everett uttered.

Simultaneously, as his feet somehow hit solid ground, outside in the open and hail-smashed sky, the weather abruptly seemed to stop. Or rather, Amy quickly realised; shelter was being created as a short, enclosed, rectangular crystal corridor, dimensionally corresponding to the huge office window, yet somehow still the size of an ordinary double-door, extended through the funnel's twister tip. Commandeering the energy of the funnel, the emerging sky-passage then snapped into existence as a straight, clean-lined corridor of sheer white light, appearing and solidifying as though fully-drawn and rendered in real-time by pens that possessed lightning for nibs and liquid mercury for ink. Instantaneously, the end of the spiral stairway was connected to the building's floor by a short, glass-edged corridor, upon which Mendoza now sprinted toward them, skidding to a dead halt as he reached the other side of the enormous window, directly facing them, his open palms slamming splat-splat against the wet outer glass, pounding on the crack that had appeared with the first strike of lightning.

For a millisecond Amy's mind understood.

Outside there was a real solid extension; it was in the rain outside, and of the rain outside; of the glass, and of the reflection of the glass outside; bound by the crystal-lines that had manifested in the air.

They had to cut the power to sever the Pleiadean anti-reflection tech so they could have a reflection to use Sirian tech...

! Ready!? !

Mendoza raised his hands as he asked, silently.

❨ *Go!!!* ❩

Amy had shocked herself at being able to reply; then the attack pattern was in Amy's mind.

She spun back as Mendoza smashed the glass into a million pieces, spilling opal into the building, which was snatched up by Amy, along with the glass, and propelled straight at the Anunnaki. The female saw it; forgetting her suicide mission she thrust her arms up, in a primal move of fight-or-flight defence, and instantly her gathered shell of opal involuntarily became a protective cocoon. The male however was too focussed, and let the explosion go. But Amy had already levitated him, turned all of his opal into glass, and shot him and his glass cocoon backwards at high speed, halfway down the massive, open office space.

'Down!'

Everyone dropped, including the other Anunnaki.

Blue blood, as blue as human blood was red, and white and blue and purple flesh exploded everywhere amid shards of glass and crystal, dark green scales and deep-lime skin. But the opal-manifested glass shell, a metre thick, radically dampened the impact, and the force of the diminished blast spread out, up and down the central ellipse, effectively neutralising all potential damage to the purely cosmetic.

'No! *No!*'

The Anunnaki woman began shaking again as she stood and looked back, clambering toward the closest pieces of her dead companion, covered in a rapidly diminishing cocoon that was obeying her command to drop from her, turning to white goo as it did.

'Amethyst Pyne…' Everett gaped as he gazed up, his hands over his head. '…that was…'

Mendoza walked in from the strange, sixth-dimensional corridor and spiral-staircase crystal-cubicle that was attached to the building outside, while the wind and rain began blasting the walls again.

'You okay, kiddo?'

He winked down at Everett.

'Hey Boss.'

He extended a hand and Everett accepted, hoisting himself to a stand.

Mendoza, olive-skinned and tanned, was wearing a steel-blue fedora, matching multi-blue, black and white patterned, short-sleeved, oversized and open Hawaiian shirt, a white singlet, and baggy black board shorts.

'Mister Mendoza – we are very grateful for your intercession here! And – Amy!'

Mendoza winked. 'Nothing like the shock of panic to trigger latent telepathy, huh kid?'

Everett looked to her, increasingly impressed.

'Are you unharmed, Amethyst?'

'Thanks Uncle Bo. But they don't call me that here…'

Everett was slightly affronted. 'They don't call you what where?'

'The Ymira, in the astral. They don't call me Amethyst, or Amy.'

'They don't?'

'No. The Anunnaki have their own name for me.'

'Do they now? What would that be?'

'Thys Pyne.'

'Fist Punch?'

'No – Thys Pyne.'

'Fist Pain?'

Amy rolled her eyes. '… actually – that will do for now!'

With that, she held up her hand, made a fist, and walked over to the Anunnaki woman. The Draco stood before her enemy; her intended, failed victim, looking as though she were standing waist-high in a forty-four gallon drum that was violently overflowing with melted bees wax. Even so, she almost made her high-chinned defiance work.

'You! You Apey – *anus!*'

'What's your name, soldier?'

'I am Ryzex! You know that! You – *dirt!*'

Thys Pyne used her raised fist to blast a pump of air into Ryzex's face, breaking her snout and rendering her unconscious as she fell into the foot-high pool of goo, bleeding blue from her face.

'There – have some fist pain, you mad bitch.'

Mitch gapped back in.

'What did I miss?'

CHAPTER 14

'The Sirians are keeping out of this one, but they didn't stop me – neither did the ship out there; it let me cut the power. In fact, I think it relayed your call. But not to worry, you're all cool, you're all together, you have some powerful allies now.'

Amy stared out at the staircase, and beyond it, to the ship.

'I know…' She allowed herself a wicked little smile.

'Hey!' Mendoza made a hurt face. 'I meant me!'

Amy turned and looked him right in the eyes.

'I know.'

She gave an even wider, more wicked smile.

'Heh, heh.' Mendoza turned to Mitch, apparently satisfied. 'Hey My Main Man; how's Heather?'

'She's good, Mendoza. How's Misha?'

'The same.' He smiled, as though this had a slightly perverse connotation.

'Umm. Okay.' Mitch smiled.

Everett stepped forward. 'Amy, what did you say before, when you gave him our location?' Everett was staring down at the goo, and Ryzex. 'Was it – Cleverco?'

'Cleverco?' Mitch enquired sharply.

'You said we were at the *Cleverco Building*. You gave the date – including *the year.*'

Amy had to try and remember. 'It was just an idea – in my mind. I've never liked the name Lever. I don't know why, but it sounds just... wrong. But it's both your names; the people who started both companies, you and Oliver, you combined them, then you gave them to us. I didn't want to be rude or dishonour that – but this is a much nicer portmanteau, don't you think? Cleverco?'

'I'm not sure...?'

'It's currently what it is...' Mendoza assured them, as though they would understand.

Amy smiled politely. 'Doza, we might need that clarified for people not currently spending most of their time in Sirian space.'

He looked at her as if to say; *Doza, huh?*

Then he continued. 'Who says I am spending my time there, huh?' He grinned. 'But; who am I kidding? We all know I am, right! Where else would I be? And lucky for you guys, too huh?' Mendoza shook his head, and scratched his ear. 'Look; I mean, okay, the Cleverco thing? All I'm saying is; from my perspective, in a year, when you launch it, that's what it's called. Cleverco. And it works. People like it – they like you guys – and her. They want more of her. But she's never here.'

'They like me?'

'TMI, toots. Spoiler City, next stop – Pyne Palace, huh?'

Amy stared at him. Then something occurred. She took out her phone.

'And these – we call these Eves, okay. Not 'Quantum Phones'. That's a thing, not a name. This is my Eve, that's your Eve. He wants, she wants, they want; we all want Eves. The middle three letters of Lever; but now it's Cleverco.'

Amy took a few steps toward Everett. He was regarding her very intensely.

'And that symbol, the human one, it's human, sure. But there's too much human and not enough *being*. I'll come up with something, don't worry, but the symbol for Cleverco needs something – dreamy.'

She stared back at the window for a second, past the staircase to the Bridge and the Harbour.

'Something poetic; but strong and familiar.'

She turned back to Everett. Her eyes were aglow with excitement; she could feel it, and knew that everyone could see it on her.

She was in.

'Lever was okay. But we don't need leverage, Uncle Bo. That's not how we do things now. We need to be smarter now. We need to be clever. We need to be Cleverco.'

Everett's eyes narrowed, then he clapped his hands together, once, very loudly.

He was staring at her with an intensity that was almost unsettling and – almost – frightening.

Then he clapped again, then again, then again. Then he was laughing, and then he was really clapping, whole-heartedly and uproariously.

'I like it!'

'Really?'

He stopped. He thought again.

'No, no; *I like it.*'

Everett laughed some more, then put a hand on Amy's shoulder.

'Well done, Miss Pyne! Send the details to my Eve!'

'That's Field Marshall Fist Pain to you, Mister Everett!'

Everett drew back slightly.

'Field Marshall are we?'

'Long story.'

Everett turned to Mendoza. 'And you see the future now, do you?'

'Sixth density, Boss. You kind of tend to live across time when you hang around out there.'

He frowned deeply at Mendoza, again in deep regard.

'Tell me…'

Unconsciously, the two began turning, moving back toward the spiral staircase.

'I believe I have a propensity for such a talent; I believe it's what the Pandora chose for me. If we can come to some mutually beneficial arrangement; will you help me develop that talent?'

'Oh, Boss! But of course, of course…!' He winked back at Amy. 'I thought you'd never ask! It's why I am here, Boss! *It's why I am here!*'

Everett stopped. 'Wait; what about that?'

'Never mind about that! Where are you going?' Amy asked, seeing that the pair were clearly about to step outside of the building.

'Going?' Mendoza shrugged.

'Without me, I mean!' Then she turned around, to where Everett had indicated. Ryzex was waking up in her own astral goo, horrified.

'My snout…! Such pain!'

'Is that what they used to call ectoplasm?' Mitch asked, looking down distastefully. 'I can see why it gave people the heebie-jeebies.'

'I think so.' Amy shook her head. 'Get up, Ryzex. You're coming with us before you cause any more trouble.' Some of the goo slithered around her; enough for her to get up and walk, but not much else.

Amy turned back to Everett. 'The goo will hold her from exploding a while, but it will dissolve back into opal; we shoud get moving, wherever it is you're going.'

Mendoza nodded. 'Opal behaves weirdly in third density, it has a few different states depending on the forces and energies acting upon it; sometimes grey dust when it's dormant. It should spread through the building again pretty evenly, wherever there are people.'

He flipped his palms up.

'Hey! Get things off to a great creative start!'

Mendoza looked at Amy.

'You wanna to show them your boat now…?'

He gave her a sideways grin.

'So-called; Thys Pyne?'

CHAPTER 15

Everett followed Mendoza, then Amy and Ryzex, with Mitch bringing up the rear. Their footsteps, once they began stepping down the short crystal corridor together, echoed like horse hooves on cobblestones until they reach the stairs, then they sounded like a bunch of urban explorers ascending a ruined lighthouse, such was the creaking and groaning of the wrought iron on the central pole.

'Your father is looking at my bottom...' Ryzex complained.

'He is not.'

'I am, but I can't help it, it's right there in front of me.'

'He has a thing for Anunnaki women; it is everywhere, everyone knows it.'

'I really don't.'

Everett's Eve went off; he took it out and apologised as he stopped to read it.

'Mendoza...'

Everett looked out; they seemed to be walking in the sky over the Harbour, directly up, in line with the building and the shattered forty fourth floor window.

'... we should get to my ship. Is there any way from here – now?'

Mendoza looked out. 'Gapping between places on the same dimensional plane is one thing; gapping between actual dimensional planes...' He looked down earnestly at Everett. 'I don't think you guys are ready for that. Not sure even I could, not safely; not directly.' He looked up and down the stairs. 'I was going to show you something.'

'We might need to do that later.'

Mendoza nodded. 'Then keep climbing. There's a point up

here; can you contact your ship?'

They started moving again.

Everett put his hand to his ear.

'Ship?' He waited. 'Ship?' He scowled. 'No, nothing.'

'*Ship?*' Mendoza scoffed. 'Really? You're not even on first name terms yet?'

'She has a name?'

'Pleiadeans sometimes tell you things by giving you an earworm, or something like that.'

'An earworm? A parasitic virus?'

'Not quite…' Amy smiled upwards. 'A song you can't get out of your head; like the first few lines or the chorus or, maybe a jingle.'

'That's right…' Mendoza had started looking left, out to sea. 'Sometimes a poem or a rhyme or a nonsense of some kind.'

Everett kept climbing, his right hand on the balustrade but his left still holding his Eve, staring into it.

'I have known the ship is feminine for some time; and I have for some days now been thinking of the word *Pleiadean* in a condensed form, as in; *Lay-de-an*. It seems – real to me, that this is… real enough to be something in my head that is being…'

Amy watched him as they climbed.

He was mildly confounded; he just needed to –

'*Lady Ann*, this is Everett. Can you find me?'

Everett's face suddenly lit up.

'Well; I'll be!'

'What, Bo?' Mitch demanded. 'We didn't hear anything.'

Everett looked down the spiral stairs to him, then looked across to Amy. She shrugged.

'She says she will meet us at the next level.'

Everett looked up again to Mendoza, happily impressed.

'Well…' Mendoza grinned down. '…better keep climbing then Boss!'

CHAPTER 16

They increased their pace for another few minutes, not speaking, until they came to a landing, made from the same shining, clear-crystalline planes, and the same shining white-glass edges as their entry-point below, with the same, strangely rickety brass-like fixtures for the balustrades, bannisters and, this time, a doorhandle attached to a frame at one end, out to sea. At the other end, there was a translucent white door that looked a lot more like it might belong to a conventionally accepted design on a futuristic humanoid-designed space craft.

Mendoza nodded. 'Through that door.'

'You do not fool me!' Ryzex suddenly announced, her chin high, her body still bound by the goo. 'You are luring me into a false sense of security! You are going to throw me into your ocean as a sacrifice to your horrific master, the Demiurge Yahweh!'

'Please be quite!' Everett snapped. 'Until you said that I had honestly forgotten you existed!'

Her eyes bulged. 'How dare you! Primate *pissface!*'

Amy tied to not laugh. 'Shut up, Ryzex, we're taking you back to the base for interrogation.'

'You are?' Mitch was stunned.

'They did try to kill us, Dad. And it is a civil war.'

'There's nothing there…' Everett said aloud, presumably to the ship. Then he cocked his head, listening; he did not like what he heard. '…do *what?*'

Mendoza chuckled. 'Well, people to do! Beings to work, places to meet; I'll be seeing you all, and you know I know that's true.' He walked to the white door, opened it and turned. Within was a glow; he was spectacularly backlit. 'And Thys, remember you owe me for this; our agreement?'

Amy spread her arms. 'Win-win, Doza!'

He pointed at her. 'You're bigger and hotter, Thys Pyne, now you've gone back home. Remember, for next time!'

Then he was gone, ducking back, the door slam-clicking behind him. Within a second, the door began to fade, then it and the frame were completely gone, revealing only night sky behind it. The landing felt immediately less real, less stable, and a lot more cold. Amy could have convinced herself that it had immediately begun to overbalance in the wind.

She turned to Everett.

'So where's *Lady Ann?*'

Everett moved along the landing to the other crystalline door, and turned the rickety brass handle. The minute he did, the door was snatched from his hand by the wind and flung open, slamming back on its hinges into the night. The weather it let in was freezing cold, with rain still swirling. Everett went to the edge and looked down. He put out his foot, however his expensive white lace-up, lashed now by rain, descended way past the point where they could expect any kind of physical continuity of the crystal landing, or even an invisible step down.

'She says…'

Everett stepped back.

'…she's right there.'

CHAPTER 17

They looked behind them.

They'd climbed on the spiral staircase higher than the so-called Cleverco building, probably another twenty floors; right below, very far distant, was the western side of Sydney's CBD. If they fell here, with the wind catching them, they could land anywhere; the end of George Street, the Circular Quay concourse, or right in the water. Dead, dead, dead.

'I've heard…' Mitch began, a little anxiously. '…that a move from plane to plane takes something. Like a plane ride, an aeroplane ride, takes time. What I mean is; like, I guess, distance takes time, and danger. Distance had a price; for most of the time, it's time. But – it's also fear; fear, based in the reality of our world, in physics and human error. Transport malfunctions; cars have accidents, bad weather, truck drivers grow weary, trains on the wrong tracks, or badly maintained infrastructure… planes crash; Heaven Forbid all of the above, but they happen. You can die. Because big moves contain risk.'

He moved over and looked down, with Everett.

'Are you sure she's there, Bo?'

Bo nodded. 'We climbed probably fifteen minutes around those stairs; working our way up toward the sixth plane; we need to get back down a plane, Mitchell. One of the starcophagi is –'

There was a crack behind them and the brass balustrades from the right side of the landing swayed as one toward the ocean, stopped, then something cracked again along their edge, snapping loudly, and the balustrades all dropped together. The dread finality of watching them spiral, wide, over and over, heavy enough so as not to be particularly effected by the wind, then crash into the water, right at the edge of Circular Quay – with a white plume so tiny it was almost impossible to distinguish from the swirling rain, made them each expel tiny, bone-chilling gasps.

Then Amy pulled herself together.

'This is ridiculous; they wouldn't leave us here to die – maybe of fear or stupidity, but that's not us and this is not the normal world, and things are not as they seem.'

With that, she walked up, and walked right out of the door, over the sea.

CHAPTER 18

The white thing shot up so quickly it was hard to know where it had come from but it shot like a bullet and caught her foot, then her other, then she was standing on a wide, white disc. Just standing, the wind in her hair, blowing and whipping her ponytail wildly, but as solid as though she were just standing on the sidewalk below.

'Holy cow…!' She realised very quickly. '…it doesn't let you lose balance!'

She felt a tug, then realised that she was descending. Then she was standing on the floor of a circular white room. She knew these walls, she'd been here twice before.

She was on the ship, on the *Lady Ann*.

Everett appeared beside her, seeming to shimmer down, in from a line of light from above. Then Ryzex, squatting tightly with her eyes squeezed closed, then Mitch.

'Nice!'

Around them, the walls seemed to fully rotate horizontally on several different levels; shining as they spun, perhaps four or five different tones between deep purple and light lavender, then they settled, and dimmed down to plain solid white again.

There was a doorway-aperture before them.

Everett was used to this and immediately walked right through like she owned the place; like a Boss back in his Office.

In the white, circular room beyond were the two deep, dark-blue starcophagi that had for several years now contained the comatose physical forms of Suzie Saturn and Holland Pankhurst. The starcophagi were placed either side of the entrance, each with the foot pointing to the the middle of the room, and the head angled one-thirty-five away from the door, the 'bed head' just against the far curve of the wall.

Sapphire Edge slept beside Pan's starcopagus in a black bed, made of what looked like the same deep, dark-blue marble material, swathed in black satin sheets, with her voluminous bright-blonde hair splayed out against her black satin pillow as she slumbered deeply and peacefully. She didn't wake at their entrance, she simply lay on her side, facing Pan's starcophagus, and sighed very deeply.

You could, Amy supposed, take this to mean that she was pleased to see them all.

This was such a startling sight, a scene of such striking gothic sci-fi / fairy-tale fusion, that it took them a few seconds to realise that the second starcophagus, which had until minutes ago contained Suzie Saturn, was open and empty.

'Suzie's gone?' Mitch seemed most surprised.

'Yes...' Amy could sense something. 'That's what the Lady Ann wanted us to come here for...'

'Look...' Everett nodded, toward Sapphire. 'She's about to turn over.'

They waited a few seconds in silence, then Sapphire squirmed a bit, rotated her shoulders a little, then rolled over and changed sides. As she did, she and the whole bed gapped to the other side. As she completed the turn, she was again facing Pan, and his place of mystical, advanced Sirian-tech slumber.

'She gets up and eats. Walks around a bit, for about an hour, usually at midnight. Gets a glass of water at midday. Smiles sernely, but doesn't say anything.'

They watched another few seconds in silence, then couldn't help turning back to the black coffin's empty counterpart. There was definitely a Suzie-shaped indentation, in what looked like a bedding of memory foam. At a guess, Amy supposed that Suzie had slept on her back the whole time, arms folded like classic Dracula.

She decided to take a shot.

'*Lady Ann*, where is she?'

Everett seemed to hear the response, and relayed it, his tone reflecting his dissatisfaction.

'She woke, asked for a glass of water, asked for fresh clothes, and gapped out when she was told there weren't any.'

'There weren't?'

'None that she liked, apparently.'

'Can you track where she went?'

'She said where she went…' Everett frowned. '…apparently. Somewhere called The Port of Ymira, on The Sea of Humanity, in fourth density – human space?'

'That's so cool…' Amy smiled, and nodded.

'How so?'

'I think – that's where we're going, too.'

CHAPTER 19

Lady Ann had no problem putting them down at the Port of Ymira.

'There's very little resistance putting humans in their place, apparently...' Everett explained. 'I think my ship is quite droll.'

The first thing Amy heard when she arrived (gapped by the ship, she assumed) was the lapping of water, and the sound of a pier; creaky wood being rocked, wind whistling through tight gaps, and the groaning of deep poles.

However, they had been transported somewhere lower, near the pier; somewhere dark, and damp.

She could smell earth; like tree roots, and sure enough...

'We're under a massive tree...' Mitch stated. '...aren't we? Is this...?'

'I don't think so...' Everett grumbled. 'Doesn't feel like Hollywood at all.'

There were burning torches along the walls, and a light from an exit.

'If we're where I want us to go...' Amy offered, somewhat gingerly. '...I have to confess; this wasn't here, when I left, not even a day ago.'

'But that's not unusual for the astral plane, is it?' Mitch walked toward the light. 'I can hear the ocean out there.'

Amy approached him, then ushered him out.

'Come on.'

CHAPTER 20

The pier was at least five meters wide, and fifty long, with no rails.

To Mitch it seemed to have grown directly out of a massive, suburban-home-sized knot of root that in turn had grown out of...

'The middle?' Mitch asked his daughter. '...it feels like the middle, doesn't it?'

...the middle of a vast astral ocean.

'You remember this, Dad? The ocean?'

He was gazing out and around.

Of course he did.

'...this is like my second home, now...' Thys muttered, not sure if anyone else heard.

The astral ocean looked almost-just like a third density ocean, but with shades of indigo and purple along with the more standard blues, greens and greys. But Amy felt that the water was too calm, perhaps creepily calm, and a little too flat to seem normal.

And, now she looked – the sky was also a more indigo shade of blue than usual; more so than the summer shade of sky, from an impossibly colourful childhood, like it usually was.

Mitch took a deep breath of astral ocean air.

'It's where we came in, isn't it? And at the end of the pier there; that's Bo's boat, the one we travelled in together? Up to the Miracle Quake? That's right, isn't it, Bo?'

'Sure looks like her...'

Mitch sniffed. 'The air smells like me when I was seven years old.'

As they approached, Thys saw that the shape of the pier, the fact that it even was a pier in the first place, was totally natural. It was as though the giant knot of root, twice as tall as Everett's boat, had simply decided to emerge from the ocean, and…

'It's grown itself into a pier, hasn't it?' Everett noted. 'For the boat. You kept using her, didn't you?' He was perplexed. 'But, this boat, this very boat, is still back on third density Earth…!'

'I know, Uncle Bo. But, I think, when we went through the portal, into the tree with Yelina, we didn't know where we would end up. I don't think we went through the Inner Earth, not exactly; I think Yelina offered that pathway, *maybe over?* – the Inner Earth? As protection for us? As safe transition to here, the astral plane?'

Everett nodded. 'I don't know for sure, but I am sure it will all make perfect sense one day.' He shrugged. 'Besides, it sounds like something she would do.' He nodded to himself. 'Smart. Away from any pathway the Anunnaki would use?'

'That's right. I think it was just available to her, after she used the same power to destroy the Hines Mansion. But when we got here, we'd all felt some variety of safety and accomplishment and voyagery on that boat – yours being the most dominant personality, or ego if you will, Uncle Bo…'

'Ego, as they say, Dear Amethyst, is not a dirty word…'

'…and well, I think we all remanifested the boat around us. The image of it, the truth of it, here, for our own safety and security. That's how things work here.'

'And as we kept going…' Mitch deduced, '…we kept manifesting a variation of the boat as we went – staying or moving on, each as was our want at the time.'

'But the astral version of the boat was here, all the time, even after I used to as a kind of – lightning cannon. I mean, you saw, right? You went on – to what is now the *Lady Ann*; but I stayed here and kept fighting – on this boat. Xylata understood; we had to make a claim, and that was me, I was the youngest, with the least to lose and the most to express, and I anchored everything here, for all of us, with this boat.'

They noticed a figure at the end of the pier, as though she had just gotten off the boat. Then, in barely a flash, she was standing right in front of them.

Mitch was momentarily startled, but recognised her instantly. 'Xylata?'

Xylata bowed sharply. 'Mitchell Pyne. My second-favourite human.'

The reptilian leader of the Ymira clan was wearing the same uniform that Thys wore; black leather with crocodile print, but just as his daughter had told him, the stripes upon Xylata's chest-plate and shoulder pads were lime green, which as it happened, complimenting her delicate scales nicely.

'I notice you noticing me, Mitch Pyne...' Xylata smiled, humming.

'Must be the uniform...' Mitch smiled, shrugging.

Xylata folded her arms and laughed, low and appreciative. She seemed lighter of spirit, yet more mature. Around her eyes, perhaps. Not so frightened, Mitch thought. More... self-possessed? More herself?

'Indeed, we moved on; there were other boats, there were ships and planes and fighters and spaceships and... there still are. The fight over this ocean went on and on. I remember coming back to this ship though, every now and then; Thys Pyne would say to me, or to Vlynk, or Gexvi or Lyveq, or any of our colleagues; 'meet at the boat!' and we would know which one she meant.'

Thys looked from Mitch to Everett, searching for something. She tried to explain more.

'When we all arrived here; well, you were both here too, right? I took to it like a duck to water. It was like an immersive video game. But after a while, I had to stop, and take stock. The first waves of Anunnaki, they just came and came, and I was able to repel them with... enormous bursts of energy.'

She had a chill, and shivered; the excitement and danger rushed back to her.

'Like I said, I was basically using this boat, your boat Uncle

Bo, as a gun – channelling astral energy, commanding it, through it, as though it were a cannon, standing on the prow like… I don't know – like one of those pin-up girls they drew on the nose-cones of jet bombers.'

Xylata nodded. 'The astral can take something from collective memory, and blend it with something iconic. You do something – and it morphs something archetypal to it before you've even noticed.'

'I basically did that to your boat, my boat here, really…'

She shrugged at Everett. He shrugged back.

'I have other boats – and I still have the real one of this one. Is this what you wanted me to see?'

'In a way. The Ymira were able to use me, the boat and what I could do, to their advantage. They were fighting the Draco; they were like winged monkeys – I mean, you saw it, right? That went on for days, and, well, it was only after the initial rush wore off, and I was…' She eyed her father sheepishly. '…hurt a couple of times…'

'Hurt?'

'I'm fine Dad, really, I don't – '

'Hurt how? Who hurt you!?'

Amy was astounded; she hadn't seen her father like this since she was a young teen.

'Dad, seriously; look, I'm okay!'

'You turn up in a military uniform and tell me you've been wounded – a few times? Manning a cannon in a battle that waged on for days?'

'Dad; I'm in the army. That's what I am trying to tell you. I'm basically a secret weapon, in dual command of the Ymira army.'

'With me,' Xylata offered.

'You?'

'That is correct, Mitch Pyne.' Xylata regarded him curiously. 'She has the power of a hundred of us, in one – we must not hide from the elephant on the pier; her expanding human package.'

'Elephant?' Thys demanded. 'What?'

Xylata leaned toward Mitch. 'How much taller is she? And her bosoms? Her graceful neck, her slender torso.'

'Xylata!' Thys was appalled.

Both Mitch's eyebrows were way up on his forehead.

'Her legs – like ostriches now.'

'Oh my God – really?'

'Your step-mother Heather Everett is out looking for clothes for you – I have informed her that you are now – *willowy,* but firm.'

'Do you want to come, Xylata? Is that it? Do you want to come to the premiere as well? Is that what this is all about?'

'No!'

'Really? Because you can come if you like! I can bring a guest, can't I Dad?'

'I; err – well…'

'See? Not a problem!'

'I do not feel left out – you cannot make me feel left out.'

'Well, I know you don't lie.'

Thys looked sideways at Everett.

'They don't even understand the concept.'

Then at her father.

'But it can seem like they lie, when their cultural norms are so different. You just have to get to the bottom of what it is about human cultural norms that they haven't absorbed yet.'

She whispered, very low.

'Like - a - child.'

'You are spending –'

It was a shock as another voice joined them. Thys turned around.

' – way too much time here!'

Standing beside Xylata was Suzie Saturn.

'And way too much time together!'

Mitch stepped up to her. 'Suzie?'

'It's my guy!'

Thys could see her father's hands trembling. Then he moved

forward, gently, and softly gave Suzie Saturn a big hug.

She was much shorter than Mitch, but Thys saw her lean in and hug back, her small but long-fingered hands gripping him tightly.

'Thank you Suzie; you saved me over and over.'

'My pleasure, dude. Hey, you were my only ticket out, after all! I mean; just sayin'.'

They let each other go; Thys could see, as Suzie gave her a quick wink, that both she and her father had tears in their eyes.

'But we did, didn't we? We made it, huh? We made it out!'

'And this is you?' Mitch demanded. 'Like us? Your real body; here in fourth density?'

'Out of the coffin and back in the… hey what rhymes with coffin? Out of the coffin and I ain't joshin'?' She made a face like she was going to be sick. 'Woah-Man! I gotta reconnect with My Muses! So we goin' to this premiere or what? I hear it's real good! Got a real shot at Best Picture, they say!'

'Really?' Mitch was pleased, but doubtful. 'Best Picture?'

'Sure!' Suzie grinned. 'Why not?' She looked at Thys, with what seemed to her like a strong affection. 'Been watching you, Thys Pyne! So ya think ya got what it takes, huh kid?'

'Miss Saturn… I just want to say…'

'Pfft! It's Suzie, c'mon! You got *laid* up here yet, kid? I gotta tell ya; it's – fucking – amazing!'

'Oh, God…' Mitch seemed go pale. 'I don't think I'm quite ready for…'

'So anyway! I just woke up this morning… this afternoon; whenever the fuck ever; and I thought – today's the day! Y'know? I could never… just, y'know? *Find the right moment –* for a comeback? You get me? Besides, I mean; people are still remembering who the fuck I was! That bitch Mistress might be gone, whoever the fuck she was, but I'm still not fully back in people's minds yet! I'm like Nelson Mandela! People think I'm dead before I'm dead. I'm not dead! There was a big hole I left, and it's gonna take a whole Earth year, maybe more to refill it!

Like I fucken retired or something! I'm the only fucken rock star ever to retire and people believe it! So hey, anyway; I gotta hang around up here so people filter me back into their whole big, swirly-messy spag-bol consciousness, you dig me? And remember; earth-plane time, I've probably been out, what? No new album, no new track for – like; three, four; five years? So, I think I'll hang around, get back to where I once belonged, right?'

'Hang around here?' Mitch seemed dubious.

'I'll look after her Mitch! I was the first one here, remember! And I was here for like – years! Learning how to survive all on my own! Who better for her to learn from?'

'…Jesus…'

'Dad; it's okay. She's winding you up.'

'Am I?'

'Aren't you?'

'Sure! Why not!' She leaned into Thys. 'Don't worry kid. We'll figure it out!'

'Miss…; I mean – *Suzie*…'

Amy, but… *maybe not Thys*, felt herself blush a little. She couldn't believe she was actually talking to Suzie Saturn, like a grown-up – *who wanted her to talk to her back!*

'…I have… so much power, up here. You will too, now you're free. We belong here, but…'

'You think?'

'…but we need to find a way to –'

'Kid! Don't worry so much! We'll find a way!'

'But, when I got here, and started wiping out Draco – the Ymira just told me to keep going, and I never really questioned –'

'Wait –' Mitch was nervous again. '…wiping out?'

'The Ymira want the Draco defeated, Dad. So do we! We both want to lessen their presence in Earth's astral plane – it's called the Terrastral Plane now, by the way. At least, that name came to mind and I said it and now…' Thys shrugged. '…it's called that.'

'That's what happens!' Suzie confirmed. 'I wanted to be Julie Jupiter!'

'Ooh!' Amy gushed for a second. 'Can I be Julie Jupiter?'

'Kid, the way you're starting to come into your own, I think you can be whatever you want without adding shitty rock stardom to the list – look where it got me!'

Amy's eyes were like a pleading puppy dog's.

Suzie relented immediately. 'Okay, okay; let me talk to Nelly Neptune and Mavis Uranus, we'll see what we can do.'

'Really?'

'Sure! No – yes, maybe – I dunno. Is this even really happening? Is this actually on the table? Maybe. I'll have my people call your people. Are we done? Did you just say Terrastral Plane?'

Thys was really starting to like her. 'Suzie, you'd better name some things, or it's just going to be me and Dad naming everything; we're like pioneers, or explorers, but in reverse up here; we're taking it back, instead of taking it from. Or maybe... we're uncovering it, after many, many... millennia? Or perhaps we're actually *making it?* I don't know! Maybe that doesn't even matter! But, whenever the first colonists or invaders or usurpers or revisionists or whatever; whenever the new wave comes through, the first names most often stick. It just happens. That's what it's like. And you are going to come up with much cooler names than we are!'

Suzie was clearly chuffed, but bluffed it out.

'Meh, I don't know about that; did you just hear me say "Mavis Uranus"?'

Thys laughed. 'But anyway – this ocean – they say...'

She suddenly noticed that there were more Ymira on the pier now. A dozen had gapped in, with more as she watched, and they were all listening.

'...they say...'

'Go on, kid! You got an audience! Grab 'em with ya got 'em!'

'...uuhh... okay... they say... it wasn't here before we showed up. Before we got here, this was nothing. Like; a desert, but not even that. An astral void; something that was made of something, for something, that has been forgotten so long, it was just dormant astral energy, absorbed back into the… I don't know. "The Plane". But, like, three hours before we turned up – a hole opened in the ground.'

There were a dozen more Ymira now, not all in uniform.

'This is the one?' Thys heard one ask another, knowing her father and Everett heard as well.

'This is the one I was talking about.'

Thys kept the story going.

'…water trickled out; then more and more and faster and faster, and by the time we got here, well, you remember – there was water from horizon to horizon, deep enough for this boat. And after you left, the more I fought, the more Ymira joined in, the more Draco we fought off, and killed –'

'Killed?' Mitch was startled.

'Well, what did you think, Mitch?' Everett asked, firmly but not without sensitivity.

'It's not the same here, Dad. They just come back a few weeks later in new bodies; they have – not complete control, but a very strong level of mastery over their reincarnation cycles up; I mean, *out here*. But the more it happened, the more we fought, the more this ocean got bigger and bigger, deeper and wider and calmer and stormier, and all phases in between. Now you have to go up, so high, to see the edges. The more we fight – the bigger it gets, the more real, like an actual ocean it gets, and the more I fight; me, personally… it gets even wider, and it gets even deeper, and the sky gets bluer and bluer.'

'That's amazing…' Mitch uttered.

'She was born for this…'

One of the Ymira had spoken, standing beside Everett.

Thys smiled at her. 'Gexvi.'

They were friends; she let her father and Everett see that.

Then she kept talking.

'The Draco and their allies send more forces, more spells, stranger traps and more bizarre monsters; mind games and fields of Rube Goldberg domino-style mine fields; but we've kept fighting, and fighting. And because we're fighting in the human astral terr – in the Terrastral Territories, the fight took on a form, an archetypal form.'

Many others had appeared around her now; the pier was half full, back to the boat.

'So now, it's an army, and we're fighting not just a a civil war, but a war of reclamation!'

Cheers went up; the Ymira saluted her.

She went to her father and took him by the hands, stared into his eyes.

'Dad, there's one thing you hadn't considered. Maybe The Dark Thing let go of you because he is *old and wise,* and maybe, it *did do its calculations,* and maybe, it decided – to cut its losses. Maybe there's never been a Pandora Sequence before? Maybe it didn't know what to do? Maybe it realised; it couldn't win?'

'Sweetie, I don't know…'

'But we don't, do we? So we have to keep fighting. This is the first time in six thousand years, in this whole iteration of humanity, of the Earth peopling, that we, the Earthlings, are back in the astral without being controlled by the Anunnaki; by the Draco and all the other toxic clans. I know it's just me, and you, and Uncle Bo, and the others. But it's a start, and we're inspiring the Ymira. Just think about our dreams – we have dreams in our astral bodies, on the astral plane, and they almost always end up being anxiety dreams, or quest dreams, or reliving-terrible-memories dreams, or – whatever. But that's because we have been engineered, genetically, by the Draco, to be that way; steered by cultural agent provocateurs to gravitate toward those base, primal psychological forces, to feed them, to feed the Anunnaki! There are humans who believe this is just – traces of evolution. Responses to primal forces we cannot escape – but how can we escape them, when our primal forces are being encouraged by the people who shape our culture? Who wants the world this way?'

She paused and looked into his eyes again, focussing very deeply now.

'Nobody. Nobody does – nobody who realises that there is a better way than exploitation. Nobody whose mind works well. But, minds and bodies are being deliberately polluted down there – in twenty fourteen, well-past the start of the twenty-first century – it's still going on, Dad. And it doesn't look like it's going to get any better. Not the way things are. But – when you're here…'

She looked to Suzie.

Suzie was listening.

'…and you're *supposed to be here,* and nothing is stopping you – here, in the ocean, away from all their shit; I mean, you can make things happen. This ocean; they can't get near it. They can fly over it, sure; send their weird shit from afar… but they can't touch it! We're making it – and it's nothing to do with them. For the first time…' She grinned at her father. '…we're creating – something else!'

There were cheers; rallying cries.

'Ymira!'

'Field Marshall'

'Thys Pyne!'

'Xylata!'

'Fuck me Xylata!'

'Lick me Thys Pyne!'

Thys shrugged at her two human elders.

'They get a bit raunchy. It's all in good fun.'

'We die in bliss for your milky white mammaries, Human Goddess!'

CHAPTER 21

Everett stood on the front balcony of the astral replica of his private yacht, two decks above the bow that extended before him, gazing out at the still lavender sea beneath the indigo sky; or, the bruised purple horizon over the becalmed lilac ocean; or, whatever the water and sky actually was, from whichever way you looked at it, at any given angle, moment or mood…

The boat was so close in appearance right now to the original that you could easily create a 'spot the difference' puzzle from the two, Thys thought, as she walked up the deck to see him; at least, from her memory you could.

'The liquid expanse, is how I think of it…' Thys told him as she arrived beside his vigil. '…until the waves come up, and it starts behaving more like an ocean. Then it doesn't matter what you call it.'

He nodded, accepting that.

'Did I ever tell you the name of this ship, Amethyst?'

'No, at least I don't recall hearing it.'

'It's… an okay story. But, in the light of recent information, you should probably know it.'

'Okay.'

Everett kept gazing. 'We always want to say…'

Amy chuckled. '….I know. "The calm before the storm". Kind of still works; the old ones hang around because they still have power.'

'Ha! I would very much like to have that sentence printed on a –'

He felt something about his clothing shift and looked down. The cream waistcoat of his evermore Sam Clements-ish suit now had a shield on the right breast, emblazoned with the motto:

"The Old Ones Hang Around Because They Still Have Power".

'Not quite a tee, Uncle Bo. But – "be careful what you wish for" – is made for this place.'

Everett nodded. 'Another old one; perhaps the oldest.'

They could see something far out upon the horizon now; perhaps…

'Amethyst; if you say, "there's a storm coming", not only will I say "I know", but I will also tell you, I know where that lines comes from, most famously.'

She made stern face and held out her hand. 'Da kize doo dah bode. Gib dem doo mee.'

Everett feigned taking keys out of his pocket, and to his surprise, actually produced a dangling set of keys. He shrugged, and dropped them into her open palm. As they fell, the keys vanished as they hit her skin. They both stared at her hand a second, then she closed it, making a fist.

'Dank yew.'

Everett made a little bow. 'I have been through Earth's astral territories once or twice; never for long. I suppose I could get the hang of it, but Amethyst; I am not suited to a world of imagination, futuristic or otherwise; I don't think many of my pre-Spielberg-Lucas generation are.' He leaned forward, placing both hands on the rail, and tensed his shoulders into his grip, restless. 'However, my information, from my time with Holland Pankhurst, and what I have seen since; what mythology and legend and the mystic texts of multiple cultures suggest, is another 'old one'. *As above; so below.* That this astral plane, here, is a reflection of our home; the physical, material plane.'

Thys half-swung herself, half-levitated, to swing her long legs over and sit upon the rail.

'I haven't seen anything to contradict that exactly…'

Around the pier, the Ymira were briefing new military recruits from their own clan, and even a few from other clans, about their cause. Many had tuned up as Amy had spoken, sensing something they needed to hear.

Behind them, Xylata spoke.

'Unheard of…' She shook her head as she walked up to lean into the rail, copying Bo's posture. '…soldiers spontaneously changing sides; clans changing allegiance. This is a new world, Thys Pyne. But the old served nobody well, other than the elite of the Draco, and their allies.'

Everett looked to Thys, who turned and smiled down at him from her perch.

'That happens here a lot, Uncle Bo. Synchronicity in this part of the astral is like wi-fi back home.'

'It's still your home? Third density?'

Mitch was walking up, behind Xylata; she didn't know from where they had gapped, but she had to assume they'd been dealing with Ryzex. She spun back and dropped off the rail, then went and gave her father a big hug.

'Always will be.'

She squeezed.

'That's nice to know…' Mitch smiled.

'But; that's not to say I won't be moving on again.' She turned back. 'Uncle Bo; it's not like – the dark world, or the upside down world, or the other side of the mirror or anything. I'm sure all those things exist here, if you want; but – this is what I am trying to tell you. I haven't seen very much of it either. I know that sometimes it seems like there is just one city, or just one building, or office, or school, or forest or… anything huge and everyday. But then, when you go in, and it's like – holographic or fractal or something. The one school contains all the schools; the further you go in, the more schools there are. And within the fabric of that dream astral world, there is one for everyone; and then within that, one for everyone's different memories of them; one, in both senses. There is one school or office or home for every person, for every scenario for every person; but there is just one, one massive archetypal one – for everyone, within which all of the others fit. That's what it's like.'

Mitch laughed to himself. 'Well, if you call Sydney a 'higgledy-piggledy mess' then what must these be like?'

Everett frowned. 'Worse than London? Rio?'

'They are all those places, all combined, all mashed up, all holo-fractally, liquid-dreamily, chaotic-catastrophic but interactively-navigably... humanly insanely – us! Everything we've ever been – all interweaved and cross-pollinated! But – this is why I asked you here – to ask your advice.'

'But, sweetie...' Mitch spread his hands. 'You're the expert! We don't know what's really happening here! From what I can tell, having only been here half an hour, neither do the Ymira. They say – nothing like this has ever happened; nothing like you, nothing like this Sea of Humanity; they say you're the one making it all happen!'

'Sea of Humanity? I wish they wouldn't call it that...' Amy folded her arms. '...or say that. Just because it started happening when I turned up, doesn't mean I'm the one causing it.'

'Hey!'

They looked down to the pier.

Heather Everett was standing there.

'What is this place!?'

They all fumbled for an answer as she held up a black evening dress and a pair of black pumps.

'How are we all feeling about gapping into a moving stretch-limo?'

Then she gapped up, to stand right in front of them.

'Because the one I've arranged gets to the premiere in about five minutes and it's going to look really weird if we don't all get out of it!'

CHAPTER 22

Heather whisked Amy down to a cabin, without her even really understanding…

'– ha – how?'

'We only have a few minutes. Where there's a will there's a way.'

'You can't just – how did you…?'

'This means a lot to your father, to have you there; and whether or not you realise, it means a lot to you.'

Amy frowned at her and tried to make a massive complaint, before she gapped back out to – she didn't know where. But she was still a bit stunned, and there was something in what Heather was saying which, despite herself, and her enormous desire to be able to be angry with her, forced her to take into consideration what had *actually just happened* –

'And I suppose –' Heather kept speaking quickly. '– it means a lot to me too, right? Okay? Because I don't think too many people here, human or not, could just pick you up and move you like that, unless –'

'Unless it really meant a lot to everyone.'

Heather held her breath. 'I don't know.' Then she seemed a little breathless. 'You tell me. I just made my best guess and headed out.' Heather lifted up the black strapless dress she'd brought with her. There was a glittering necklace in her hand as well. 'She's a designer we're helping out. Just a bit of private development funding. It's diamond; I think she's a channel, it's very Sirian, right?' She raised the shoes. 'I had a choice of three, wasted time, went with these.'

Heather extended them.

'Two minutes real-time and counting.'

Amy shot out her hands and accepted them.

Heather turned her back. Amy noticed that Heather's number three cut, which had been part of what had completely startled her so much, the first time she had seen her in her father's arms, here on this very boat… had grown out. She was just a beautiful woman now, with sexy-messy, French New Wave-ish chocolate hair, who loved her Dad.

Heather somehow knew she was looking.

'It was weird that you saw me then. That it was your first impression of me.'

'How did you know that's what I was thinking?'

'The intuition thing; it's getting better with me. Like Uncle Bo. Must be in the Everett genes. I knew, the first time I saw him, that I would be with Mitch; okay, probably not the first time but definitely the second time I spied on him. There was that feeling of; man, this one's going to take some work, a real fixer-upper but, when you get that feeling…? Actually, I don't know if you know that feeling yet. Are you going to have a twenty-first?'

'I've –'

'Don't talk, just dress. Let me know when I can turn around.'

'I – nearly…'

'There was just something about the way he just loved movies. Even when he was sad, and depressed. Even when they were bad; the way he cared about how they were bad. He had a perspective. Not a lot of people do, you know. Not one that isn't spoon fed. Not one that's their own, that actually comes from them, that's developed over time. The first time he saw me, I had those dreadlocks, which was part of my cover. I was so over them. I could tell, he looked at me, the first time he saw me, and thought; now there's a woman who would be very attractive if it weren't for those dreadlocks. Now, don't think I go around trying to look good for men, let's just nip that one in the bud, okay?'

'I…'

'I knew he thought that, because that's what I thought every time I looked in the mirror. He says now he barely noticed them, but – I shaved it all off that night because I wanted to forget that job, undercover with The Pan, spying on your Dad, trying to forget Holland Pankhurst… and I wanted your father to know that's not who I was.'

She slowed down a bit.

She seemed more anxious than Amy had ever seen her.

'Because sometimes, you know; men put on a nice outfit because they know a certain someone is going to be at a party. Women put on makeup. I didn't know what my next assignment would be, I liked him, so I made a statement.'

She sped up again.

'It was spur of the moment, but, my God, Amy, if you ever get the urge… it takes so long to grow back!'

'It was very short. And it did make you look… fairly – hostile.'

'Well it was kind of a hostile thing to do. Remember Britney? It's a massive call to the universe for change. And well, I got that, didn't I?'

'We all did.' Amy told her. 'You can turn around now.'

Heather turned around.

'Holy shit!'

Heather held out her hand.

Still, a little standoffish, almost despite herself, Amy took it.

'We're going – now.' Heather threw her head back and shouted. *'We're going – now!'*

'Wait.'

'What?'

Again, a little unsure of her, almost despite herself, she took Heather's other hand and they stood there, holding hands, facing each other. Only then did she realise that Heather was dressed as well; ready. They both looked amazing; they both looked like… Heather had made it so… they belonged together. They complimented each other.

'Heather – am I ready?'

'No.'

'What?'

'Nothing prepares you for this. It's batshit. Stay with me. Or your Dad. But try and stay with me. Smile and don't engage; if they force you, don't answer any questions with anything other than how thrilled you are to be there. You'll get through it.'

'Okay.' Amy heard her own lack of confidence. 'Fuck.'

'Amy, look at me.' Heather squeezed both her hands, and looked into her eyes. It was hard, she was nervous, but Amy looked back. She didn't really see anything. She was freaking out.

What the hell was she doing???

'After tonight, will you come back and see us a bit more often? We're doing things together, but Mitch has his own projects, and so do I. I could use your advice on some of them.'

Amy wasn't sure.

'Heather, look…' Amy took a breath. '…Dad, and Uncle Bo, they don't really like the astral. They don't feel comfortable with things being able to come out of nowhere, with the flow of it. Some men are like that; some older men, in particular.'

'Okay. Your Dad's not that old, you know.'

'You know what I mean; it's why I took to it so fast, I think. My generation are going to be able to handle what's coming, the flow of things, the fluidity – at least, if we can get a handle on all of that now.'

Heather was shaking her head, tensely.

'You think I'm too old?'

'Heather, it's not really age – it's conditioning. And I don't mean…' Amy huffed. 'Look, Heather, what I mean is – I think you'd be fine. I think I might – *need you.* How about – you come here more often, and see me?'

'Me? Here? You?'

''Uh huh!'

And with that, they both burst into tears.

CHAPTER 23

'Come – on!' Heather insisted.

Mitch and Everett turned around to see that Heather and Amethyst had gapped back onto the top deck.

'But...' Mitch was confused. '*We're* waiting for *you.*'

There was a commotion from the pier.

'Actually,' Everett acknowledged cheekily. '...I believe; we've all been waiting for her.'

Yelina was making her way, with a small entourage, out of the huge root system and along the pier. She was simply walking, followed by six young women, in a quite unassuming manner. Only; she was a goddess, and nothing she ever did came across as anything but possessing a kind of natural poise, and gravitas. Somehow, the pier had become not just a catwalk, but a stage upon which a legend, some kind of mystical, Earthen, planetary royalty was making a grand and spontaneous entrance.

It was only then that Thys actually took full note of the root-entrance behind Yelina, and realised...

She leaned toward Heather.

'What is it with her and the female anatomical portals....?'

Heather muttered from the side of her mouth.

'...I know, right?'

Then she looked at her again.

'What....?' Thys demanded. It was quite a penetrating look.

'You have more than one aspect here,' Heather noted keenly.

Yelina was dressed in brown leather jeans and knee-length black boots with gold buckles; a long, woolly, burnt-ochre coat; and a breezy, low-buttoned, untucked shirt that featured something like Incan or Aztec patterns (Thys was never sure) in zig-zag blocks of orange and ochre and red and black.

Behind her were six young women, all dressed in casual street clothes, all of whose outfits were completely different. They had come from different parts of the world perhaps, in a hurry, uncoordinated, but for the matching earth-tones tones that corresponded with Yelina's fabulous casual ensemble.

In quick succession, the top-deck Pandorans all followed Everett as he gapped down to the pier, even as all the Ymira along the way stopped what they were doing to observe her entrance, with a dozen or so returning via gaps, as though sensing another kind of disruption – or maybe, more likely, an approaching spectacle, just as Thys had also sensed.

Everett walked up to her and they kissed warmly.

'Hello Pandorans!' Yelina exclaimed, as they both turned, arms around each other's waists like a Presidential couple who were so evenly matched, you would never know which one held the actual title. Up close again, Thys had forgotten how beautiful Yelina was; some kind of voluptuous, mainline-Latina aspect of the Earth Goddess in the flesh. Not South American, not Mexican, and not American, and yet parts of all of those expressions of a very ancient feminine archetype. She went way, way, way back, but she was new, and powerful, and she had the ear and held the right hand of the re-emerging Gaia. She was not to be messed with, but she was their friend; and she was here, Amy knew immediately, to help. As soon as she'd had that thought, Yelina walked up to Thys and smiled.

'May I, Thys Pyne?'

'Help? Of course!'

'This is your world, here; I presume nothing. Just as I presume nothing when I am on my Bo's great white ship.' She winked, just gently, and her voice lowered half a melodious octave. 'Feel free to take that as euphemism, darling, everybody does.' Then she paused and examined Thys more closely. 'Oh!' She placed a gentle hand just above her hip. 'My sweet young lady, you must come to me; I have something just right for you!' Then she turned away, leaving Thys feeling just a little more sensual about herself than she had, a mere three seconds previously, and for way too long since.

'However; why I am here. The Great Malevolence that came though; he burned. He burned down; and this ocean, and this pier, is the result of the dimensional rifts he created. They are not evil, not foul or contaminated of themselves, but they must be consecrated, and blessed, and properly nurtured – and pruned of his residue.'

Heather approached her and they embraced, lightly but warmly, with a familiarity of which Thys was momentarily jealous.

'You mean…?' Heather spoke as the greeting occurred. '…this has come up, from Earth? Through the downward dimensional rift?'

Yelina turned and gazed up at the giant, umbrella-like root system. 'It has; but it also provides an opportunity. A focus point through which natural energy can be creatively channelled, rather than randomly dispersed. This portal has grown itself, through from the Inner Earth, seemingly through want of a – a nexus point? A station, it seems, on this plane? We must locate the link in Third Density, to honour and consecrate this strange new alliance we are making, and secure it in the name of the Pandorans, but for now…'

She gestured back to her acolytes; the six young women who were standing and gazing about, their focus aimless, but their faces happy and amazed.

'…these are my dryad sprites; they are sleeping, and they know me in your world, Amy, however sometimes this, guiding them in semi-lucid dreaming, is the best way to ease them into their roles, to prepare them for exposure to their true heritage.'

Thys recognised one of the dryad sprites, but Mitch was ahead of her.

'Yelina, this is a Miss Lavé, a young woman I rescued – just this evening, from –'

'Mitchell!' Yelina beamed. 'You do look well.'

'Thank you, Yelina. You *always* look well.'

'Very well...' Yelina smiled, appreciatively. '...your confidence and good nature continue to recover nicely.'

Mitch folded his arms, but his expression remained that of a giddy school kid who had somehow become regularly acquainted with his screen crush. 'We've encountered each other enough times now Yelina; I know what you're doing.'

'Indeed you do Mitchell, indeed! And you are correct; these young human women are all my descendants, seeded generations ago within my family tree; they have each been exposed to highly unusual elements of reality beyond their normal spheres and have coped very well, and so they have each, in their way, sought me out and found me. In dream, I give them apprenticeship; in your reality, my lover provides them internship, and even some, a – trial position?'

Yelina again deferred to Thys; and somehow, Thys felt it was sincere.

'I bring them here to honour you, and to please me; may we be permitted to fertilize and accelerate, just a sprinkle?'

Amy dreaded what this meant, ever so slightly.

'Do not fear; I understand, we might seem overwhelming, however, I can assure you, we only mean to provide a more stable station for the –'

Thys didn't know why she was hesitating.

'Of course, Yelina! Of course; we owe everything to you, you showed us the way that afternoon in Los Angeles, please; it would be *amazing*.'

With a beautiful smile, Yelina somehow indicated to her acolytes that the path was clear for them to begin whatever ceremony had been planned. Immediately they reached into their pockets; skirts, jackets, jeans, trousers, and began throwing fistfuls of something into the water. It seemed clear somehow, almost immediately, that they were casting seeds; one girl threw small seeds that hit the astral water in multiple tiny splashes, while another cast handfuls of what might have been acorns, which plonked as they hit, then floated a while before slowly sinking. Yelina herself held out her hand and what looked like a small melon shimmered into her grasp, materializing as though through a different kind of dimensional gap; one perhaps more gaseous, made of mist, and a twister of sand. The melon spouted right there, in her palm, springing vines from its top, surprising even Yelina with its speed of growth. She moved quite fast, to hold the melon out, over the edge of the pier with both hands, then she moved quickly along, muttering a series of low, songlike incantations, before dropping the rapidly bursting, ferociously fertile melon, with vines and flowers and writhing tendrils now high above her head, as close as she could to the top of the pier, down between the boat and the edge.

Pop-plonk!

'Well…!'

Yelina gasped, stepping back again amid mutterings of wonder and amazement from the surrounding Ymira.

'…this is a fertile plane!'

Within a second of her bringing her hands gently together in a soft clap, trees of all kinds began to burst forth from the ocean, splashing up and rising from the edge of the pier, but becoming closer as they grew, their trunks increasing in thickness, as each tree shot higher by the second. Although they had sprouted randomly, they seemed to somehow accommodate an evening of their spread as they developed and expanded, their branches and leaves moving between each other as they sprang forth, stretched out and arose, weaving to create a vast canopy, higher and higher, and a further network of piers and walkways. At first all the new planks, planes and flat extensions were even with the pier, then they too were grown and pushed higher. Then, another set appeared, as if by design; the trees all growing new levels and sprouting even more interconnected paths as they went, then rising again. The canopy was three or four storeys high now, Thys saw; then there was another growing, then another, until she was able to discern perhaps five distinct levels beneath the wide, lush canopy; all shades of green, yellow and brown, with perhaps even more happening on top. Only then, when the fifth or sixth (she was still unsure, the highest levels were so far away now) had stabilized, did the growth slow, and the wild, creaking sounds tone down to a more leathery, squeaky shifting of bark on bark friction.

Yelina was staring up, her mouth agape.

'That was supposed to take five years!'

She turned to the others.

'I must admit, I did not expect our first effort, in so long, at full-physical cooperation to go *exactly right*, however...' Yelina laughed in deep amazement. '...I could not have predicted such...?' She turned back hopefully to Thys and Heather.

'...success?' Thys offered.

Behind, above and before Thys now was now a kind of massive treehouse fort, the size of a major city railway station. It would have been difficult to look at it all and not see the genetically programmed – Thys had to assume – design of some kind of pre-envisioned port complex, of a dense but sensible system of piers and stations, all created from the same over-arching, above-water, umbrellalike root systems, each a hub of their own, with arcing branch-walkways over and under, and rope-like vines, braided to create stairs. There were very clearly rooms, if not also a system of open-offices above, beneath and within the enormity of the canopy-cavern. Even as Thys realised this, she saw that it would be difficult to look at it and comprehend just how expansive the new astral port was. Or indeed, could be? Presumably, it would continue to grow? Certainly it was absoluetly, minimally five floors high; but how wide exactly? The view from where they stood had been blotted out entirely, but... what would it look like from above?

'Yes... succuss!' Yelina uttered. 'Let's go up and see shall we?'

CHAPTER 24

'I only just realised. There's no sun?'

There were several circular lookouts spread across the top of the new port's canopy; Yelina had transported them to the most central, which was the only one not to have a tree-lined canopy of its own.

They arrived holding hands, as Yelina has instructed.

'It takes a while to realise, doesn't it?' Thys released her father and Heather, and walked to the edge. Below it seemed as though a massive jungle stretched before them, at least a kilometre in each direction. She had an odd, swelling sensation beneath her, a deep but subtle sense of throbbing underfoot; a sense of slowly rising which told her that the jungle had not quite finished its expansion – or was at least ready to burst again when the time was right.

Xylata was already up there.

'There is a sun.' She turned in response to Everett's remarks. 'This is the astral plane; the light is the light of all suns.'

'What does that even mean, Field Marshall?'

Xylata shrugged, but Amy could tell she liked Everett's tone of respect. 'I don't know; I am not a mystic, I have no interest in questioning the Anunnaki Arcana.'

'The...?'

Thys began suddenly.

'I didn't think we would see it this way...'

She pointed out, toward the ocean horizon.

'But – there. Look. That is the Dracopolis. If there is an actual Karma Forge, a mechanism, a machine; that's it. That is where virtually all of the dream energy, the psychic energy; the opal dust, created by human dreaming, particularly anything filtered through Western Culture, goes when we sleep. It is stored in our bodies down there on Earth during our waking days, and brought here by our astral bodies in slumber.'

Thys turned back to them all.

'And this whole ocean that we have created, or birthed or summoned or whatever; Xylata, the Ymira and me; it's done nothing.'

'What do you mean, sweetie?'

'It's not doing anything to the Dracopolis, or the other clan cities that control any of the other dominant human cultures; they just go on, regardless. This ocean has been here six Earth months. I go back every now and then, just for an hour or so, alone...'

She saw Mitch and Heather exchange glances; their girl was a grown up, out there now, working alone, without always checking in.

'...and nothing has changed. Our culture is still a higgledy-piggledy mess, being collectively piggybacked by competing Anunnaki clans, still using hacks they made six thousand years ago that keep us as close to the Dark Ages as possible. So; that's where you go, when you fall asleep on Earth. The Occupied Astral Territories –'

'The Occupied Terrastral Territories, surely?' Mitch corrected.

'Is that right? The astral shouldn't have territories...' Heather offered. '...at least, not from what I've read?'

'Indeed...'

Everett kept staring out at the vast metropolis; a black-smoking, chimney-lined, jagged-towered infestation; an endless array of black steel pylons and bunker-concrete shafts, coal and grease-smeared; packed tight, inhumanly, unliveably tight, with the shrieking, squealing, violation of sound, of pressure against pressure; vocal, metal, refining and mining; projecting from every blackened window, endlessly, always, along with a horrendous energy frequency that might have been... a combination of a million abuses; conscious, unconscious; deliberate and accidental;

forced upon and surrendered to; horizon to horizon.

'...behold, the post-Industrial astral expanse! The Dracopolis! The Karma Forge!'

He looked to his niece.

'It is true that there should be no astral territories; but we just happen to have manifested them, as we have on Earth, as we have come into conflict with one of the most aggressive and psychopathic clans from one of the most aggressively expansive alien races in the galaxy...'

He raised his hand. There was a cigar, burning.

'…and if this is where they herd us when we sleep…?'

He looked to Thys.

'Look, Bo – out there, you can see their temple-refineries. They just call them towers, head offices; but that's what they are; part temple, part refineries.'

'For… opal?' Mitch wanted to know.

'Opal is what happens to matter from here when it gets taken back to third density; only the strongest manifestations of it can survive being carried there. Here, astral matter is all sorts of energies. They correspond to everything we have back home; states of matter, different minerals, different psychologies…' She looked to Everett. '…and because generating our psychological states, and siphoning off our emotional energy, takes the form in the astral of what they are doing – they are, at best, refineries. Just as my presence here, my resistance, takes the shape of a war.'

'Then this is where we must fight them, no? In these astral hellscapes? Defeat them at their own game? On their own ground, on their own terms?'

'They are horrible places, Bo. As bad as the worst of us ever came up with, through history. Refined refineries with nobody to rebel or stop them. Because nobody knows they exist.'

She looked to her father as well, then to Heather, and finally to Xylata.

'Until now.' Xylata held her chin up. 'It is possible to think of the astral plane like your Old School Heaven, hovering above the clouds. That can be manifested for you, if you desire, in dreams. But the Anunnaki colonization of the Terrastral Plane is greater than that; it contains that as just one section. There, in the Draco City, is where thought and emotion are power; they are like currency. If you think of a stock exchange, with calculations being made, constantly assessing how much things are worth, who owns them, accumulating that, dividing it into shares and stocks, then comparing it against the judged worth of all the other companies, and corporations, and entities within that reality; the lower astral, where we Anunnaki live and work, is like that; but we trade primarily in units of emotional energy.'

'That's abominable...!' Heather uttered.

'How...?' Mitch scowled. 'How on Earth does it work?'

'Oh, Mitchell Pyne; there are a great many answers to that question. Do you remember there was a President called George Bush Junior?'

'Who could forget? He's almost as bad as –'

'Of course; they are all as bad as each other, depending on the lens through which you view the world. Through one lens, people would say 'God Bless George Bush', through another, 'George Bush is a moron!' Many people, when people think about their lives in a country like America, would also think about the President as they did, no matter what other aspect of America they had on their minds. The President represents all that they hope for, or all of which they strongly disapprove. But the President is just a man. He eats, sleeps, had dreams; has anxieties, has desires. He laughs and he cries, he poos and he wees, he has the occasional dark night of the soul, he has the occasional blissful epiphany. But it is the image of the man; the iconography, the symbol, which becomes the "real thing" people think about in association with; as – America. That is what becomes an avatar for the power of America; the "dream symbol" replaces the "real man" as "reality".'

'I understand all that, but how did it all – happen?'

'Originally, Mitchell, it was all just an ecosystem; the same as your world has an ecosystem. Everything was in a kind of Dream-Darwinian balance, as above, so below. Initially, we fed off the energies of anxiety and satisfaction from the lesser species, just as your primitive ancestors fed off of the sun and the water and the air. But then, as it does, astral life evolved. We Anunnaki evolved intelligence within the fourth dimension just as you did within the third. Rather than continually adapt to our surroundings, we began to adapt our surrounding to suit us. We discovered that we could herd the lesser species...'

'Us?'

'...to increase the output of astral energies; we could go amongst you and lead you into mass production of the refined energies that empowered us; into slaughter if we so desired. And like your own cattle; you would not truly recognise us as we walked amongst you.'

'Until you became completely dependent upon us?'

'Until we convinced ourselves that we were. So thought the Ymira. So thought many who have joined the Ymira now. But the stronger clans; they were, they are, the people behind the scenes. The people behind the people behind the scenes. The powerful middle-men; the wormtongues; the King Makers. Our agents have been recorded in history, but we remove or refine or reattribute those mentions within a generation, so that they are not remembered past that generation. But now that is becoming more difficult. Not impossible, but harder.'

'The internet?'

Xylata smiled. 'Nobody foresaw it. Nobody knows where it will go, past this Earth year of twenty-fourteen. But it has hastened the plans of some of our more powerful enemies.'

'But not you? Not – the Ymira?'

'There are some of us who you might equate with your human movement of... put it this way; we wish humanity to become a sustainable resource. It seems clear to us that we have become you; but you, too have become us. You have depleted something you require to exist, almost to the point of no return. That's why the higher-again races, like the Sirians and Pleiadeans are returning to take an interest; what you've done here, what we've done under you influence, it's unsustainable. Not just for us, and you, but for the whole cosmic ecosystem!'

'The influence of the Anunnaki...?'

'Has made everything worse; including ourselves. This is why we fight – it is pointless, inefficient, cruel and wasteful.'

'Only that?'

'No. Many of us, we Ymira, are experiencing an enlightenment also. We have desired change for many centuries. It has been horrific, yes, for those many centuries. And now, it must end.'

'Dad, you've seen them right? Or sensed them?'

'Yes… yes. Although, you don't really see them, do you sweetie? They're just too…'

'They're too overwhelming to actually see, in the conventional sense of – there it is, in the middle of the city, towering above. Where they are – they are the city anyway. They are the main event. Like, just; massive oil rigs for our despair, huge smoke-billowing Dickensian factories for our weaknesses; nuclear power plants to distil our self-loathing. They're hard to get near; that's just the impression I got, but they're all connected to logos and icons and companies and corporations. They treat them like cathedrals; depending on the clan they have temples, and priests and ranks of acolytes. Somewhere in there they take the joy and the love and the pleasure as well; that's like gold and silver and diamonds to them. But, I can't get near. All I can do is keep fighting them off, and this ocean, this vast field of liquid astral energy, it just keeps growing.'

She stared back now, at the Karma Forge, a fire in her eyes.

'We were able to get this high, before. To see it, once in a while. But now – we have it in our sights, for good.'

She turned to Yelina.

'Thank you, Gaia.'

Yelina bowed. 'She is humbled by your gratitude, and offers any further assistance required.'

Again, Thys returned her attention to the Dracopolis.

'We couldn't see it at all for… quite some time.' Xylata had not taken her eyes off it since they'd arrived. 'I believe at some stage – the physical quality of this liquid ocean spread, and deepened. It raised the boat, Bo Everett, raised it eventually so we could see the smoke; then the tops of the towers and chimneys; then we started piloting out craft, higher, to see. But I have never seen it like this; from so far away, as a whole. It disgusts me now, more than ever; more than when I first saw it filtered through the consciousness of Sapphire Edge. I see without question that it must go.'

Everett stared at her, his eyes piercing.

But she just kept looking out; her own lime-yellow eyes seemingly lit from behind with the same fire that had become stoked in Thys.

Then suddenly, someone spoke from behind the group.

'Hey! Ah…' There was an audible gulp. '…guys?'

Someone new; they all felt the odd vibe immediately.

He was a late-middle-aged man, with a thin face and healthy eyes, framed by a white beard and ponytail.

'…guys; heya. Hi. Ahhh; so, see; I wanna to help. Whatever it is you're doin' here? I wanna help.'

Thys was shocked. 'Who…?'

Shocked that the shock was so... pleasant.

'I was just – drawn here, y'know? I sometimes lucid dream? And I kind of woke up and I was, like, walking around the city, trying to get out, as you do, y'know? When you realise the city is, like – dank and miserable? And then, suddenly, I felt – something else. Maybe because – I, like; I'm a kind of enlightened dude? You know? Back home? I have classes in the Hills – yoga and meditation, mystical systems and self-realization; all the good stuff, yeah? I kind of woke up a while back, to the dream city being – dark? Like, dark to the core? But this time, there was, like, a cave? And the cave was round? A round cave in the sharp and angular and miserable dream city; I mean... you gotta go through, right? Cause, there was a symbol carved, above the cave, and it was – cool, you know?'

'A symbol?'

'Carved real well, like, you know? Old, but new? Timeless?'

'What kind of symbol?'

'Like – a moon?' And, ahhh...? Something else?'

Thys walked toward him, holding up her finger.

As she did, she traced a symbol in the air before her; it seemed to hold integrity, to be made out of the opal dust. It was two curves, joined to make a crescent moon, with a bright star beside it. Even as Thys drew it, it seemed to take on a golden, storybook, Nouveau quality.

'Like this?'

'Yeah, dude; exactly like that!'

Amethyst looked back at Heather, and her father, and her Uncle Bo.

'That's it; that's the symbol I had in my head for Cleverco!'

CHAPTER 25

Everett took a few steps toward the man.

'Who are you, my good man?'

'You know me, yeah?' He nodded, smiling, friendly. 'Yeah, I had my moment. I was in a band near the turn of the Millennium – we were right on the wave of hard gypsy funk at the end of the eighties, man. We were huge.'

Suzie Saturn suddenly moved; until then she had been near-invisible against the background sky.

'The Smudge! Right? Yeah, I heard of you guys!'

'Oh hey; wow, yeah! Like, Suzie Saturn! I love you, man!'

Suzie spread her hands and gave a huge shrug.

'Who wouldn't, man?'

She laughed; he laughed, then they nodded at each other, grinning.

'You were the bass player, right?'

'Yeah, and backing vocals. You really remember? We had a huge fight with this other massive band, Wellsprung, right at the start of the new millennium! They got the number one album, but we got the number one single, on the only charts that count - the indie folk rock charts!'

Heather frowned. 'Did they even have them back then?'

'We knew man, *we knew*. I think my name is Jason. Jason…. uh… might be Axelrod?'

Mitch was grinning. 'Jason Axelrod!'

'Yeah man!'

He clicked his fingers. 'The Smudge!'

'Yeah!'

'I have all your albums!'

'Of course you do, man!'

Everett shrugged. 'I was a Wellsprung man, myself.'

'All cool, heavy dude. To each their own.' He clearly did not completely feel this way, but was doing his best.

Everett put his hand to his ear.

'*Lady Ann* says if we want to go to the premiere still, she can get us in the limo before it leaves, half an hour ago. She says the film is excellent; we should all go see it.'

'Where is *Lady Ann?*'

Thys suddenly looked up, and sansed her presence.

Everett looked up, following her gaze.

'Apparently, she is The Port of Ymira's first arrival.'

CHAPTER 26

The attack had come quickly.

Enormous faces in the sky, screaming down.

Old school teachers; disgruntled ex-lovers; disappointed parents; bullied siblings; jealous siblings; toxic grandparents; just to name a few, and each of those things, what they were, what they represented, to all of the people on the docks, all at once.

Mitch shouted. 'What's she shielding us with?'

Everett shrugged. 'Nothing – the air! Or, whatever the equivalent of air is out here!'

Heather had her hands over her ears.

She shouted.

'She turning the air into shield!'

Thys heard and told them:

'It's the opal-crystal rainbow dust! I can make it do things!'

They all heard another exchange, between Ymira:

'This is the one you and Xylata are following?'

'Yes! She is the way forward!'

'This is a good idea. I will follow her as well!'

Ryzex had thrown herself at Thys's feet.

'You are the Astral Saviour; she who comes from the without to save the within!'

'Yeah, yeah.'

Thys was gritting her teeth. The fear-faces were powerful, and would have broken all their minds. She couldn't figure out if they had appeared to attack the *Lady Ann*, or if *Lady Ann* had appeared just before the attack. Regardless, *Lady Ann* was teaching her, telling her what to do, and helping her find new paths to new reserves of power. Soon, the fear-faces would give up, stop bullying, and run crying home.

'I just hope we can still make the red carpet.'

CHAPTER 27

Everett nodded and folded his arms as the Olivera Studios logo came up.

He hummed distastefully as he stared out at the screen.

Amy leaned over to him.

She was pretty sure he was going to walk out once it started; this really wouldn't be his kind of thing.

'What should I do, Uncle Bo?'

'I think you should keep going.'

But Everett hadn't spoken.

It was her father who'd answered, sitting on her other side.

Everett turned to them and spoke past Amy with a big, wise smile.

'Oh, Mitchell.'

He guffawed.

'Clearly, my son! Clearly!'

Phew.

Now she could sit back and enjoy the movie.

THE PANDORA INHERITANCE

PART (_)

DEBUTANTE

CHAPTER 28

Amethyst Pyne watched her father in a moment from his past.

Mitch stood in the middle of a Los Angeles street.

He was still as buildings shook and collapsed all around him, awaiting his own death.

'You keep returning here...'

Amy was mesmerised and didn't respond.

Heather Everett had started running toward him, still almost a block away, her eyes filled with pain and longing, knowing that she would never reach him. But even as the world was ending around them, Heather ran. And even though Amy knew that this had already happened, that her father and Heather did not die, that it all worked out in the end, Amy shouted a warning.

'Dad!'

Beneath the street, something exploded. Enormous flames blasted up and claimed Heather, even as a subway train smashed up through the street, flared in the orange plumes. The engine jutted up, high for a second at forty-five degrees, then slammed down on Mitch like a whale landing on a rowboat.

'No!'

Amy ran forward, but couldn't move. But, she *was running* –

She was running but making no progress, as though on a treadmill.

But again, Amy knew.

'Wait. I can't be seeing this. It was years ago. I wasn't even there when this happened. How can I stand here, in his memory, like it's some sort of....?'

'That is correct, you were not there...' The voice was angelic. '...Mitch returns here often, dreams about it, and you are standing in his dream...'

'Oh. I'm dreaming?'

'No. You are *standing in his dream*. The dream is extremely vivid because it was essentially the climax to the most traumatic period of his life – his mind will make him relive it, over and over, until he has properly processed what happened. The human brain does that after being traumatized, it processes things over and over, makes you relive them over and over, because it is… what's that word humans use? Oh yes – glitchy. It is quite, really *very quite* – glitchy.'

'But… how can I do that? How can I stand in someone else's dream?'

'The Pandora Sequence.'

'The what…?'

'The Pandora Sequence. The coffee and the nougat and the peach flavoured bourbon; the cigars and the Turkish Delight and the – what was the other thing? Anyway, all the things you consumed together in the bathroom, with everyone, at Oliver Hines 'party.'

'Oh. *That* Pandora Sequence.'

'Yes. That, and time. More time has passed now.'

'But – what an odd thing to say. Time does that. It is what time does, surely? It passes.'

'To you, that's how it seems.'

'Oh.' Amy intuited something. 'What did you say about the brain being faulty?'

'The human brain. Many, many faults; very, very exploitable. I'll remind you about all of that later.'

'Should this make sense to me?'

'Now?'

'If not now, then when?'

'And if not you, then who? It's all about the Pandora Sequence for you now. That started everything… so now, you need to go on.'

'Go on? To where?'

'Figure it out, *Amethyst Pyne*. This is your story, now. Here is your invitation, and there is your door.'

'My...?'

There was a symbol. A moon and a star; Art Nouveau.

'They want to see you, before you return.'

'Who do?'

'Your fans.'

'Fans?'

'In the good seats.' The angel smiled. Had that been a joke? Had the angel just made... a remark? 'You'll see.'

'But...'

'Don't be afraid. Everybody loves you.'

'Everybody...?'

'At least they will.'

'They will...?'

'In time.'

CHAPTER 29

Then, all of a sudden, there seemed to people standing around her.

What? Where had they all come from?

Strangely, simultaneously, even as she was standing in the gossamer hall of the angelic cocktail party, her father was still there, still in the distance, still at the end of the street in Los Angeles. She checked herself, checked her surroundings again.

She was definitely at a party, although she could not remember whose it was, what it was for, or even how she had arrived there. But apart from that, the scene with her father and Heather, at the end of the world, or… what might have been; could have been, *would have been,* if it had not been for her father and Heather, was still happening at one end of the room. Was she at some kind of cocktail party for the apocalypse?

On the street, Mitch was talking to… a woman. A short woman, attractive with sharp features, who Amy had seen before. On Everett's boat. During the storm. She'd seen her again, since then, but again she could not remember how or where.

Cricket. It was Cricket Wilde.

No longer in her twenties, Cricket looked to be middle-aged now, with grey streaks in her (still rocking the) black pageboy cut.

It was the same person, Amy was sure, but there.

On the street in Los Angeles, much older than she had looked on the boat.

But the boat had been just a few hours before – surely?

'rhyme …riffing-ear…'

Had someone spoken then? Beside her?

'I said time is different here.'

There were two very tall and slender elves with Cricket and

her father. Or, hippie gurus, or angels, or aliens or… or were they fashion models?

Had one of them just been talking to her – before?

The way the four of them were talking… while one of the fashion model angels – super-tall, androgynous and svelte – held Heather in his arms…

It was weird but it was – so important.

Heather was asleep, by the look of her; but not dead. She had not been blown up, just as her father had not been flattened, just as virtually nobody in Los Angeles had been killed in the earthquake. Heather was asleep, and Mitch was – negotiating?

That's what it looked like, anyway.

'This isn't a dream, is it…?' Amy realised.

'Not quite.' Her guide remained beside her, watching with her. 'You were closer, observing. But now you are watching, through a window, from The Intersection.'

Amy felt a strong gust of wind, as though she were high on a hill.

She saw enormous white curtains billow before her, as the Los Angeles street, her father, Heather, Cricket and the two Elohim faded away.

Then she remembered; what she always came to see.

Her father's lips; the words, at the end, always, before it always faded away.

'Okay…'

His father said to Cricket, to the two angels.

The street was gone and all of the people, the muttering voices that she had sensed around her, became more apparent.

Now she was properly at the shimmering cocktail party.

But she still heard the last word her father said to them; the Elohim and Orion.

'Deal.'

CHAPTER 30

The party was being held in a long, wide, open-plan apartment, surrounded by glass, but she immediately recognised that the view here was unique.

It was night. Late.

Later...?

The Harbour Bridge was to her right; a cruise ship in dock, lit up, The Rocks behind it; the Opera House to her left, with a smattering of people wandering about; Circular Quay ahead, below at about forty five degrees, with two ferries in dock, two coming in and two heading out, white trails of surf in their wake.

Behind it all, the glittering skyscrapers; helicopters, light planes, a few stars.

They were high, over the water, above the North Shore...?

She knew that she had seen this view before, although...

Seeing the famous Harbour from this angle... should be...?

She couldn't quite get her bearings.

This was confusing.

Not the North Shore...

Maybe out in the middle of the water?

The middle of the...? It was as though they were in the air, stationary, above the middle of the Harbour somehow?

But no; she shook it off.

Enough.

This was someone's apartment, someone wealthy, she remembered that now. She turned around and examined the apartment, to make sure, to remind herself, to forget the view and how it didn't make sense. The scene was minimalist, like retro-fashion Swedish modular from the seventies. Over this, everything was back-lit from behind free-standing window frames and door frames and picture frames, a light from within them causing the gently billowing, translucent-white curtains to glow, like an eighties music video. Around her, everything was clean; the hors d'oeuvre and drinks trays, the nibbles and drinks themselves, all seemed to possess a quicksilver quality within lines so smooth they blended into the fabric of the space-time bubble around them…

What thoughts she was having!

Everyone was so beautiful.

Some people were in grainy, nineties black and white, some in clean Millennial CGI. Some looked like they were from television in the fifties, some were simply drawings of themselves in the air.

And some were just human, like her.

Her angelic guide spoke again.

'Perceptions… filters and lenses. Turn the kaleidoscope, it's all new.'

'Where am I?'

The guide was silent, but a new woman walked up to her. This one was one of the people who were as solid as Amy; she was an actress that Amy recognised but could not name. Amy was pleased to see her; the actress was a friend, an ally, someone with whom she was especially bonded, from within her own plane of existence. The actress handed her a drink in a long-stemmed glass.

'I thought I'd find you here. You're still at The Intersection.'

'Is that a club? Were we invited?'

The actress stared at her. 'You don't remember? You're on your way home, but they invited you, asked you to take a detour.'

'So exclusive up here!'

The actress sipped her quicksilver champagne. 'Yes, it's quite a big deal. It's only my second time.'

Amy looked around at all the beautiful people.

The actress sounded droll. 'An honour just to be nominated.'

But, Amy considered, she wasn't beautiful enough to be up here, surely?

Even as she'd had the thought, several of the guests, tall and fair-haired, slender and serene, with a silver-violet sheen about them, looked at her as though they had been listening in, and with that notion she had committed some terrible faux pas.

The actress stepped between Amy and the Pleiadeans, and ushered her off in a different direction.

'Don't worry about them. They're –'

'Pleiadeans, right? Was that Uki?'

'Yes. She still holds a bit of a grudge; or whatever they call it to make it sound nicer. A concern for contamination.'

'That doesn't sound nicer.'

'The Pleiadeans are, what you would call, in your science-fiction slash fantasy vernacular, empathic and telepathic.'

'The portmanteau would be *telempathic.*'

'You're always making up these nerdy words.'

'I like doing that.'

The actress had linked arms with her and was moving them through the party; slowly, but surely.

Everyone was smiling as they passed; she and the actress smiled and nodded back. They were all observing and approving with their smiles, with their eyes and their shimmering, their glowing, their projecting, their ghostly presences and their passages back and forth and up and down through space and time.

The actress slowed them down, as it seemed to be going well.

They were simply wafting now.

'To them, at an occasion like this, expressing self-doubt is tantamount to bad etiquette. Think of yourself as a kind of Eliza Doolittle figure. An ingénue being presented into society. Right now, you're making your first walk through the guests…'

'I am…?' She could feel herself becoming something close to thrilled at the prospect, although she didn't know why.

'Not really of course, but that's just a vulgar analogy to make you understand. Emotions to the Pleiadeans are like sound or movement; they have their own vibrancy, their own rules as to exposure and use, their own impact. They can see emotion, feel it;

your being uncomfortable makes them uncomfortable.'

'How?'

'Think of it as emotional vibration. Everything to them is about energy, and density; waves of vibration and intent.'

'Is it?'

'Yes. They prefer it when we gracefully acknowledge our own beauty; inner and outer.'

'But – how can they do that? How can – I do that? Just – *feel beautiful?*'

'They just do; and you just do. Imagine this were a real party, in your world. They can detect self-doubt and low self-esteem like you could detect someone who has rushed here, unprepared; someone who hasn't washed and has body odour. Or someone who has come to a black-tie event in a tee shirt and board shorts.'

'But I didn't even know I'd been asked –'

'It's okay, they want you here. This is your debut, so to speak.'

'Debut?'

'At The Intersection, yes. It's just, they're not used to it. They're not accustomed to being in such close proximity to fourth density, let alone with someone from third density. But this party is being held here, in, as they call it, The Intersection, so you're going to meet all sorts.'

She tried to see who was talking to her, which actress it was, who'd handed her the glass. She looked a very deep and natural green, somehow.

'Are you a crocodile?'

There was smattering of laughter throughout the party.

Was really she on show?

Was she really – being introduced?

'We're both crocodiles.'

'Really?'

'Yes, we're the boss crocs; you're the pink one, the rare albino one; I'm the big momma green one; but you don't remember because they snatched you out of a gap halfway home; your astral amnesia was going to be bad enough already, with how long you've bene gone this time; now it's going to make things difficult.'

'It is?'

'Look; don't worry about that, and don't worry about them. Before long, you'll feel right at home here.'

'I already do feel at home here, strangely...'

'That's because they've hired out party deck of the...'

From another room, there came another smattering – doubtfulness and disapproval.

Then a burst of shock.

Amy couldn't quite comprehend what she was experiencing. The shock was more of a wave of feeling than sound. Although there had been sound waves too; audible gasps.

So, this was definitely a physical place.

And she had felt air – at least, something discernibly tangible had shifted within the solid atmosphere of the room. Suddenly she had butterflies. Suddenly, there were butterflies, hovering around her.

Two figures approached.

They were beautiful, a mother and daughter, she sansed, although the daughter was hovering behind the mother, like she was...

...shy?

Why?

Why shy?

The pair moved as though they were astronauts on the moon, within a lighter gravity, yet conversely, their movements were not at all restricted by that – but even still, that was not quite it.

Maybe, Amy reconsidered, it was like they were walking underwater, but unrestricted by pressure, even though they were still moving through the volume of the water...?

Again, not exactly – not even close?

But – closer?

And the closer they came...

Lines of light glistened about them, as though the duo were

dressed in flowing crystalline togas, surrounded by their own currents of space and time and movement, their auras constantly forming and reforming with ice, or ice crystals, or even diamonds, with the sun catching and reflecting and glistening upon them; sharply, perfectly, mesmerizingly.

Were they, themselves, animated crystal energy? Or were their gossamer costumes somehow crystalline; seamless, organic, diamond-armour, toga-style evening gowns?

Then, they stopped moving.

They were humanoid; they had flesh but not as Amy had flesh. They were shockingly attractive; curvy, symmetrical, sexual and sharp, with billowy, low-cut garments, tied at their hourglass waists. They had complexions of light blues and soft greys, sapphire and crystal quartz, summer skies and diamonds.

'Look mother, she sees us!'

'Yes darling. Her father has seen me, and now we are beholden to them.

'As a courtesy?'

'As a pledge; for honour. And, we like them. We like their human strangeness, and boldness, and cuteness. Her father and his offspring and familials will always see us now.'

Behind the Sirians – and she did not know how she knew them to be Sirians, but she did – some of the Pleiadeans moved forward.

A man spoke.

'Greetings. We helped him also, the Mitch Pyne one.'

There were several Pleiadeans, but the two of them who came forward were clearest to Amy. They too were humanoid; they too had flesh, but not as Amy had flesh. They moved gracefully, their voices serene, their attire, their adornments colourful, yet cultural; harmonious with their faces and bodies, gorgeous and graceful. They were rose-pink and violet-lavender; they were fully robed in white but nude in all tones, and they held all colour in balance.

The female Pleiadean spoke as well; this was not Uki, this was a different person.

'If this creation is to have agency, then we should show unity, collaborate.'

Misha nodded.

Misha.

Misha noted her remembrance. 'You know the name your father gifted me; you have been able to see how we met, as you see the dreams of others now. The knowledge and memories that exist between generations blur here; he knows me now as you will know me and that ripples outwards from your physical presence in your own density.'

'Okay.'

People laughed; this was perceived as innocent, yet beguiling and charming.

'These Pleiadeans are Eya and Iba. They also know your father, and have interceded in events on his, and Pan's behalf.'

For a second she was okay about being there, at her own debut that nobody had told her about, and for some reason this allowed her to sense that there were many other people at the party. She understood quite suddenly, but quite naturally, that her introduction to society, such as it was, was not the single purpose for the party; gatherings at The Intersection occurred with reasonable regularly. However, her being brought here and seen, as an expression of the cosmic consciousness that was potentially of great interest to other, like-minded expressions of the cosmic consciousness, albeit many more ancient, wiser and more experienced than the expression that was she, was a highlight of this particular gathering.

She was a special guest.

'Every full moon…'

As opposed to the information she had just intuited, which had, she saw again on another layer, been telepathically communicated to her, this was someone whispering directly in her ear.

'…you can get here from the Earth plane every full moon.'

Amy took that on board.

She sipped her drink, some Fizzy Lolly Water, which was her favourite, which she hadn't had for a very long time, and it therefore felt delightfully special, as she gazed around some more. She saw and sensed intuitively – *sansed* – (...that ever so helpful notion again...) that there were twenty-seven different kinds of beings here with some kind of physical presence, all from different levels of... density?

The Sirian with the shy daughter...

Misha spoke again.

'Density is the name you 'humans' have given, the one that we 'aliens' have in turn accepted – to the stable manifestations of dimension from which other conscious life has evolved in the cosmos.'

'It is?'

'Yes. It is.' She smiled and Amy felt... oh; so worthy. 'Our physical evolution either occurred within or evolved into a plane of existence that was lighter or heavier than your own human existence – or density, as you would have it.'

'Our reality?'

She smiled again, and Amy almost swooned.

'Amy, out of all of the potential, from all of the other races who had evolved in this section of the cosmos, within all the different planes of reality, twenty-seven distinctly different ones have chosen to take an ongoing interest in Earth. Many others have chosen only to observe and advise, and they will remain in the background. However, of the twenty-seven who have chosen to come and see you here, nine... perhaps ten of them have had direct influence upon Earth. Four or five of these civilizations have become involved enough, for long enough, so that they remain intrinsically connected to the karma field of Earth's collective consciousness.'

'Karma field?'

'The reincarnation cycle, you would call it. We can explain all this to you later, in greater detail. Much of it you know already, but have forgotten. The situation itself is not unusual, though;

although, it is more rare when involving a planet such as Earth, which is in isolation.'

'Isolation? We've been isolated?'

Misha smiled sadly, softly, but sternly.

'Again, dear young child lady; these are matters for another time. The main thing I am here to tell you today, is that some of the races who have involved themselves with Earth's progression weren't necessarily races who were immediately more evolved than humans, as would usually be the case.'

Amy was suddenly aware that, nearby, watching, there were great men and women in black suits, who looked like wealthy bankers. Then, as she tried to observe them directly, they shimmered into living expressions of mathematical equations. There looked to be a man, however, old like her grandfather had once been, before he had become unwell and died, but spry and wiry.

Also, there was a woman who was standing… behind Misha? Or…?

She seemed like a matriarchal siren of stage and screen, photographed in stunning monochrome. Then again, as Amy attempted to observe her directly, she was clearly occupying the entire room; the entire building, or structure of wherever they actually were, and then she was everything around and outside of them all; and then, for a shocking second, so was Amy.

Then there was a budgerigar on a windowsill beside her.

She thought to ask…

'What is the other reason for this particular debutante ball?'

A wave of pleasure hit her, a flow of light and approval, and the whole room –

CHAPTER 31

She was dressed head to toe in tight but comfortable black clothes. They felt like a second skin to her. Her thick blonde hair was tied back into a long ponytail and her calf-length boots made her several inches taller than she already was, which was tall. Still, many of the other people at the party were taller, despite them still preferring to remain at the back.

She felt good about herself in these clothes, in this outfit; all of a sudden, she didn't know or care if she stood out.

Everybody else at the event was more solid now, but still ethereal. It was as though the idea of a debutante ball had always been there, but now the details had been plucked from her mind and elaborated upon; now, suddenly The Intersection had become a composite set piece from every movie or novel she had ever read with a debutante ball in it, and even one or two she had been actually attended when she'd had a brush with very wealthy people on the North Shore, years ago now.

And, while always her debut in theory, the fact that her choice of veneer was the one to which they had committed, and were now elaborating upon, was something of an honour, she felt.

She felt it deeply, and was glad to feel it.

This was it; this was how it worked.

Already there was more of a New York art scene vibe occurring. There were frames on the walls, not paintings but not windows either. Within each frame, the image seemed to recede out; stretching into a star field; across the grassy planes to the forested hills; endlessly ploughing into enormous ocean waves; epic vistas across snowy mountaintops; and yet, amongst them, there were actual... what she would call "paintings", there was actual "photography". Beautiful and modern and stirring and fascinating and challenging and strange, as though, underneath it all, this was a real place, a real apartment, a real party, a real debutante ball, in a real grand hall, that was somehow embracing a real New York gallery.

'My family are the hosts, this time…' Misha offered. 'You might recall that, at Pan's wake, there were also some space-time installations…' She frowned. 'Oh no; I apologise; you were not there. You and your father are so similar.'

'Space-time… what?'

Misha smiled. They were walking together; Misha was her chaperone. 'We use astral energy to map, then wrap third density locations around and within each other; then guests can attend the function from many simultaneous planes and remain at their desired level of visibility. Part of this event is being held on your friend's ship, *Lady Ann*.'

'Uncle Bo is here?!'

'You can see him afterwards. *Lady Ann* had succeeded in creating…' She paused as though she were a beautiful dog who had heard a pitch of a frequency just made for her. 'Oh! It appears that my daughter wishes to speak with you! How delightful, she has overcome her shyness. She is what you would call – a fan.'

'A fan of what?'

Amy was a fan of most of the big franchises.

'A fan of you, of course, Amethyst Pyne!'

'*Me…?*'

'Would you indulge her? She is ever so excited that you are here.'

Amy was going to pursue this, however they had entered another section of the mansion, a series of interlocking antechambers where the guests were admiring a procession of objet d'art, displayed freely on wide glass podiums, and sealed within long, wall-to-ceiling cases. Each of the antechambers seemed to lead off from a central chamber, into which Misha ushered her.

'Let's see if she's in here?'

CHAPTER 32

The central chamber was dark; all the wall-planes and angle-shines and crystal-ware, and everything, everywhere, so far, at the party had been shining white, if not varying degrees of pure diamond transparency.

But this one room now had black walls.

Or...

If not *black walls*, then somehow *no walls* that receded into a deep surrounding desperately aching collapsing calling void of utterly pitch –

No; no, black walls, that would do.

In the middle of the circular room was a down light, under which had been placed a diamond so big it would only just have rested in her open palm.

'It's not really a diamond. And it is amethyst in colour because I thought of you, and your family, when I created it.'

'It's not... *me,* is it?'

There was was silence, where they were.

'It's called The Arcana.'

Amethyst started at it.

'The Arcana was commissioned by a very powerful friend. It is a data crystal. Within it; the true history of Earth.'

'The true...?'

'Not just this one. All five iterations of humanity. The history your planetary race and resultant civilizations, from the first peopling of this world, right up to – well... to right now. To your debut, and the presentation of this crystal to the community.'

'I don't know what to say...'

'How could you? You have not yet examined the data. And you may; after this event, you may come here any time you desire.

You, and the other Pandorans, any time, to make use of the information contained therein, as you see fit.'

'Why… have you done this?'

Misha smiled. 'You will see. And then, you will see.'

Amy smiled. 'I see.'

'You do. Others do not, but it is too late now. The Arcana exists, its existence is revealed, and it cannot be removed now.'

'It can't be destroyed?'

'Once data is assembled in this way, it becomes irrevocable.'

'I see.'

'No, you do not. In that regard, you will be most fortunate if you ever do. But you must trust that I do, and I have your best interests at heart; the greater sights, I must see for you.'

Amy could hear music in the distance, but she couldn't tell what it was.

'How delightful.'

Amy was tuning in; Misha was too.

'That's one of my fav – … wait.'

Amy suddenly understood.

'…this world, this field we're in, it takes things from our minds and manifests them.'

Misha turned to her.

She placed a hand, very softly against her cheek. It felt like being in an outdoor shower on a private beach after a relaxing swim on a warm midsummer morning.

'Only for those very strong with that ability. That is why you are here. You have been using that ability; for some time now. You do not remember. That is natural as you return home. But you will remember. And when you do, that is when you will begin to understand the burden of the journey ahead of you; your part in the story.'

Amy looked into Misha's eyes. But she couldn't see them clearly. She simply perceived the idea of eyes, very beautiful eyes, looking out from a powerful, yet caring and adoring maternal force.

'Before, you were going to say it was interesting…' Amy intuited. '…because the song is a song we both enjoy. It's one of my favourite Earth songs.'

'And one of mine.'

'And you know it because…'

'We have been watching you, my daughter and I. We have heard it whenever you have played it. It 'caught on' with us.'

'Watching me?' Amy was slightly alarmed, then she understood. 'Okay. That's okay.'

'We would not have been watching you otherwise.'

CHAPTER 33

The song ended and another began.

It seemed to be playing on a scratchy old gramophone, and to come from a different room, far away; perhaps even another party. She wanted to follow it, find it, dance to it and allow it to make her remember, and to cry in melancholy pleasure from the heart for lost, remembered things.

There was food around; she was hungry, but it was out of reach. She had a sense that there was someone here, or there, at the party down the hall, on the other side of the mansion; that she should be looking for them, but also that she should move on now, that they might have left already, and she would miss them, that she should hurry now. That she'd left the house without her shoes, and had to get back – but if she did that, could she find her way back here again? And by that time, wouldn't it all be over? Did they want her here anymore anyway? And why had those others she knew left without her…?

Wait; what time was her train?

'They're letting you leave – these are basic dream cues. You'll be immune to them before long – but they want to talk about you now.'

'Why?'

'Don't worry, you'll be home before long…'

'Home?'

'Yes. Or something like it.'

'Who are you…?'

'Safe and sound and all fucked up –'

'All – ?'

' – tucked up nice and warm.'

'Why – Who – ?'
'Where did you go…?'
'Why…?'
'Where – ?'
'Who…?'
'Wh…'

CHAPTER 34

But then –
Shock.
All of a sudden –
Shouting.
Suddenly, out of nowhere –
Accusations.
There were sudden –
Recriminations.
And suddenly –
Insults.
Again, a sudden shift and –
Threats!
Departures.
'Am I awake now?'
Collapse.
The clear walls were gone.
Fury.
No, she told herself, realising.
Danger.
'No; this is still the dream.'
Fear.
And the tone had shifted…
Flight.
Running down a dark corridor from something she couldn't
see.
Suddenly.
Distinctly.
Nightmarish.
There was terror behind her, but a dog running beside her.

Her father's dog, that he had owned before he had married her mother, that little Amy had known and loved as a little kid; the first thing she cared about that went away forever. But here he was again; to scale, big, like he had been when she was still little.

'Chesterton!'

The dog told her; 'It is the dream world. But you are not asleep. Not yet.'

'Chesterton, I don't understand!'

'You do; you have just forgotten.'

'I think I just want to wake up and be at home in bed!'

'You are awake. You were awake before. You're still awake. This way, child!'

These were normal walls now, of a normal house, but they were labyrinthine.

'Where are we?'

'Corridors of time, hallways of memory.'

'Is one of these bedrooms mine?'

'They are every bedroom you have ever known; this place is that for everyone. There are billions of Earthlings across this plane, simultaneously, always. Do not talk to anyone!'

Now that Chesterton mentioned it, there were ghosts everywhere.

'Don't look at them! Maintain your focus, child – it is one of your human gifts, it is one of the reasons you were asked to The Intersection!'

'What happened?'

'A thief in the night!' Chesterton barked.

'A thief?'

'You must go on alone from here, and wake up. Follow your instincts; try to wake up at home.'

'Chesterton!'

'At home!'

'Don't go!'

But he was gone.

CHAPTER 35

Just a dark corridor now, on and on with closed doors.

There was light though, and she could see something at the end of the hall; rooms, a home – a kitchen, a living room, a television, a couch… warm and safe from the cold and wind and rain outside. There were bedrooms all down the hall on either side.

A woman exited the nearest room.

'This way, come on!'

She knew the person that she was following was a friend, that she could trust her, but she did not understand why everything was – suddenly – so urgent.

'What happened?' Amy demanded.

'I was having quite an interesting evening with you – you've never been to The Intersection before.'

She turned around. The woman turned around. She was Anunnaki, in a natural, reptilian Anunnaki body, with bright yellow-green eyes and a zig-zag of bright green scales up the middle of her head that gave the impression of a Mohawk. They were dressed in the same kind of tight-fitting black leather outfits with crocodile prints, like sleek and professional cat burglars; this was something, this was what they all wore now, all her clan.

'Xylata?'

'Yes, Thys Pyne?'

Relief.

– Thys –

Amy remembered – her name was also Thys now, that's what her friends called her here –

'I've never come back down to Earth this way before, have I?'

Xylata smiled. 'I am not sure anyone has. But no; certainly

not since you took The Pandora Sequence. But this time is odd. Special, and odd, yes, odd; and disorientating for the best of us. Especially with what just happened back there. Beings will be talking about this one for a while; all manner of beings.'

'Why? What happened back there?'

'I lost track of you. But when a Sirian elder comes and takes you away to her private art gallery, there's nothing I can do.'

'There was a diamond as big as a rock melon!'

'There was, I know.'

'You do?'

'You came out with her and you were talking about a song you both liked; getting along famously, it appeared. Then suddenly the proverbial stones hit the proverbial glasshouse walls and the shards were flying everywhere and believe me they were sharper-than-sharp and they are still coming down the hall after us…'

Amy turned around. There was indeed a flickering, searing kaleidoscope of white, angry light coming after them. Splintering light – and a form of darkness as well, which was shrieking, angry, spiky and speeding; and grey, smoky ghosts and ghouls and –

'That's what they all look like when they're pissed off and out for blood!'

Thys Pyne knew this meant that she was still somewhere on the astral plane.

Then another door burst open, and she was pulled –

'What happened?'

'It's okay – I got you out of the way.'

The Anunnaki held out her hand.

The Ymira clan.

'Did you get it? Where is it?'

'Xylata?'

'Did you get it?'

'Get what?'

'You know what…' The Anunnaki smiled.

'No, I…'

'Show me.'

'Show you what?'

'Show me!'

'I don't –'

'Show me, Amy!'

Amy?

All Ymira called her Thys; none of them called her Amy anymore.

This Anunnaki was not Ymira.

This was not Xylata.

Xylata had a jagged lime stripe; but this woman had a dark-yellow racing stripe, kind of like a safety helmet. She was taking a huge risk; if she was caught in a uniform of another clan… the result would be karma exile; executed and thrown into the Karma Forge.

But in her current state of disorientation, of near-amnesia… she did not know who it was.

The Anunnaki snarled.

'Okay then, Amethyst.'

'My name is Thys.'

'I am going to kill you, and you won't see it coming, and then your name will be Nothing.'

'I –'

'Unless you do as I say. Right now. Somebody stole the Arcana – and I know it was you. Now show me, hand it over!'

Her claws extended; blue-blood all over them, bones from her fingertips like glistening white porcelain –

'Or I will gut you like –'

CHAPTER 36

There was a fuss.

'Run!'

There was a fight, there was more blue blood.

'Run, Thys Pyne! There will be more!'

...but she found an abandoned shopping mall, ran past some urban explorers, slid down the side of a dead escalator, and ran on.

She was alone now, trying to find her own way out.

In the courtyard, she found the party again.

There was nobody left; just a few drunks on the couch and people who had brought sleeping bags. Maybe someone was cooking something in the kitchen, concocting a plot. She was leaving though, she'd had enough; she was heading back out of the big double doors at the front of the house. Looking back, she saw that, back down the hall in the party, what was left of it, what was left of the whole palace; place; play; plane; something distressing was still happening. Something she had missed. Or, they had missed. They had missed her, doubling back. But, she hadn't meant to double back. She hadn't deliberately snuck back around; she had been completely lost. Those last doors had just opened that way; the empty hallways had simply led back here!

She sensed that many of the people who had still been there, perhaps waiting in the shadows, had departed, quickly, as this new force had returned. This somehow made the apartment something less. Elements of fragrance and colour, of integrity and spaciousness that she had not been consciously aware of...

...vapor now.

Back down to star-stuff, gas and dust.

Something dark, down the hall, was demanding to know

where she was; if anyone had seen her.

Something angry was demanding to know why she had not been destroyed.

Something vicious was expressing fury at missing the opportunity to destroy her.

She turned around and saw that the main doors to the house were not there, where they had been, just a second before.

She could feel that the structure of the house remained, crystal and solid.

So, she knew, the Sirians, at least, some of the Sirians, were still resonating influence.

And she could see that the house remained decorated, was still at least a nice suburban home; no longer a sky mansion, but still welcoming.

So, she knew, the Pleiadeans, at least, some of the Pleiadeans, were still resonating influence.

She could see a pattern within atomic sparkles, and feel purpose in her heart; the Orions and Elohim had not abandoned her.

But the darkness; the three forms of darkness that wanted her ended; they had the house surrounded. And through the windows, high glass windows with no upper frame, she could see that there was only space outside.

She had become aware of the void beyond the stars.

She was frightened.

Where was Xylata?

'This way...'

There was a man, and he opened a door for her, as though spiriting her back through a forgotten hatch, unconsidered by high-ups; it only gained access to servant quarters. The door was strange; it opened inward, into a descending set of steps.

It was dangerous; access from this side, a trap for your players from the other. The man remained within the low light beyond, at the top of the descending stairs, with only his arm extended, along the inner door, still grasping the inside door handle.

Then, with his free hand, he beckoned her with a quick series of circular waves.

'Hurry!'

He whispered in her ear as she rushed through.

It was like a defensive door at the top of a lighthouse you would use to keep people out.

She scampered barefoot down the lighthouse stairs, willingly and effortlessly, her nightgown billowing behind her, into deep and embracing darkness.

'The audition's over…'

CHAPTER 37

She emerged into a theatre lobby; one she knew from childhood.

'Didn't they tear this place down? I used to come here with my school, for plays.'

'Go through.'

She went through the doors to the auditorium, and stood there behind the back row, far away from the stage.

As far away as you could get, and still be inside.

'This is a dream.'

The man next to her nodded and spoke, resonant and silky.

'Merrily merrily.'

She looked at him.

'This is what you look like when you're not inside Vance McLeod.'

'Sometimes.'

'Sometimes?'

'Somebody pulled you out of your journey, and got you into the Intersection. Somebody took you out, just at the right time so you would be addle-brained when you get back to Earth. Somebody stole the Arcana; somebody, one of yours, accused you of doing it; wanted it for themselves. And somebody wants to rub her tits against yours, to suck your tongue, and eat your pussy.'

For a sharp second, Thys Pye remembered herself.

'Or, is that just you?'

He laughed. 'Five different people, I promise you, none of which is me!'

'Promises? From the Lord of the Tricksters?'

'Lay back. And remember, when you get back, you will be as vulnerable as you are now.'

She was sleepy, despite herself.
'How vulnerable am I now?'
'As vulnerable as you will ever be, hopefully.'
She mumbled.
'...you want me to go back...?'
'Almost everybody does.'
She was forgetting herself.
'I can't trust you.'
'Sometimes.'
'You're trying to trick me.'
'Sometimes.'
'But not today?'
'Not today.'
She was asleep, about to dream.
She sighed.
'I bet you say that to all the gods.'

THE PANDORA INHERITANCE

PART TWO

AMY

CHAPTER 38

Amy found herself standing in her bedroom.

She was immediately disorientated.

Somehow, she was dressed in a tight-fitting, one-piece outfit, black with knee-length boots and a high collar, the front zip done up, right up, under her throat.

Why was she standing in her bedroom, dressed like this?

Hadn't she just come back from her mission with The Pan?

Where had her black, Ninja-like paramilitary fatigues gone? The ones that she had worn when she had boarded the helicopter with April up front, and Lorena and Capri, and Terry and Franco and DJ in the back?

Her gun and her rifle and her helmet were gone, too.

This was more like a… a cat suit?

No; not really.

More like a… wet suit, or a… she didn't really know what it was, to be honest.

She was tired.

The stupid costume made her feel… vulnerable.

She thought hard, thought back, and remembered getting onto the chopper.

Flying to the boat –

Okay. That bit was a bit hazy, actually.

It was all a bit hazy, coming to think of it.

But – she had done it, right?

She remembered having done it – just not the exact details.

And, she had gotten back okay, because, logically, here she was.

Back, and okay.

Back home, standing beside her bed.

Right?

…right.

Yeah.

Yeah; okay.

She was figuring it out.

She remembered Trudy, her Aunt Trudy, or at least Pan's sister Trudy, who she still thought of, despite being an almost nineteen-year-old adult person, as Uncle Pan and Aunt Trudy…

God, her mind was a muddle!

She remembered Trudy – right? Trudy telling her that sometimes after something stressful, like a rescue mission that devolved into armed combat, you could wake up in a panic and not really know what was going on. Not quite PTSD, or maybe mild PTSD, but along the lines of something like a bad stress-hangover, she'd suggested.

'You're home…' Trudy told her. 'And that's a relief. But you don't remember where you've been, what happened, or how you got back. Not immediately anyway. It will start to come back to you, but you can't force it. You have to let it trickle back.'

'This is that…' Amy told herself aloud, somewhat assuredly, as she stood by her bed.

It, or, something like it.

So, she was standing here, in her…

Why had she disguised herself as a sci-fi-themed cocktail waitress?

To get into a party? Had she done that?

No. Noooh. Why would she have done that?

That was absurd – that was –

That was part of the dream she'd just had.

Wow, and what a dream!

That had been *crazy!*

But she refocussed on reality.

The mission. That's right. The mission had been completed, then they'd all gone out to celebrate and somehow… she'd ended up in this outfit?

Sure! Why not?

And, she'd probably just come back here and dropped straight onto the bed. She'd had a nightmare; about the crystal queen and the lizard lazy; and it had freaked her out; and; she'd woken up; and she'd stood up from her bed, like she was now; stressed.

Her bed, which was still made, and unslept in.

She checked carefully, felt the sheets and the quilt with the palms of her hands.

No. No kind of indentation. Not even slightly warm.

Although; she could convince herself that it had been slept on.

On, not in...

...even if it was tightly made, with hospital corners and military precision.

She could ignore this of course; that there was no indentation. She was going to. That's what people did. Ignored things like this, dismissed them, and moved on. Got on with their life. She didn't know why she hadn't done that immediately. She didn't know why it had occurred to her to even check the bed in the first place. Why she had elected not to believe the story that her mind told her to believe; that she had come home, stressed out, had a nightmare, leaped out of bed, and would remember in a second how the Pan mission on Everett's boat had... well, panned out, she supposed.

But as she stood there, and waited, and thought about how she should try not to think, and not to allow the gathering low pressure system in her gut to start creating anxiety, that memory did not come.

So then Amy decided this: that she had effectively been sleep-walking, and sleep-prepping. Sort of. The mission had been a great success! She had established that.

She was back here after all, wasn't she?

In one piece?

Even if she couldn't remember what had happened.

However, it had also been extremely stressful.

Right?

So she had come back, crashed out, and in the middle of the night, she had woken and dressed again – probably thinking, 'for a mission', but she had actually sleep-dressed in the clothes she had come home in, after a night of partying.

Yes.

Yes, it all made perfect sense.

She had even made her bed, military style with hospital corners, although *shutupshutup* she never did that, The Pan was not paramilitary *shutupshutup* at least not in that way and she was not really a soldier so much as a group leader for a bunch of enthusiastic *shutupshutup*…

Her brain froze. Then it told her:

Baby, you are so frickin' tired….

She stared at the bed again, then pulled the top of the sheets and quilt back and started to feel drowsy.

Go to sleep, girl…

She seemed to undress herself in a dream.

Go to sleep, go to sleep…

She couldn't really tell what the one-piece material was, but it was soft and very comfortable, and she almost didn't like to remove it. Still, as she did, a fine, rainbow-mist seemed to appear before the zip as it lowered.

Like a rainbow.

Off a waterfall.

Multi-coloured rainbow sparkles seemed to catch her eye, crystalline, like mites of opal dust floating in a sunbeam… but also strangely pastel; shining mid-tones…

– but big sparks of primary colour too! –

…and the same again, with the knee-length boots, as she zipped each one down the side; and a big puff when she pulled each of them away from her feet, like you would expect dirt from working on a farm, or sand from a day at the beach.

She was very sleepy now, dreamy.

She unclipped the strapless bra, which was a relief because, wow that thing had been *tight*...

And let it fall.

As she slipped into the bed, there seemed to be some kind of residual… what was it? Sweat? Moisturiser? It smelled… sugary. Not part of her. Some kind of residue?

Residue of the dreamland…

Turning to dust as it made contact with the air.

Forgotten.

Huh. What a silly thought.

Nice, but... so silly.

Then out of her undies, chucking them aside with a stardust sparkle, punching her legs down to free the tightness of the hospital tucks, then with her arms under and in, and the sheet and doona up over the shoulders and body to the side and the head-drop *whoomph* to the pillow like a stone and –

CHAPTER 39

((They're coming.

...

...

Amy woke on her right side, blinked and looked around.

She felt better now, immediately better.

She was somehow naked, which was unusual for her, but she was warm as toast, all fuc–

...all tucked up.

Huh.

Odd.

She could feel that it was cold outside, cold in the room, with no heating on. She did not feel like moving and, to be honest with herself, could not recall anything particularly urgent she had to do today.

Presumably, at some point Trudy...

...

((Amy, you need to get out...

...

...Trudy would come and see if she was okay after what had happened on –

That boat.

Did that boat even have a name?

Everett's boat?

...after what had happened on Everett's boat, and they would debrief.

She shivered, remembering how cold it had been, in the middle of the storm, out at sea. But then, why was the room so cold? Was it winter? She was still hazy. Was it a winter's night? Winter's morning? Early? She couldn't recall. She'd been away though, right? She'd expected to have been gone a few days. She thought she remembered turning off the automatic air-con settings before she'd left. That was all. The heater hadn't kicked in, hadn't warmed the apartment. Switched off the heater; ergo, the room was cold. Occam's Razor; simple as that.

But, still…

…

((Amy?

…

Now she was more awake, she could not ignore the fact that had just escaped her, on the edge of falling asleep last night.

Her bedroom had changed.

She tried not to panic.

She tried to think it through.

Amy was a *reasonably* organised person.

She liked to think that she knew herself *fairly* well.

She knew that, more often than not, she woke up in the morning on her right side.

So, she had put things there, in her right-side line-of-sight, so that she would see them each morning. Things that she liked, things that reminded her of not just who she was but who she wanted to be, what she believed in, and how she hoped that would manifest in her life – or within herself.

Wow.

((Amy, you need to tune in

((I can't reach you.

((They're coming.

Wow; like, wow. She had never really realised that before. Never formulated that personal equation, not even to herself, within her conscious mind. But that was it, totally, wasn't it? Through the prism of pop culture, that was what she had done; she had tried to inspire herself. Give herself symbols of the idylls she hoped to live up to. And she had never fully realized that about herself –

Until those things were gone.

((Amy! Amy, they're coming, Amy, dammit, you need to –

She tried not to panic again, lying there, snug.

Tried to think it through.

Had she… moved her things herself?

She was aware enough to be aware, paradoxically, of how hazy her mind seemed to be right now – morning or night. But right now she needed to remember, and to be sure.

Before she'd gone on the mission – had she cleared her bedroom of all here personal stuff?

Because right now, from what she could see...

Everything was gone.

CHAPTER 40

Amy's apartment was a tight but very liveable, bog-standard maisonette in a block of twenty-four which were almost all exactly the same; cream walls with cream tiles, subtle caramel swirls, and white marble surfaces. The front door, which was accessed from wide, third floor hallway, opened from the apartment's left corner, directly into an open living space, enough for a five-seater couch and coffee table, entertainment wall, with a neat, four-seater kitchen table (dining in a pinch) in the corner. A set of stairs led directly up from the front door, along the wall, directly to a landing that overlooked the lounge, where the bedroom and bathroom were situated. Both were big enough, with plenty of built-ins, and the bedroom had a balcony that faced the suburb and passing freeway outside; standard, single-person, three and a half stars.

'Twice the space of a normal hotel room, and they charge three times the nightly rate. Don't worry; you don't have to pay anything.'

Amy had been very happy for the offer; she had wanted so much to join Trudy, to help her and Pan. The two-dozen identical apartments on the top floors of this hotel, she had quickly seen, were being used to house Trudy's personal new recruits to The Pan. Amy had been assigned a nice one, a corner with an extra balcony down the side that led back to the inner landing. It was hers though, she was assured, to do with as she liked, and so she had modded it with bookshelves and display cabinets on every available wall-surface, and framed and hung her favourite movie posters and art on the wall surfaces where storage would have been too tight a squeeze. At nineteen, with an ex-movie critic father, she had already seen way more movies than most in her so-called Millennial generation. (Although, she was still not sure if being born in 1994 put her in that category, or at the end of Gen-Y. It seemed to depend upon who she asked, so in the end, she had to pretend like she didn't care, even though it actually drove her just the tiniest bit nuts.) She actually, openly cared a lot more about things like realising that there had been wall-space for only fourteen framed A-1 movie posters (five in the living space, one on the kitchen wall, three up along the stairs and three along the landing, one in the laundry, one in the loo) and that was nowhere near enough for the list she had composed of her favourite movie posters, let alone her list of great films.

Being 'that kind of person', Amy had compromised cleverly with her dimensions by purchasing some statues and maquettes, which consumed a different kind of space in the apartment, and made it so she was able to represent a greater number of her favourite things.

Accordingly, she made it so that whenever she woke, on her right side, she would be looking directly at the bureau and desk beside the bed, upon which sat her PC, laptop, tablet and phone, and all the paraphernalia that went with it; her important papers and purse, and her designated space for 'the things she had to deal with today'. But even more so, she had made it that primarily, surrounding these things, she also saw a maquette of her favourite incarnation of The Doctor, another of her favourite Starfleet Captain, and a third of her favourite Jedi, then her favourite Marvel character, and her favourite DC character, her favourite Cascadian, and finally, her favourite of The Dolls. These seven eighteen-inch statues framed all of those other items, upon, around and over her desk, as her holy septet. Above and around that – hardcopy corner; shelves of books and box-sets and collectors-edition Blu-rays, CDs and vinyl, and a stack of drives. These were all of her favourites, the ones she returned to again and again, and combined, all of these things were her treasures, her precious things, her life so far.

And now, all of these things were gone.

She blinked, and blinked again, hard, repeatedly.

Still gone.

She pushed the sheets down, felt the cold acutely, swung her legs over and felt the carpet on her bare feet.

Strangely, apart from the heater being off, that last part all felt – normal.

This was her bed, her carpet; how she got out of the bed and touched the carpet with her feet, every day, her bum right there on the same spot on the edge of the mattress.

But – all her stuff – was gone.

She gulped.

She reached for the remote, almost as a comfort response. At the end of the bed, the TV was still there – bolted to the wall. But the contents of the shelves, above and behind it, that she'd put up herself, with more discs and books – all the big series, Oscar winners, cult biggies, and serious literary ones that she loved; superhero figures, doo-dads and nick-knacks, were gone too.

Along with the remote.

Maybe - she was in the wrong apartment?

But – how?

But – no.

No, that was stupid – these were her shelves, she'd put them up herself, where she'd wanted them. This was her room, there was no mistaking that. Each of them, each member of The Pan, had made their apartment their own, and this was hers. Her shelves, her TV, but just with none of her stuff.

This was her place!

Her first home away from her childhood home!

She would know it anywhere!

Even, as it seemed right now, after being totally and completely – cleaned out.

CHAPTER 41

Almost a year ago now, just after her outburst on her eighteenth birthday, her 'Aunt' Trudy had found her.

Amy had actually left London, returned to Sydney and gone hunting for 'Uncle' Pan, but it had soon become apparent that he hadn't been around and 'Aunt' Saph had vanished with him. Weeks later, Trudy had heard about her turning up in Sydney and had found her in a grim but very independent and alternative suburban share house. She had been trying it out for a fortnight, all she could afford, and the boys who had offered her a spot in the dilapidated three-bedroom had been, as boys just out of home had want to be, utter pigs. Still, it was all she could afford on the dole, until she found herself a proper job, and she had been minutes away from co-signing a six-month lease.

'Think – Greenpeace; think – Occupy.'

Trudy had pitched to her.

'We're going to organise protests, and occupations, and maybe a bit of light paramilitary-style sabotage. But – against the psychopathic elite who control the banking system, and the corporate power grid; never against the ordinary people. We're going to try and agitate our way into getting a say in our own form of social control. Violent, maybe, sometimes, but never homicidal.'

Amy had learned that The Pan's new recruits were being trained and housed in an old hotel in Paramatta, owned by, but of completely no interest to Bo Everett. Apparently, after some kind of epiphany that had been caused by her Uncle Pan, Everett had decided to change the world along with The Pan.

'Like a lot of his ordinary real estate, he has no idea he owns it, or that one of his companies owns it. There are so many addresses he owns, so many levels down from the mansions and penthouses that he actually lives in, city by city, and they all just kind of form the foundation of, and pump up, his net worth. This is one of them.'

The hotel was nice. It had been recently renovated. Amy could not imagine anyone not remembering they owned it.

'How many levels of wealth up, before that happens to someone?'

She'd heard herself say it. She'd fallen into the habit of asking things out loud to herself, since her eighteenth birthday meltdown.

Trudy had heard, and smiled; as though she considered the question, and everything the question represented, to be a very good sign.

'The thing about this place is that people still use it. It's a solid three and a half stars, just a middle-class budget come-and-go, neat and nondescript, well-maintained. Members of The Pan will have the apartments on the top two floors, which they hardly ever rent anyway, and we'll train in the old ballroom out the back. The lower five will just continue to function as a normal hotel, business as usual. The staff are all ours, but if anyone asks, we tell them we're a modern dance company on government arts funding. Nobody asks any questions after that.'

Amy smirked. 'I guess that's the world.'

Trudy had smiled. 'Maybe. But remember; you earnestly want to be part of a group that genuinely wants to change the world for the better.'

Amy shrugged affirmatively.

This time, Trudy smirked. She was a little younger than Amy's father, with natural jet-black hair, porcelain-skin, and bright, sky-blue eyes, under thin, sleek back eyebrows. And, usually, just the right amount of a-little-too-much mascara. Trudy and her notoriously, gorgeously handsome brother were often mistaken for twins; both were lean and angular, and both almost exclusively favoured blue jeans and black tees.

When Trudy smirked, it was sexy; cool, confident and knowing. Amy saw in that instant why the movement had coalesced around them.

'If we tell people that we earnestly want to be part of a group that genuinely wants to change the world for the better, everyone will try to stop us. That is also the world.'

Amy nodded.

'Oh, and Amy, just so we get started on the right foot, if you think you're going to get preferential treatment because I have known you since you were a baby, and think of you essentially as my niece…?'

'Oh, Aunt Trudes, I didn't – !'

'Don't worry, that's totally going to happen. Your father would kill me, and I would die myself, if anything bad ever happened to you.'

'Oh! I –'

'We're new and I'll need people I can trust. They'll know you're family to me, so I will treat you like family. A lot of them won't have anyone. I want them all to know, to see, how we treat family, so we all treat each other as family. Stay close and learn, you'll be my Number Two.'

Trudy smiled and extended her arms, pulling Amy into a big-sisterly hug.

Then she whispered into her ear.

'That's the world too.'

CHAPTER 42

Amy looked around the empty apartment.

Her world was gone.

Someone had cleared her world out, left her world bare.

What the *actual fuck?*

What had happened?

She was cold – she needed a shower.

But if her room had been cleared out…?

She got up and went to the built-ins, slid the door across and saw – white plastic coat hangers.

She turned and slid her chest of drawers open – empty.

She left the room and went out to the balcony.

Sure enough, all her framed posters, from up here and down there, all over the walls, all her favourite movies, were gone. Looking down into and across the rest of the living space, all the personal décor, all the things that had been her own, *been her –* had also been taken.

There was a small linen closet on the balcony and she flung it open. White towels. But at least they were there. Like; eight of them. She took one and went into the bathroom, determined to shower. The fact that she need not have, that there were already two thick, fluffy, generic white hotel towels, just neatly hanging there, like her home was just some generic fucking hotel room, made her furious.

She started the shower. The tiles were cold on her bare feet. The water was steaming hot in no time. There were hotel soaps and shampoos there like it was just…

'For fuck's sake! This is my bloody home!'

Her hair had apparently been in a tight ponytail, but had come loose and had tangled in the night.

It must have been a restless one, she figured grimly.

She ripped out the hair-tie and let it fall and slide across to the shower drain. The weird film that seemed to have gotten onto her skin shone again; opalish-rainbowy...

She fumed. 'Fucking chemicals they spray all over new clothes these days, just to make them all shiny! Jesus!'

She washed, trying to think.

The evidence had been there last night – or, whatever time that had been. What time was it now? She had to find her phone. Maybe she should just call down to the lobby? No, not yet. She had a weird notion that – she hadn't been burgled. It was something else. The bed. It wasn't as simple as the fact that her bed had not been slept in. Her bed had been immaculately remade to the extent that it was effectively a complete reset. She could not ignore that, because she never made her bed. Ever. Once in a while she changed the sheets, until it became such a mess that she changed them again. Again, she reasserted to herself; The Pan was not that kind of paramilitary organization. Trudy demanded commitment, but she couldn't have cared less about how tidy your bedroom was. She just wanted people who cared about the fact that the world was run by an elite layer of highly intelligent psychopaths. She wanted people who were prepared to take matters into their own hands, under the guidance of herself, and her brother, and Bo Everett; people who were prepared to do something about it. Of course, it just so happened that a lot of the people that The Pan had attracted absolutely were those kinds of people; the kinds who made their beds every morning, with hospital corners. But there had been others, like her, who liked a rough and tumble quilt, and many others of all degrees of OCD in between. But this, today; this had not been her. The whole apartment had been remade.

She thought it again.

It was a total reset.

Her stuff hadn't been stolen; her home had been cleared.

Like – she didn't exist.

Like she'd moved out and didn't even live here anymore–
What had happened?
Had something happened on the mission?
She tried to remember –
She tried to think it through –
The mission had –
The mission had been planned –
Planned – to run about fifty-two hours, including a lot of travel time to the middle of the Pacific by chopper. She remembered –
She remembered –
Why was this so hard?
She remembered – the weeks of training, the driving to the helipad, the anticipation on the flight, the nerves, and then the adrenalin as –

CHAPTER 43

Amy stood alone now, in the kitchen.

Fifth floor, apartment sixteen, corner view.

Out of the elevator, down the hall, last on the right.

She had wrapped the huge, white, hotel towel horizontally around her body and wound it, right up tight, under her arms, tucking the corner in, locked down, just above her right breast.

Something she had done a thousand times.

Still, she felt vulnerable, and alone.

But at least now she felt clean.

And in control of her own towel; and that was always a good thing, right?

With no fresh clothes, she had been forced to wash her socks and undies with soap in the bathroom sink, then stand around another fifteen minutes while they tumble dried.

She had used that time to ascertain that this was, absolutely, the same apartment, her apartment, the one she thought of as home, but which had been completely –

Well, gutted.

She had gone out and looked out of the balcony, it had been the exact same view of the river and the overpass, the expanse of trees and houses.

The – exact – same.

After a brief assessment, she determied that what remained of her old place, aside from the basic toiletries, was; the solid king bed; the bureau and wardrobe, both built-ins; two plasma televisions, one up, one down, bolted onto the walls; the marble kitchen bench and the rotating built-in cupboards, also built ins; and the washer, dryer, fridge, dishwasher and oven; all bolted in, all the same in every one of the twenty four apartments.

They (she had begun to think in terms of *they* now) had literally taken anything that was not bolted down.

Her couch, her tables and chairs, her players and consoles, her PC and laptop, collectables, frames, even cutlery and clothes...

◊ *Amy, ignore everything else; do not give in to your fear; they're closing in, but –* ◊

But; the bed she had awoken in, this marble benchtop...
This apartment.
They were hers.
She was trying to focus upon that.
Not to mention that her were little things that she could immediately point out, things that confirmed for her absolutely that this was indeed her apartment; the apartment she had spent the past ten months living in. There was the red wine stain on the carpet by the bench. Blue-tac stains on the wall-paint there, and white Velcro strips up there; plus, every time she went up and down, the third step from the top that squeaked.
Eh-ah.
'Wait...'
She suddenly noticed.
Her hands went to the top of her head.
Her hair was dry.
When had she...?
She had been in the shower, thinking about the mission, trying to remember. She remembered getting out, drying, putting the towel around her, finding the dryer in the bathroom cupboard, standing there with the blow-dry shriek-blasting... taking forever... and coming down, the third step; *eh-ah*, again confirming again that it was indeed her own –
What had she been thinking?
As she had showered, and washed, dried her hair, redressed and...
What the hell was I thinking about?

'How long have I been back here now…?'

She still didn't really know what time it was.

She'd thought back to –

(… wh…?)

Damn it, then where *was* her stuff?

She'd had quite a bit of stuff in this apartment, actually.

Quite a bit of stuff!

Important stuff!

Stuff that meant a lot to her, you know?

Stuff she'd like back!

Damn it! Her thoughts kept skipping.

Skipping away from –

Whatever she'd been thinking in –

She couldn't seem to think back.

Back to what she'd been thinking in the shower.

Or what she'd been thinking when she'd been drying her hair.

Although…?

Had it been harder than usual? Her hair? To dry? Denser somehow? Why would that matter? She had to remember what had happened, not that she needed to book with her stylist, or to use more conditioner! She was going to. She was damn well going to –

She was damn well going to want her stuff back.

Maybe she should go out? Check next door.

Maybe it hadn't all been stolen?

Maybe it had been packed up?

After all, maybe –

She shouted to herself.

'*…what the hell is happening!?*'

She went to the door but there was no swipe key; she could get out, but without her swipe she would not be able to get back in again.

But… this was her room.

It was, right?

She looked around again, centring herself.

Yeah. It was.

The red wine stain, the traces of Blue-tac, white Velcro strips...

All the things she had checked for herself and confirmed, wrapped in the white towel, with the sound of the clothes tumbling.

To make sure, fully sure...

When had that been?

Minutes?

An hour ago?

It was!

It totally, totally, *totally* was – her apartment.

So... there had been an admin error?

Someone must have cleared her apartment by mistake while she'd been gone.

Right? That made sense.

Sort of.

Enough sense.

Enough sense so that all she had to do was go down to the lobby and talk to someone – the concierge was always one of Trudy's people – and they would have all her stuff brought back in no time. It wouldn't matter that she didn't have a key to get back in – they would recognise her, see what had happened, and return it to her.

Wait – where was her purse?

No!

No, wait – she could sense... some part of her, the same part of her mind that was blocking her thoughts, her memories, of the things she had been thinking; of the things she had remembered, in the shower; and at the clothes dryer; this was the part of her mind that wanted her to make an assumption, act upon it, then become involved in a stupid drama when that assumption failed to play out.

People do that all the time.

There might not be one of Trudy's people downstairs, right? Even if there were; they might not recognise her – right? They would make her wait, or worse, chuck her out, creating a whole new set of problems on top of the ones she already had – leading, no doubt, to more problems, right?

Cops, maybe?

Suddenly, almost cannily, she was somehow seeing her own thoughts – her own thought patterns, more clearly.

That, quite often, she didn't think, or, at least, didn't think enough, didn't think things through the way they ought to have been thought through.

That she followed her impulses.

Emotional impulses.

Which was okay, sometimes, but sometimes – sometimes part of her just wanted to get into more of a bind, to –

To what?

To – bind herself even more…?

In – *the world?*

No, no – what was happening?

Wait. *Waitwaitwait.*

CHAPTER 44

Something had gone wrong.

There had been death.

Her friends had been killed –

Her father, and a woman, and waking up on a bed beside a huge man –

Then, Bo Everett, and Oliver Hines –

She had taken something –

Some kind of potion –

Made by Uncle Pan –

There had been a huge tree, shaped like a massive vagina –

CHAPTER 45

A what like a *what?*

She snapped back again, out of it, reaching for the door handle.

To trap herself outside, get involved with the outside, the drama of impulse, running with the world, the world that sucked you in and bound you –

She was shaking now. It was just like when she'd had the epiphany on her eighteenth birthday, about how the expensive gifts, and her bickering frenemies, and the plans that her mother had made for her; made for her, her whole life; would not make her happy.

They would just bind her more and more within the bullshit.

She had joined The Pan, come here, lived and trained and made friends here, then gone on the first mission and –

The training.

She remembered.

The training and the tips and the tricks.

She turned and went quickly back across the lounge and up the stairs; *bop-bop bop-bop bop-bop eh-ah*, across the short landing, past her bedroom to the second balcony door. The extra door, a Suzie favour; the balcony extension that only the corner apartments had. She didn't have a key, right? No matter; she unlocked the balcony door – if she got locked out, she could get up here via the fire escape and get inside again.

She turned and went back down the stairs again.

Focus.

In the movies, when people hid things, the things were taped to the back of the u-bend under the kitchen sink, or the one at the back of the loo... or in the cistern, or in a tub of lard in the fridge, or buried in the ice cream in the freezer.

(She would never do that; she loved ice cream so much…!)

But, the fridge was empty and her cupboards had been professionally cleaned, like new throughout.

'Think of something else,' Trudy had told them. 'If a hiding place can be easily thought through, change it. If you see your hiding place in a movie, change it. Think hard; sometimes you think you have thought of an original hiding place , but it's from a movie you saw five, ten years ago. If anything really serious ever goes down, it might save your life that you put your essential escape shit in a smart, permanent place.'

'What could go down?' Capri had asked.

'What could go down – that serious?' DJ had demanded.

'We are still working out how much of Pan's information is…'

They awaited her every word.

'The government of this country, probably others, will want to know what information we have; what we know. About possible alien influence within other governments, within corporate structure, but most likely, any corporate espionage we're planning. Once we get cooking, it's not unlikely they'll try and take us in for interrogation. Just be ready. Have your stash somewhere only you know; fast but complicated is good, as I understand it.'

When Amy had looked for her hiding place, she had walked her apartment up and down, with deep focus. A permanent place. She had looked at the marble kitchen benchtop and thought – now that is permanent. That is heavy. And she had read-up.

The marble slabs were the same in every apartment. They had been bought in wholesale sets and installed all at once over a couple of days (like every other part of the identical apartments had been over a couple of months). Each set came in two pieces, one long piece for the breakfast bar, and one pre-cut with a cavity for the kitchen sink, forming a standard right angle bench. The bench slab did not have a join; it was three metres long and went right to the wall.

That was okay.

Some marble slabs apparently just sat on the base cabinet, but some were supported by a substrate. Some installers charged for substrate, didn't put them in, then pocketed the money. After all, who was going to lift up a marble benchtop and check?

Huh.

Substrates, she discovered, were thick wood sheets that sat between the countertop and the base cabinet of stone benchtops, installed for extra weight distribution. The benchtop surface generally overhung the substrate by several centimetres; several dozen centimetres for a breakfast bar.

Making them essentially invisible.

Right.

Searching on, it appeared that not all contractors sealed the substrates down; it depended upon how heavy the stone benchtops were.

She stopped searching and cleared her engine.

Trudy always said there was no need; Everett's security was the best, but she was thinking like a spy now.

She gave it a try, but this marble benchtop surface, at least, had been sealed. So; she found out where it was sealed, took out the drawers and got under the bench and into the cupboards.

It was decided.

She would need a drill, and noise cover.

Saturday nights, Pan recruits had their own time; alternate weekends of group-getways and alone-slash-family time. There was often a band in the (still functioning, she had to remember) hotel bar until one in the morning. Sometimes Amy went down for a while, if the music was... well; all music was good to someone. But if it was *her* good, it was easy sometimes to hang down there for a few hours, like a normal person, enjoying a normal Saturday night. Regardless; hotel bar musos always set their sound to eleven. You could not hear your own voice; you wouldn't hear a nuclear explosion outside; despite how noise seemed to carry all through the building, you would not hear a drill five floors up.

The apartments above and below and to her side were all ,

technically sound-proofed to international standards... probably eighties standards; but did that cover a twenty-first century power-drill?

The answer had come from nowhere.

"From the universe..."

...as people said.

April had knocked on her door.

'Hey you know how you said you wanted to pimp out your apartment with shelves for all your nerd gear?'

Amy considered this. She supposed that when put together, several of the things she had openly mused about over the past few weeks might have been summarised in that way.

'Well, I'm goin' back to Darwin this weekend, and almost everyone else in the block is away. I dunno know why, but I put it together when I saw the maintenance room. You seen it? There's drills and ladders and shit, everything you'd ever need. It's in the basement, across from the laundry. You measured the place up yet?'

Amy actually had; she'd known exactly what she'd wanted for some time. That afternoon she got supportive but cautionary clearance from Trudy, a key to the maintenance room from the front desk, then drove down to Paramatta Bunnings and ordered shelving cut to her own specifications, which she had been calculating for weeks now.

Saturday night she got a power-drill and released the brackets that were keeping the substate bolted to the base. Then she used solvents to separate the long marble breakfast bar from the second peice over the kitchen sink.

It was fucking heavy.

So, she ordered pizza.

Family-sized.

And classic Coke.

A big one, thanks.

Amy was tall, and young, and naturally somewhat physically uncoordinated. However, thanks to several months of fitness training with Everett's security people, she was more aware of her body, and how to use it, than ever before. With the help of a couple of sturdy A-frame metal ladders, angled to support each raised corner, she had managed to raise the slab literally one step at a time.

Then, she watched the new episode of *Dolls* while she ate half the the pizza and drank half the Coke.

The thick wooden substrate sheet was three centimetres thick, and had been glued well, but in a hurry. She applied some pressure at the join, got some leverage, made a gap, dribbled some solvents in at forty-five degrees, and; there it was, coming away.

"Release the substrate!"

(...she had desperately wanted to cry out, but had not. She had been making enough weird noises already without actually, formally announcing her cunning plan.)

She lowered the wood panel, heavy enough on its own, from the still-upright marble, then took the hole-saw she had also borrowed from the maintenance room, and drilled a circle two-and-a-half centimetres deep, with an eighteen centimetre diameter.

She'd never seen this in the movies.

Passport, burner flip-phone, vanilla smartphone, untraceable debit card. Then she drilled another circular cavity for the three-grand in cash bricks (three quarters of a sum she had persuaded her mother to give her, claiming she needed to bribe an agent to get fast-tracked for reality TV auditions, the other quarter of which had paid for the new shelving and a new Sideshow Collectible statue to christen them) and a loaded gun.

Trudy had insisted, and had issued her with one.

Trudy had told her.

'I will find someone to teach us how to fire them.'

'Us?'

'I have one as well. When we go on missions, we'll use tranqs. But these will be the real thing. I'll ask one of Everett's security people – that's who I got them from.'

'We're going to need these?'

'Hopefully not. And just these two; one each, nobody else. You're the only one I trust to be responsible. Your father might have gone to ground, but people used to know his name. And your mother is married to that bloke who thinks he is the new David Attenborough.'

'He thinks he's the new Brian Cox.'

'Oh dear. He's as much the new Brian Cox as Brian Cox was the new Paul McCartney. But regardless, if it comes out you're with The Pan, people will go for any association that will bring them greater attention; and there's nothing like celebrity.'

'I think I understand.'

Everett ended up dispatching a very fit-and-proper Englishperson from his personal security detail, not a day later; a woman named Jo Sara.

It turned out, she had considered Amy an excellent shot.

'Jolly good; hand-eye superb, balance, timing, grouping, all that. Just as well, I hear you're perfectly unable to fight your way our of a wet paper bag with a knife and fork.'

'What?'

'No matter my angel, we can't be smashingly special at bally absolutely everything, can we? Now if you would be so good as to do me one very special favour, will you petal?'

'What's that?'

'Never ever let yourself find an excuse to use it? There's a good luv.'

Later, Amy had relayed all this to Trudy as they'd shared breakfast at the hotel restaurant.

'She's right. Never use it. But only use it if I give you the code.'

'What's the code?'

'I'll tell you later.' Trudy had looked down at her plate. 'You know, sometimes you have to ask, and be clear, but it's always worth it.' Then she had looked back up, right into Amy's eyes. 'Eggs benedict is better with both ham, and smoked salmon. There, I said it.'

And they'd laughed.

Right there and then, in her empty apartment with the happy memory, Amy had been content again for a second. She imagined that she could still taste the family-sized pizza, and the classic Coke, and feel the satisfaction of slowly, carefully lowering the kitchen bench back down over the substrate, sealing her secret stash, beneath the marble in her carefully carved circular cavities, like a proper secret agent.

Content.

Until she heard someone running down the stairs, and almost wet herself.

Then she realised that it was just her heart beating.

Real fast, real hard.

She had a sense, a feeling, an intuition…

The thing that she had done, that had gone wrong – it had consequences, and now those consequences were on their way.

It was –

They – were – coming for her.

((Amy get out they're coming!

Oh.

She could feel it now.

The rising terror, like a nightmare; they were coming.

She looked around her empty apartment; it was so white, so clean and new and un-lived in. She had never lived somewhere and left it before, not like this, not on her own, from a place that had been offered to her, and she had accepted herself. It stung that she was going to leave it behind, her first home as her, as Amy Pyne; not someone's daughter or sister or little girl.

But she had nothing; just a towel and the catsuit and an escape kit that felt radically too Jason Bourneish for her to even think about using.

But, then again –

'This isn't a game, you know.' Jo Sara had stated as she'd bid Amy farewell. 'What you are doing will get hot, and when it does, it will get hot very fast. And at that moment you will discover what kind of person you are.'

'What kind of person?'

'Some people can only tell other people to pull a trigger. Some people can't pull a trigger unless another person orders them to. If someone comes for you, you need to be the third type.'

Amy knew; straight away.

'...I need to pull the trigger without being told. For – myself.'

There was a knock at the door.

'Room service!'

((Amy, don't answer the door!

◊ Amy, answer the door ◊

((Amy they're almost there, don't answer the door!

She could hear the voices now.

Perhaps because there was a second one; it had made the first voice more distinct.

◊ Amy, answer the door, stand your ground or there's no going back ◊

((Amy!

◊ Amy, answer the door ◊

Or maybe it was just the thumping of her heart that had made her internal monologue seem stronger? More like actual voices in her head…?

Voices in my head?

The phrase triggered alarm bells.

She wasn't crazy!

But she had instinct; to push against the stress and the fear, to be strong against the panic that created the crazy…

She yelled.

'Wait a second!'

What would she do though, with her things?

Guns and phones? Was she really going to answer the door to room service? Yes, yes she was. Her instinct was clear. Answer the door, be calm. The opportunity had presented itself for her to explain herself and rectify the situation. Maybe she could find out where all of her gear was being stored? Yes, yes, of course that's what had happened. She hadn't been robbed, she had simply been covered. The Pan were moving, because of what had happened on the mission, and this would be the message – what to do next.

She needed to accept the message, then get out.

Be calm, be strong, be sane.

She undid the towel and folded it quickly, draped it on her right shoulder, lifted the marble with all her might and got herself under it. The slab was very, very heavy but she had practiced this. (Sometimes, even with a bath towel.) Not for months now, but; she knew she could do it...

Brace herself, rest the slab on the towel; immediate weight, force, pain, but; left hand in, quick-grab the first sealed baggie, hook it over and slide; quicksmart the second baggie; the third; hissing softly down the marble to the corner of the long, raised bench like a slide, coming to rest in the corner under the coffee mug cupboard where the microwave and espresso machine used to be.

Pain now, lower it, easing, back in place; done.

Gasp.

A second.

Okay.

'Coming!'

She wrapped all her spy shit in the towel and shoved it behind the u-bend in the cupboard under the sink. Then she scampered, barefoot up the stairs, jumped the *eh-ah* and ran into her bedroom.

'One second!'

Only, when she reached the top of the stairs and was in the room, the catsuit wasn't on the bed where she'd left it.

Not on the floor, not on the bureau...

She checked the bathroom; not in the bathroom.

No.

No? What was...? Who was she kidding?

She had *definitely* left it on the bed!

She remembered, unzipping…!

With the boots!

She went back, thinking the catsuit was camouflaged somehow, the way things sometimes could be when you were in a hurry.

((Amy you can't trust any of them, not any of them!

But there was only dust on the bed.

Dust that looked like crushed opal, and a lot of it; where the catsuit had been, and on the floor, where the boots… she went to the corner of the room behind the door, where she habitually threw her underwear, when she was tired. Shiny, silvery, colourful dust there, too. But even as she looked at the dust, it was dissolving. Even as she went to touch it, there was nothing left. But no – no, she had taken the clothes from here, and put them in the dryer! Yes, that had to be it! As she swung back toward the door, she saw, on the bed – the same thing was happening! The harder she gazed, and the quicker she reached for it – had her clothes…?

They had!

Her clothes had disintegrated in a pile of atomic fairy dust!

◊ Amy, you have to stand and fight… ◊

((Amy, if they get you, they will never let you go!

◊ Amy, I am on my way, they will not get you! ◊

((Run!

◊ Fight! ◊

((Don't trust her!

◊ Trust me! ◊

The two bickering voices echoed through Amy's mind, filling it and demanding total attention.

She didn't know whether to listen or not; what was real and what wasn't any more!

Which one?

Which one was right?

((-- Amy, remember who you are!

◊ -- What? ◊

((-- Who is this?

◊ -- I asked first! ◊

((-- No you didn't!

◊ -- *Yes I did!* ◊
((-- *Oh my goddess!*
◊ *Sapphire???* ◊
((*Xylata???*

CHAPTER 46

There was a terrible, stand-offish silence, for which Amy was extremely grateful.

She went to the landing and reopened the cupboard. She looked for the robe. Hotel rooms all came with them now. She couldn't find one, got out another towel, realised that it *was* the robe and threw her body into it.

'Just out of the shower!'

She grabbed the second towel from the bathroom and wrapped her hair in that, thinking, again irrationally, that there was more of her hair than there had ever been, damn it! And, that it was thicker now, and harder to wrap, and so much harder to put up; harder now it was *goddamn dry* than when it was *goddessdarn wet*; so difficult for some *stupid reason*, probably nervous, and done, cord tight around her waist, and down the steps, still nimble in bare feet, *eh-ah* - damn!

Still her place; *it was still her place.*

'Almost there!'

She held her breath and went across the short section of tiles to the door, poised as she steadied the towel in its enormous hair bechive, then brought the handle down and pulled.

Nobody.

Just a breakfast tray.

It seemed that room service had already gone.

She paused.

Just as opening her door was a totally familiar movement to her, so was the sight outside; a central corridor in a nice, three-and-a-half-star hotel corridor. Fire exit door at the end of the corridor, just to her right, elevator doors way down the other end. Fourteen doors with room fifteen, April's room, directly across.

Quiet.

Quiet in the corridor.

Quiet in her mind.

She planted one foot behind her, keeping the door open, and slowly squatted. She concentrated. She kept the towel steady on her head. Slowly, she raised the silver breakfast tray, one thick white sleeve covering the tray handles on each side, checked left and right again, then slowly stood, backing in again, with the weight on her towelled head making her feel like she was in some kind of bizarre finishing-school test for deportment under pressure. She saw the door swing automatically closed as she backed in again, hard at first, then slow as the pistons kicked in for the requisite soft close.

Just as the clunk should have come, an *eh-ah* came instead, as did a sudden black shoe, struck through the gap in the closing door at the very last second.

CHAPTER 47

She thought; the landing balcony door.

She saw the sharp black shoe move further in, saw the door push open with a confident shove.

The assassin was holding his gun out like a pro. He was a clean, good-looking man in a crisp black suit, maybe in his early thirties, white-blonde hair cropped in a low buzz, high-brow, tiny nose and mouth. She knew instantly who he was, from the feeling she got. It was a shock; she remembered being on the boat with her father, and him talking to Heather about aliens and other dimensions as though it were nothing.

Black Ops assassin, controlled by Orion Renegades.

'Where's the lizard?'

The voice was so cold, it made her every orifice clench.

'Can I put this down?'

'No ma'am.'

The gun was aimed right between her eyes.

'It's heavy.'

'Keep it there ma'am.'

A lifeless man who had devoted his entire life to killing.

He wanted something else, or she would be dead already.

She had made two mistakes; initially to assume he would be human, and secondly to draw him in. But for the next few seconds, until he could ascertain that she was alone, one cancelled out the other.

'You're The Pandoran.'

'The what?'

'Where's the lizard?'

'The what?'

'Back up, two steps.'

'The tray is heavy.'

'Two steps. I know you have a gun in your hair towel.'

'You do?'

'Your hair is dry.'

Two silencer shots went off, blowing out her robe from beneath the breakfast tray, impacting with his chest.

She had figured, from the angle she had, the head shot was a stretch.

'Telekinesis, moron.'

He instantly fired three times, off-aim, as he staggered backwards into the door. There was nowhere for her to go; running either way would see her flat on her face with multiple bullets in her back, but she stepped backwards and to the right, in case she needed the wall or the stairs to prop her up.

Instantly she stopped levitating.

The empty cotton arms dropped.

The hotel robe fell from her shoulders as she moved, exposing the extended gun she'd tucked, along with her folded forearms, steady under the tray. The silver tray and lid slammed to the tiles with an almighty, echoing clash as the second volley was exchanged, simultaneously as they were both slammed backwards, then fell to the floor.

The first two of the three bullets of his first volley, each an intended head shot, had whistled straight past her ear as the silencer puffed, but the third had penetrated, straight though her ear.

She felt the sting, and the pain, and a terrible roaring, and the echo of the metal tray hitting the tiles, the jangling cutlery and waft of Hollandaise and eggs, of hot smoked salmon and ham; felt the splash of blood against her check and the side of her eye, focussing as she had been taught on her target no matter what, his second volley – pfft-pfft-pfft – slamming her shoulder against the wall, missing, then dropping her as the sixth bullet blew out the flesh of her left thigh.

But by that time, the Orion Renegade Black Op assassin was

dead, down against the door with his legs spread in a wide V, his face angled up and his jaw dropped, stuck against the door with the back of his own head, a kill-shot through his eye.

She saw his spirit glow, deep inner white surrounded by shitty-brown and blood-red marble swirls and smears, and a hard black crust, all of which broke away and dissolved outwardly, into the space around him, an astral space only she could see, as all he ever was or would be here dissolved from third density, into cosmic memory, cosmic record, cosmic attention – as the white sphere of his original essence, what there was of it, blew out and dispersed.

His ego's last words sounded depressed, rather than resentful.

Fucking Pandorans…

She waited a second.

There was blood everywhere.

The apartment stank with the passing of his foul karmic residue. Poor bastard would be working that off for the next thousand years.

But that was Planet Earth, after all.

She couldn't move.

She breathed for a few seconds, making sure she still could.

'Well?'

She felt she had to ask.

'Are you going to help?'

CHAPTER 48

The small section of the tiled floor by the door, four meters square, upon which she was now face-down, had once been reserved for a vintage hat and coat stand she had found at a garage sale, that had come with matching bureau…

Gone now.

Just pain.

There had been a bowl on the bureau. She'd always thrown her swipe key, and her car keys, and her purse in it. Where were her car keys now? Would her car still be in the hotel garage?

She was drifting.

Shock, blood loss.

But there was someone else here, with her.

'I know you're…' Thys uttered. '…there. I heard you.'

The tiles were cold, and she was naked again.

It was all tile; cream with pale caramel swirls, but basically off-white. She was six foot, one-eighty-three, taller in sneakers, and her body, and the fallen white robe, and the silver tray and lid, and spilled food, took up most of the other space.

She'd gone back, into the wall, her knees had given out and she had fallen forward, bashed both knees on the tiles and, slap, onto her bare tits like a belly-flop, with barely the presence of mind to brace her head up.

Still, she'd clonked the right side of her skull.

She could still hear the thud of it.

Terrific.

She addressed the other presence again.

'I heard…' She tried to swallow. '…I heard the stair squeak.'

'I cannot help.'

'No kidding.'

Silence.

Laying with her head to the side, staring out, into the empty apartment, she could hear herself breathing.

She tried another tactic.

'You smell like… I don't know. Primrose?'

'No. Not really. But, imaginably. One supposes. From your current perspective, my scent may manifest within your senses as one of many things.'

It had taken her a few moments to realise that the red, shapeless lump on the tiles right before her was her bullet-dismembered ear. It was just across the floor, beside the edge of the robe. And the other thing must have been the silver breakfast tray, which had indeed fallen flat.

At least, it looked like the top part of her ear.

Whatever that part was called.

Pink and pointy and mangled and bloody.

Or… was it ham?

Then, she saw the tip of a sword.

A long, thin, glistening silver blade descended, right in front of… yes; her severed ear, then pinned her severed ear, and raised her severed ear.

Then it was gone.

Poor severed ear.

'Oh. You came to kill me, too.'

'Yes. Perchance.'

'Too late.'

'Perchance. No.'

She sounded like an upper-class British woman; like any one of those nice ones who appeared in movies based on classic novels. A foot came down where the ear had been, and stepped into the blood. The foot was strange to her eyes.

'You are one of the Pandorans.'

Thys couldn't move. Even thinking about moving shot pain through her, everywhere. So she just remained still, the front of her thighs and her stomach and boobs on the tiles, blood-soaked, bleeding out, her head turned into the apartment but unable to see anything much past the discarded white robe, the silver tray, and where her poor severed ear had been.

'Apparently.'

'Yes, that is the name people seem to have chosen for you all.'

'Apparent – lee.'

'One imagined, coming to find you, a group of colourfully costumed superheroes with mystical titles, and amazing abilities, then one finds that – like many things here, that newfound skills are limited to the initial parameters of one's genetic makeup.'

'You're telling me I am shit at healing.'

There was a pause. A slight shift of her garments as she moved.

'You possess many skills and strengths. Imaginably, self-regeneration does not appear to be your greatest.'

'What gave it away? The gallons of blood pumping out of all the open holes in my body or the fact that I still only have one ear?'

There was silence, but she sensed, if not sansed, a great and unexpected swell of curiosity.

'I can feel you applying what energy of that nature you are able to generate. The first bullet blew you back into the wall, the second dropped you to the floor; but your power of potency, it did not fail you.'

Thys could see her own blood now, spreading from beneath her, across the nice tiles.

'Potency?'

'The little prediction you made. It is notoriously difficult for those existing within third density to predict even seconds ahead in a crisis; or were you just lucky?'

'I knew I was going to take a hit. I knew that going right was better. I went with it.'

'Yes; you saw that moving right and being slammed against the wall by two injurious bullets was better than moving left and falling completely backwards when the first bullet hit you, exposing yourself to a cerebral kill-shot that would have had you dying instantly as you fell to where your coffee table used to be; either than or getting to a run and taking bullets in the back. Somewhat shameful, one imagines. Either way, the man would have had his way with your body while it remained warm, in time to kill anybody who came to help you; too late to help you, they would have discovered to their fatal detriment, in the instant before he engaged them. But you moved against the urge to move to the open – and the illusion of more options. Although, no human would believe it was anything but luck.'

The room, her home, still smelled awful, might always now; might never get him out.

Drifting again, fading, as the assassin crapped on and on.

But who was she kidding?

It wasn't her home anymore.

Mere minutes ago she had stood here; no clothes, no possessions, no memory, no plans, no idea; assessing the total emptiness of her space. Now she was losing all her blood here as well.

No blood, no life.

Dying here.

How many more signs did the universe need to give her that she was being rebooted?

'Rebooted?' The second assassin sounded amused. 'Perchance. Unlikely.'

'Trudy doesn't know I'm here. She's the only one who could –'

The assassin moved.

Her hand descended like a whisper and removed the silver lid from the dropped dinner tray. Beneath was scatterd a mess of breakfast muffin, yellow sauce, egg yolk and egg white, splashed everywhere, with shaken slices of ham and smoked salmon folded into each other amid it all.

'Amethyst. How many times have you returned to third density since you first ascended to fourth?'

'The battle over the ocean… it seemed to go on a long time.'

'Did you sleep there? Or here?'

'Sleep? There, I suppose. Wow, you know… it might have been more than a week since I walked through that earthy tree-tunnel.'

'Tree tunnel?'

'Wait. No; I… came back. Yelina. Made a tree port. I went to see that movie.'

The assassin's foot moved. She had been moving in boots before, but now she was barefoot. Her foot was pale, a beautiful silvery-lavender. From the floor, she watched as the assassin's heel rose, and her ankle pushed the graceful arc of her instep downward, stretching the slender muscles and well-defined tendons with the poise and elegance of a ballerina. She extended with what any human would expect to be toes; but there weren't any toes. She stared at the tip of the smooth, toeless foot as it rippled, one wave, just as a human foot might, and the assassin dabbed the slightly off-centre point into the pool of blood.

'What…?'

'You are a better telekinetic than almost anyone I have ever sensed. Which makes you a princess in the astral. And an enormous threat there, as you have shown.'

She was still staring at the blood-tipped foot.

The blood from her ear was… clearing?

The assassin's toe; it seemed to be vacuuming the blood from the tiles.

'I have met your father, Amethyst Pyne. Very briefly. He has enormous gifts for traversing, and perception. It is my family's belief that, if the greatest of dark forces are trying to destroy him, and taking enormous risks to do so – then he must represent an enormous threat to the established order, in which the old, dark forces hold so much power.'

'Huh…' Amethyst Pyne sighed. 'So… I am the daughter of a powerful man?'

'What a strange way to frame your own abilities. You are a member of a powerful family. You stood your ground here. If you ran for the balcony, I was waiting for you.'

'To kill me?'

'A fall perhaps. That would limit your progression. If you showed lack of personal integrity.'

'I thought the Pleiadeans…'

'We all think that; wherever we are from. You trust your democracy. And yet, every manifestation of governmental power on this planet you would consider civilized, and right, has Black Ops, protecting its interests against lesser states of organization, correct? That is the way of government; correct?'

'I… believe so.'

'It is very bad here; that much is true. Worse than it should be; worse than it ever has been on Earth, considering the current population. Six thousand years of exponential misrule. But we understand why, now.'

'Well, there's a first time…'

'For everything, yes. Very droll, for a dying lady. Regardless; the Principle Interest must be protected. Here, and on all other planes. And so I am a Shadow Pleiadean, protecting that interest. As is my third mother; as is my seventh sister.'

'By allowing me to bleed out?'

'Perchance. We have learned to harness and direct the collective shadow-psyche of our race-pool. The Principle Interest must be determined for each of you. More will be revealed in time. Perchance.'

'… to dream, I get it. If I ever get… back…'

…eh-ah…

She was fading now, losing a lot of blood.

She heard the balcony door open. The Shadow Pleiadean gave her a tone of encouragment.

'Try to live.'

I've done my best.

'…bye…' Amethyst Pyne managed to say.

But her sense was, as she passed out, that they were coming, and everything would be –

CHAPTER 49

– snapped right back into reality.

'She's back...'

A woman, behind her.

Two shocks.

First, she couldn't see, but she felt and quickly realised that she'd been blindfolded.

Then; she was cold all over. Her nipples were erect, super-sensitive, stinging with the chill; then the shock passed and, angrily, she realised that she had been tied-up-naked.

Fucking: Seriously?

Her neck was tight and her shoulders were pinned back, because her wrists were restrained with plastic zip-cuffs. From the feel of her bum, the way she was positioned, the way her legs stretched right out, and down, and from her sudden sense of balancing herself, not to mention the wooden stair jutting into her gathered mid-forearms, just above where her bound hands now rested behind her at her lower back, she knew that she was sitting about half way up the steps of her apartment, with her ankles also bound in zip-cuffs.

However, she was alert, and aware; unwounded and restored to an extent that all but shocked her.

'She's come back strong – I warned you!'

The woman behind her again. Her voice modulator sounded deep, resonant and foreboding, like the movie trailer guy, back from when movie trailers had narration.

In a wrrlllddd...

'She looks confused.'

Another woman – to her left.

'But is she there? Is her mind there?'

A third woman… difficult to pin, more distant, again to the left, with a whiny American accent.

Then she regained more of her bearings: they were all to the left; she was on the stairs; there was only wall to her right. She attempted to visualise, to pinpoint them all as they spoke, as they moved. All of them using voice-modulators to make their tones distorted and unrecognizable.

But that wouldn't stop her, when the time came…

Wait. Something was wrong.

'Put the fucking robe back on 'er, I don't wanna se 'er tits!'

The fourth voice had come from a man. He was Australian, someone old and gruff, and clearly thought of himself as being in charge. He was essentially standing right in front of her, at the bottom of the steps. A second voice came to her though; a deep, *Scream*-type modulator. Even through the distortion she could sense an American male.

'Leave it. She's hot. We should take pics, they might be useful later.'

'You will do no such thing.' That was the whiny American woman again, who was hard to pin. Oddly far away. 'This is a business negotiation – you will *not touch her.*'

Anger spiked within her; hard, gut-wrenching, intolerant.

Just on pure instinct, she fucking hated these people.

But she also felt… caution.

And as she felt caution, she felt…

Intelligence creep in.

And greater instinct.

She felt… clever.

But there was no doubting – she had been mortally wounded, before. She had definitely been bleeding out, had almost totally bled out, by the time she had lost consciousness.

But… she searched, lucid.

There was no memory of returning to the astral.

Really?

Had she not been passed out long enough for her consciousness to even…? And now she was sitting up, on the stairs, with her hands behind her back, and –

'I said cover her the fuck up!'

'Shit no! Leave 'em out! I wanna see 'em!'

The much-older Australian snapped back at him.

'I don't fucking care what you want, ya fucken Yankee dildo!'

'Shut up both of you!' A French accent, probably.

Not disguised, but… was he speaking from a Skype call or something, maybe?

'Stop acting like fucking children. We just want a fucking deal from her. We get her to go along with us – and all of this other tedious shit goes away.'

Someone muttered to him; it sounded like the woman who was distant. Yes; yes, that was it – they were both on the same Skype call. The Frenchman grunted agreeably and continued. 'Try and remember that we want her on the team, unharmed. Remember, gentlemen. This is a very long game.'

She wanted to try and figure out what that meant; then hands moved on her head and she freaked. She knew they would have seen it, it was a primal, full-body flinch, no chance of even trying to suppress it. The hands had been clasped over her scalp, so still that she had not even felt them over her hair. She had not been aware that the hands had been there until the person behind her had slowly removed them.

She'd been healed – quickly, and extremely well.

By those hands.

'Can we bloody hurry this up please?'

She was startled again.

There was another gruff male Australian in the room. 'Her bloody lizo-lezo mates will be here soon!'

No less crass than the other one; but she intuited from the accents that the first was working-class Sydney, the second upper-crust Melbourne. It revealed something.

She could sense the tension in the room.

Nobody liked each other very much.

She needed to get them angry, get them nipping and barking at each other. She leaned back, feigned a greater level of discomfort, and brought her tied ankles up toward her. She could feel the cold air on her labia as it was exposed toward the end of the stairs.

The third step.

Eh-Ah!

Someone stood suddenly.

'She's really waking up! Your time is running out!'

Just as she'd supposed, the gruff Australian arced up again.

'Fark! I said – put that fucken robe on 'er! And fucken ditch this eggs benedict shit! Jesus Christ! I nearly fucken trod right in it! Who has fucken ham and fucken smoked salmon both at once?! Jesus fuck! Make a fucken choice for Christ's sake!'

The feeling of thick towel came down on her shoulders, and then somebody shoving it about her, bringing the lapels in over her breasts. It was damp, and a little crusty; still wet and thick with her own blood, she supposed.

The gruff Aussie went on, addressing her.

'Listen, girlie, you fucken owe me for this. You were checking out, fucken flattline, seconds to spare when we turned up. We knew this was the one place you'd turn up eventually. Fucken Norion's had their man here, got to yer first, and yer mates weren't gonna get 'ere on time, so we had to call in a favour. You hearin' me Pyne?'

Norions?

Ohh. Okay.

Probably this guy's nickname for the Orion Renegades.

But sure, she was hearin' him; she could hear it all, just fine. In fact, she could hear extra-well now, given that someone had grown her ear back for her. Good healing energy worked like that, and this had indeed been tremendously powerful; fast and exact.

Again, she tried to work things out, quickly.

The Shadow Pleiadean had been here first, and watched how she had handled the 'Norion' – these guys must have been right behind him. This crew had probably the heard shots – waited for the Pleiadean to leave, then rushed in and stopped her gapping back to the astral. If she'd done that, she would have been able to slow down her rate of decay until her friends had arrived to heal her. Instead, they'd brought their own superhealer, and tried to make it look like they'd saved her.

But why hadn't her friends arrived?

They must have been able to get here in less than – what?

Two minutes?

They must have been close.

But, the fact remained; they were not here.

How long did she have until help did actually arrive?

'She lost 'er fucken voice or what?'

Who could do healing like that, besides Trudy?

Had they expected her to be wounded?

Or had it been just lucky that there'd been a healer with them?

She supposed, if the apartments had been monitored, and she'd had time to shower… fifteen, twenty minutes away? These goons could have come from anywhere. Could have been alerted, wrapped up business, gotten together or come separately through dimensional portals… wait, no.

This was it.

This was the thing, the potency that the Shadow Pleiadean had talked about. The idea that an expanded consciousness could feel – what? Things approaching? Potential situations? The skill Aunt Saph had supposedly been really good at? The ability that Mitch was so terrified that the higher beings possessed, to godlike, or at least, demigodlike degrees?

However, now she knew it was there, and something she might also be able to use, it seemed like something more; it was presenting as yet another kind of *sense*. She was picking up their general un-conscious thoughts; where they had just been, what they were doing here, what they had to do next; and the sum of those parts, those psychic impressions, she supposed, was informing her collectively… *what was going on, just generally, without anyone telling her.*

Also, Jesus; she was starving.

She could still smell the ham and smoked salmon; Trudy's signal to use the gun to defend herself, of course – that those coming for her would not hesitate to do so first, and efficiently. The signal had never been used before. That had been for the Norion, presumably?

'She's definitely awake, and thinking.' The nineties trailer voice on the squeaky step again. 'You need to amp that thing up, she's super-powerful now; if I can read her, she'll be able to –'

She tried to stretch out, trying overtly to deploy the potency.

'I said amp it up! She's trying to stretch her conch!'

She could sense three people thinking intensely about her from a distance, and two of those three were on their way, worried like crazy, desperate to get to her; they would be here soon, but they were being deliberately held up for this – charade, as it turned out. The paths of the two people coming for her had been sabotaged, and slowed; that was murky, she could not see exactly how, because…

Ah; she got it.

They protected that, even when they were not aware. Somewhere between unconscious and just under their general, conscious guard; *this was a secret*, collectively categorized and maintained as clandestine activity, and unable to be simply plucked from the air, so to speak, as she was doing. It was a thing they all knew; *always knew*, even when they weren't thinking about it.

Getting through *that* would take more power.

But it told her something new; it told her that her friends, who were coming, were not people that these people – whoever the fuck they were – felt comfortable engaging with; either physically capturing, or holding back. These people were too scared to openly move against her friends – but; *not her.*

She wondered; *why not me?*

She tried to open her sphere of perception some more, to find more power, to find out more, but couldn't.

The thing was stopping her.

What was that thing?

There was a thing here.

What was it…?

What was it doing?

She couldn't see it, but she could *feel it*. It was small, and sharp, but generating a lot of… no; it was hoovering in a lot of power. Sucking in the opal dust that had been all over her, and in her room, and on her bed when she had awoken, but in an entirely converse, negative way. This thing was kind of like a reverse air conditioner that absorbed opal, like a vacuum, and then pumped it out… grey.

Not dead, just – neutralized.

'She's still pushing to see – she's very nimble with it. She's going to be big trouble for you all unless you do something.'

'Yeah. I got ya. We thought that.'

You all? Not – us all?

Was… squeaky stair girl - someone for hire?

❨ *Are – you – for – hire?* ❩

Nothing.

❨ *Are* ❨ *you…?* ❩ ❩ … ❨ *for* ❨ *hire…?* ❩ ❩

Still nothing.

Okay. It was time for some more provocation.

'Who are you?'

She directed the question at the old Sydneysider, in front of her, at the same time thinking both; never ask a question to which you do not already know the answer (one of these gruff old Australians was Wyatt Styger) and also; if in doubt, ask an open question anyone can answer. You might find a crack. She hadn't necessarily been taught that in Pan training; someone else had given her that one.

'That's for me to fucken know and you to find out, girlie.' She felt him crack, right then. 'Jesus I said cover her tits! Jesus Aitch, we're not fucken animals here, for fuck's sake!'

Again, she'd done it herself, shifting her shoulders slightly, pulling her arms back so that the robe draped apart again, attracting his attention to her physical presence simply by asking him the question – knowing that her nakedness would make him uncomfortable. He was one of those old idiots with some kind of perverse and contradictory code of honour toward what he perceived as 'ladies'. Still, the douchebag *Scream* boy pulled the robe in again, over her chest and breasts. But he fondled her simultaneously. She immediately tensed, but the offender's indecency had indirectly exposed him.

What had that big, bodyguard man – Harding?

What had Harding said to her father?

'Remember, pay attention to the spikes.'

Well, she had a big spike now.

She could feel them. The old Aussie wanker in front of her was a human, as was the other old Aussie who spoke with the Melbourne accent; there were several powerful men who had similar accents, but she was sure that this one, right there in front, was Styger, the third first-son of a first-son to run Styger Corp.

Styger was now in his seventies; her intention, as she had squirmed her robe free, had been to give him a heart attack right here and now. But what the American's touch had provided was that there were more people in the room than she'd thought. Most of them had Anunnaki passengers; everything from full possessions and day trip piggybakers.

That was all-so troubling, in oh-so many ways.

'She's sensing us...' The American man said.

'Good.' She heard Styger utter. Then he moved closer. 'Okay, girlie...' He maintained the superior sneer in his voice. '...what are ya gonna do about that, then? So maybe ya got a neutral body deal with ya mates in whatever tribes are on your side of this fuckin' nuisance civil war ya started, but these guys here are fucken hardcore, they don't give a fuck whose bodies they hijack.'

She let out a breath. 'Understood.'

'Hah!' Styger started laughing 'Hey?' He cackled. 'Ya get that?

A woman of few words! How fucken refreshing! Understood, eh?'

Suddenly she could feel that he was right up in her face, the hot breath of his words right on her lips.

'Well ya betta bloody understand, darlin'. Ya fucken betta!'

She squeezed her mouth shut as she smelled the fresh lager on his breath, the edge of a cigarette. But there was something else there, aged and foul. She tried not to retch, and only just managed. But they had her; she couldn't use her powers just to indiscriminately bust out of this predicament. The Anunnaki had simply possessed a bunch of innocent people, and were using them as human shields.

'Now look down.'

He moved back and somebody slipped her blindfold up, just enough so she could see her own lap.

Immediately, an iPad was placed there.

Her life was coming back to her now.

She had been on the astral plane, and seen a lot.

She still couldn't remember a lot of it, but she did remember that you needed to keep focus when you were there, like anywhere else really, if you wanted to get anything done.

Or you could get lost.

Kind of like the internet; a seemingly infinite expanse of ever-morphing clashes of people's deepest hopes and fears, made manifest, maintaining focus from notion to motion, but rarely ending, rarely finding satisfaction, and in the end, still alone. And again, just like the internet, when one was conscious and within the astral, other people's fantasies, dreams and nightmares became addictive. So; she had seen – a lot. Every kind of flesh, every kind of sex, in every possible permutation. But even after all that, what she never expected to see, what she never wanted, ever, to see, was this.

'That's my sister.'

'That's right.'

She tried to play it blasé. 'Who's the guy?'

'Does it matter? Someone she hired.'

'Hired?'

There was another spike as someone else arrived, through a generated dimensional rift. She heard the sharp clip-clop of heels on the tiles as they came through, then someone spoke through yet another voice modulator. This one sounded like one of the male *South Park* kids.

'Shit.'

Someone who wanted their identity kept secret had just given away the fact that they were wearing heels, and was therefore ninety-eight-plus percent likely to be female.

These people were not used to doing this kind of thing.

Who the hell were these people?

'Have you shown her the video?'

'Just then.'

'You brought one of those fucken things too?'

'It's a voice modulator, you fool. I told you to bring one. These other fools all did.'

Nobody protested, which spoke volumes.

'Fuck!' Styger growled. 'I thought you said voice *moderator*. I wondered what the fuck you meant.'

She sighed. 'But you didn't think to ask?'

'No, I thought it was some new politically correct bullshit.'

The newcomer sighed. 'Never mind. Listen, Amethyst. We know you've been causing trouble on the astral plane. We know that your body absorbed the genetic formula, the so-called Pandora Sequence at Oliver Hines' party, before the Miracle Quake.'

Styger snapped. 'I hate that fucken' name.'

'Only because someone else came up with it.'

'Fuck. True enough.'

'When has anything I have said ever not been?'

Amethyst.

Amy.

Thys.

She had not yet thought her name; she felt her focus again.

'You've caused a lot of trouble for us there, dear Amethyst. Our informants tell us that you seem to be able to transport your whole body back and forth, that this is something to do with – Anunnaki DNA, was it? Is that what Holland Pankhurst was doing in Peru? Dissecting Anunnaki and splicing their genes with humans?'

The old bastard chimed in again. 'We wanna know where the formula is. Who's got it, how much and where.'

'Ritual!'

The shout had come from somewhere that seemed so far away that it was impossible for it to have come from somewhere within the room, and yet it had almost certainly come from someone standing just beside the articulate woman.

'What?' Styger snapped, paused a second, then ignored the voice, returning focus to his captive. 'And another fucken thing – we want to know who the fuck else at the party took it!'

The Frenchman spoke up, over the Skype connection.

'We know who was there, Amethyst; we just need confirmation of who else changed their DNA to Anunnaki. Who else can do what you do?'

'Ritual!'

This time, it felt as though all the air had been sucked out of the room; but she saw the sharp thing, shining in her mind, where her coffee table would have been. She saw it glow, then sparkle – working overtime. The thing that had spoken had brought with it more, a lot more, opal dust to neutralize.

'I'll do it.'

The main woman in heels stepped forward again.

'Amethyst Pyne; this information is usually coded, and must be sought and found to be believed. However, you have gained fully-conscious access to the astral plane and therefore, this must be spoken as verbal contract. There are rules, and laws, embedded within the total consciousness of the universe which dictate that as parts of that consciousness expand and begin to gain full comprehension of the universe, they must exercise free will. This means that you must be informed of the cosmic truths that effect your quality of choice and decision-making; they must be stated in such a way that they are present in the everyday. People, consumers, can choose to see them, recognize them, they can choose not to see them, consciously or unconsciously; but they will see these messages, and they will understand them – even if their immediate response is to deny or reject them, or pretend they are not there, or that they did not in fact see them at all. Naturally, they do see them – everyone does – and they do understand. Everyone does. All the cabals, the old conspiracies and secret societies, understood this. It is a law we break at our own karmic peril, with very certain and dire consequences should we choose to do so.'

'Why you?'

Amethyst Pyne could not believe she'd asked that question; perhaps she hadn't. Perhaps this was all part of some deeply imbedded ritual which existed within the fabric of consciousness itself, and she had asked that question merely as a function of the progression of that ritual. It certainly felt like that to her, in the moment.

'We are just the spearhead. The cabal moves organically, beneath the surface; we were jostled to the top. But we are, believe me, just the tip. Just the voice through which, each of us, thousands speak. And listen. So listen well, Amethyst Pyne. You are currently being addressed by a cabal of representatives of extremely powerful human interests, allied with alien and extra-dimensional interests, who aim to control the entire population of this planet. We are very close. We have competition; there are other cabals, but that is who we are, and we are the closest to succeeding. Abundance, Information, Sustenance and Death. These are the four quadrants of third density existence we make paramount; we control them all, and are taking steps to ensure that this control is ours for the next millennia. There are a lot of other details, but we know that you know them already. Do you understand?'

Amethyst Pyne felt strange.

Compelled by something way larger than herself, she spoke truthfully.

'Yes.'

'And do you understand that this is the game on a level with which you are able to engage? We are the New Cosmic Mafia, Amethyst Pyne. And do you understand that you – are positioning yourself as the new cop on the cosmic block who won't play by our rules? If you want one of your movie references, you are the "Astral Serpico." Is that clear enough for your pop culture personality to understand?'

'Yes.'

The deep and powerful thing that was in the room, but far away, touched her in the middle of her forehead.

'Her consciousness has potency; she understands.'

Styger was fast to jump in; he clearly did not give a shit about any of this cosmic ritual bullshit.

'Then we want names, girlie. Names, ya hear me?'

Amy.

That was a name.

Amy could hear them, just fine. But she had to not-think about any of it. The squeaky dobber on the third stair would pick up on anything.

'Are you listening?' The woman with the *South Park* modulator clip-clopped once toward her. 'No more trouble, or we upload this video of your sister and her toy boy to Porn Central and alert the media. Understood?'

Amy waited a second. She couldn't help herself now. She had to speak. But she didn't want squeaky-stair spy-girl picking up on what she knew and dobbing her in.

So she decided to provoke some more, distract and divide.

'Firstly, I am not my sister's keeper. I have no idea why she has done what she has done –'

'I can answer that for you.' Her clipped tone shut Amy

down immediately; she was well-practiced. 'Your little sister has some stupid notion that she is going to – "get out ahead of her celebrity", I believe is the idea. Firstly, she doesn't seem to understand that – not only is the celebrity sex tape passé, with the advent of easily manipulated video programs, but now it is free and easily accessible, pornography itself is passé – at least it will be as soon as the Boomers all die off.'

'Careful, lady.'

Someone slid the iPad off her lap, but she had long since stopped looking there. She'd seen enough to know that the video had been long, well-lit, well-staged; even semi-professionally produced. They pulled the lower edge of the blindfold back down so she could see nothing again.

The high heels clip-clopped over again and the woman leaned in.

She was wearing a distinctive scent, an expensive one. It reminded her of a kind of bubble gum her father had collected – that had come with bubble gum cards of superhero movies in the late nineties, one of her first remembered smells; the last of their kind.

For now.

Nothing ever went away, nothing was ever wasted, everything was recycled.

You just had to know where to look.

'Now, Amy, you are no doubt wondering – well, what would be so bad, then? You are not your sister's keeper and in this day and age she may well profit from a well-produced illicit video. It's just a blowjob, no penetration; nothing too scandalous. And, like yourself, she has certainly inherited her parents' aesthetic appeal. Well, try and remember that we have technology ten years in advance of anything available publicly, fifteen-to-twenty years ahead of whatever the lowest general population can access. We can make it look like she is sucking the big, fat cock of – anyone. *Anyone.*'

'Everyone knows a fake when they see it now.'

Amy regretted that instantly; it was stupid, as stupid as the people who read tabloids, watched morning television, spent all day on social media and clicked on any bait they were told to click on.

'Ha!' Styger cackled. 'I've seen that look. She knows what we can do. We can make it so the gutter-press and the outrage sites never let up. We can make her not just notorious, the way she thinks she wants to be – but shamefully notorious. Her life will be over; her mind will be broken; her spirit will be destroyed. Believe me, I've – '

'Silence!'

There was, indeed, silence for a few seconds.

The woman leaned in again.

'You would think, wouldn't you, that the kind of low-level video manipulation that is available to the general population right now was so primitive as not to fool even the most gullible want-to-believer. But child, it's already worked.'

'They don't know the fucken difference!' Styger snapped. 'Or don't care! They just want the outrage hit – they just want the hate and the dark adrenalin!'

Heels ignored him. 'With the digital tech we have at our disposal right now – and the cash to put it into play, we could make the man in that video look like… well, let's say… *your own father.*'

Amy was going to be sick. The eggs benedict smelled rancid now, somehow.

'Or, worse still…?' The woman continued leered. 'How about… The President? And because we have this to work from, it will be so real, so undetectably fake, nobody will be able to prove it's veracity one way or the other. Or at least, by the time they have, the tabloids will have done their job…' She paused; she was looking at Styger. '…and made your lives a toxic hell that's not worth living.'

Stairway girl chimed in, sounding uncomfortable. 'She's trying not to talk. But, she's still thinking that nobody will care. She's hanging on to that. Who will care about her sister? She's… oh!'

'Nobody will care?'

'She doesn't know. I… don't think she's been back to actual, real Earth for a while. Maybe… a long while.'

'Wait.' The woman moved; she turned to the Americans. 'What's that thing you lizard people are always saying about time? In the astral? Something about time and the astral plane?'

'Yeah, I know that one.' Someone spoke up gruffly. A third American who'd been silent until now. 'It's – don't call us 'lizard people', *ape lady.*'

There was an awkward silence. Amy did not need any experience with the astral plane to determine that it was palpable.

'I – apologize.'

The woman's vocal inflection raised sharply as she spoke this word, which to Amy meant she was more upset at being called out than having offended an Anunnaki colleague.

'Time works differently in the astral.'

Squeaky dobber on the stair had said it.

She was right.

It was a thing, people said it, all the time.

'Amy…' The apparent Anunnaki racist bent down again, and spoke mock-sweetly into her face. 'Darling, how long were you in the astral this time?'

Again, she couldn't help it; something had gone wrong, and they had the advantage. She needed to know why; she answered.

'Weeks. Maybe three.'

There were mutterings, some were aghast, some were – like, typical.

'Amy, a lot has happened, since you've been gone. The last time you were here, I believe, was to attend a movie premiere, many months after the Miracle Quake, after Bo Everett and Oliver Hines merged their companies together and created something called… *Lever.* Is this right?'

Was she giving her the astral protocol check?

'Yes.'

She'd been back and forth a few times; *and their shitty cabal hadn't noticed.*

'Everybody hated them, and hated the name. And everybody hated your father, and Heather Everett, because Lever was transferred to them. Completely transferred. Incalculable wealth.'

She clicked her fingers.

'Practically overnight. Now, we, our organisation, know what they did to earn it; or at least, we have a clue. However, so far as the rest of the world was concerned, they did nothing.' She sneered. 'Oh! Such jealousy and vitriol!'

Amy gulped.

'But then, dear child, something happened. Everett and Hines – vanished. And Mitchell and Heather - changed the company name. They changed it in a very small way, subtle; but it worked.'

'Cleverco.'

'Yes! So – you do know!'

'I've heard.'

'No strings attached to the wealth – and believe me, we've searched. We've tried. But almost overnight, as soon as they changed the brand, and the logo, something strange happened. Amy, your family, including your father and your soon-to-be, when *will they* set the date stepmother, your brat, star-fucking sister, and your desperate housewife mother, are all major personalities in the world spotlight now. They are – well; properly famous. As is anything to do with them – with your family. And you, my dear, are not only the primary heiress to the Cleverco fortune of multi-billions; no. You are also a notorious recluse – given that nobody has set eyes on you since you walked down the runway to watch that atrocious Achilleos indulgence – precisely three years ago today.'

Amy spoke. 'Three...?'

'Give or take an hour or two. Darling.'

CHAPTER 50

Amy blinked.

Of course. It explained everything. There was always the sense of waking up after a deep sleep when she returned; a sense of bewilderment while she got her Earthly bearings. And she had returned to Earth before now, every now and then, in secret, to see her Dad, and Heather; see Jade and her mother; see… the few friends she had managed to stay tight with after joining The Pan.

She had let them know… that she was okay.

At least… she had returned, here and there… in the early days.

But she knew now, this was true; she had been gone, been there, a long time, an extended period. Maybe not the entire time this woman was talking about, but… maybe one third of that?

A year, maybe?

Since she'd last been back?

Time worked differently in the astral.

This was true.

That was a thing.

Everyone said it.

And she had lost track of it.

For a year, surely, apparently; more or less.

'I can see I have rattled you. Good. Think it over, Amethyst Pyne. Have a good think before you speak again.'

'You stay out of the astral from here on, girlie – and do what we fucken say. As of right fucken now. Or this will not end well for you.'

((where are you?

◊ what's happening??? ◊

She blinked again.

◊ what's happening? Are you still there? They have created stupid

delays for us, and think we do not know, but they are effective. Are you there? What's happening? ◊

((Amy – are you still at the apartment?

'What's happening?' Styger demanded.

Squeaky stair girl dobbed again. 'Her people are talking to her – telepathically. I can't tell who, unless she responds to them.'

'Right. We need to get the fuck outa here. Wait. What's she doing?'

She blinked a third time. Her tears were running down her cheeks, under the blindfold. He had just noticed them. He came forward again.

'That's right. You should be afraid, little girlie. And here's another thing. We've been protecting you, and your bloody thick bloody family, all this time you've been gone. But that's over now. Do as we say, or we remove that protection, like that.'

She heard him click his fingers as well, clearly thinking it had worked so well for the woman.

'And you'd better believe that if we do that, all the Anunnaki you've fucked over will want a piece of you – not to mention those Norion fanatics. Starting with –'

'Stop.'

Stair girl had suddenly spoken up.

'What did you fucken say? Nobody tells me to –'

'She's not afraid! She's not afraid of any of us – she's remembering!'

'Remembering what?'

'Remembering who she is!'

CHAPTER 51

Franco had been okay, but DJ had been better than okay.
Amy had liked DJ, really liked him.

So... she'd been gone for a long time.
A long year in a long three years...?
More?

Back then, with The Pan, they'd been at a party, at someone's
house –

...had that really been - five years ago now???
She supposed, now.... that was true.
Three years since the Kamikaze Anunnaki; she had been twenty,
then. Eighteen in The Pan, when; DJ...

Trudy found all her recruits somewhere to unwind once a
fortnight. They'd been to a lot of parties by then, but she had
wanted him since the first party. He had been so nice, every time
they had been together, and while he had circulated – after all,
they had not come together, weren't together – every time he had
been with her, she had felt like the only person in the room, and
the one that he really had wanted to be with all night, all along.
Finally she had gone to the bathroom and when she'd come
out, he'd been there.
'Wait for me...?' He'd smiled so nicely.
She'd listened to him wee through the door, and wash his
hands, and then he had come out of the bathroom and kissed
her, just like that, against the wall of the slim hallway that led
to the bedrooms of whoever's house it was. They had kissed and

kissed, really rolled tongues and clicked teeth, and she'd never really understood kissing until that day. She remembered - she'd been eighteen and three months, and really, it had not been all that long ago, not in the scheme of things, even though, to an extent, it felt like… everything.

When someone had started up the corridor from the other end, DJ had grabbed her and in a whirlwind of opening and closing doors she had found herself outside, in someone's garden on a warm night, up against a back fence. They were under a tree and they could see out from under it, but nobody could see in. They were rubbing up against each other with their thighs pressing hard and he'd told her that she could take 'it' out.

If she liked.

Although by that time she had been very familiar with the internet, and her own body, she'd never seen a penis in real life, let alone one that was fully erect that she was being asked to touch, and handle, and to deal with. She knew from reading, and from adult videos, that there were a few variants as to what she could do next, but she'd taken a deep breath and put the head in her mouth, hardly visible, even up close in the dark – just to see. After a while, he'd told her to use her hand as well, and showed her, like she'd seen the porn actors do in the videos, and she'd asked him if he could stop pushing it in so hard, or she would gag. With that established, it had seemed to work, they had seemed to figure it out, and just when she was thinking she would like to try and go further there had been an enormous flash of light; white, and pink, and red, and she'd found herself being spat at, with something actually quite hot, and was covered in something steaming and thick and wet, and it was all over her. Then he'd made an excuse, and she'd said it was okay for him to go back in, she would text a friend and get them to come out with a wet-wipe or something, to a clean her top. April had come out with a fresh tee-shirt. Amy had been wearing an OCP tee and a casual leather jacket; April waited while she cleaned the stuff off the jacket and changed the tee. Back in the party, she told Terry, the one person who'd asked why she'd changed her top, that she'd managed to spill tzatziki on the other tee, and he'd taken her to the laundry, where she'd been able to soak it. He'd noticed her earlier tee because he'd been a huge Verhoeven fan, and then he'd wanted to know if she wanted to go out for coffee some time.

She'd been noncommittal, but they'd enjoyed talking about something other than corporate conspiracies, even though they hadn't, really. Terry was good looking enough, and really smart, really engaging; but he had been one of those guys who...

Never mind.

DJ hadn't said anything about it later at the party and neither had she; there was nothing to be embarrassed about. The party went on. They had sat beside each other on a big couch in the middle of the living room with about six other people and he'd put his arm around her for a while, but they had 'gone home' separately, with a promise that they would catch up after training one night, and a polite kiss goodbye. They did, after all, live in the same hotel.

Trudy had never made any rules for her young recruits. That part of the briefing, as such, had gone something like:

'You're all eighteen, some of you are early-twenties. Just be responsible, and don't cheat.'

Amy had been a virgin.

'Sorry I rushed away, it all happened so fast, I was embarrassed.'

'That's okay. I can deal with all sorts of situations.' Amy had smiled widely, charming. 'It's what they train us for, after all, and, after all, it all came out.'

She suddenly realised how that sounded.

'...in the wash, you mean?' DJ grinned back.

Amy found herself blushing. 'Yes. OCP. Totally clean. Nothing to see here!'

She had been a little worried. Her training was not going as well as it might have. As it turned out – she wasn't that good at fighting. But DJ was. She had worried that he might not like her as much, now it had turned out that she hadn't the natural, innate aggression that was required for combat.

DJ had smiled, again.

Such a lovely smile.

'We all have different bodies, different minds; different genes, and different programming, from childhood. And then all that all gets fucked up in the school system, and we spend the rest of our lives figuring out what we should be doing with our lives. My Dad says that school is like a prison in a jungle; he says that people who work that one out can break out, and that's the first smart thing they will ever do. The people who take to prison life stay in the workforce. The ones who don't learn to make a home of the jungle. My Mum says that if everyone's different, that can't be true – but it is true for the people who are meant to be on those different paths. She told me to stay in school.'

'Did you?'

'Sure. The Pan is basically a scholarship, right?'

They had laughed, and talked a lot more.

And now he was dead.

CHAPTER 52

She remembered.

On the mission, after April had landed the chopper on Everett's boat, there had been a second boat, and people on that boat had fired incredibly powerful bullets at them across the ocean as soon as they had jumped out of the chopper.

They had all followed their training, she had led them as she had been instructed, as had been planned, but the snipers had waited, assessed them, then attacked so quickly that there had been no time to respond. The snipers had been able to discern things within that short time, tactical things – like, the fact that there was a weak spot where the helmet joined the body armour. They had shot DJ, the bullet had impacted there, in the weak spot, and it had practically decapitated him. Seconds later, Franco had gone down the same way.

They had shot other people with darts, to capture them.

But her, and her friends, The Pan, they had aimed to kill.

CHAPTER 53

All through the week after the party Amy had wanted to go to DJ's room, but there was something a little bit unromantic about that. It was not a seedy hotel, but it was still somewhere ordinary. Instead, they had waited until the next weekend. Every second weekend they were encouraged to go and see their families, whatever that meant to them; to Amy it meant calling her mother, Janine, and catching up with her sister, Jade, usually for way too many drinks.

Sometimes it meant building bookshelves.

Her father was still somewhere in Sydney but she hadn't spoken to him for nearly two years. Janine had told the girls that he was depressed, and drinking, and that he would get in touch when he came out of it. She didn't even have his number.

'I have his number...' Trudy had told her once. '...it's a landline, he's staying at one of Pan's flats.'

She took it, thought about it, but didn't call.

She hated him when he was drunk; he was a domineering, sarcastic and inevitably self-righteous and judgmental dickhead. Disappointed with himself, but projecting and pretending and even believing he was disappointed with her, then making mean decrees about her poor life decisions and lack of ambition, that he would either have forgotten the next day, or pretend he had forgotten. No shame, and never an apology.

If he ever came out of it, she thought after the last time, it had better be soon.

But Amy could drink too; just as well as her Dad could.

She had the gene.

She had learned, quite fast, that she could hold more than other girls, and many of the boys too. That she did not throw up, or pass out; at least nowhere near as quickly as they did. She was thinking about not drinking at all, because of that, but was not listening seriously to those thoughts, even though they were serious.

That weekend, they had called their families and told them that they couldn't make it. Amy had cancelled her plans with her sister so that she could have sex for the first time, and lose her virginity (an achievement her little sister had so easily unlocked and demolished at high school level).

So on the Friday night, she had allowed it. She had thought; he is handsome and cute and polite, and when he was around, her body felt like it wanted to be naked, with him; like she almost couldn't stop herself making that happen, both of them naked and pressing together, right there and then – wherever it happened to be. She thought about him when he wasn't around. A lot. She had heard stories about boys, doing a number, getting you to have sex with them, lying, and then turning the cold shoulder; she was not stupid. She understood hormones and conquest and how the human mammal was hardwired; how some men couldn't help but sleep around, and sometimes, for so many reasons, they were impossible to resist. Further still, she understood the great worst-kept-secret of the so-called sexually liberated west, slowly being whispered into society at large… that there were women who were exactly the same, and men who could not resist being consumed by them. She had read, and studied, and gone looking for more information, a lot. And even if one did not do that; there were songs, movies, books, shows, all about all this.

With all that… how could anyone still seriously fall for all that bullshit?

But when it came time, something inside her, something that seemed to be required within herself to bolster her courage, was able to say to her and make her believe; maybe he will be mine forever, and she realised; you fell for all that bullshit because you were hardwired to fall for all that bullshit, even if you knew, rationally and completely, that it was all bullshit and you were an idiot to fall for it.

He told her that he hadn't slept with many other girls; but that she was special, that she was different to the handful of others he had slept with.

She had heard in songs and seen in movies and read in books and watched in shows that this was often a complete line. The other thing in her that wanted the bullshit to be true, believed it. Even took pleasure, great pleasure, in believing it.

He loved her, he said.

This had to be a lie, but she wanted to believe it, and the part of her that wanted that – did not believe it.

CHAPTER 54

She was not that stupid, and his bullshit was not that good.

Still, she proceeded, and ignored it all the same.

The hotel apartment where she lived seemed different when he was there, and when all their comrades-in-training from The Pan were away for family weekends.

He had gone slow, and managed her. The way he had done this told her; this is certainly not his first time sleeping with a virgin, nor is it the confidence of a man who has not slept with many girls. The way he proceeded, smoothly and efficiently, to arouse her to a point where she had gone beyond what she had been able to achieve for herself, with her plastic tools and bookmarked European erotica, confirmed to her that he was no freshman wannabe lover, but a natural; experienced and cocksure.

Her first experience was not awkward, and painful, as other girls, particularly older pre-internet girls had found, nor was it rushed, and rough, as with post-internet girls and their boys who bull-headedly forced some very high, porn-based expectations upon them. Rather, it was slick, and professional. It was not impersonal, but neither was it true. She did not feel cheap; he took her there, then stayed afterwards, and they watched a movie. It had felt – friendly. When he asked if she wanted to go again, she had found that she could not refuse. The second time, he had blown her mind with how far he had been able to take her. Where she would naturally stop herself, and take a breather, he gracefully pushed on, and glided through, without her even knowing that was possible. Everything had seemed glorious, and electric, even at the end when he had let loose all over her again, like he had under the tree at the party, and she had realised it wasn't an accident; that was what he liked to do, it had been deliberate. But still, it had seemed as amazing a natural occurrence to behold as a Leonid meteor shower.

They'd lain there in a soft embrace, then cleaned up, ordered pizza, chatted, and fallen asleep.

In the morning, he'd woken her lightly to tell her that he was going.

All of this went completely against her expectations; it was supposed to have been confusing and painful, and he was supposed to sneak out.

They had been flirty and friendly and kissed secretly here and there all week during training, not wanting to make it public, wanting to keep it private, dreamklike, unsullied by peers.

He had called her that Saturday afternoon.

He'd told her that he would like to come around again after his band practice, and he would bring dinner. He had brought dinner, and flowers, and desert. He had taken note that she was thinking about not drinking, and so had brought several different cans of American import soft drinks along with the wine. She was being seduced, he was making it easy, she was making it easy, and she did not care.

Their Saturday sex had played out almost exactly the same, and she did not care; in fact she was somewhat excited that the whole thing could be so easily repeated, and feel just as good.

He'd woken her softly and vanished all Sunday, and she did not care.

Once more, they had agreed to wait until the following weekend, and stay at the hotel when everyone else went out for the fortnight party, and that's exactly what they did.

She called Jade, her little sister, and told her what was happening. Jade had been impressed; her first sexual experience had been over in under three minutes.

'But you have three vibrators...!' Jade was excellent at dispensing the sharp backhander. 'I hate all that shit!'

Amy wished she hadn't called.

'By the way, it's Saxe now. Or just Sax. I haven't decided.'

'Saxe?'

Wow. Amy had almost forgotten. That was her real name. Saxe was an ancient German word, or something like that, for blue – or what the medieval Germans had thought that the medieval French had called blue, or… something like that. Janine had named her daughters Amethyst Sky and Jade Saxe; in other words, purple-blue and green-blue – her two favourite combos.

'It sounds like Sex.'

'It's like saxophone. Sax. Sex is an entirely different word. Plus, you lightly pronounce the 'e' at the end. Like Sax-hh.'

'No you don't.'

'I do. People do.'

'People don't. Americans won't, especially.'

'I don't care, Amy.'

'Fucking mother, she is so fucking clueless. Naming her daughter 'Sex'.'

Saxe, or Jade as she had always hitherto been, had gone all quiet after that and ended the call quite brusquely. One out of two calls with the Pyne sisters always seemed to end with one of them doing something like that.

Still, things seemed to have gone well, by comparison.

She'd had sex with DJ eight times, in three weekends.

Was it really – years now?

More than two full years since the day on the boat?

Amy had started to believe that maybe it was, actually, for real. That his line wasn't a lie, and they were really, truly…

Then, Jade-Saxe had called her out of the green-blue.

'I thought you should know. He goes back, to his hometown, out past Lithgow, on those family fortnights, when you're supposed to be out partying with me, and he stays with his girlfriend there. He's been with her since high school.'

Despite herself, she'd let her sister hear the first of her tears, and then cried herself to sleep.

CHAPTER 55

Trudy had heard the tears, and noticed the puffy eyes.

When Amy had explained, her aunt, friend and leader had nodded, somewhat sternly.

'He's also sleeping regularly with a girl in a second Pan group we have over on the North Shore.'

She'd heard herself moan then; the sound someone makes when they can't quite believe they've let themselves be so naïve, and stupid.

Trudy had been great that day; what you really want an understanding aunt to be.

And Amy got it, she really did.

He was just too good-looking. She'd heard stories about Uncle Pan. So good looking. So many girls, secret girls, all secret from each other. Until he'd met Aunt Saph, and then he'd been faithful, for three years, until she had broken it off and come back from Peru. More beautiful, by an n'th degree, than he was handsome. Beautiful enough to leave him, not because he was unfaithful, but because he would not leave Peru, and the jungle, and his work, and give her children.

Trudy had told her many things during that afternoon, and night, when Amy had shown her aunt how she could drink, and not throw up, or pass out, and they had still been on the beach swigging vodka when the sea-side breakfast café had opened.

'Amy, I know a lot about guys like that. Good looking guys who… well, look, it's just a fact, with men that handsome. And cute men, too. Women, a comparatively high percentage of women, can be seduced by them. They will allow themselves to become willingly entangled with them, sexually. In a way they thought they would not with anyone, sometimes. In a way they didn't think themselves capable. Risky ways, dangerous ways; emotionally, and to the stability of their lives, their relationships, their marriages too. In ways that, as often as not, they later consider to be a lapse in judgment. But it's an age-old story, it's something that happens. A large percentage of women are attracted to men like DJ – and my brother Pan – and they will go against their own rationality to become engaged with them, sexually, even if it's just the one time; even if its longer, and they know it *will not last*. Because they know that, when it is over, men like that won't make a fuss. They won't come for them, won't ruin the marriage… all of that. I've grown up with those women, those my brother collected around him like Pokémon. I've seen it. Beauty trumps rationality, it even trumps trust and truth; ninety-nine-point-nine percent of the time.'

Amy looked at her. She was the flipside; Pan's sister, just as hot as her irresistibly hot brother.

Trudy saw the look and leaned in.

'Amy, you are not as hot as me, or Saph.'

Amy had been shocked.

'Yet. But you will be, when you are a few years older, and have some real world experience in your eyes. You have a weird combo of Mitch's good looks, and Janine's beauty – and something else. Can't quite put my finger on it. But, it's something.'

'Really?'

'Really. But I can tell you what it isn't; it's not aggression. You're not an angry girl. You're a… a serious girl.'

'Serious.'

Trudy laughed. 'It's good that we're proper friends now.'

'We are?'

'Oh yeah. So I don't feel so bad telling you that we're taking you out of fighting training.'

'You are?'

'Amy, darling, you can't fight your way out of a wet paper bag.'

'No!'

'Yes.'

'But –'

'*But* – you can think. You see through people. You saw through DJ.'

'But I didn't!'

'What? You're in love with him?'

'Oh, God no!'

Amy had been startled by her own response.

'That's what you're crying about. You're not in love with him. You want to be. You look good together. You think it would be like Pan and Saph. But you're not, and he's not, and the sex was routine. Am I right?'

'I don't… really have anything to compare it to.'

This time, Trudy was startled by her response.

'Seriously? He was your first?'

'Yeah. I mean; I don't really see…' Amy shrugged. '…I'm okay handling all that myself – until, you know… fireworks. I suppose.'

Trudy had smiled, a big smile.

'Amy, we're going to put you in change of this group. You're The Pan's first Group Leader.'

CHAPTER 56

Amy and her father had been on the boat together, when DJ had been killed. Mitch had been different; the same man, but a different version of her father, a version she had never seen and would never have believed, caught up in the middle of something crazy and talking about aliens, and other dimensions, as though he had been talking about them with this amount of blaze conviction his whole life. And then, she had been caught up, and become the same. She had found out afterwards that her father though had only been in the early stages of becoming a different version of himself. But she had stuck around to see it happen, to see him fully bloom. She had asked him about it.

'You saw me become a different, better version of myself, but you just became yourself – you have always been the best version of yourself.'

She had asked him about it.

So, she had not been gone this whole time.

Yes. She must have come back; she had remembered correctly – she had!

Once or twice, surely?

April had flown the six of them to the boat.

Tick.

Bo Everett's boat which, they had been told, had had been left in dock somewhere up north, then "stolen by pirates".

(All bullshit as it turned out.)

DJ, Franco, Terry, Lorena, Capri, April and herself had been trained to fight the pirates, who would not put up much of a fight, they were told, and to dart them on sight. Then, to put them in the life boats, and set them adrift to be picked up shortly after, as reported to the authorities.

Tick.

Instead, Everett had actually been on the boat, along with a host of other people who had vanished-presumed-dead as of three months prior – including her own father.

Cross.

Then they had all been attacked, DJ and Franco had been killed, and her father had killed the sniper.

Big, horrible cross; a skull and crossbones.

Then, the enemy boat had gone, but not before doing something that had knocked her father out, and nearly killed him. A storm had started, a terrible storm, which she had slept through, after having yet another emotional meltdown in front of everyone, including her father and Bo Everett.

Cross, cross… question mark?

She was still embarrassed about it, even though all the grown-ups who'd heard it seemed to think it had been something… healthy?

She didn't really know.

Some indication that she was… okay?

That she was… one of them?

Tick, tick??

Then she'd fallen asleep.

CHAPTER 57

She'd slept deep, she knew, very deep, but she'd had no idea for how long.

The huge man beside her had awoken at the same time.

She looked at him and could see that he had been thinking the same thing.

'Hello.'

He was South African.

The weird thing was, she had felt fine about waking beside him.

Same bed, but it was big, and they were both still clothed.

But it had somehow been as though….this huge South African man with a weather-beaten face and a silver-fox buzzcut… had protected her somehow, as she'd slept?

'Hello.'

He had then stared at her oddly, squinting, as though examining her.

He was propped up on both elbows.

She was on her side, facing him, on one elbow.

'What?'

'You look like someone I know.'

Amy had smiled and fallen back onto her pillow, staring at the cabin ceiling.

'My Dad. You know my Dad. Mitch Pyne. I'm Amy Pyne, his daughter. Everyone says I look like him.'

'That's because you do, girl.'

'I'm not a girl.'

'Don't tell me my own perspective, girl.'

She had rolled back and looked at him again then, and something about his attitude had made her smile.

'I suppose I am a girl to you. I don't feel like one.'

'That doesn't matter.'

They lay in silence a few seconds.

'I saw two of my friends get killed. Decapitated by bullets.'

'I'm sorry. You were on the helicopter?'

'Yes. We thought Everett's boat...' She sighed. 'It doesn't matter.'

The big man grunted. 'I work for Everett. It should have been me that saw them off. Those darts. Lucky shot.'

'Are you – *Harding?*'

'Yes. You've heard of me?'

'Trudy told us to look out for you.'

'I see. Trudy Pankhurst.'

'Yep.'

They were silent a few seconds more.

They could hear the ocean outside, and the rocking of the boat had become more apparent to them as they had become more awake, and alert. But the storm had stopped. There were distant voices, footsteps on the deck above; people were active.

'They used bullets on you and your friends?'

'Yes.'

'I am sorry you had to see something like that, so young. There are parts of the world where somebody your age would be lucky not to have seen such a thing by the time they were even thirteen. But if you have not been born into that kind of insanity, it is unfortunate that you would be exposed to it ever. It changes people; does not make them any better off, in my experience.'

'Great.'

'I can help, so it doesn't happen to you.'

'What? How?'

'I have ways. Mitch is a good man. He doesn't see things as clearly as he should. But he will. I would be happy to help you.'

'Thanks. I guess.'

Amy was already having trouble getting the images out of her mind; all the blood, where it had come from, what it meant.

DJ.

'Do you love your father?'

She had loved DJ, in the end, in some way.

'Yeah. He's a bit of a luddite, and a total dill, but…'

'So, it's your mother who is the real problem?'

She sat up again. 'How did you know?'

'Your father has that look in his eyes, when he looks at Heather Everett. Like he knows he should risk something, but it cost him too much, the last time he took that risk.'

Amy stared at him. She had found something. She wasn't sure exactly what; but it was something. She heard herself say something quite bold, and out of character for her.

'When we get back to shore, we should have a drink. But I don't want my father to worry.'

She knew she had changed. What had happened had changed her. Life was shorter now, more precious. The shortness added up to something bigger, somehow.

Harding shrugged. 'Okay.'

'Do you want my number, or – ?'

'No girl. I will find you.'

'Oh.' She smiled to herself. 'Yeah, right. Okay.'

CHAPTER 58

Amy had been with Bo Everett, and his wife Yelina for a while after that. Yelina was not really his wife, and they had apparently known each other less than a year, but they went about the world like they had been married for thirty years. She was a good deal younger, it seemed, but it wasn't weird, or creepy, like some super-arrogant, super-wealthy, super-industrialist, sociopathic narcissist had married a voiceless model one third his age. It was more like they had been married forever and had an incredible shorthand that went with their massive agenda; an agenda you knew was massive just from who and what they were.

'Supernature has seduced Progress…' Yelina had told her, quietly, out of nowhere, as they had stolen the cocktail waitress uniforms. 'It is a strange love, but it is true love. It may not be doomed.'

April had flown them away from Everett's boat in the Pan chopper, and they had left her father behind with the promise that they would see each other soon. And they had. Everett had immediately praised April's skills and offered her a job as one of his personal pilots; she had thrown a ridiculous sum at him and he had laughed, and agreed. When they had landed in Los Angeles, Trudy had appeared and tried to whisk the other surviving members of The Pan mission away, but Yelina had asked that Amy remain. And so Amy had bid farewell to Capri, and Lorena, crying and hugging as the bodies of DJ and Franco had been unloaded behind them. But Terry –

Terry had vanished, straight off the chopper and into the sunrise.

Everett had approved; Terry had gone his own way, it was to be admired.

They had all regrouped by essentially crashing a party held by Oliver Hines, in a big seventies rock-star mansion on Mulholland Drive… and from there, things had quickly escalated into a series of threats that had at once seemed insane, then all too real, and now – they pretty much ranked as everyday.

'Ohhhh.' Amy aired to herself, half-forgetting where she was, tied and blindfolded on her own staircase. *That's where the outfit comes from…*'

'What?' Styger demanded. 'What the fuck is she saying?'

'We stole them from a box in someone's car boot, then changed in the garden…'

The other older Australian man stepped forward.

'We do not have time for this. We need her to agree to back off, do we not? We need her word, isn't that correct?'

He sounded like every Australian private school principle she'd ever dealt with.

Jesus; suddenly she twigged.

He was a Minister. In the Australian Government. People knew him, and hated him, and believed him to be weak, and ineffectual. She couldn't remember his name, but she recognised the speech pattern instantly – and she had never trusted him, because despite being considered weak… he had been around for at least three decades.

'Yes… we do…' The elder woman practically purred through the *South Park* modulator. She was the real dangerous one, Amy knew that; could hear that so very clearly. 'We need her to tell us something.'

She could practically feel the woman beginning to regard Amy as a more serious threat; a kind of admiration, coupled with a burgeoning hatred. Genuine regard, nevertheless.

'But she is beginning to see through us all.'

The Minister didn't care. 'Doesn't that mean something here? For her? More than a blood contract, or a karmic debt, correct? Her word – it means everything at this juncture?'

'So I've been away fighting that war, since *that day*…' Amy was talking to herself now really. '…for five years now?' She couldn't quite believe it. 'And underneath everything, still wearing that outfit… *for a whole five years?*'

'What's she talking about?' Styger was becoming increasingly frustrated, just as she had hoped. 'We need her to focus on the matter at hand!'

'Five years!'

No wonder all that opal dust had come off it.

With that thought, however, Amy saw something.

There was light; there was substance – beneath the blindfold.

Was there… twinkling?

Was it just within her eye, like those little stars, from the pressure of the blindfold?

No, it wasn't that tight. Or was it…?

Oh.

Oh right.

She remembered what it was.

Her tears for DJ, and Frankie, had brought it out.

Styger lost it now.

'Give me that fucking pistol, dickhead!'

There was a shuffle.

The woman clip-clopped back. 'I wouldn't do that…'

But she did nothing to stop it as Amy felt something cold and metal, upright-rectangular, pressed against her mouth. There seemed to be a large circle over her top lip, and a small circle on her lower, pushing the inside of both lips against her teeth.

'Now…'

Styger pushed a little harder, pushed up and down to make her lips part. As she felt this pressure, the twinkling that she could see behind the blindfold began to glisten.

'Stop that!' The Healer sitting behind her gasped.

The Dobber, on the squeaky step, was standing now, and echoed The Healer.

'She's right Old Man! Fucking stop that right now!'

'No….' The Healer was shaking all over. 'No! This is evil!

You're an evil old arsehole and I won't – !'

'*Shuddarp!*'

Styger had power; from where, who knew? But everyone in the room froze.

The older American spoke up, angry. 'This holy healing-power freak shouldn't be here – we should never had agreed to this – she needs to go.'

The barrel of the gun in her mouth was bigger than she'd expected. A proper modern handgun. High and hard. He was slowly forcing her to open wider; it still wasn't in past her teeth. She was making it harder for him.

The Dobber snarled. 'I did not sign up for this!'

Styger ignored everyone and addressed Amy.

'Now listen here, girlie. We have spent decades, and billions, and billions, and fucken endless billions, making sure that the world is equally divided between Anunnaki clans and human corporations, between the four fucken quadrants on every plane of relevant existence, making sure that the alliances are strong; making sure that the percentages of malnourished, uneducated, inbred morons are finely balanced with enough high-intelligence, fine-faring, inbred psychopaths, and every degree in between; that the wheel will never – stop – turning! We've divided up the continents, and the races, and the classes, and the systems, and the cities, and the suburbs, and the streets; all just enough to ensure that the exact equation of this planet has the perfect ratio of friction to the lube; enough slaves and enough masters; enough victims and enough perps; enough cons and enough marks; enough useless idiots and enough enlightened sages; enough naive radical bullshit and enough fear-mongering conservative horse-crap; enough fine art and enough fart jokes; enough men, enough women, enough kids, enough elders; lezzos and poofs; trannies and transphobes; on and on; enough of everything – all just-so; just so that the friction is perpetual and the lube secretes itself. On and on, just the way they set it up for us, six thousand years ago, so that we have an endless supply of pointless pain, and misplaced desire, unattainable goals and endless competition. All four quadrants, working the lower four chakras; intelligence, emotion, challenge and pleasure; all working for us, all nice and primal. Now sure, not everybody's in on it; but we always stage the dance, we always write the songs, and we always rig the race, and we always tell the stories; and we always, always take the lead. And now, finally, this planet is exactly where we all want it.'

He pushed and she let the gun barrel slide fully into her mouth; she didn't resist at all as it went right to the back of her throat.

The Dobber was fuming.

The Healer was crying.

'The Karma Forge Equation is balanced in our favour.'

The Minister made an approving moan, as though he were back in Parliament.

'Nnnnnn....'

'But what we don't want – what we can't have – is gnosis. Just as surely, we have spent billions, and billions, and trillions even, making sure that the old religious system fails, that it falls apart, falls to the Abyss, and rots in Hell. Ensuring, as it thoroughly decomposes, that even as the world moves into its Third Industrial Revolution, and as the new millennia's technology takes shape and infiltrates every sector or reality, that it will be ours, our technology, and it will infiltrate, replicate, improve and surpass every-single-fucken-system that pre-existed it, and, so far as I can bloody see; that our so-called spiritual and religious and even meta-fucken-physical values remain as unattached to all of this as we can manage, *and we can manage a lot;* and, that what remains of them is pummelled, as deep as we can shove 'em, into the smouldering embers of the fiery pit of the Dark Ages until they finally go the fuck out for good. And when they finally do go out, and we have promoted all we have to, to ensure that the soul is a part of an insanely overpriced sneaker made by slaves, that spirit is a sugary medicine made by machines to help you forget, and that all that matters is the physical – with those lovely fucken four quadrants again – winners, sinners, health and wealth – workin' overtime; *minimum wage, overtime;* then and only then, will we say we have made progress. And if ya drew the losin' genetic hand there, and ya can't win, can't sin; ya sick and ya poor; well, don't worry, cos we can endlessly film and broadcast the arseholes who have won the genetic lottery, get away with everything, love to fuck all the time, and never run out of money! Not while they're being filmed they don't! Cos we keep payin' em! So you can endlessly watch them, until you die. Until you die – *expensively.* And when you do die, and everything you ever had and were rolls back to us, everybody knows that reincarnation is just a cynical means of class oppression; everybody knows that there is nothing out there in the rest of the empty universal void worth shit; and if there is, it's too bloody far away; and no bloody aliens thanks! Or they would have landed on the Whitehouse Lawn by now – am I right? I am right! There's – just – nothing. Nothing but this, forever; never, ever, anything else, for ever and ever and fucking ever. And anyone who tells you otherwise? Well, we know now. It's been proven beyond doubt. Those people are mentally ill. Sad but deluded; nothing for it but to lock 'em up, or let 'em write screenplays. Same fucken thing really! Consciousness is a freak of evolution and that is snuffed out when you die and there's nothing – nothing, ab-so-fucken-lutely *no fucken thing,* other than *that fact.* No meaning to anything – not even 'no great meaning' – no meaning – at all. If ya really desperate after all that, well; there's our new sell – if life has no inherent meaning, *then that makes the meaning we give it all the more important.'*

He cackled, and the gun clicked on the edges of her front teeth.

'So buck up, people! It's the new catch cry of the clinically depressed, casual narcissist. *Life is meaningless - make up your own meaning!* The meaning for the "Me Generation!"'

The woman spoke softly. 'The Me Generation was decades ago.'

'They're all the fucken Me Generation and you know it! We

all know it, and they all know it! And that – is all they get.'

He pushed the gun a little further, trying to choke her a little.

'And they get that – and they like it. And the more they like it – the more they fucken thrive on it. And you, girlie, are not gonna fuck that up for everyone, by coming back and forth and making a fucking scene, about the real truth of the matter – which is that *none of that is fucking true!*'

CHAPTER 59

Styger sneered, his voice suddenly directed away from her, across the apartment.

'How's that for yer fucken ritual, or could ya not fucken hear me from way out there?'

There was no response.

There was silence in the room.

'I undeh'and, h'ully...' Amy told him, relatively clearly with the her lips over the gun barrel. 'Gn'ister H'yger.'

'You little fucken cunt!'

He was right on her now. He stood and she was forced to angle her head further up.

'I am gonna shove this thing down your smug fucken neck and blow a bullet out your pussy through your heart!'

'Dear God!' Someone shouted, an older man from the back.

'This is absurd! You can't kill her...!' There was a fumbling of cloth, and something else; the leading woman was removing her *South Park* voice synthesizer. '...you know that, you insane old arse! She is part of the larger equation!' Without the modulator, she spoke harshly, but her voice was soft, with the edge of a European accent. 'They all are! If she works with us, she can take us to the next level – to the goddamned penthouse and beyond!'

Amy could feel the gun trembling.

'I don't *wanna* kill 'er...' His tone stated the opposite.

'Then; don't.'

Amy could feel – he'd done this before. They knew he could do it; when he saw red, he was erratic and bloodthirsty, and everyone in the room had seen him see red before.

'...but, I *could* do it. And then, they would all be shattered, wouldn' they? I could pull the fucken trigger, now, an' put a bullet through their whole fucken Pan-dildo-dorian fuck-family. And they'd never be the same, they'd never recover! Their First Daughter. So sad, so senseless – *so brutal!* Their anger and grief and pain would overwhelm them all, and they would, *they will, they will crumble and –*'

Amy drew her lips back, exposing her large white teeth, upper and lower.

Revealing her nice, pink, healthy gums.

Revealing an enormous, toothy, fuck-you grin.

'Don' you fucken test me girlie, I am three fucken seconds away from…'

Amy bit down hard; a savage, complete bite, right through the barrel of the gun, then wrenched her head to the left, toward her captors, severing the offending tube clean off and spitting it out at them. Swiftly, so that the room barely had time to react (most of them had been stunned into paralysis anyway, having no next move for this scenario) Amy snapped her cuffed hands apart and raised them from behind her, pushing her blindfold back in one fluid movement. There were gasps, cries and curses. Immediately she glanced down the stairs for Styger, to eyeball him, but someone had shoved a hood over his head, even as his hand, still trying to pull the trigger, had reduced what remained of the liquorice handgun to mush.

Then, he screamed –

'Ants! Fucken bull ants! The gun's made of fucken ants, there's ants everywhere!'

– over and over, until a massive black-hooded figure behind him clamped a hand on his shoulder, there was a spike and they vanished. Whisked away by his Anunnaki bodyguard.

There were further, increasing gasps of shock, and guffaws of disbelief, and a massive tension filled the room. Everyone seemed to be focussed upon the white-robed European woman. She was, as Amy had intuited, in the centre of all this.

Somehow this woman had put it at all together.

Their deal, this deal.

She was surrounded by a crest of others, also dressed in the same clean, white, deep-hooded robes. All eyes turned to her and she stiffened, straightening her posture, and raised her hands to her hips.

'I see.'

She had not restored her voice modulator. Her lips were thin, no lipstick. Her mouth was wide, her jawline sharp; tough.

'It's going to be like this.'

She remained still.

Everyone awaited her judgment.

Amy exploited this pause and used it to take everything in.

The spear, the glowing thing, was still there, but she could no longer perceive it in her mind's eye – now it was physically blocked from her vision by a clutch of people in enormous robes. These robed people were everywhere, grouped by the various colours of their voluminous garments, packed tightly to fill the apartment with virtually no room to spare. But the more startling thing was what they were all doing, and watching, aside from Amy herself.

There was light everywhere, but different kinds of light, competing for space and obscuring everything and everyone – holographic, three dimensional displays of data hovering between multiple eyelines; light-streams cascading down commandeered sections of the apartment walls like an array of indoor waterfalls; and yet on other sections, solid readouts, like massive car dashboards or game consoles, right down to LED and digital, or even basic monitors with contemoprary devices attached. There were even a few small podiums, clustered in a central group, where laptops and smartphones had been opened to face her, streaming her image back to other members of the cabal, watching her through the bannisters of the stairway upon which she still sat.

All watching, just watching.

Until that moment, she must have looked like a prisoner to

them.

To them all.

Amy's heart was beating incredibly fast.

All of them, so many; they could easily overwhelm and kill her, and she did not know if she could pull off another stunt like the one she just had.

She'd only worked out, by the electron of an inkling, that although their spear device had been blocking astral energies – somehow – a skerrick of the twinkling, opal energy that had returned with her from the astral, that had been on her, and all through the outfit that she had, apparently, worn there for so long, had been with her on the costume; the catsuit and the boots, between her skin and the material and the sweat of her body, maybe even *under her skin*… so much that even after laundry, even after a shower, even with the neutralizing device, somehow there had still been some left in the corners of her eyes, in her sinuses, triggered by her tears, dripping down the back of her throat – only perceptible to her restless mind when one of her most dominant senses was hampered, then forcing her to pay attention to whatever was there, with her, in the blackness. Somehow, from that; from her own opal mucus and eye-dust, she had been able to generate enough astral power to reshape one of the most deadly shapes known to humanity, to reshape matter with imagination and will, literally by the skin of her teeth.

But now, she had to do something else; she had to make them see, definitely, that she was strong.

'Mmmm…'

She bit into the wrist restraints again, and started chewing.

'Cherry.'

She gave them as wide a Cheshire Cat grin as she could manage; showed them her bright pink gums.

'My favourite.'

The European woman, her adversary, did not flinch physically.

'She is much stronger than our intel provided.'

If Styger's disappearance seemed to trigger a chill of mass

concern, then this pronouncement triggered an Ice Age.

Everyone froze.

Amy smacked the cherry liquorice on her molars.

'That a problem?'

Clearly it was, but she could sense the woman's dilemma. She could not show weakness, but would not risk a confrontation. The intel she had on Amy was bad; indeed, this could still all go very, very bad for everyone. Her only solution was to rely on the weakness of others.

'If this disturbs you –'

She boldly but assuredly addressed all the others, all the robes standing behind her, as one.

' – go.'

It was a mass evacuation.

Everything happened very quickly amid a similar, heightened chorus of response; gasps of horror, cries of outrage and curses of sheer vulgarity. But through all that, Amy thought she saw almost all of them, even if just for a millisecond, even as they all scuffled, shut down and vanished, even as the boss woman kept totally still, staring at her, her lips ever-more pursed.

Amy watched at least a dozen figures, of indeterminable characteristics, gap out within the space of three or four seconds, some under their own power, some grasped on the shoulder from behind by their alien transporters. Some were wearing thick, deeply-hooded robes, with large rubber masks underneath. The largest group wore royal-purple robes and masks of classic movie stars; then there was a group with blood-red robes and masks of American Presidents, almost as numerous; then a few with dark-gold robes and masks of US talk-show hosts past, with one in each group who had full nose and mouth distortion apparatus connected to the lower parts of their faces, like mini gas-masks, with large reflective sunglasses to totally disguise their faces. Clearly, these were the spokespersons, the tips of many spears; one vocal member for each group.

Beyond that, she sensed several other levels of etiquette, of power structure, but she was not interested.

There was movement in the kitchen; sub-cabals, hitherto un-noticed, drawing attention to themselves in the act of leaving. People in Hazmat suits there, vanishing as well, which drew her attention again, somehow to perceive another whole level of audience. Presences, beings from above, from around, from within the walls, or just hovering, now receding away, expanding away, or just blinking out of her perception; a dozen different ones, gone, gone, gone.

People had gathered on the landing as well, draped in deep, dark-green robes. Some of them simply melted away, but others ran out of the balcony side-door. It looked suddenly to Amy like the entrance to a small, midnight forest had just separated and vanished, taking with it the illusion of the forest that had been behind it. She heard the balcony exit doorframe banging against the wall as people continually thrust it back behind them as they ran out in panic, people in ordinary earthy-brown monk robes, who had been disguised by the forest, then the glass in the door frame shattered. A woman screamed, and a man cried out, then there was a lot of shouting and swearing. She heard them begin to clamber down the metal fire escape and couldn't help breaking her poker face, and smiling, imagining what it must have looked like from outside – you could see that side of the building from the park, and the freeway.

A couple of the remaining cabal members on the living space floor raced past her, hugging the front wall of the apartment with their robed bodies, one eye on her, one on the door. Upon getting past her, they immediately took flight down the hotel corridor outside. Seeing that she had seen them, some terrified stragglers held back, too scared to move past her. Amy just watched, her face a passive mask of disinterest, chewing cherry, then turned to the rest of them.

'Get out.'

They did; another four, stumbling into each other. She heard their sprinting footfalls down the corridor outside as the front door swung shut again, ka-clack.

At her rough estimation, there had been fifty, maybe sixty people crammed in here, along with all the aliens and entities. It had been like a surprise birthday party, the kind they used to have in eighties sitcoms, with the conceit of the "the wrong address book" leading to an over-attended, overcrowded party filled with people the "birthday girl" didn't actually like.

They'd been quiet as mice, most of them.

The European woman remained, with her companions in white robes.

The human shields had all collapsed to the floor, unconscious; they were clearly just people from the hotel downstairs who had been temporarily piggybacked by Anunnaki foot soldiers, commanded by the people behind them, whichever clan, or cabal that had deployed them gone, and sleepwalked up here as human shields. Then, all of a sudden, they all woke, almost as one.

The European woman had clearly been here before.

'Go downstairs and get a drink.' She made suggestion firmly. 'Forget all this, go to bed.'

They obeyed, walking out as though hypnotized guests on a stage show; Amy knew they'd wake in a few hours, with no memory of the events, feeling weird, but probably never drink in a hotel bar again.

Behind the European and her white acolytes, several other people still remained. There was a group of six, wearing burnt-orange robes; a trio in deep burgundy; another trio dressed in baggy, white one-pieces, with crash-helmets, like race drivers; and one other in a definitely darker shade of blue, that nevertheless stood out as being lighter than the six other shades that had been represented by lesser, or less-interested clans, before they had all vanished.

The ones in the orange robes were trouble; all of them were training guns on her.

One of them moved forward, pushing two of the white robes aside.

'We have an offer.'

The European was clearly astounded. 'How dare you!'

Amy tried to hide a genuine spike of terror. 'Are they handheld automatics…?'

She could feel her heart beating very fast again; she might be able to leap out of her body before they opened fire, but her physical form would be destroyed. She would never have this, the Amethyst Pyne physical form again; never experience thought through these filters, matter through this prism, or actualize these memories into this personality.

She, effectively, would die.

She tried to sound nonplussed.

'One bullet should be enough, surely…?'

'Those things bring new meaning the term overkill…'

Still sitting on the steps, looking left though the balustrades, Amy glanced reflexively up over her shoulder but saw nothing; that had been Squeaky Dobber though. She looked back and saw her bare knees and feet; she saw that she was five stairs up, her feet on the third, pale white and caked in blood. The robe was around her, also very bloody. She didn't feel like putting it back on, but she didn't dare look any further down at herself, at her own naked body – she just pushed on with her chin up, still chewing the cherry cuffs, supressing her self-consciousness and bolstering her self-confidence from some central reservoir around her heart and gut, a reservoir that seemed to be drawing from somewhere, somehow, and ignored her physical self.

' – you want to shred me? Is that it?'

'Nobody wants to kill you; not today, not here anyway – Field Marshal Pyne.'

'Field Marshal?'

Oh yeah; she remembered telling someone after that first battle that she remembered hearing somewhere, sometime half asleep in history class probably, that the term Field Marshal was the highest military rank in the most important army. So the Anunnaki, *her Anunnaki,* had started calling her that – she didn't even know if it was true or not.

She had been called that, and Thys, Thys Pyne, for what seemed like a long time now. Maybe even five years.

'Field Marshal!' The European scoffed. 'She's barely out of wet nappies!'

That was great, Amy knew; a chance to ignore her.

Amy stood now.

She just finished chewing, looked straight ahead at the door, pushed down with her hands on her knees and stretched her legs with all her might – and stood.

Then she placed her left hand gently on the handrail and turned her head back to them, again, chin up.

Covered in her own blood.

'You're Chenek clan Anunnaki, right?'

She stepped down without looking, keeping her gaze fixed directly upon his own; finding each step over the blood-soaked robe, one step, two, three – finding the floor, with bare feet on the cold tile.

'What do you want here?'

He pushed his hood back, removed his voice synthesiser and sunglasses and addressed her.

'You don't know this face. But we have known each other these past years – you know my name, and you know I am a force you cannot deny.'

With the disguise gone, she could see the lapel-tops of the suit he wore underneath. It was a certain kind of slate-grey, but if you'd been on the astral, if you had anything of the expanded perspective fourth density offered as to colour, you could see a green weave through it, repeating a symbol-pattern that was not unlike hound's-tooth. She had also seen a rust-coloured variant, more of a corkscrew symbol, that belonged to the Psohla clan.

'We're at war – aren't we?'

'War?' The Healer gasped. The Cheneks ignored her, but Amy looked back up the stairs, directly at them for the first time now. Both the Healer and The Dobber were indeed still present – sitting on the seventh, middle stair and standing on the second stair from the top, respectively. (She had figured out the squeak and moved, Amy supposed.) They were both in black robes, virtually gagged with full Bane-style voice-modulators, plus reflective goggles. There was no way to tell who they were, not without it being homicidally dangerous. Amy suspected that the main reason they had not departed was that they had been the only truly third density humans in the room; psychic humans, but humans nevertheless. They dared not make a move now, or reveal themselves – but could they even see anything? Or, was it that their employer remained, and still had them under contract? Not time to tell. Amy looked back to the Cheneks.

'– are you trying to take me alive?'

The Dobber spoke up. 'Jesus, Pyne; hurry up and work it out, will you? Everyone wants you on their side. Working for them. They want you obey them, do their bidding.'

The Chenek growled. 'She will not do that…'

He was handsome, but nondescript; the same as Don Eissley, the same as every corporate guy she'd ever met. She knew that when the Anunnaki entered into an agreement to possess them, or simply bullied them into submission, that they altered their DNA subtly, so that their hosts now possessed the kind of good-looks that were easy to trust, but just as easily forgotten.

'No…' Amy turned back. 'I won't.' She huffed. 'Let those two go.'

'We didn't bring them. They have been abandoned by their employers – you provoked the tiny old Australian into exposing too much. They are not cleared for that; they are not ready. Maybe – the next life will be the one they rise within.'

'What…?' The Healer uttered, as the third stair squeaked.

Amy knew the subtext; either they were dead, or they were her responsibility now.

'You can't.' Surprisingly, it was the European who spoke up, and addressed the Chenek. 'You can't kill them, Ealo.'

'We might *take them*.'

Both Amy and the European grunted in disgust; neither were allowing that. The second Draco seemed to sense that the first was not doing well, and swiped back his hood and modulator as well. Amy knew this guy, she couldn't remember from where, but she knew him. Ealo was the good-looking type they preferred to deploy, but she had learned that there were several types; this guy was the completely nondescript type, just like The Minister; different riffs on the same spruiking wormtongue archetype.

'We want Vgyrl released. If you agree to the possibility we can discuss terms.'

Amy bluffed. 'Vgyrl? Was he the one…?'

'Don't pretend. He and Don Eissley nearly killed you.'

Again, The Healer was shocked '*What?*'

Amy turned back to her. 'What did you think you were doing here? They try to kill me ten times a week!'

'They said you'd been in an accident!' Her modulator sounded like Princess Leia, when she had pretended to be a bounty hunter. 'I – I know who you are! You're Amethyst Pyne! I had to save you!'

Amy swung back. 'Let her go, she's got no idea, she can't possibly process any of this and turn out to be anything but a useful idiot!'

'Give us Vgyrl.'

'I can't do that.'

'You will.'

'You don't understand. I can't.'

The Dobber spoke up again. 'Pyne, they're stalling, it's a distraction.'

'We are not.'

'Then they've been left behind as a distraction; there are more Orion Renegades; this mob call them The Norions; they're coming, can't you feel it?'

Amy looked to the space in the room where, when she had been blindfolded, the angry, disembodied voice had come from, and demanded ritual. If they were coming, they would come through there.

The European hummed to herself. 'You can sense it, can't you?' She was keenly interested, very impressed. ' – you can pinpoint even the traces of the wormhole that the voice came through…?'

She walked up to Amy, slowly – clip, clop, clip, clop, her thin lips rubbing together in measured consideration.

'But you can't control it, can you? It's still wild. It's still acting out of your unconscious… no?' Before she could even respond, the European pushed back her hood and removed her glasses. It was another set of features Amy recognized, another public face. 'I call parlay! We need to talk – at length. We have been going about this entirely the wrong way!'

But Amy was astounded. 'Rio DeVora?'

DeVora seemed genuinely taken aback. 'I am surprised you recognise me so readily, I have not been –'

'You've won two Oscars!'

DeVora stared at her, almost lost for words.

This was something neither of them had expected, and for a bizarre second they had no choice but to treat each other as normal human beings.

'Now, I know you think that, but it's something that happens sometimes; people think that I am an actress, another person. I've never been sure which one they mean, but –'

'You're Rio DeVora. I know who you are. Why are you doing – *this?*'

This seemed to surprise DeVora even more. 'I made *two films* in my twenties, which none of the critics enjoyed. So I turned my focus elsewhere.'

Amy stared at her. 'You're telling the truth, aren't you?'

'I always tell the truth, child.'

'But then… this can only mean one thing….'

DeVora almost took a step back. 'What? What can you possibly be talking about?'

'Either you weren't always an acclaimed actress, or you weren't always –'

'What? What are you saying?'

There was a spike – someone was coming.

Amy turned away from the wormhole to the front door.

'It's coming from there!'

Everyone tensed.

'Fair warning Amy Pyne, if it's the O'Renegades, they will kill anyone who does not immediately vacate or venerate.'

The dimensional gap flashed open and was gone.

Standing there was Queen Elizabeth II.

CHAPTER 60

It took Amy a few seconds to process.

But this was not 'The Queen'.

Clearly.

Indeed, the face had at first seemed oddly familiar.

Then, strikingly familiar in a really odd way.

But really, this could not be –

But it was.

But then, it was, and it wasn't.

Because – this was not the Queen of England as she was now, but…. as she had been, in her mid-twenties…? When she had been… crowned?

In the nineteen-fifties!

'Wait… *what?*'

The young Queen, as such, was enwrapped in a vibrant royal-purple robe with lush, white-fur trimmings, and a multi-diamond encrusted, silver-spiked crown that arced over her head and shimmered like an angelic halo. However, the young Elizabeth the Second had also struck a musical diva pose, with both hands raised and poised above her head, with her chin raised sharply, in high in profile. With her above-the-elbow white gloves and strapless, ankle-length, silver-white gown, which in this pose, given the royal aspect, seemed almost indecently to only-just defy gravity, she seemed to possess the confident glamour of some kind of Monroe, or Material Girl. Further still, she was also holding an old ice-cream-cone microphone in one hand, and the metal rod that looked like it really belonged in the bottom half of a microphone stand in the other, with the rod over the back of her royally-robed shoulders like a lightweight dumbbell. But perhaps the most amazing thing about it was that she just stood there, apparently totally oblivious to the apartment's other occupants, who had all frozen as well.

She had literally stopped the show.

Suddenly she flicked a gaze at Amy and uttered out of the side of her mouth.

'Got it yet?'

'Monarch or Monroe or Madonna or Mercury?'

The two closest Draco retrained their guns on her as DeVora snapped.

'You're a look alike, of course we get it! Now deliver your message or state your case and get on with it – this is life or death business being conducted and we do not appreciate interruptions! Who are you with? Who sent you?'

The Queen dropped her arms, then the pose entirely, and swung the microphone and the stand down before her, planting it upright with the loose end hitting the tiled floor with a sharp clack. Now it looked like some sort of exotic cane.

'Look *alike*? I'll have you know that I am a look-*exactly!* Then she huffed. 'Oh you're really not getting it, are you?'

◖ *it's you, right?* ◗

◊ *of course it's me!!!* ◊

Amy played along, stood back again, and really took her in this time.

'Wow.'

'Yeah.' The Queen spread her arms again. 'I know!'

◊ *they're coming, hold the line; there's nothing we can do, we just have to stall* ◊

'I mean; you've got the voice and everything!'

'I – *know!*'

◖ *who?* ◗

'More distractions!' DeVora shouted angrily. 'We need to settle the matter at hand!'

Amy nodded at The Queen again. 'Well, yes. I mean, I actually attended a private school in London for five minutes, and her coronation portrait was in the staff foyer and, okay, I give it to you…'

'…you really do look exactly like The New Queen of England! But given that I haven't ordered any kind of novelty message, I am assuming you are some sort of – Anunnaki Candygram?'

DeVora snapped. 'Amethyst, the O'Renegades are on their way, and they will kill us all if we do no seal our business – !'

'Enough of this!' Ealo was losing patience. 'Release Vgyrl from the crystal cage!'

'Shut – up, Ealo!' The Queen protested. 'I have not finished making my entrance!'

Ealo stared at her, suddenly like a police dog sensing drugs.

'Field Marshal Xylata?'

The Queen was becoming frustrated. 'Well, yes! Couldn't you tell? It's a surprise – ' She turned back to Amy. ' – we've put our deal into operation, about taking human bodies. Or rather, not taking active human bodies of real people that exist in present time. If you take my meaning.' She grinned a regal grin. 'It's part of the Amethyst Covenant!'

'The… what?'

'The pact that Ymira Clan has made with Astral Humans. We thought about the Xylamy Accord, but it was a little on the nose, some people felt.' She eyed Amy doubtfully. 'Although, not all of course.'

DeVora stepped forward.

'I am human, I am not bonded to any alien race, I owe nothing to anyone other than the human people of my world and I am not beholden to any covenant, or accord, that that Amethyst Pyne has made on behalf of humanity –'

'Your people have a deals with the Draco, and the Cheneks!'

'Business deals! I do not allow them – *inside me!*' She turned slightly from Ealo and hissed. 'Like that – *pervert.*'

Ealo raised a pistol at her head. 'Your insults mean nothing to us! Your years are like weeks to us! We can kill any of you and you will return in another body with another personality that is still the you that has always been you and we will still make the same deal with the essence of you – the you that wants to deal, has to deal, will not stop dealing, and will – always – deal!'

'How dare you!' DeVora was livid. *'You – filthy – snake!'*

She was dead; he was pulling the trigger and nothing could stop it.

Until there was a sudden feeling that Amy recognised as depressurization – on the plane, on the way back from London, there had been a lightning storm and turbulence; the plane had dropped and everybody had been bounced up and down in their seats quite violently. This was kind of like that, but as though everything around her had been suddenly, massively widened and then condensed.

'Holy fuck…'

'They're coming –'

◊ *They're coming!* ◊

She knew where it was coming from – the same place the voice that had demanded ritual had come from – the same connection to this room from so far away it was unimaginable.

And then, they were there.

CHAPTER 61

In the middle of that wall, when her room had been completely her own, there had been a poster for the movie *Reservoir Dogs*. The echo of that remained – perhaps Orion had been watching her the whole time through that cosmic peephole – and it was there again now; with the five figures on the poster starting to move; breaking their iconic, frozen pose and walking again. Walking towards her, toward them, from far away, slowly now but gaining momentum.

The front door cracked, but nobody could move.

A Black Ops agent in the employ of the Orion Renegades, a 'Norion' as Styger seemed to have named them, entered. He too seemed to be walking in slow motion, like a moon-walk.

Had they taken the idea from her mind, from one of her, and her father's, favourite movies?

Did it mean anything or was it just… navigation?

She glanced back down the tunnel to the eighth plane of existence.

◊ *remember, Orion is eighth density; as old as the Elohim, the angels in seventh density; they are the ageless management of the cosmos, they greenlight every design, allocate its construction – anything less than a Sirian or Pleiadean is a tool to them, a foot-soldier, at best a random, precocious child; they do not care, as we care, but they are not evil, they are not psychopathic – until they turn Renegade, when they descend to the lower realms of eighth density… that's when they start making their own judgments; deconstructing and disassembling; and that's when people die…* ◊

'What's happening?' The Healer was terrified.

'Whatever it is, it's not something we're supposed to see.' The Dobber was grim, resigned. She thought she was going to die.

Amy was starting to remember something of the self she had become on the astral plane. She felt her own hand raise, open toward the two of them, then heard herself speak.

'Stay where you are, you're with me now.'

The Orions opened the movie poster, which wasn't there, like a door opening into the room, which wasn't there. They were dressed as the characters from the poster; but they were certainly not ordinary people in the suits.

The suits appeared – empty.

Animated by invisible entities she couldn't –

'You are the "Amethyst Pyne?"'

'Yes.'

And she was ripped apart.

THE PANDORA INHERITANCE

PART THREE

AMETHYST

CHAPTER 62

Five-or-so years ago, give or take, Amethyst Pyne had spontaneously jumped into battle and started a war.

…not that this had been her intent, of course.

However, back then, the charge had been instantly irresistible.

She had been made for this, it had seemed.

Been.

Was.

Was now.

But after it had started, after she had started it, the stream of engagement had not seemed to stop.

Had not stopped.

Was not stopping, even now.

And, neither had she.

For a while it had been fun.

Like a game.

An extremely intense, first person…

Whatever. Anyway.

The endless engagement on the astral plane had been dubbed…

Wait for it…

"The War of the Terrastral Territories."

Amethyst Pyne had been inventive and outrageous; bold and daring; aggressive, and victorious.

And so, the first time she had not been victorious, the first time she had actually been hurt, been physically wounded after several weeks in, it had come as a total shock.

CHAPTER 63

'What do you mean – I can get hurt?'

Xylata, "Leader of the Rebel Anunnaki Ymira Clan" as she had thought of her then, had looked at her strangely. Xylata had also been hurt during the battle, and was also being tended by a nervous Anunnaki medic.

'What do you mean; *what do you mean – I can get hurt?*'

'What do you think I mean? I mean; this is basically a dream, isn't it? I went through that portal, with the others, and now we're all asleep back on Earth, aren't we? This is just my astral body, doing this on the astral plane... right?'

Oh dear... the way Xylata had looked at her.

Then Amy remembered.

Someone... no, not someone. The Earth Goddess, Yelina; she had explained it all to them. All of that business with the Los Angeles earthquake felt like ages ago now...

But really, it actually hadn't been that long ago.

Amy was starting to see...

Time here wasn't the same.

Memory.

Thought itself.

None of those things were the same here.

There were... spirals, where there should have been straight lines.

Corkscrew waterslides in place of elevators.

Figuratively and literally.

And that was just for starters.

She wondered then, just briefly, how long she had actually been gone.

How long had she been away from Earth?

Her Earth?

Then she realized; now was not the time for that.

She was hurt, here and now.

But, even so; back then, at the start, Yelina had explained things.

That, while it was true for normal people that only their consciousness (in the form of their ghostly, glowing astral body) appeared on the astral plane when they either dreamed, or sometimes when they meditated (or even when they were medicated; usually self-medicated), when they fell, in any of those or several other ways, unconscious, this was not true for the few humans who had been changed by the genetic potion of the Pandora Sequence.

For them, when they consciously went into another realm; higher, lower, inner, outer, wherever, they took their physical bodies with them. They did not even need to be asleep or unconscious. Their physical bodies, in fact, changed as they travelled from dimension to dimension, in order to accommodate existence within the dimension to which they had travelled. Those physical shifts between dimensions were part of what the Pandora Sequence did to a human; had done to her.

In a way, it was who she was now, and why she was here.

'Oh.' Amy began. 'So, to all intents and purposes…'

'To what…?'

'To all intents and purp –'

'No!' Xylata laughed.

'What?'

'No, it's 'to all intensive purposes'. Don't you know how to speak your own language?'

Amy was quite sure. 'No it isn't.'

'I am very much certain that it is.'

The attending Anunnaki medic, whose name was Tzaebi, glanced nervously, but weirdly at Amy. They had all come to respect her now, perhaps almost to fear her, without her even trying. This just frustrated her even more.

'Look, I don't know how you Anunnaki speak English up here in the astral…'

'Out here.'

'What?'

'Out here. The astral plane penetrates, surrounds and extends throughout everything. It is not above the Earth. It is part of the Earth. Your Earth. If anything, it is coexistent, as are all the other planes within reach. Your idea that it is 'above' comes from ancient, two-dimensional maps, made many centuries ago in a dark time, when the collective consciousness of your race was extremely stunted.' Xylata then whispered. 'Do not use such analogies in front of the troops, it does not look good for their leader to seem so consciously stunted.'

Tzaebi glanced at her again, a slight nod, as though she should listen and take heed.

Thys frowned. She was starting to realize that Xylata was her friend; that the Ymira clan were behind her, that they wanted her to be… something.

This was Xylata's way, and she meant nothing by it, other than to help.

Thys took a deep breath.

'So, 'to all intensive purposes', when I am 'out here' on the astral plane…' Thys considered. '…or is it 'in' the astral plane?'

Xylata laughed.

'In?'

'Not 'in' then?'

There was a slight twitch about the scales Tzaebi's dark-pine lips.

Xylata kept laughing. 'No, not *in*.'

'Okay, okay. So when I *am here*…I am just the same as you? I am like a human Anunnaki?'

Xylata burst into hysterics.

'Oh, oh, Thys Pyne, you are very funny!'

'I am?'

'Very funny! Human Anunnaki! So funny!'

Amy looked to Tzaebi. She nodded, once, briskly, desperately trying to suppress a full smile.

'Wait; what did you just call me?'

'Thys Pyne.' Xylata beamed. 'Well, 'to all intents and purposes', as a 'Anunnaki Human', you must have an Anunnaki name. That sounds much more better.'

'More better? It's just 'better'. Not 'more better'. That's how children talk.'

This was too much for Tzaebi, who ran away giggling.

'Oh…' Xylata was laughing, quite happily. 'Thys Pyne.' She put her hand on Amy's shoulder. 'I hope you do not die.'

And then, strangely, Amethyst Pyne knew that for the first time in all her nineteen years, despite the love of her family, despite the camaraderie of The Pan, she had truly found somewhere to belong.

CHAPTER 64

Right from the start of the Terrastral War, Amy had become immediately embroiled, to the extent that she had become its central participant and symbolic epicentre practically overnight.

Pretty quickly, she had found that she was spending so much conscious, lucid time in the astral, where ordinary people slept and dreamed, that her actual, human, three-dimensional dream life was no longer serving its natural function; which was to help her make sense of her actual life.

Amy equally as quickly decided that this was…

…fairly ironic.

Regardless, the upshot was that she was not processing her thoughts properly, and that this had become a problem. She was making poor decisions, forgetting things, and becoming overly emotional at times when even she knew that it was unwarranted.

In ordinary life, this would be dangerous enough.

In a war…

In a strange realm…

In a time when…

Wait.

She wasn't a late-twentieth century movie trailer.

She was just… *tired*.

So tired that… well, now she had been injured.

It hadn't been good. Then again, it hadn't been *that bad*.

In fact, it could have been much worse.

(Or, as they said in Anunnaki-speak; 'could of been much worst.')

Astral bodies were bodies, but like time here, they weren't the same.

That time, Amy and Xylata had been injured when a massive

school of pirate cutlasses with frog eyes had swarmed through the under-ocean wreck of an archetypal Bond-villain complex and mass-teleported into the arcade game forest where she and her troops were just setting up mushroom beds for the night. The frog cutlasses hadn't been spotted because all the point-sentries had been spiked with circuit-bread weed-pies and could only see yesterday; the frog-eyed swords had been certain enough of themselves though, and shocking enough to Amy, and the others upon first sight, that when they had seemed to spew out of a gaping, angry-red butthole with giant squid teeth, they had actually instilled panic throughout the whole camp and made them all believe that they were actually underwater and drowning in chowder, despite that being impossible on any sane level within an astral ocean.

The astral blades of the frog cutlasses had also actually cut through astral bodies.

Several troops had taken the hit for Amy as living shields, but one had found its target.

Upon being hit she had instantly found herself gapped back into her childhood bedroom at her old family house, screaming in agony and terror, with an antique privateer's sword penetrating completely though her left flank, terrifying a teenage boy who had simply been trying to crack his neighbour's wi-fi password. She'd had the wherewithal to gap immediately back to the astral, where Xylata was in the process of pulling a similar sword from her own leg, just as Tzaebi and the Ymira clan medics had descended upon them both.

It wasn't that much, not in the astral, and the wound had been easily healed.

But that had been enough.

In the aftermath analysis it became apparent the attack had been long-planned, taken a lot of enemy power, and had clearly been aiming for a war-ending, seven-chakra, ego-death, spiritual kill-shot that would have reincarnated both herself and Xylata back down to Earth with no recollection at all of their previous existence.

Game over, Ymira clan; game over, astral revolution.

War of the Terrastral Territories; nuked from orbit.

And Amy had been so worn out that she had not seen it coming, not even a bit.

CHAPTER 65

Having realized all of this quite early on in proceedings, Amy had sought out, found with surprising ease, and begun to consult often with the recently returned Suzie Saturn.

'A seven-chakra, ego-death, spiritual kill-shot…?' Suzie had grumbled, nodding, frowning. 'Huh. Get your head around that one.'

Amy grimaced. 'I don't like the sound if it much…'

Suzy was working it out. 'Ass, pussy, gut, heart, throat, third-eye and crown.' She nodded, looking angry. 'Nice.'

Amy nodded. 'Basically.'

'So coordinated, too. Determined little bastards.'

'About a dozen of our girls jumped right in the way, they saved me. It was like… rocket-powered underwater ballet. They all lived; it was a group effort. We gave them all medals.'

'We?'

'Me and Xylata. She's okay. Like, really okay. We're in charge now. Somehow.'

Suzie, being a friend of her family, had welcomed the regular chats with the girl who she now saw as her astral superstar 'niece', coming to her wise rock-and-roll aunt for sage advice on being 'astrally famous'.

'They call it the Seven Out, like craps.'

'Do they now?' Suzie considered a few seconds before calling it. 'I think I'd rather be back in the black starcophagus.'

It was a huge relief, speaking to Suzie like this. Not only was she the only other conscious human who had experienced anything similar to what Amy was going through, she was also the only nonparent elder that Thys knew well enough to speak with about something this strange, not to mention oddly personal, who wouldn't completely freak out, and try to ground her, or send her to her room or something. Especially given her father's earliest reactions to the notion of her becoming 'hurt'.

'Just a few days after this last time I got hurt…'

'You got yourself hurt again?'

'Yeah…' Amy nodded. 'A few times now; they've really stepped up their game the last week or so.'

'Uh huh.'

It was nice that her rock-and-roll astral auntie pretended to be nonchalant, in exactly the way Mitch or Heather or even Janine would be unable to.

'Anyway, just after that, I started to realize that I was no longer… defragging. Or deciphering, or… sorting through my shit while I slept anymore, you know? Like, working through my actual, waking life…?'

Suzie shrugged. 'Because you are living your waking life in a physical body, on the astral plane, where you would usually go to dream. Right?'

'Yes! I live, and work, and fight, and kick back and… everything else, on the astral plane. I – sleep, physically sleep, on the astral plane!'

'Yeah. I had that. You're no longer reflecting upon your general conscious existence on the Terrestrial Plane from the perspective of another realm, like the Astral Realm.'

'I'm not?'

'No. And that ain't how it's supposed to be, kid.'

'No… I'm not, am I? And, it isn't, is it?'

Amy suddenly understood; everything became clear. She was a physical part of the Terrastral Territories now; she lived a physical life on the astral plane, like she had emigrated to another country or something. To the Astral Realm. She breathed, ate and slept…

But… she hadn't been actually dreaming.

Not properly.

Not – unconsciously.

In fact, now she thought about it; now she actually stopped and properly reflected; even when she was sleeping, she knew she was sleeping, and dreaming. And therefore, strangely enough, even though she was always in the astral, always in the world of dreams, she was never, actually, technically, dreaming.

'Oh my God and Goddess. All my dreams are lucid dreams. I am *permanently lucid*!'

'Kid, calm down, it's okay, we've all been there!'

'All?'

'Well, I have. And now you have. All two of us. Dig it?'

'I...?'

'Kid, it's simple!'

The iconic rock star made a sudden booming declaration to her warrior-general niece.

'What you need; is – !'

With a finger pointed to the sky; wide-eyed, wild-haired, and in a thunderous baritone, she declared:

'*– a decent mattress!*'

Then she calmed right down.

'Or something like that. Bed, mattress, bunker, nest, hole; you'll figure it out, kid. Whatever's best for ya.'

'I do? I will?'

'Sure you will! Actually – that's it! Exactly! Just – will it!'

'Will what?'

Suzie sighed; realizing that yes, she would need to 'spell it out' for her.

'Pyne-kid, you just need something, somewhere, hidden away. Something, somewhere, *protected*, where you can sleep, and nobody knows you're there – or where to find you. That's all it is. If you're lucid in the astral, people can, technically, track you down and find you, and they will disturb your sleep. They will find your astral body walking about, trying to get lost in all the iconographic architecture and... I dunno, ask for your fuckin' autograph or something.'

'Seriously?'

'Seriously? Believe me – it happens. You think about it; what happens when you lay down to sleep these days; here in fourth density?'

Thys did. She thought about it.

'I… sort of float around… in my astral body…' She looked up at Suzie. Looked her straight in the eyes. '… and socialize!'

'See?'

'With people; normal people from Earth! And, troops, and other Ymira! And… just people, from everywhere! Like I'm… *not even asleep!*'

Suzie laughed. 'There you go, kiddo!'

'Suzie, I'm not sleeping!'

'I know! You just said that.'

'But – really!'

'I – really – know.'

'But…' Amy frowned. 'I can't!'

'You can't?'

'I've tried!'

'How hard?'

'Very hard, Suzie! I go back, and I go to sleep in the real world…'

'Real world? You mean, back to third density? The boring old Earth Plane?'

'Yeah, there – I go back and sleep there, in my normal bed, like, a normal night's sleep on Earth, but then I forget all this!'

'All this? What? This? Here? The Astral Realm?'

'And what I do here; what I've done here! I come back and I don't remember anything for days. I have to be re-briefed and re-minded and… it becomes a whole production just to bring me back up to speed! And then I'm so exhausted, all I want to do –'

'Is sleep, yeah, I get it.' Suzie nodded, grimly. 'I know. I lost a metric fuck-ton of lyrics and hooks and even… *old school pen and paper ideas* – in just that exact same way.'

'I mean, I come back and I've forgotten half of the plans I made with Xylata and the Ymira. Or, what happened on a whole bunch of yesterdays here.'

'I know, kid, and I hear ya, believe me. You live here, ya sleep here; ya probably die here in the end.'

'What?'

'Well, you are fighting a war here, aren't ya?'

'I…'

'Forget that for now. Wipe it from your mind.'

'But I just said that I don't want to –'

'I mean, figuratively, kid! Jeez. Okay. The thing we need to focus on now is; you need a place to sleep in the astral, on the astral plane –'

'I knew it…!'

'What?'

'Nothing.'

'Okay…?'

'It's just – *I knew I was dangerous.*'

'Everything's dangerous in the right hands with the right application, Pyne-kid. Don't sweat it or you'll lose your grip. Especially here.'

Thys's shoulders slumped. 'Okay. I guess.'

Suzie pressed on. '…you need a *private place*, in the Astral Realm, where you *actually sleep*, that's all! And trust me kid; you *absolutely can fall asleep here*, actually fall asleep, and actually dream. So that your astral body just goes wandering unconsciously and randomly like normal. Nobody will know you; nobody will give a shit; it's the opposite of *Cheers*. Nobody knows your name. It's *Jeers*.' She sang a moment. '*You gotta go / where nobody gives / a shiiiiiit.*' Then she gave an enormous smile. 'Very therapeutic!'

'Sounds… like Heaven!'

'Well, I'm sure it does to you, right now. You probably haven't been alone, or stopped thinking, for… how long you been here anyway?'

'…months…?'

'How many months?'

'How long since that movie premiere and the red carpet?'

'Jesus, kid. Do you need this or what? How long since you got laid?'

'Ummm…'

'Oh Mary, Mother O'Mine; you need to *think about it?*'

'I –'

'You even – takin' care of business?'

'Business? Of course!'

'Really?'

'Yes, really!'

'Okay. Okay, then; woah-man do you really need this or what? Just find your secret place, Pyne-kid. Find it, and kip out, and trust me; before long you'll just be another wandering go-go.'

'Go-go?'

'That's what I call 'em; us, when we dream. Ego-ghosts; go-gos. Wandering go-go-schmucks, floating around, running down corridors and bumping into fuckheads you went to school with and dipshits you didn't even know you had a crush on in the first place, never finding closure…'

'I will…?' Thys was so happy to hear this.

'Sure. Why not? Sometimes you even bring back some inspiration.'

'They do…' Thys stated quietly, helplessly. '…they really do. I mean; as soon as I sleep here, as soon as I float away and go wandering, they just find me. I never realised, not really. And they want to ask me questions. I'm lucid, and…' She suddenly stared, wide-eyed at Suzie. 'Oh my Goddess! I am – *so sleep deprived!*'

'Okay, we're at the going round in circles part again.' She shook her head, then stared her suddenly right in the eyes. *'No shit, kid!'*

'I haven't dreamed properly – slept properly – since I've been here!'

'You already said that – you're so tired you're repeating things back to me that you said to me, that I repeated back to you. Again. I think.'

'I am?'

'I dunno, kid. I lost track. We should have had this conversation in normal bar, on Earth. Like *Cheers*. Wait. Did we have the *Cheers* talk already?'

'Wait. Aren't we in a normal bar…?'

'Wow, kid. You really need a solid eight. Make that a solid eighty.' Suzie threw her arms up. 'Great, now I'm doing it!' She leaned into her niece. 'It's human rule number one, kid! We all need our sleep! Perchance to dream, you know?'

Amy tensed and looked around.

They were no longer in a bar; they were sitting on a long tree branch, legs dangling, looking down on a dense jungle, high enough so that they could see that there were thousands of people in the jungle; walking, running, bolting; looking, talking, screaming; alone and calm, bumping into each other, fleeing from each other, fleeing from nothing; feeling from themselves; fleeing from something massive and dark and deadly; running to find something they didn't need, running to find a treasure, running to find nothing and everything and everything in between; running to find each other, running to find themselves. There were children playing, teenagers lost, adults hunting, and adults fucking, and adults completely bewildered about how they got here in the first place, some late for work, or school, or that big event, with no pants on.

'Oh my God!' Thys looked down and assessed them all. 'I was down there once!'

'In the Twilight Woods?'

'No… I mean…' Wait. Had she? 'Yes, yes, I was – and in the Infinite House Party, and the Platform To All Stations, and on and on; everyone I meet, they just want me to make endless decisions for them; decisions they should be making for themselves! Like I'm some kind of… giant Tarot Card Reader In The Sky!'

Suzie flinched. 'Hey. Mind if I take that? That might be a song title. Or maybe lyrics?' She hummed a quick tune that seemed to simply come to her, like a puppy she'd called out of nowhere. Then Thys saw; there was actually a puppy, biting Suzie Saturn's silver shoelaces on her black lace-up boots. 'I'm gonna take it anyway, okay?'

Thys shrugged again, and mumbled. 'I don't care.'

'Cool.'

Suzie picked up the puppy and stuffed it into the breast of her baggy leather jacket, where it poked out its little head and started gnawing at her shirt.

Thys sat up. 'The thing is Suzie… I guess I actually *can help all these people*. You know? I can help them make better or more informed decisions, but… just, not all the time, and not like this…' She yawned. 'Not all night, every night, all at once!'

'Now you sound like a real rock star. Just don't take amphetamines, and don't take sleeping pills. Trust me.'

'I do.'

'I know. So, go build a bed. In an astral shack, on a dream island, under cloud covers, in the sleepy snow. Or in the desert, in a bunker, under bed-rock and sand, man! Behind a nuclear blast door! Build a place from scratch if you have to. But you gotta do it. Ya hear me kid? You can't help all these restless dreamer people if you can't help yourself; that's a fact. That's one of those 'Golden Rule' things. From the Bible!'

'Really?'

'I dunno, kid. Sure, why not?'

Thys nodded, lost in her own thoughts.

'Build it from scratch?'

'Sure. You're good at that kind of thing, or so I hear.'

'What kind of thing?'

'Making things appear in the astral. Building, manifesting, attracting and focusing. Shouldn't be too hard for ya.'

Amy, or Thys… she wasn't sure which one she was any more…

…which ever, was quite taken with the idea.

'I can see you're quite taken with the idea. They call you Thys now, right?'

'Yeah.'

'So, there's just one trick to it all, so-called Thys; and it's a good one.'

'And that is?'

♪ *you have to trick – yourself* ♪

'Meaning?'

Then Thys's mind topsy-turvied. Suzie's lips hadn't moved.

'Wait, Suzie, what did you just do?'

Suzie grinned, very beautifully, a fully rock-star portrait for the ages grin.

'What? Haven't found that yet?'

'Found…?'

'I thought Mendoza shook it outa ya?'

'He spoke to me like that, but…?'

♪ *meaning, kid – not even you can know where this place you create actually is…* ♪ 'You dig?' ♪ *It has to be secret, even from yourself!* ♪

'But…'

Thys saw something in Suzie's eyes that told her not to say anything about the – inner-outer voice – she was using.

What did they call it in sci-fi? Telepathy?

'But… how can I not…?'

♪ *you have to start from nothing… from nowhere… as no one* ♪

Thys didn't quite understand – but she tried to speak the way Suzie was speaking.

☾ *Nothing? No one?* ☽

♪ *oh wow kid, what a stunning astral voice you have!* ♪

☾ *Thankyou! Yours sounds like music!* ☽

♪ *and this is the first time you've used it? It sounds like the voice of… it sounds like you really belong here, kid…* ♪

☾ *really?* ☽

♪ *look kid, you gotta find this place to sleep; then you'll find all sorts of other things here, thing's you're too blasted to even think about might be there…* ♪

☾ *I still don't…* ☽

♪ *…you find the place, then you put a thing there. A thing only you know, only you understand, and only you will see. Something, one* *thing, you will never forget, and nobody else will ever really see the way you see it. Unique. Okay?* ♪

'You've done this?'

♪ *…of course I've done this. I'm not crazy am I? You think I'm telling you all this for fun?* ♪ Then she frowned. ♪ *Of course; I didn't realize I had done this, this thing with a nothing seed, until you just asked me; and, I did just name it a 'nothing seed' then because it needed a name, because it needs to be explained to someone in human terms for the first time. Ever…* ♪

'Ever?'

'Yeah. I think. Ever in this now, anyway.'

'This now? Wow.'

'But that's how we learn, isn't it? Especially about ourselves.'

'Is it? How?'

'How else? By getting interviewed, kid!'

'I suppose…' Thys nodded. 'I think I'm going to have to – go. Lose myself. Get somewhere – get nowhere… without me knowing how I got there.'

'There you go, kid – you got it! Metaphorically speaking.'

'Metaphorically – of course.'

'Of course.'

'Now let's get a drink. Talking to you makes my head hurt.'

'In a good way?'

'A good way? Sure kid, why not?'

CHAPTER 66

The thing that everyone now called 'The Amethyst Palace' had developed slowly.

First, Thys had done as Suzie had instructed.

She had gone to a Ymira meditation spot, which was basically an automatic gap to flat rock, surrounded by foliage, beneath direct sunlight...

'Anunnaki meditation is sunbaking...!'

And there, to the best of her abilities, she did as she had been trained to do by her yoga instructor one afternoon several years ago, and did her best to ignore her thoughts and contemplate nothingness... and think of nowhere.

It didn't work.

So she gave it some time, re-read the best books, listened to guided audios, and did her best to go within and quiet her mind, observe the silence, and become... no-one.

And after a while, just for a second; she had.

She had been in nothingness.

She had been nowhere.

She had been no one.

And then, within that, she had panicked.

Her mind, her ego, had become instantly terrified; and pulled her right back into her psychology again. However, in that fraction of an astral millisecond, after the nothingness, and just as the panic had come, the 'nothing seed' had been the thing, the first thing, that had given her comfort, and memory, and *something to hold onto;* when she had realized that she had been nothing, nowhere and no-one.

When her mind had panicked, and reached out for something to secure itself, it might have been a nipple, it might have been a teddy bear, it might have been her Daddy's hand.

She had laughed, when she had realized what it was; what her nothing seed actually was. This nothing seed, this basis for something, had appeared out of nowhere, when Amy-Thys had been no-one. But now it was something, and she was someone again. She had remembered, straight away, that it had appeared with a purpose; to answer her need for a slumber sanctuary.

She had thought of a bed.

A secret bed.

She had thought childishly, innocently, of a bed made of clouds, protected by angels.

And there it had been; billowing into existence right before her. Expansive wings, extending all around; forming a space. Spherical walls, but with a translucent floor, just below the central circumference, that she could walk upon, up to the side of the bed, and so that she slept right in the middle of the space. The bed had short steps leading up to the side, and was like a giant cradle. Like a boat, sailing on the clouds. Then suddenly, but slowly, peacefully but surprisingly, the *angelcloudbed* was right in the middle of the *silverbluemoonroom* and the *silverbluemoonroom* was right in the middle of the *allthelovelybigquietemptyrooms* and the *allthelovelybigquietemptyrooms* were enclosing the *silverbluemoonroom* but surrounded by the *mobiusspiralstarbalcony*, looking over the *gossamerspacemoat*…

…and so on.

Thys had been in, and asleep, and dreaming, before she had even known she had succeeded. And for the first time in ever-so-long, she dreamed a normal dream.

– of being late for high school exams.

CHAPTER 67

Just as time worked differently in the astral dimension, physicality was fluid there as well.

'But if certain things manifest often enough...' Thys had explained a few times, to a few select people who cared to understand. '...they become reliable. It's how the astral temples work; they're tied to reliable, repetitive symbols. Imagine how worship and manifestation could work, if we knew how to do it properly? Without intervention, and misdirection, from psychopathic astral alien invaders? No offense.'

Thys had been thinking about it, quite a lot in this regard.

She knew that she had no idea where she slept, no idea where the *angelcloudbed* was situated; just as Suzie had recommended. She didn't care; she didn't want to know; and she knew that was a good thing. She had slept very well for many nights in a row now, and for the first time in ages felt focussed, healthy and even sometimes, on her very best days, good and powerful.

'None taken. And, I know you don't know where it is...' Xylata told her. 'We've looked.'

'You've what?'

'Well, not we. Me. I have looked. And, if I can't find you, nobody can.'

'You looked?'

'For a long time. I still try, once and a while.'

(Thys said nothing.)

'You're not saying anything. That means you are pissy with me.'

'I am not 'pissy' with you. Who told you that word?'

'Nobody. Certainly not Suzie.'

'Suzie taught you to use that word?'

'No.'

(Thys said nothing.)

'Yes.'

'You think it's in the middle of The Amethyst Palace, don't you?'

'Everyone does. That's where Draco assassins go looking for you.'

'Assassins? Plural?'

'No.'

(Thys said nothing.)

'Yes.'

'I thought it was just the one assassin, just that one time?'

'There might have been more than one.'

'Might have?'

'No. None. None more.'

(Thys went to put on her 'say nothing' face, but –)

'Twelve!'

'Twelve?'

'Yes, twenty.'

'Twenty?'

'Five.'

Thys huffed. 'Well, is it twelve, twenty, or five?'

'Both.'

'Both?'

'All!'

'All?'

'Twelve different attempts, twenty-five assassins altogether.'

Thys shook her head.

'It's okay. They won't find me.'

Xylata nodded.

'I know. I've looked.'

CHAPTER 68

It was there, still, where she slept to this day…

☾ Wait – where am I? What's…? This has already happened, this was before I came back this time! ☽
☰ She is resisting ☰
■ She cannot ■
☰ Yet she is ☰

…after years in the astral; where she kept her own counsel, maintained her own private sanctuary and inner sanctum, and where nobody knew where she was.

The *silverbluemoonroom* was a little room (she thought of it that way, when really, when she thought about it some more, it was quite a big moon… room. She meant room. Moon?)

It had of course initially materialized from her mind's-eye-idea of a child's nursery, but it had since evolved into something far more ornate, with deep, dark but vividly navy-blue night-sky walls, speckled with white stars and silver skirtings and cornices, shining brass fittings and elaborate wrought-iron spiral staircases and rich-timber balconies. In the little (but not really little) *silverbluemoonroom* she had dreamed into existence for herself, the little cloud she had made for herself, her bed, stayed permanently aloft, floating right in the middle of the broadly spherical room, above the strong, polished, gleaming wooden floor boards that extended across the middle, and the rolled-out magic carpets that floated peacefully, undulating softly all around; aloft beside all the bookcases along the balconies, and below the starlit observatory (that led out to the *mobiusspiralstarbalcony*) which nobody, not anybody, could ever see into, and only she could ever see out of;

out to the *gossamerspacemoat…*

…and all the stars, out on the astral plane, across the Astral Realm.

    ● She cannot be allowed ●
    ≡ She cannot be allowed to stop ≡
    ■ Stopping her is everything ■
    ○ Stopping her will end everything ○

But the best thing, Thys thought, and the one thing she could never tell anyone, was… that she could see quite well from here. She could see out, but they could not see in.

    ≡ She can see out but we cannot see in – astounding! ≡
    ● Where is she? She is hidden from us! This is intolerable! ●
    ≡ The fact that she can hide must remain hidden ≡
    ○ She must remain secure ○
    ■ Bring her before Obsidian! ● Resolve this! ● Now! ■
    ○ ≡ we concur ≡ ○

CHAPTER 69

'What's happening?' DeVora cried out. 'This is – outra…

As soon as the men had arrived through the *Reservoir Dogs* poster, Amy had started to shudder. Nobody had been able to move to help her.

First, blood had streamed out of her nose and mouth with the speed of lightning, and flooded into the first of the black suits. Within the ghostly garment (weirdly complete with white shirt, black tie and black lace-ups) there had appeared to be some kind of body forming, some kind of being – made of Amy's blood.

Then, all of the remaining water had been drained from her; at first, for a few seconds, sweat had been sucked, streaming from her now anaemic form, then it had swirled around her body and been siphoned off into another suit.

Then, all her remaining flesh had disseminated through her skin, and into another suit, forming a gross, brown, muddy, mushy being, who stood third in the row, beside the water body in the second suit.

Finally, her body simply vanished, with the rest of her becoming gaseous, and filling the last suit.

What remained of her, standing there in the abandoned living room apartment of a place she had once thought of as home, was a glowing astral body; a kind of glistening, bright-blue outline of Amy, now facing down a bizarre audience of four grotesque, besuited humanoids, created collectively out of her own flesh, blood, water and bone; the most nightmarish talent show she could imaagine.

'What the…?'

The four suits simply stood there, like soulless judges, waiting for their cue to begin the show. From somewhere she remembered someone, someone powerful, telling her that her audition was over.

Then what the fuck was this?

…geee…ous!' DeVora moaned in seeming slow motion.

Amy was stunned. 'What is happening? Why have you done this to me!?'

'She's right, this is outrageous!'

Amy looked around.

Everyone else was frozen, except Xylata, who stood there in her true Anunnaki astral body. The body of the young Queen Elizabeth II had collapsed on the floor of her apartment.

☾ Xylata! What the – ? Who – ? ☽

◊ …there's no point conspiring to speak without them listening, Thys Pyne; they can hear us however we speak ◊

The cloud-like person spoke first.

'We do this, all the time. So very quickly. People never notice. But it informs us of all we ever need to know about your being. We scanned your mind for symbols, to which you would be able to relate – we believe representation of the four states that your civilization refers to as "the basic states of matter" would be best. I am Cloudia. I am gaseous. I believe you are important.'

Amy and Xylata exchanged glances.

'Thankyou…?'

The muddy, fleshy body spoke next. 'I am Stonic – I am solid. I believe it is important that you are erased from history along with all your friends and everything you have ever influenced.'

'Oh.'

Amy and Xylata again exchanged glances.

'Fuck… you?. I… guess?'

'I am Bloodbold. This is Floodfold. We also disagree, fundamentally. Floodfold is liquid. She wishes you destroyed. I am plasma, and I wish your lineage to dominate. We have requested final adjudication from Obsidian.'

'Obsidian?'

Amy looked down at her astral body.

'He gave you permission to do this? Not even the Draco are low enough to trap someone in the astral without their body…!'

Xylata cleared her throat. 'We did actually trap Suzie Saturn, and Holland Pankhurst. They will do it to you, if you're not very clear with them.'

Amy was agog, but turned back.

'Why?' It was an absolute demand.

Stonic, her fleshy self-confessed enemy, took one step forward. 'We do not need to explain! We created this galaxy!'

'Upon the request – ' She reconsidered her words. '…within the agency… of a higher being who made sure we had free will – correct? How do I have free will here? You've stolen my body and bent it to your own sick will!'

Floodfold stepped forward beside Stonic; she got the sense that Floodfold was feminine somehow, Stonic masculine. Bizarre incarnations of water and flesh, allies in her desired eradication from reality.

'Her every thought is a corruption of divinity.'

Bloodbold folded his arms. 'She will learn.'

Stonic turned to him. 'She already has allies, massing. You see them, sniffing and licking and pissing and ejaculating, all around her; her entire family, making alliances with matter, with our matter, that they have no wisdom to manage, that will destroy everything!'

Floodfold nodded, once, her face rippling with anger.

'I support the acceleration of the Karma Forge. There is no further use for this world – the humans must be dispersed; this planet will re-people itself, perhaps with canine or feline. Obsidian will see sense – we will return in thirty thousand years; maybe there will be an avian race. It almost happened one other time here; I have not seen one for many millennia.'

'…just; no more monkeys…' Stonic uttered, sounding exhausted.

Suddenly the two turned as one to Cloudia, as though some sudden signal had come from her.

Amy had heard nothing.

'No…' Cloudia uttered, softly but with great trepidation.

It was not, Amy learned in that moment, at all comfortable or reassuring to hear an ancient and still extremely potent demiurge react with anything like anxiety.

'What?' Stonic demanded; neither, Amy also realised, one quick moment later, was it okay to hear a demiurge become testy.

The other three all seemed to receive the message at once.

They all cried out.

CHAPTER 70

Amy's little cloud bed reminded her of one of those art installations that science-artists made where it somehow rained inside, and only inside, a Manhattan loft, even though it was sealed in, and sunny outside.

It was there, the little cloud she went to, every night. No more constant streams of little 'hope I'm not disturbing you' rat-a-tat-tats upon the giant wooden storybook bedroom door in the Amethyst Palace, no more ghostly invasions; no matter how innocent or spiritual or presumptuously grateful, of people who required her assistance or advice.

Just slumber, and dreams.

Sweet slumber, sweet dreams.

There was even a soft, heavenly glow that seemed to emanate from the side of the cloud bed, where a night light would be. Would be, had the presence of an actual night light not reminded Thys, almost unconsciously, of an actual bedside table, and an actual alarm clock on the bedside table, and an alarm itself; of pressure and anxiety, and what her life might have been, without the Pandora Sequence, in the real world.

But there were no such things as those stupid things in the *angelcloudbed,* within the reality of the *silverbluemoonroom,* where she slept in innocence, surrounded by an enormous but not at all intimidating library of volume upon volume of wise, satisfying, practical answers to all of the questions she would ever have.

And yet, the *silverbluemoonroom* also seemed to have special properties that worked to her practical, real world advantage; something – again – about time being different in the astral. The *angelcloudbed* seemed to allow Thys to sleep one or two average-length, ninety-minute sleep cycles and, in doing so, restore her completely, to the equivalent energy levels of a full, deep, uninterrupted eight hour slumber in the ordinary astral. And so, there, in and upon her cloud, she could relax enough to allow her physical form, her flesh and blood mind, the regenerative power that sleep provided; to literally dream within the dream world.

Mind you, it had been from there that she'd had… would have? …the bright idea to contact Linh and Brooke and Emily…

(in… around five, six years? …or so, she thought. When the astral war ends and the other thing starts…)

The Sirens…!

…which she would do on a whim, as soon as she woke, in two thousand and nineteen… or twenty.

Whenever that was supposed to happen…

So… so what? So what that the ideas she dreamed up there weren't always that great? Even if they were, juxtapositionally, always important?

It was hers, and it was magic. And she loved and treasured it without even thinking about it. Indeed, it seemed as though that central core of isolation, that keyhole thread through to the Astral Realm and back, might now have become a vital part of discovering what the hell was happening to her, and her friends and family, and for that she felt another level of gratitude entirely toward the little (but not actually that little at all) room, and its powers.

But technically…

She did not know about some of that.

Not just yet.

Time, you see, works differently in the astral.

CHAPTER 71

' – rageous! Utterly outrageous and I will not – '

Amy screamed in sheer, savage agony as her body was pulled apart, atom by atom, repurposed, then came back together again, all in the space of a millisecond.

Like, really screamed; she had never felt anything like it, just for a second, but it was so terribly, mind-killingly acute, that as her throat had reformed, she had felt the air rush up and her chords retract and the shrill, sharp scream of agony had shot from her body like a trapped ghoul that had just been freed from her bowels through her gullet.

She fell to her knees.

'Fa–ar – fu–cking – ou–ut!'

Beside her, Xylata, in her Queen body, was getting up again. But instead of fully rising, she crawled over to Amy, put one hand on her shoulder and used the other to steady her as she stood. The feel of Xylata's hands on her bare skin, on her shoulder and under her rib cage, felt like a slap to sunburn – but she knew she had to hide it, to grit her teeth and stand.

'I should never have come back to this shitfull plane of existence!'

Xylata rolled her regal eyes. 'If I only had a dollar...'

Everyone else was still there; the sole figure in the blue robes; Ealo, his advisor and the other four burnt-orange henchmen; DeVora; the mysterious trio in burgundy robes; and the trio of helmeted race drivers. But now, there was something else happening. The four suits that had, for what Amy now recognised to have been less than a millisecond, trapped her and extracted and distilled physical form, had appeared before everyone in the room. They were empty, ghostly, but still upright, and slowly being filled with energy, with matter. But this time, thankfully, not from her.

'Who are they?' DeVora demanded. 'Where are they coming from?'

Something dawned on Amy then.

'Where's…?'

'What?' Xylata wanted keenly to know.

'The fifth suit?'

'What?'

'There were five suits, coming down the tunnel…'

Immediately, she noticed that there was another man present. He was camouflaged; he blended in exactly with the pale cream colour of the blank wall. Then he moved, and he was tall, and gaunt, in an expensive cream suit. He had a gold necklace and rings; a gold and white and beige tie and waistcoat, and white-golden hair. These things were forming, Amy realised, as she looked. Becoming real as she accepted them. He looked like that actor who her father was always saying would be an excellent Doctor in *Doctor Who*, but was too famous now, or too old, or had turned it down or –

Because this new, fifth Orion representative had taken that notion from her mind as well.

As an insult to her, and her father.

Involuntarily, DeVora stepped back.

'Are you – Obsidian?'

Amy had to wonder if she was beginning to regret her decision to remain, her show of power; this was now, she was sure, way above her pay-grade.

The new man looked at the four suits as the physical forms emerged within them; as Amy had guessed, two women and two men. Two, Floodfold and Stonic, wanted to kill her, and two, Bloodbold and Cloudia, wanted to save her – but she did not remember which were which.

'Obsidian could not be here. He does not see the threat of the Pyne-Everett manifestation.'

Amy's heart sunk. 'Oh. Fuck.'

'What?' DeVora demanded.

Ealo uttered. 'He is High Orion – but he is not Obsidian. Obsidian can be reasoned with, but this one –'

'Is going to kill us all…'

They all looked back behind them; The Dobber, and The Healer were still there.

It was The Healer who'd spoken.

Amy looked at her – there was something about her. Something she wanted to protect. She looked up at The Dobber. The woman cursed under her breath and pulled back her hood, removing the voice synthesiser.

'I'm not going out anonymously. Fuck this gig, I knew I should have blown it off!'

As the psychic Dobber on the squeaky stair revealed her face, Amy saw a very striking young woman with a short, shoulder-length, bright blonde shag cut. Her large eyes were so blue that Amy could see how blue they were from where she was standing, well away and below.

Xylata stared up at her, her royal eyes assessing keenly.

'I know you – I saw you many times when I was possessing Sapphire Edge! You work with Heather Everett!'

'My name is Mirabelle Contrelle!'

Amy stared a second.

'People call me Belle! Amy, we've met; briefly, but we've met!!'

'You were spying on me!' Xylata proceeded to accuse. ' – on us – on Sapphire – with Heather! What are you doing here?'

Amy was stunned.

'What are any of you doing here?'

The new, white-gold man had spoken suddenly; not so much demanding an answer with his tone as making any tone obsolete.

'Obsidian's Second Orion Directorate has run its course. I am here to disband, dismantle and reassign it. Before this section of evolution is complete, Obsidian will be superseded and retired. He has been here too long. Become enmeshed and involved.

Gone native. The Karma Forge Equation will soon be balanced, formalized and activated; I intend to oversee the great purge myself, to govern the exclusivity. You decide here and now if you want –'

Amy stepped forward. 'Who are you? What do I – ?'

'Gordian. I can already see that you will accept no deal that I offer.'

He was right – but she hated his arrogance.

'Amethyst Sarah-Jane Pyne, you are forming a renegade consciousness cluster that will lead to an imbalance of the karmic reservoir of this world, establishing a rogue trajectory that will be irreversible –'

'Good!'

'You are… misguided?' Gordian pursed his lips and his jaw rolled from side to side. 'Obsidian has spent too many millennia of energy balancing psychopathic impulses, and fending off catastrophes; corralling your species' propensity for self-destructive violence into theatres and stages of war – well now we are going to set you free; we are going to give you free reign over your own DNA, your own ability to replicate, your own limitless growth, and see an end to it. Or a new beginning – but the odds are radially against it.'

'I'll take those odds.'

She desperately wanted to add, *'motherfucker'*.

'No you won't. They are infinitesimally small, even by what I am able to observe as small. This process will be a natural and useful end for your species; the last days of the planet known as Earth, inhabited by the genetic cluster known as Earthing Humanity, Iteration Five, will continue to be a highly valuable and instructive karmic location in which to manifest or even incarnate, if there is still time – a space to learn, to practice endurance; to experience loss and sacrifice; hope and longing and desire. Your world will sink, with a less than infinitesimal opportunity to swim, and with that edge, these experiences will be pure, unmanufactured, untainted and unique.'

'You're talking about... just letting us – destroy ourselves? And – higher beings incarnating here as we do? To – learn a lesson? As a – teachable, cosmic, high-karmic moment?'

'See how easily she comes to the realization?'

'You fucking monster!'

Gordian ignored her. 'Do you not see, "Human"? How this end is held within the minds of all "Humans"? That it therefore must end this way? That it must come to pass, as this?'

'As... *This.*'

Something clicked.

◊ *Thys* ◊

'Ingenious!' Ealo nodded, and smiled as his burnt-orange followers seemed to exchange telepathic glances beneath the robes. 'The highest bidders for the most excruciating karmic purge...!' His nondescript companion smiled sharply as they exchanged nods of agreement. 'We would like parlay; we desire accord with Orion.'

'He... is not... true Orion... anymore.'

They had almost forgotten about the four suits. They were emerging as people, at least, humanoid in form, but it was difficult to tell what kind of people. The transition seemed as agonising for them as the reinstitution of her form had been for Amy, but theirs was occurring in slow motion.

She remembered her father telling her that Misha, the Sirian he had encountered, had lamented Obsidian's sacrifice; to come to Earth and exist in third density space. How agonizing every minute must have been for him. But these three seemed younger, not the old man Obsidian had been described as; these Orion entities had perhaps never reduced themselves to this density before. She wanted to ask them; which of them wanted to save her, to help her? Which two wanted to work with her to banish the psychopathic grid that the Anunnaki had placed over the Earth? She wanted to appeal to them, and try and help *her two* manifest more quickly than the other two somehow. But they were not even really able to be helped – they were still collecting stuff from the air, still processing energy in the patterns that they had stolen from her; somehow, bizarrely, still representing those four states of matter.

The one who had made the declaration, essentially announcing that Gordian was now an Orion Renegade, was the one named Floodfold.

Amy remembered thinking; Floodfold wants to drown me.

The statement had not been a warning to her – it had been a statement of pride, and honour; she was aligned with Gordian.

Floodfold was now also Renegade Orion.

Welcome to your valuable lesson, she thought grimly.

Welcome to The Last Days of the Karma Forge.

Welcome to Earth.

Gordian addressed Ealo. 'You wish an alliance? I will require foot soldiers, and recruiters. Agents. I intend to put an end to this, soon and irrevocably.'

'I am Chenek – but I am sub-clan Ienjch; Ienjch will serve the New Obsidian!'

'No…' Floodfold spoke again. She, for this one was almost certainly emerging to have a woman's face, turned to DeVora and smiled, even though, somewhat horrifically, her skin and flesh were still composed of a transparent film, filled with clear liquid, and she was trembling in pain. But, her teeth were there, in an awful, rictus kind of smile.

'We – are – O – Renegades!'

The Orion water ghoul seemed to snigger, almost fully laugh.

'O'Renegades!'

And she laughed again.

Behind that, somewhere, there was a high pitch.

Sounding, from far off.

Amy looked for a sign as to its source, but saw DeVora instead. To her credit, and despite despising her, Amy could see that her human enemy was totally disgusted to have had anything to do with their manifestation, or the nominal formation of their plans.

Gordian stared balefully at Amy again.

'You will not take any offer from me. You could join with the cabal who will benefit, join the cabal who will side-benefit; join the cabal who will survive, and perhaps rise to become stronger than all of the most intelligent of the human subsets who wish for power. But, no. No; you will do none of these things, and you will not discuss these matters with me. And so you must be stopped. But I have already seen this.'

He waved his hand.

The whole room exploded with colour, as though a massive sphere had been created out of thousands of rose-shaped, stained-glass windows, then had been struck exactly at that moment by a heavenly blast of high-summer sun, right in the middle of the room. At least, that's what it looked like at first.

'As you can see! I have already seen...'

Then, the closer Amy looked, the more disturbing it became.

'...so, so much!'

Shifting her head, the map, for it was surely a cosmic map of some kind, became kaleidoscopic; multi-dimensionally so. She could see multiple images come to life on any of the sprites of colour, or thin strings of plasma; every grain of light, viewed correctly, contained a moment of time that, when focussed upon, revealed multiple scenarios; and there were connections, like small explosions in slow motion where the shrapnel connected with other pieces of debris... and one thing led to another. She was suddenly reminded of the movies where the serial killer's lair, or the paranoid's plotting is revealed; even the obsessive cop's theory, or the fantasist's world-building. This was all that, but on a truly cosmic, incomprehensible level.

'You think I am insane, but I am so, so close to completing my map! I can read this as you would find directions to your local fossil fuel station, to buy your salt and sugar, to go to an alcohol binge and indulge in carnal flesh and psychological torture; but it is missing only three data lenses, before... ah, there she is!'

He pointed his finger; and there she was.

In the garden, giving DJ a blowjob under a tree.

'I can end all of this, here and now. Your little pretense will play out; you will not believe me, you will forget this, you will convince yourselves that I am insane and this, my cosmic cartography, is proof – but you will fail, and here is why; the one...'

He activated it much as one would a holographic computer; by moving his fore-fingers and thumbs, with the interface understanding the points of his physicality, his important extremities, and the pre-programmed manoeuvres. He was, however, magnificently efficient, and fast with it; bedazzlingly so. But she could not help thinking, not for the first time where aliens were concerned; that this was just technology.

In the end, it was technology that looked like – a God Map, in this case. And yes, she had to admit; it really did look like a section of God's Plan For Mankind; the Cosmic Scheme of Things as applied to Earth and All Her Permutations.

'And all you need do, Amy-Thys Pyne, is hand one over.'

It zoomed, pivoted and zoomed in again; out, then in again; spinning on one section like a wheel of fortune showing a different possible scenario playing out in each wedge.

For each moment in time!

– she saw Mitch and Heather and Janine and Jade (or Saxe?); she saw women, many women she didn't recognize, huddled together – she saw Everett, and men she did recognize but could not quite...

She saw herself having sex with people she knew – but had never had sex with, and realised – *he is bewildering me; these are all permutations of the progression of my life –*

...it was a ploy, and then she forgot them, as she would in a dream, as the next shifting scenes and images and further-bewildering permutations came forth... over and over, flickering, as he zoomed in and out, out and in; at least eight directions or permutation each time; all possibilities cast aside like Cosmic Tinder, left, right, up, down – telling herself, he is trying to impress and frighten and bewilder you – Xylata and Tzaebi; film stars, young, dead; film stars...? Ice; freezing to death; Ice. Love there; love not there with same person – two streams, but – love! And – *sorrow…*

◊ *He is trying to bewilder us!* ◊

☾ *Yes I know!* ☽

– realizing in the end there was a big, big –

Sorrow and heartache and – friends dying – the same friends living – the same friends – hating her –

Ω chunk missing Ω

Hating her, loving her, hating her, betraying her, loving her, saving her, never meeting her; meeting too soon; too late; wrong place, right time; right time, wrong place; never happening; all happening –

End all this and agree to serve me.
Run the Karma Forge with your Pyne-Everett Dynasty!
Rule Earth – and have what's left!
Ascend!
Ascend to Orion and be the Gods and Goddesses…
…of Earthling Humanity, Iteration Six!
All you need to do…
Is give me…
What you stole!
Give me –
The Arcana!

CHAPTER 72

She could hear a kind of weird throbbing from upstairs.

In what had once been her bedroom.

Someone had come through the broken glass and was setting something up.

And the high pitch – the high pitch was still building.

'This is it, Amethyst Pyne. You can see – the level of mastery I already possess over spacetime! Jahova shall tremble before me, and Lucifer shall be ascribed to but a footnote in the canon of Trickters! For I have The God Map, as you see it! Or better still The Gord Map!' He laughed. 'Yes, yes; do you see how the words, how the names; how the plans and the plays come together?'

Gordian was stating his case.

'Of course you do! Clever girl! And so you must now recognise; there is only surrender remaining! Your only move is to hand over the data lens; hand over the crystal arcana! And you may go on, to Orion, just as Cricket Wilde has done; you can best her for me, and serve there, spinning your weave, your womb, throughout spacetime in my name! After all! All is said – and – done!'

Tech, she told herself.

There is a power, there is a purpose, there is a plan; but he is just an alien with a higher perspective and better tech; he is an insane Orion with an obsession and a God Complex; he is the one her father warned her about, the one Mitch Pyne foresaw; looking down from on so, so, high...

'Or...' His voice dropped. He spoke sadly now, with disappointment. '...there is progression; and you will never succeed; and this is the price. I have stated my case in real time; – *ah!* – I have known in the greater circumference of your sphere of endeavour that you are – *kah!* – destined never to align with me, however – *jah!* – *what is that throbbing?'*

He put a hand to his temple.

Thought for second.

Then he turned to the door.

The man who had entered with the gun.

He was still there.

It seemed like an eternity ago now that he had entered the apartment.

He too had faded into the cream wall.

Now he stepped out again, and raised the gun, pointed it at Amy's head, between her eyes.

Amy turned away and stared at Gordian through hateful eyes, speaking through gritted teeth.

'A slide show is still a slide show, I don't care how advanced the God-damn tech is! Do what you need to do, *psycho-rion!* Destroy my body! I don't care – I will come back from the astral for you, and trust me, I will still be Iteration Five and *you will not like –'*

But it was a distraction.

That was not the threat.

The apartment door was kicked in and there was another person there – in golden mask, like an Aztec, with a black and red robe, holding a rifle, already raised. Amy craned her neck back, was seeing this at forty-five degrees, as the sniper, at close range, aimed the weapon and fired.

Distractions!

DeVora was on the floor with her arms over her head.

She knew – distractions.

Time – slowing.

Amy looked into the map.

Gordian still had it set on her timeline; but it had passed as he had looked away, to give the order.

It was there, the memory she needed.

Amy reached over, into... *into the map* and grabbed it.

She grabbed her timeline with her left hand.

It burned her; her hand, her arm, as she felt something, some kind of vibrating, metallic, liquid sac; she reached in further and hit solid, painful, hard; crystals, spikes, shards, razors; immense gravity pulling her hand off her wrist, fingers off her palm, joints disjointed and nails sliding off. She thrust in her other hand and in her mind's eye she saw, with her left hand:

...her father and Heather, about to kiss on the boat, during the storm...

: and with her right hand:

...her own death, alone on the cold asphalt, fallen and wounded beyond healing upon the promenade at Circular Quay, where the ocean liners...

..."sail slowly over the horizon; and are gone...":

:and then she grasped with both hands, screamed, and wrenched at it, just like a bundle of wires, just like the tech it truly was.

The map sparked from that section, then spun around her arms like she had them somehow in a washing machine, back and forth, jostling and lurching; then, as though reconfiguring, the loose tech seemed to pause itself, hovering and wavering, even quivering just a little, with her arms still stuck.

Flood-bitch was on the floor, screaming up at her about ruining everything.

One of the other Orions came at her, still unformed; she could see nothing but the animated suit, but from behind, another of them ran up, planted their leg on the first one's calf and brought him down, coming down on top of him and flattening him on the floor – there was an explosion of rocks and stone and dirt and something in cloud-form, gaseous in a suit, wrapped itself around her body, tightened onto her shoulders and chest and upper-arms, and wrenched with her.

Time seemed to slow even more.

The piece came out like a dagger, like a shard, like a splinter of the beginning and end of all time. It was sparking with colours she could not comprehend, but vanishing into corners of reality right there in front of her that there was no acceptable point of reference for her mind to latch onto. She could not forget this – it was too important; this was the thing that would save her, remind her of what she needed to remember from the cosmic cartography of her would-be Orion master. There was almost nothing in her hands anymore, it was all just disintegrating into atoms around her, but it was still there, still connected in the pattern.

How could she contain it?

Thought struck; something about the analogous stained glass image she had seen, made from the Orion tech into a cosmic-kaleidoscope; the beauty, the colours and the construction; it was closer to whatever God was than anything – yet it remained an impression; an interpretation; a... a...

An!

An abstract!

It was – art!

Art!

She plunged the splinter, the line of time, with her left hand into her right arm, and the whole thing vanished through her fingers like sand.

CHAPTER 73

Cloudia vanished from around her, sighing in relief.

But the sound of the single percussive explosion echoed, and somehow slowed everything down even more.

Turning, Amy could see the bullet from the rifle, still moving in a direct line, halfway between the gun and The Healer.

What the - ?

The Healer?

The Healer is the target – ?

The other gunman squeezed the trigger of his handgun, the shot that was aimed directly at her. Aimed at her getting out of the way, aimed at preventing her from saving The Healer.

◊ *The Healer is the target!* ◊

❪ *I bloody know!* ❫

Someone big jumped over the balcony.

The deep background throbbing that had been building all this time, pulsing ever more apparently – along, Amy could still register – with the high pitch that was closing in as well, threw everyone backwards from the new entrant.

It was as though some sort of sonic weapon had been deplo –

Ohhhh, Amy registered.

◊ *A sonic weapon is being deployed!* ◊

❪ *I know! I know!* ❫

All the remaining Anunnaki, including Xylata, who had been moving to push Amy out of the path of the headshot, seemed to be singled out by this strange new vibrational power. They were all cast violently backwards, staggering but not quite falling against the apartment walls, shouting in alarmed protest but momentarily impotent. There was a bright flash of the opal dust, as though that too had just been blown out of the centre of the room and, with that, Amy started to see, and remember, at least a part of the full picture.

The big man landed on the floor beside DeVora, incidentally rolling her over, even as she cowered there.

The throbbing was coming from a staff that the man held, a long white rod with a glass sphere on top, within which, attached to the top of the staff, was a polished, brilliant-ivory human skull. Just beneath was a small flag, fluttering as the man landed; the British flag; the Union Jack. The big man landed expertly, on both feet, still holding the shocking staff upright. He was huge, he was tough, and Amy knew him immediately; he was Harding, and, just as he had promised on the bed, on the boat, he had found her.

Gordian staggered backwards, away from Harding, clearly shocked and appalled at not just him but everything that had so quickly and violently transpired.

'No! What have you taken! No! You cannot take yourself! You cannot *have – yourself!*'

Simultaneously however, throwing Amy's perception and consciousness into complete disarray, came a sudden, brutally natural rippling over the tiles. For a second she thought it was hallucination; that she had somehow been spiked with LSD or something, as though all this other frequency distortion wasn't enough. Then, clear as day, a swarm of cockroaches, and mice, and rats, all shades of all kinds of brown, moving as one, burst out from the cupboards, out of the drains, poured over the landing and onto the kitchen bench, onto the floor and launched as one all-enclosing wave that directly targeted Gordian. More grey possums than she had ever seen in one place smashed the air conditioner out of the wall from behind; it landed on one of the Cheneks who had been pushed back against the wall, and with a grimly final crunching sound, he lay still beneath its bulk. Dozens of feral cats and wild dogs burst in through the still-open front door, right behind the rifleman, while at the sound of more smashing from the balcony door, two dozen magpies plus a dozen huge, white, sulphur-crested cockatiels flew in like a catastrophic blizzard, backed up by a dozen black ravens and finally, an enormous, swooping, seemingly very-determined wedge-tailed eagle.

All of the disparate creatures ignored each other to pummel, bite, peck and bloody Gordian as the whistling sound increased to a terrible shrieking pitch.

Gordian fell backwards under the onslaught, but stretched out a hand to Amy, shouting in outrage.

'Give it to me! Give me the thing that you stole!'

Amy just stared, amazed.

There was an underscore of burgeoning incomprehension and an edge of panic now, as his shouting continued.

'The Arcana! I require it for the completion of my ascension!'

As his cries began taking more of a frightened edge, the enormous pile-on of writhing, clawing, snapping fur and claws and teeth began to sink into the floor, as the creatures finally overwhelmed him.

'I will find you – Arcana! Pyn-naaargh!'

The writhing, pinching, clawing, snapping and swirling mass then started to pass through the floor, as the substance of the tiles dissolved beneath them all. Then it was like a giant drain, a sinkhole of fur and feathers, down which he was clearly now descending, below floor level but without falling totally, like a net, a funnel, a trampoline tunnel with ever-increasing weight forced down against it, with most of the wild creatures following him down and through, into the cosmic drain.

It was all too late though.

The bullet was going to miss Amy.

But, it had never been intended to hit her.

Just to startle her, and get her out of the way.

The real target was not so lucky.

The bullet was there; Amy watched it penetrate The Healer's hood, and beneath, above and between her eyes, on her forehead.

The Healer's head jerked back.

The jolt seemed quick, even through the slowed time; but the sheer, efficient brutality of the missile in question, accompanied by an explosion of blood that splashed violently down over her sunglasses and voice-distortion mask, made it shockingly and appallingly apparent that the bullet had just penetrated her skin.

The forgotten figure in the blue hooded-robe, so quiet as to be almost invisible, moved forward.

'This is the moment! *This is the moment!*'

The wedge-tailed eagle soared in an arc; Amy didn't see anything but a brilliant flash of light, and then The Healer and the eagle were gone.

The hooded blue figure came forward.

'Yes! How – how did she do it?'

The blue hood turned to Amy.

'You – you are the only way it can work!'

Amy collapsed then, her ability to process and comprehend finally burned right out, her arm of Art on fire, her consciousness not just fading but closing down, no longer knowing which end was up, or where the floor was, watching all the birds who had not been sucked into the cosmic sinkhole fly back out over the landing as her vision flared to white then faded to grey, then brown, then black, and she knew that if she were going to get out of this one, she was going to have to –

CHAPTER 74

She saw a fountain in the middle of a village.

An old village, in the mountains.

Something told her it was European.

Maybe Greek or Italian…

It looked deserted, but that was just because it was so old.

There was a village shop, almost modern, but then again, decidedly not.

She smelled coffee; amazing, fresh coffee.

As the clouds drifted across, to allow the light through, she felt a mild draping of sunshine on her face, against the crispness of the cold air.

The aroma of the coffee was so appetizing; irresistible.

Heavenly. To die fo – oh. Really?

'Have I died? Is this Heaven…?'

Somebody laughed.

'No, no, but where have you come from?'

She tried to answer.

'Oh!' The voice was more distant now. 'Did you see that? She vanished! Into thin air!'

'Well…'

She was almost gone now.

'…nobody wants to vanish into fat air!'

…

…such laughter…

…

..

.

CHAPTER 75

Someone or something had her hand.

Was pulling her back.

Squeezing her through the tightest, most dense hole, pulling her back, atom by atom; and the atoms were shocked. The atomics had never seen anything like it, and because they had never seen anything like it, they realised that they were seeing something; something real.

Something else.

From elsewhere.

For the first time.

The first time – in a **time** long. time,. *time* – anyway; …and … time … … was

… … … very

… … … … slow

… … … … … … … here

((((and after a --- long --- stretch of time

and

some very strange communications))))

…

..

.

pop

(.)

THE CHRONICLES OF THE REALMA

BOOK ONE:

ENCHANTRESS PRETENDER

PROLOGUE

Tharomak lay dying, propped to a sitting position against the trunk of the ancient oak. The battle had been fine but it had not gone to him. He had not disgraced himself. Hardly. But the battle had been lost, nevertheless.

There had been great pain initially, in both body and soul, but both had passed as he had realized that the battle had been mighty, and would be remembered. That the outcome, his loss, would be remembered, but as a noble loss.

Tharomak had allowed himself a tear, just one, in sorrow that that he would not be king, that he would not grow any older, that he would not see his remaining children grow old. But many had died today and he would be one of the last. His body had not failed him, despite his injuries, any of which would have killed a lesser man. He had been struck, and dispatched, then struck again and, again, dispatched. The third and ultimately decisive blow had come from a knight who was laying not far from him at the edge of the field of the dead.

The field of the dead was hot and steaming, high into the air, to at least the height of a tall man. Down the rise, from where he sat dying, propped against the old oak, the body of the knight who had dispatched the death blow had ceased to steam, had run cold. But the other bodies, strewn for maybe a mile out from the oak and the rise, still gave up their heat, collected together as they were, broken man upon broken man, with the last of what their lives had generated wisping up and out over a mile of battlefield that would forever remember the blood, their guts and their piss and their shit, and seed within its soil the remembrance of their collective pain. The field would be marked; a place of honour and suffering. Hair would rise on the arms of travellers as they crossed, women would urge their rides to go faster, and those with magic in their veins would pay their respects to what they knew was a place of dread-memorial. Perhaps they would even deem to stop and scrape some soil for their spells – they would be welcome; it would be, at least, some use.

Regardless of how time would come to see the field; it was, to Marmantuan, victory.

Figures moved across the fields in the distance.

The assessors would come from there, from the west, from Marmantuan's course of approach. Counting the bodies, identifying who they could from their sigils, markings and coats of arms. Mercifully dispatching those in ultimate pain, taking home their own wounded to see if the ultimate pain could be forestalled, and if Marmantuan was as good as his reputation, taking Tharomak's wounded to the sorcery groves for their ultimate decision. Life, freedom, servitude or death. Only the sorcerers could decide.

It would be death though, for Duke Tharomak, before long.

Long before the ponderous assessors would reach him across the wide field, he would no longer be here.

There was one assessor though, who was moving more swiftly than the others. This one was moving directly toward him, over the bodies as though she; yes, she, had not a care for them at all. She sailed through the blood-steam as though the dead were not even there. She came swiftly. Tharomak thought he must have passed into sleep, a minute or two, for her to arrive so soon.

'Duke Tharomak.'

The woman was plainly beautiful. She wore white robes and a white head scarf. She was slender and wore no undergarments, but was decorated with thin gold chains and a white-gold headband. Her bright sapphire eyes gazed serenely upon him over gaunt, sharp cheeks and full, pale lips. She spoke softly.

'...it saddens me greatly that you will not be king.'

Tharomak heard the voice clearly and recognized it. He had

only heard it in dreams, and had not heard it in the world before. He had not remembered in the world that he had heard it in dreams, spoken by the woman in dreams. Perhaps more. Perhaps they were friends. No. Not friends. Consorts.

'Yes… you can see me in the world now.'

'But; you are not a phantom. I am dying, but I still live. You are in the world.'

'I can come into the world, when the one who sees me can never be sure. Those close to death often see spirits, of those they have known, or will come to know; some see their deities, some even their gods and goddesses – you will die, so the proof of my existence here and now will pose no challenge to your faith. You will not require faith, henceforth.'

'Faith… is then, indeed, the engine?' Tharomak enquired keenly, turning one of the basic tenets of his court's religion into a question.

'Yes.' She smiled and nodded softly. 'Faith is the engine.'

Tharomak looked closer. Of course. It was absurd that one dressed as such, so fine of feature, would be here at all.

'You are Gilethreia, the Sapphire Goddess…'

'Yes.'

'I have prayed to you…' Tharomak blinked. '…we have spoken in dreams.'

'We planned this day. It is not to my liking that you are dying.'

'You are all but forgotten; but you came to me. I never forgot the Sapphire Path.'

'I know. It is not to my liking that the battle was so close. It is not to my liking that you have no heir who will honour the deities and allow me some final purchase here. I would have it that you won this battle. Alas, that was not to be, and we must adjust the course and make plans anew.'

'I am sorry, my goddess…'

'No, please, do not be; you did not fail. This was fair, but unfair. You did all we planned, all that was asked. Now you have made the ultimate sacrifice.'

'My goddess… forgive me…'

'But I believe I can make some amends. Your member. Is it still intact?'

'My…?'

'Your cock. Do you still have it?'

'I cannot feel…' Tharomak winced. '…since I crawled here and propped myself against the tree, below my heart, it is not there…'

Gilethreia nodded. She stepped toward him, stood astride him, raised her skirts and squatted over his hips. His vision became bleary and for a moment he thought he could see through his own armour, to the bulbous resting head of his cock amid the rough bramble of greying black. He thought he saw her garment evaporate into something like the body-mist of the corpses, yet white, and an opening; the lips of a woman but smoother, undulating like a milk churn. He thought he saw her queer but beautiful nether-regions hover as her pale, slender hand lowered to touch the head of his cock. He felt pain, for a second, as she made contact, and his bowls clenched. The flaccid head spat blood, then began to rise, erect within seconds, and she lowered her quivering, creamy opening upon him. She did not ride him, as such, although he felt it, keenly, with great pleasure, as her rippling inner energy, like muscles, undulated; contracting and expanding the length of his cock and back, repeatedly. She even rose and floated down, rose and floated down, slightly, smiling at him.

But not for long.

He shot what felt like an enormous load, seven or eight times, right up into her.

Then, as he jerked the last few short spurts, and his muscles involuntarily relaxed, and his body fell yet lower, only then did he begin properly to die, with the two processes so mixed as to be virtually indistinguishable.

Within her gossamer figure, he saw his bloody expulsion of semen strike up through her, like the upward spouting roots of a tree, as though she were fully transparent now, then reach where her skull would be, if she were mortal, if she were a real woman, then descend again, to her deity's womb. The child emerged fully formed, into her arms, and she lost all pretense at appearing even half like a mortal, just a second, as she looked upon their child for the first time.

'In such times, this is permitted.'

She looked down at Tharomak.

He had died, and his spirit was a boy. A handsome little boy, from the time when his grandfather had died, when his spirit had first truly become aware of death. In spirit form, Tharomak looked down at the dead body of the thing he had become, in life, in flesh, and sighed.

'I might have been king one day. The battle was so close.'

Gilethreia nodded. 'That was the assumption upon which this battle was set.'

He looked up at Gilethreia, and the demigod they had conceived.

'I will find her a home. When she comes of age, I will come to her, and she will know her birthright. Because of this, you will be here in spirit form until she too passes over.'

Tharomak looked over the field of the dead.

'That might be interesting.'

There were many spirits on the field, but they looked lost, and alone.

'They will find their way?'

Gilethreia smiled. 'Yes. But; for many, the way is not home. Not yet.'

'I had a whore in a village outside of Festroon. She was clever. Too clever for whoring. If I was victorious today, I was to make her a concubine-consort. Hide the child with her.'

Gilethreia stared at him, as though unaccustomed to being told.

'Is there...?' The child spirit of Tharomak was already plotting. '...is there a boon you can bestow? Whores can take residence outside the village in the cluster of wise women. But there is nobody left to buy her out, now I am dead. If you want to raise a child to be king...'

'Queen...'

Tharomak stared at the baby and a second later she let out her first scream.

'...then she will definitely need the tutelage of the wise. Is this possible?'

'There will be a price, but, yes. It is possible.'

The crying of the baby had caught the attention of the assessors, even a mile away.

Gilethreia was still staring at Tharomak as though surprised.

'The child will bring attention. We must leave. Do we fly there?'

She kept staring. 'Curious. This is not your first time. You were not fully mortal. You incarnated.'

'Did I?' The boy had no idea.

'You would never order me such, otherwise.'

'Wouldn't I?' Again, no idea.

Gilethreia shrugged. 'No grief. Such is The Sapphire Path.'

'So, shall we fly? Like gods?'

'We have a mortal child. We walk, like mortals.'

Tharomak shrugged. 'Is has been a long time since I walked with the legs of boy. Shall I lead the way?'

'As you wish. Not so fast. When we find this woman, we will teach her the ways of the Three-Handed God, and how to walk The Sapphire Path. And then we shall see – what we shall see.'

CHAPTER ONE

'Nobody knows how Realma came to be.'

Zyxi had heard this one.

Nobody knew how the world came to be, only that it was formed from The One, who split itself into The Heavenly Consorts, Ah and Ou. They remained ascended, but birthed the Stellar Consorts Boua, Haak, Rouz and Yina; then the Sixteen Astral Consorts...

Zyxi listened as the other children chanted their names...

'Cithrilc, Endryzal, Gobreeus...'

The Sixteen Astral Consorts mated, and between them created the Eight Earthly Realms, decreeing Four Territories in each, erecting Two Citadels in each Territory, and allowing One Regent for each Citadel; the two Regents could only be vetoed by The One – or the representative of The One on Realma, and that One remained in no place, only appearing where they were needed. Nobody had seen The One's Representative so long as anyone could remember. But one day The One would appear, and...'

The children chanted.

'...and all our needs will be met, according to our purity of heart, integrity of thought, and devotion to The One.'

'Zyxi Xyxiz!'

The voice triggered something in Zyxi's guts, like a fist in there had clenched, and sent pain through her body. Her hand tensed, her shoulders clamped and she could feel water welling already behind her eyes. Wasn't it enough that her name itself indicated to everyone that she held the lowest status in Vaaa? Where names could only be four letters long, and none could begin with anything higher in status than a V?

'Do you think you are too good for the Gods?' The question

was a terrifyingly familiar one. 'Too good to speak their names are we? – oh!'

The last syllable was uttered in shock; too late Zyxi realised she had not only failed to mouth by rote the list of Astral Consorts, but she had succeeded, instead, in mouthing by rote the standard threat Matron Wyxa always thoughtlessly offered when Zyxi was caught failing to do so.

Speak – their -names – are – we…?

Zyxi hated the school room.

'How dare you!'

Matron Wyxa was going to go wizard, completely wizard, and although Zyxi had been in this position before, she was still afraid.

'Stand – up!'

Zyxi was at the back of the room, where all the difficult children sat; the dumb and the restless and occasionally the privileged, at least by this village's standards, who didn't have to try.

And the poor.

Zyxi was a double disappointment to everyone; she was not only restless, she was also poor, and according Matron Wyxa, dumb as well. That was why she hated her. She had singled her out from day one. Seen her as a disruptive element, decided that she should be sacrificed for the betterment of the other children, singled out and made a constant example of. She would make her rise and mock her. She would make her come forward and strike her. She would make her stand at the front of the room and humiliate, then banish her. Banishment was the best; as least then it was over. But it was still horrible, because in her mind… it wasn't over. The humiliation would play over and over, as Matron Wyxa always knew it would. Even when she went home, even when she did her chores, even when she played and went to bed, when her head hit the pillow, Matron Wyxa was still there.

But this time, Zyxi had gone too far.

The playing over and over in her mind of Matron Wyxa's constant chastisements had overflown, out of her mind into the real world.

The school house was half way up a rise that looked out, across the town,

CHAPTER 76

It was Mendoza's hand.

The Three-Handed God had been Mendoza, calling her, all this time.

Holding out his hand, all this time –

All that time, and Amethyst –

and Zyxi had felt it, all this time, across valleys and oceans and voids of time and space; and she had responded to its call, its measure and meaning and symbolism and intent; come to it on her quest, assembled all the keys to the mountain labyrinth and –

Mendoza pulled her with all his might, back up through the hole in the floor.

Zyxi grabbed the edges, but they were falling away like sand at the top edge of a dune; her feet were scrambling beneath her as the ground turned into a slippery wall of wet mud, and her other hand,

but one Mendoza was so tightly grasping, and had been for – what seemed like forever in the first place and; years, surely, in the second place, and he and her God would not let go even as –

Zyxi started to cry as she realized that she would never see her friends, her allies, or her creatures, ever again. But she had fought and almost died for them; they had fought for her, and some had died – all to get her to the end of her quest and back home.

'Come on, Thys!' Mendoza urged. 'Kick it baby! This is where it all comes together!'

'Pull harder, Harding!'

She kicked.

People had died to get her here. Her friends, people she loved; because that's what people did there, where she'd been, but also because... you have to earn it, for people to do that, even in a place where that was what you did anyway, you did it anyway for the people who earned it, earned the accompaniment upon the quest, earned their protection, their love, their support and their honour; but she had, and they had, and –

'In the name of The Sapphire Goddess; *I will find my way home!'*

'That's it baby – kick it baby, kick up, kick up!'

'Always yanking Pynes…'

There was another hand, and now it had shifted to her lower arm, pulling, pulling, and she kicked and kicked – and was finally, almost; then, from way below –

somebody pushed –

somebody weeping as they pushed –

"Goodbye my friend, my Queen, Great Zyxi – ! You were the bravest of us all – and we loved you!"

CHAPTER 77

'…out of the jaws of a demon!'

And she was through.

Back.

Home.

Harding stood, his enormous muscular arm now practically single-handedly pulling her out of the hole in the floor, dangling her above the fall through to the ruined floor, into the apartment below.

It had been Harding, not Mendoza!

But wait; either side of Harding; Xylata and Mendoza were standing, and their three hands were – meshed together, in an incredible combination of flesh and light. Even as she was watching this, Mendoza wrenched his hand free, relinquishing the crystal-blue matrixes of energy his force had provided, over Harding's tightly-tensed forearm. Xylata was pulling her own hand free, or rather, Harding was pulling his arm so high, to raise Amy so high, that Xylata's arm could no longer reach his.

But it was okay – they had her; she had found them, found the hand, grasped it and they had pulled her out of –

Harding's face was before her now, sweating under the silver buzz-cut, his white teeth grinding in a grimace of focussed strength and concentrated power; he was essentially pulling himself free of the astral energy that Xylata had provided, and the Sirian energy with which Mendoza had sealed their combined might; both as aide to his sheer human physical force, to pull her out of the hole…

Two lifetimes ago, it seemed –

--- --- ---   **it was**   --- --- ---

It was in deed…

 She had fainted, after wrenching whatever she had wrenched from the cosmic kaleidoscope, and fallen in; right in, along with Gordian.

Harding let her go and instantly caught her again, his huge arms snapping simultaneously out, snatching her around the waist, spinning her as he turned and dropping to one bended knee, then laying her flat, as gentle as can be, on her back.

She was staring up at the ceiling now, crying.

'Amy; Amethyst; Thys Pyne!' Xylata, still in the body of the Young Queen Elizabeth the Second stared down at her, as concerned as Amy ever remembered seeing her.

Remembered seeing her.

How long had she been gone?

'I'll never see them again!'

She heard herself saying that, over her crying; over her sheer weeping.

'They loved me and I loved them; we did everything for each other and they did everything to get me back here – and I'll never see them again!'

Xylata stared down into Amy's eyes.

'She can't keep making naked jumps like this! From plane to plane, dimension to dimension, density to density! I need to get her back home!'

Harding nodded sharply. 'Mitch and Heather's apartment. I know the way.'

'No; she doesn't live there anymore. She is going to die unless I get her back to The Port of Ymira!'

Mendoza squatted down and assessed her.

'She was in first density. Who knows what she saw there – how her consciousness measured it? When we tuned into her, she'd been in second density, in the Inner Earth, for…'

Mendoza looked to Harding.

'How long did we have our hands shoved down in that mud hole?'

Xylata shook her head. 'Sirian, you know as well as I do – if her consciousness was truly separated, and her consciousness somehow responded with the abilities that the Pandora Sequence gave her, each one of those levels of density, each one of those planes, those dimensions, those experiences, could have been an entire lifetime for her…!'

DeVora was still there, still on the floor, but as she stood, the Cheneks moved with her. DeVora looked back at the discarded blue robe, then to Mendoza.

'Hiding in plain sight, this whole time. Spy!'

'Go fuck yourself lady.'

DeVora pointed sharply down at Amy.

'She is too powerful for this dimension! On behalf of all humanity, I banish her to the Astral Realm – never to return!'

For a half-second, everyone stared at Amy, half expecting her to vanish; such was the intensity of DeVora's insane conviction.

But when that didn't happen, DeVora turned to Ealo.

'On pain of death – correct, Ealo?'

Ealo looked back at the Chenek whose skull had been crushed by the air conditioner. He looked to DeVora, then down at Amy, then back at his advisor, and his remaining three troops.

'Kill them all – now.'

CHAPTER 78

They were saved by someone shouting up from the hole.

'What on Earth is happening here!'

It was a young voice that carried a lot of authority, which none of them were expecting, which gave Harding the split second he needed to shoot the fastest of the Chenek to raise his weapon, before he could shoot down and kill Amy. This in turn allowed Xylata the split-second she required to throw herself over Amy as the second-fastest Chenek shooter did fire down. Xylata's royal body took three bullets in the back as she rolled over Thys, grabbed her and kept rolling them both straight over the edge and down into the hole.

There was a loud thud.

'Jesus; Mother Earth!'

The same voice cried again from below, followed by another woman screaming.

'Call the police!'

Mendoza took a few flesh-shredding bullets as well, but only in service of protecting Harding, Xylata and Amy, then jumped down after the two women. Then one of the other robed figures, one of the trio in the burgundy robes, smashed one of the Chenek from behind with both fists, enclosed together and held high, brought down upon the back of their hood. Before anyone had known what was going on, he had grabbed the hooded Chenek again and brought the hood, face-first, down on his raised knee, then taken his victim's gun and opened fire on the closest burnt-orange robe – two fell, before Ealo, total confusion in his tone, cried out.

'Abort!'

The remaining of the burnt-orange Cheneks vanished in a

dimensional flash; just Ealo, the advisor, and perhaps miraculously, one of those who had taken fire from the burgundy assailant – but not before Ealo took a bullet in the shoulder from Belle, spinning him backwards, just as he disappeared.

Harding immediately had a gun on her, but she was already in the hands-up pose with her gun on the step below her.

'All good, dude! Choosing a side!'

'Then pick it up again and keep it on her!'

Harding pointed at DeVora, who had backed away from the now-departed orange Cheneks, against the side of the stairs – perhaps aiming to snatch the dropped weapon herself.

Harding looked to the burgundy robe.

'Who are you?'

'I'm human, I'm human!'

Amy was half-watching, half-sensing all of this from below; she felt strangely out of body still, as though watching it all from way above, although not completely in or out of herself. She wondered where the three motorcycle-helmeted bystanders had gone, then realised they were standing in the kitchen, down here with her and Xylata and the two newcomers.

'I think my consciousness is broken.'

'I know… this lovely… regal personage… certainly is…'

She had fallen right on top of Xylata, as her friend had arranged it. She had sensed the Queen-body wince hard as they'd hit the ground, then heard Xylata grunt, a lot, as blood had squirted across the floor, exiting from the several bullet wounds, as all the breath was blown from her lungs. Amy pushed herself off and rolled over, falling again, flat on her back, and found herself staring at the other side of the hole – now in the ceiling – looking up. She watched as Mendoza leaped down, his bullet-torn flesh flying off him like streamers, being instantly replaced by shining blue plasma, then saw as Harding turned and hoisted himself over the edge, hanging by his hands, then dropped to a stand not far from her. He turned, almost mechanically, and assessed her through his hard, steely-grey gaze before coming down again on one knee, and scanning her more closely for wounds.

'The ceilings are not high, the fall was not far…'

It was a lie; they had both fallen two floors, down onto the cream-tiled floor of the empty lounge area beneath.

'I'm okay, I'll live; check her – check Xylata…'

Harding nodded curtly and moved over, still squatting.

Amy watched Harding's face as he assessed, then addressed.

'Your name is Xylata?'

'Yes.'

'You are a warrior?'

'Yes.'

'Then I will be direct. You are too far gone, there isn't a hospital close enough.'

'I thank you for your honesty. Now, here is mine; I am Anunnaki, I am an astral being in a human body, that was created like armour for me to walk about in the atmosphere of this dimension.'

Harding nodded, and looked over to Amy.

'True?'

Amy nodded. 'She's my Number Two, and I am hers; believe everything she says.'

Harding looked back to Xylata.

'What can I do, Lizard Queen?'

'Ah!' Xylata practically squealed. 'So close! Nobody got it – I was Queen Liz! *Queen Liz! It was so obvious!*'

Queen Liz then coughed up quite a lot of blood.

'Talk softly, moron!' Amy snapped. 'Don't get excited!'

'I have transport.' Harding offered.

Xylata raised a shaking hand and wiped blood from the royal lips.

'Not yet. Better not to move humans when they have holes. My people will be signalled automatically. They have mobile transport. They will be here. We just need to wait.'

Harding nodded. 'I'll try and plug the holes. Is this robe

important?'

Amy groaned. 'Is it genuine?'

'It's all genuine!' Xylata guffawed. 'What would be the point otherwise?'

Harding started ripping fabric from the base of her gown. 'This will do better anyway.'

Mendoza extended a hand and helped Amy up.

Amy stood, still feeling creaky, then stretched out, even taller again. She groaned and sighed and belched and farted as she forced herself to stay balanced, and remain standing up.

Mendoza smiled, friendly. 'Nice outfit.'

Amy looked down, forgetting that she was still naked.

But she wasn't.

Mendoza smiled. His eyes were still a dark and brooding brown, but there were now flecks of shimmering ice-blue, and Sirian-azure within them, complimenting a variant of his blue, black and white Hawaiian togs.

'You don't really know, do you? You didn't notice? You thought you were naked. You knew you were, this whole time, like a nightmare, or a dream; and you decided not to care. That – everything else was more important than your modesty, your ridiculous base-human shame. But while you were talking to DeVora, your old catsuit reappeared on you.'

'Wait. You know it?'

'Yeah, I know the outfit. The one you've been building on ever since you got there and started the war, with her.'

'Building on?'

'It's what happens. We build. Build layers. Build strong foundations, high castles; shoot rockets to The Moon from their highest towers. You've still got the astral amnesia; what you've been doing, nobody's ever done. I don't know what's going on in your mind, or what's happening with your sense of time, but you will come good eventually and remember. In the meantime, we've crossed paths a few times since the Kamikaze Anunnaki; fast but satisfying.'

'Oh; no, we didn't..?'

Mendoza seemed almost offended. 'No we didn't – but; oh, never mind.'

'I'm sorry, I have a type. I mean, I know you're considered very...'

'Shall we just drop this line of inquiry, Pyne? It was all good, all trading messages between you and your family, collaborative war efforts against Team Draco, all cut and dried. Very important, very cool, very you and very me.'

He smiled and raised an eyebrow, as though that meant something she hadn't quite remembered yet; something very important, something massive.

'No?' Mendoza sensed that she was onto something.

'No – nothing.'

'Well, it'll come back to you. You've been through a lot. But I did remember the outfit! And the white robe you were – shot in?'

Amy nodded.

'…you saw it on the floor at the bottom of the steps, but what you didn't see was when it dissolved, into clouds and fluff and feathers, then manifested around you, on you, while you were facing down that idiot Gordian. You didn't even know you were doing it, did you?'

'I...'

She looked down at herself. She was fully dressed, but hadn't even realised.

But, how she looked – *what she was dressed in…*

'She must be banished or killed!'

They looked up. DeVora was staring down at them through the hole.

'Just because I don't have one of those things inside me, don't think I don't know – Sirian! Sixth dimensional magic is not unfamiliar to me – neither is your story! Others were there that day, watching – not as sympathetic to your faux-Egyptian mistress! And others have encountered you since – running about, doing her business, her bidding!'

Mendoza threw his head back.

'Shut up you cow!'

Then he looked back down at Amy.

'We used to bang. Back when she was – "an actress". Huh!'

'Pornographer! Don't think I didn't understand everything that went on here today; she is more powerful than anyone has ever been on this plane! She went to first density – to the atomic level of consciousness! She existed there! She was in the Inner Earth – she led two different lives in five minutes! What will she be – when she unpacks that – remembers what she learned? When she can harness that!?'

Belle appeared beside her. 'Shut-up! This is all your doing, all because of your meeting, your – *thing*. You nearly got everyone killed, you bloody mad-woman!'

DeVora turned and looked at her, square jawed and hard-eyed, Hollywood New Wave meets chiselled European power.

Straight into the barrel of a gun.

'You don't fool me, you upturned mop of scarecrow's side-girl! You're not a murderer, you're a surveillance expert. A voyeur! Your hands are clean; *you just like to watch.*'

They stared it out a few seconds.

'True.'

Belle shoved the gun down the front of her pants and stared down the hole.

'Now how'd he do that?'

She quickly threw off the robe, revealing blue jeans and a white tee underneath; a cool pop-culture print that Amy half-recognised. They were kind of the same, she figured. Her skin was very bright, very pale, very white-pink; like Amy, she was clearly something of a several-generation blonde Anglo-Saxon descendent who almost never went outdoors. Then she got down on her hands and knees, turned around, looked like she was going to swing her legs backward over the edge, but then quickly gave up.

'No fucking idea.'

'Wait!'

They all turned to the door.

The two women who had shouted; one of whom had effectively saved Amy from being riddled with bullets, were still there. One was middle-aged, maybe fifty, while one was younger, around Amy's age. The younger one was tall, like Amy; at first glance she looked very striking, but very compact, fit and thin, with short, neat black hair, minimal makeup and mocha skin, dressed in plain black slacks with a white shirt. The shirt's long, sharp, draping collars seemed her only concession to fashion.

'Just – everybody – wait.'

She stood very upright, perhaps tense but certainly having a discernibly excellent posture; the middle-aged woman seemed in many ways her direct counterpart. She was also staring keenly at them all, with an icy gaze from within a round, plainly Northern European face. She had mousy, unruly hair over a high brow and small eyes behind enormously framed silver glasses, seeming to have a resting-face of general disapproval. Having visually assessed the scene quite thoroughly, she now hugged herself in a huge shawl; red and white with sharp black patterns.

'You people need to immediately identify yourselves. You there – aren't you Amethyst Pyne? Your parents were looking for you!'

Amy was caught by her demanding manner, but it returned something to her. They weren't. They had been in touch. A long while ago, maybe… but not now; now, they were good. She was either lying, or out of touch, or – most likely, Thys sensed, being overly dramatic. Maybe all three.

The taller woman seemed equally at a loss, equally as confronted by the scene, but took a soft step backward and remained still.

'This is my hotel – you people and your psychotic shenanigans are no longer welcome here – I thought I made that clear to Miss Pankhurst – six months ago! Look at this damage! Who is going to pay for this!?'

DeVora leaned down.

'Hines?'

Hines looked up. 'DeVora? That's you up there? What is all this nonsense? What are you consorting with these ruffians for? This path leads nowhere, you know that! To nothing but chaos and disorder!'

'I know, I know!' DeVora sighed, loudly and broadly. 'But tell me – Oliver and Bo Everett *gave you* the hotel chain? I thought your brother had departed to – "walk the Earth" or some such…?'

'Don't be ridiculous! Maybe he has, but he still has a phone, and satellite connection!'

Hines turned to Amy.

'Your father and Heather Pyne had a teleconference meeting with him, not a week ago. They were all wondering when you would come back! Such a disgrace this generation! Years away without so much as a picture post card! You should contact your father, let him know you haven't been killed – wherever it was you went!'

She turned back up to the hole in the ceiling, to DeVora.

'This chain has been mine for years now; I just happened to be here, in town, to finalize some other business! My brother sold everything else to that Irish scoundrel Bo Everett, you know…' She shook her head, disgusted as she turned back to Amy. '…and Everett gave everything to your awful failed-film-critic father! Calling it "Cleverco"! A more ghastly portmanteau I've never heard! Lever was far superior! Much stronger; so much more respectable!'

'He and Everett left you… the entire hotel chain…?'

'Yes! Dear Oliver, he always looked after me! He managed to withhold this one thing from the deal; the fifth largest hotel chain in the world, would you believe? Keeps me busy!'

'I don't know how I could have missed that…' DeVora guffawed down the hole, then shouted. 'I should say so my dear!'

'I'm still finding acceptable people to run it! But I will be wealthy forever because of it, so there is that!'

'But, this hotel…? It has… a certain… significance..?'

'I don't know about any of that, DeVora! Trudy Pankhurst doesn't trust me, because I don't hold with all the mystical-spiritual, alien-angels-and-demons, woo-woo-mumbo-jumbo that she does! Oliver told me everything that he thought happened! Nervous breakdown I say! Quite mad, the lot of them! I think dear Olly circled the wagons around the hotel chain to allow me to keep away from all their collective-insanity, New Age, pseudo-religious idiocy! And yet here I am – mopping up all the blood, once again!'

She shot another steely blast of disapproval across at Amy, then down at Harding and Xylata, who was still laying prone at his side. Then she sighed heavily, almost sadly, and for a few seconds became another person entirely.

'I know it's all real, of course…' Hines huffed softly. 'Which makes it all the worse…'

Then her nastier side returned, and she looked up at DeVora again.

' – and look at all this! Look at the damage to property!' She looked back down. ' – and this dreadful woman on the floor! All the senseless bloodshed – *all the blood!* Every time the other worlds come in contact with ours – destruction and bloodshed – and the longer they are here, the worse it becomes!'

DeVora kept staring down, but this time there was silence as DeVora and Hines held their gaze.

…a very intense, private silence, that everyone present felt suddenly almost bashful to behold.

Then the younger woman stepped forward, and broke the spell. She seemed quite stunned by it all, made a few sounds, but then started talking – just staring down at Xylata.

'I heard… that Oliver Hines had been planning some sort of genetic regeneration line; it was going to artificially but 'naturally' reverse the ravages of time upon a physical body, through genetic manipulation. But, the rumour was that Hines had cracked the total exploitation of the human genome, or was close to it, and that anti-aging was just the first of it…'

Amy wondered who she was, why she was there.

She had a very strong sense; she was going to be trouble.

'There were also plans to release a line of treatments that could accentuate or diminish both one's active and dormant genes for physical appearance, providing a menu of possible celebrity look-alikes to anyone with the money to pay for it.'

She took a few more steps and stared down at Xylata.

'My great-great grandmother told me that the very idea of it nearly destroyed the world…'

'…she's flipped…' Amy uttered, thinking only Harding would hear.

Instead, the woman swung her gaze, her whole body, across at her with a hateful look.

'You clearly have powers, start using them for good! And get this woman to a hospital!'

Amy was appalled. This woman clearly, really thought that Amy was the problem here; the cause of it all.

'It's not – I was just – Harding said –'

'Your mercenary assassin? A doctor as well is he?'

'I've stitched more organs back into people than you've had birthdays, little girl.'

'So… not a doctor, then? Proud of that are you? A trail of sanctioned corporate murders and emergency amateur triage across the globe that's led you to the delusion that you're capable of life and death medical decisions?'

They stared at each other – the room went cold.

'So much drama with you humans…' Xylata sighed heavily, staring at the ceiling. 'We can't get to my people, we must wait here for them to find us – I don't know where they are…'

Hines exploded again, shaking a stiff finger.

'Extreme cosmetic genetic manipulation! Out of the control of the world authorities!'

Amy turned to her; addressing both Hines and her slender companion.

'She is an alien from a civilization that is five times as old as ours and she is making her own call as to her life and death fate –'

'Ha!' DeVora cried out, still shouting down the hole. 'Hear how the astral warrior, the representative for the human race, defends the alien conquering colonists! Didn't take you long to go native!'

'You were just in that very room negotiating with at least five different clans!'

'Over you, you stupid girl – over you and your sudden, sinister presence here in this dimension!'

'But – *what?*' Amy was stunned.

'Hear hear, DeVora!' Hines clapped, very loudly three times. 'Keep these insane other-worldly dimensions where they belong – behind the dimensional barrier! These walls between us are part of the natural order of things! There for a vital purpose! And isn't that, in a nutshell, the reason we had such a problem the last time!? My brother almost died!'

Harding had had enough.

'Listen to me, Madame Hines! I saved your brother! Saved him from – well…'

'Satan!' Amy cried out. 'He saved Oliver Hines, and my father from the darkest creature in the cosmos!'

Hines just ignored them. 'Assassins who look like Queen Elizabeth The Second! It's a profane disgrace! The whole science, the whole philosophy, it must be brought to heel – gathered and contained and distributed according to the established world order!'

'My dear Hines…' DeVora practically gasped. 'I could not agree more! Stay there, I'm coming down. We need to talk – there is no dealing with these people; some dinner perhaps?'

'Oh, very well.' Hines huffed. 'You might as well descend here with me, and take me out, then!'

Hines batted her eyelids.

DeVora looked around, suddenly regenerated with a purposeful energy.

'Do the lifts still work?'

'Apparently.'

Amy spun around.

Belle was standing at the door to the lower apartment. Behind her was the man in the burgundy robe, still struggling to undo the knot. At first glance, Amy thought that he looked like a man befuddled with the flu who desperately needed a wee, but had accidentally tied his dressing gown cord a bit too tight. Then he looked up at her.

She was shocked.

'Terry?'

'Hi, Amy – great to see you.' He rolled his eyes. 'Alive, anyway. Cool vanishing act. Fake death? Nice one.'

'What – me? But, you – you were the one who vanished!'

'Simultaneous mic drops? Call it a draw?'

'But…?'

'He didn't vanish!' Belle scoffed. 'He did the opposite! He just ran straight off Everett's boat and splashed his experiences all over the web! Told everyone his crazy story!'

'He what?'

'He's a fucking conspiracy podcaster!'

'A what?'

Terry shrugged. 'I'm a podcaster – it's a new thing, like recorded radio you can download – it's starting to take off online and really make –'

'Yeah right!' Belle scoffed. 'All the true crazies have their own one, especially since the Holland Pankhurst one shut down! Terry here does some show with his loser mates about corporate conspiracies and alien intervention and Illuminati sorcery!'

Terry looked to Belle, almost pleased with himself. 'You've heard of me? I mean – us?'

Belle ignored him and took a few more steps inside, toward Amy.

'Look, I've come back. I don't mean you any harm. I'm asking – please don't try and come after me. It was a job, I skimmed your thoughts for DeVora and Styger – they hired me.'

'How?'

'I'm still in security, but I'm freelance now. I didn't take a Pandora pill or whatever happened to you and Heather, and Bo and Mitch; I've been low-level like this my whole life, but ever since that Miracle Quake, I just – spiked. I got a whole lot better at it, like, overnight.'

Hines scoffed. 'It's an abomination – too much freakish power to random people off the streets! It's not – proper!'

Belle didn't look at her, merely held up a firm middle-digit as she continued talking to Amy.

'Look, Amy, a lot of people did 'step into their power' that day, relatively speaking. I mean, you have to know this, right? You're some sort of – astral traveller? Don't you guys – meet up?'

Amy blinked.

'No, I don't…'

She tried to remember.

'…I haven't been – travelling. I've been fighting. On a giant boat, on a giant forest port, over a giant astral ocean – for, I think – all these years!'

Belle didn't really know what to say about that.

'I don't really know what to…'

'Really?' Terry uttered. 'Really; that's what you've been doing? You haven't just – been in a coma? And like, woken up and wandered out of somewhere?'

'No!'

Terry shrugged. 'Sorry.'

For some reason she sympathised. She remembered seeing him, after the deaths of their friends. On the chopper, getting off Everett's boat.

Leaving.

Never coming back.

'No; I mean, that's okay. I guess that's a fair assumption. But – no, I've been… away. Trying. Trying to make things better. Trying to – to make room, I suppose!'

Belle stared at her, like she couldn't quite figure out whether she was crazy, or –

'Look, I know what I do is real, but; all this alien stuff? Are you okay? I think you might have – I mean; I've seen people with PTSD. Whatever you've been doing…? I think you should go see Heather. I think – you need someone you trust, who is – like you. Human, but like you. Heather is that, right?'

Amy looked at her.

There was something about her she liked.

She was professional, hardcore, but – she was trying to help.

She was okay – maybe one of the good guys.

And maybe she had a point.

Maybe she should just go see Heather? If nothing else, to ask about Belle. Maybe – that's what Belle wanted? For Amy to go see the one person who could both help set her mind straight after all this chaos was over – and who just happened to be the one person that could verify Belle.

Ahhh. She got it now.

Belle was not just good; Belle was clever.

Amy needed clever.

Belle expelled a sharp, frustrated breath. 'Look, whatever. I can see I've stirred something up. But what I mean is; I can make good money at this telepathy stuff – it's the real deal. Better strike rate than with electric surveillance; I've been doing it more than a year now, but until now, I've always been anonymous.'

'You said…' Amy frowned. 'I might… come after you…?'

Hines snapped at them. 'You can't trust them! Don't deal with any of them if you mustn't!'

Neither Amy or Belle seemed to know to whom the warning had been directed, but Belle became restless. She rubbed her hands back through her platinum shag, as though she hadn't really listened to either of them.

'Okay, okay; I've got something for you.' She reached her hands simultaneously down into her jeans pockets. 'I can work for anyone, and nobody can read me, because of these.'

She extended two genuine polished opals, one in each hand. Each was thick and flat, very highly and beautifully polished, with the bright, primary blue and green shining brightest. 'Anyone who's anyone in this business carries one. They say someone in Coober Pedy who calls themselves 'Siriusandthem' makes them, but another guy brings them in, locally.' Belle extended one further. 'I have a few on me. It's all I can offer right now.'

Neither of them moved.

But beside Belle, the white-shirted woman extended her hand.

'I'll take one. If you're feeling contrite.'

Belle was clearly a little taken aback, and probably didn't want to part with more than she had to, but she glanced at Amy, wanting her to see that she was making amends – although for what exactly, Amy wasn't sure.

'No worries, I have a few.'

The woman took one from Belle's palm, then Belle moved forward and offered Amy the other, holding it out. Amy extended her hand and Belle dropped it gently into her open palm. Amy felt something; a magic, a programming, then Mendoza snatched it out. Amy sighed at the bold assumption, but then he dropped it back.

'Genuine. I'll look into it.'

Amy looked back to Belle; she seemed relieved.

'Amy, I've seen some stuff, working with Heather, and the others, for Bo Everett.' Belle frowned. 'But, look, all this stuff here today, about aliens? I mean, I saw some shit, but who's to say you saw the same shit I did? Who's to say what someone like The DeVourer, or Beans Means Hines here, aren't pumping psychoactive laughing gas through the air-conditioning to make us hallucinate…? Alien conspiracy? Anunnaki and the corporations? I mean, is it? Is it really, really – ?'

The other woman stepped forward to stand beside Belle, clutching her new opal as she confronted Amy with a little more aggression.

'Is it true?'

Amy looked back and forth. She wasn't sure what to say.

'It's true. I've been out there, out where they live. Years now, I think. I'm trying to stop it, stop them; roll it back somehow – but they've been here six thousand years.'

'The Lizard People?' Terry demanded.

Amy shrugged, helplessly.

'How many others are there like you, Belle? Who can just do the psychic stuff? Who were made stronger by the Quake?'

'Yes, how many?' Hines puffed herself up again, and demanded. 'How many street people with delusions of psychic grandeur are there to help shift the intricate and delicate and insanely complicated established pattern of order that has held the world together for six thousand years? Do tell – we're all – *so very interested!*'

Belle sneered. 'You really need to learn to go fuck yourself lady.'

Hines stalked up to her – she was at least a foot shorter than any of the shortest of the three taller-than-average women present and standing, but she puffed herself up and sneered back, baring her long, white teeth and curling her nose up.

'I am the sister of the wealthiest man in the world. Three to five times a day I have a different *gorgeous woman,* a different one each time, each more gorgeous than any of you three – *willow witches –* ' Conversely, her gaze scanned them all up and down desirously as she continued. ' – to service me in ways you've *never dreamt,* ecstasies you *can't imagine* – and then I go about my business, my life, my interests and hobbies, until the next one arrives, *and services me again…*'

She smiled, really smiled, with her eyes; and her teeth fully bared.

' – they are an extension of my wealth, my money; a service I pay for, a tool I command – that wealth, an extension of me, myself – and so, little *tight-pussy tree-trunk,* with your *pert tits* under your *punk tee-shirt,* you are teaching your grandmotherfucker to *suck cunt* – because I – through my wealth and position and freedom of mind – have been *fucking myself* with my wealth and my tools, my gorgeous, expensive, *exclusive tools* – since before you had your first *nipple tweak* – you skinny, uppity, *albino carrot!*'

They were pretty much all speechless as she kept smiling, but backed off, just a little. Then she cried out:

'Next!'

'Jesus…' Harding uttered. 'Do not mess with that one.'

'Thys…' Xylata groaned. 'There are more than a hundred in Los Angeles. We've talked about this…'

'Yes…' Amy remembered. 'They won't come near us – come near the war, in the astral, like Axelrod did…'

'There have been more like him, finding the Port…'

'But not enough!'

Xylata huffed; as though they'd had this conversation too many times before.

Belle shrugged. 'Well, I don't know anything about that. I don't really know what Port you're talking about. But I know that the spike in powers was focused in Los Angeles, where the Quake was; where, I'm told, the energy that triggered our abilities was released strongest across the board. But I hear there are maybe another two-hundred or so worldwide? I mean, these corporate guys pay us, sometimes they talk. Sometimes we see each other and have time to swap notes. There are chat groups, but nobody's really open. Nobody's sharing too much. I mean, they pay really well; this was thirty-kay up front. Just for an hour. We've got a good thing; nobody wants to blab too much, risk fucking it up. I mean, not even Everett paid that much; I mean, I would never have asked him for that much!'

'You can travel – dimensionally?'

'The teleportation stuff? No. Just the reading. Others are good at other things – but I can skim thoughts. Do it well; but that's it.'

Amy nodded. 'Go find my father, find Heather. She trusts you, right? Tell them I sent you. Tell him what's happened here. You want security? You work for the Pynes now, okay?'

'Okay.' Belle let out a breath. 'Okay; we're cool, then?'

Amy shrugged. 'Totally. We never weren't. Go back and ask Heather…' But she could tell that Belle wasn't listening – she had her idea of the world; maybe based on something she'd already seen, that she wasn't shaking it off. Certainly, it seemed, not just because she'd met someone nice on a bad, or at the very least, very weird day.

'Look, Belle; it's cool; we'll meet again, you'll see. Tell Heather – tell Dad; I'm going back.'

Belle nodded, then Belle was – gone. Not running, but moving quickly; out the door and down the corridor, with a vibe like she had a lot to get done before she would ever feel safe again.

Amy thought of Trudy. The way she described herself.

Great at the healing, terrible at the dimensions, so-so at everything else.

Then she looked at Mendoza.

'So?'

Mendoza shrugged. 'The Sirians make them, out where the opals come from; there are aliens everywhere in the outback. Those things work – there's really no hiding from Orion or the Nephilim, but the Orion Renegades are lesser once they split from Orion as a whole – still too powerful to face off on your own, but once you move, they won't be able to find you while you have these things. Nor will Anunnaki or anyone else – lesser than seventh density. Maybe the Sirians have a backdoor, but I don't think so, they value integrity and efficiency too much to corrupt their own tech with duplicity.'

'Maybe having a backdoor is part of the efficiency?'

'That's a third density attitude, doesn't fly with the Sirians.' Mendoza shrugged. 'Not as far as I can tell.'

Amy assessed him. She was remembering. He was right – she'd had dealings with people, and beings, in the time she'd been gone, been there; he was one of them. But something was wrong; he was nervous, not his usual verbose self.

'You don't know – do you?' She asked suddenly – one of those questions she didn't know she was going to ask.

'Know what?'

'Who that was, that just got shot? The girl; The Healer?'

Mendoza shifted his posture uneasily. 'No – not really, but I don't think…' He looked at her and there was a terrible morbidity in his eyes.

'Don't think what?'

'I don't think you should ask.'

'Should I know?'

'No. No, I suppose not.'

'But…' She didn't like how it had felt. Didn't like how this was feeling. '…did I – know her?'

'Maybe. Maybe yes – but…' He slapped his hand on his large bald spot and rubbed anxiously. 'What you should be asking, I suppose –'

DeVora was at the door now. Terry jumped, startled, still fumbling with the robe knot.

'Jesus, lady!'

She ignored him totally. ' – is who.' DeVora stated clearly. 'Who shot her? *And why would they?*' She nodded, superior, like she had him in a bind. 'Remember what he said? "This is the moment!" And there was something else, too...'

Amy assessed him carefully.

'You asked yourself, "how did she do it?", didn't you? I remember now! Who? How did who do it? Who is *she?*'

Harding looked up at DeVora. As he did, Amy noticed; Xylata had become increasingly, more noticeably white, more pallid.

'Was it you, woman?' Harding demanded.

DeVora assessed Harding and Xylata as though she might spit upon them. 'I am a corporate animal; I don't murder, and I don't *hire murderers*, I use my brain, my mind, my instinct, my personality and my cunning – of course it wasn't me.' She looked at Hines and smiled, her whole face changing at her renewed proximity. Almost as an afterthought she whispered. *'How dare you.'*

'On pain of death, wasn't it?' Amy accused her suddenly. 'If I return?'

'Theatrics!' DeVora was still staring into Hines' eyes, still with reciprocated desire. Her tone had become a lot more smooth. 'Heat of the moment! But you no longer belong here – I am no fool, I have studied you people. If you return, you will bring nothing but pain, and misery, and death…' She broke her gaze with Hines, as though she had suddenly remembered what she was talking about. Both of them turned and stared angrily at Amy now. ' – to no greater purpose; no end other than the worst kind!'

'Indeed!' Hines huffed, stomping toward her.

'Come along, Hines dear…' DeVora hooked out her elbow, and Hines slinked her arm through. They looked strangely adorable, Amy found herself realising, if adorable could also be completely sinister. '…it's been too long – and too long in the company of these *lesser folk;* we need a cab, and get out of this godforsaken suburb!'

'Absolutely! You – girl; what was your name?' She pointed at her apparent companion. 'Make sure this is all cleaned up before tomorrow, or else, there will be Hell to –'

'My name is Tarni. Tarni Lavé. And I don't work for you.'

'What?'

'Apparently, according to some ancient answering service, I still work for Mister Everett, but actually, I am only here as a courtesy because it's the only number you could find when the alarm went off. I was under the impression that you were some kind of innocent, bumbling old techno-fearing dame; but I can see you are an overindulged, criminally wealthy monster; one of a kind that this world is truly over and done with, but who will not lay down and decide to be a decent human being. So, no, I won't have this cleaned up. There is blood everywhere, people have been shot, and I am not the person to deal with it, nor clean it all up, not at all, Miss Hines. I'm calling an ambulance for this woman, then the police, and then I'm reporting back to…' She turned to Amy. '…well, your father, as it happens.'

Amy was shocked.

That name.

Tarni Lavé.

Why did that ring – ?

'Enough!' Hines threw up her hands. Beside her, DeVora was stunned, open-mouthed. 'Really; enough!' She wrapped her shawl about her, preparing to exit, stage right. 'I wash my hands of the whole deplorable incident! We'll see!' She threw her head back and walked out, puffing. 'Come, DeVora! We have each wasted enough time this evening on these – *delinquent delusionaries!'*

DeVora pointed at Amy.

'Mark my words. Demigods do not belong on Earth!'

And then she, too, had made her exit.

CHAPTER 79

'What horrendous people…' Amy whispered to herself, then turned quickly back to face Mendoza. She could tell that he had anticipated her demands by the way he held up 'surrender hands' and took a step back.

'Pyne, seriously…'

'Who shot her?'

'Thys, you know I have to be very careful…'

'Don't call me that!'

'That's what everyone calls you now.'

'Mendoza, I have at least four different lives and six different existences in my head right now, all competing versions of me from different dimensions, with different divisions within those dimensions, all with different names – *Amy will do for now.*'

'You do?' For a second, Mendoza seemed both amazed and impressed. 'Okay, okay; *Amy* – I don't know for sure who that healer was. And I don't know for sure who shot that rifle. I really don't *fully know* what happened, okay?'

'But you know something.'

'I –'

'This is the moment? How did she do it?'

'Maybe. Maybe I know something. But I tell you this; what I *do know* – if my theory is correct…'

Amy moved in, even closer.

'You know, Mendoza. I know you know.'

She gave him this; he seemed genuinely conflicted.

'I know, Thys! Amy! And you have to trust me – time is different out on the astral, you know that, we know that; everyone says that, it's a real thing! But it is also bigger, and wider, and clearer, and more navigable, from the spirals of Sirian space…!'

Amy's right forearm itched.

'What are you saying?'

'Amy; you can't know.'

'What? What do you mean?'

'I don't know, yet, what just happened up there. Or to you, down here, wherever down here was for all that time, for you. But you – you cannot know –' Mendoza glanced up through the hole. ' – what just happened up there!'

'Jesus Mary…' Amy was in no mood. *'Why not?'*

'Not now, not yet!' Mendoza stared up again. 'Can you see that, Pyne?'

'No, I can't.' She didn't even look. 'But – what you're saying, it implies…'

'I know! I know you know! But Pyne, seriously; you can't see that?'

Amy still refused to look up at the hole in the ceiling; the hole in the floor of the apartment that was no longer her home, and hadn't been for ages.

'You know – that I *do know* the people who did this!' Amy's eyes bulged. 'Wait – *do I know her as well? The Healer?*'

Mendoza looked away from the hole for a second, into the distance; his eyes glazed over and he rubbed his head again.

'We'll see…' He hummed. '…it depends…'

Xylata stared up from the floor. 'I see it…'

Amy would not let Mendoza go.

'We'll see? *It depends?* You're not my *mother*, Mendoza! I'm not asking you if I can go to my *first metal gig!*'

But he wasn't listening. He was talking to himself now, mumbling.

'If that was who I think it was, and the other one was too…?'

He hummed again. To his credit, from his creased expression, he was attempting to unravel a riddle that would stop a nuclear explosion and save five million lives. '…in whatever form she was in…? She's no more than a – and then maybe she – exploded? Divided? *Imploded?* Into… something different; or the same, but

– divided, exploded, imploded? But then again; if she's who I *think* she is – or, *was…*'

He looked back at Amy.

There were tears in his eyes.

One rolled down his cheek.

'…she was the most powerful human healer I ever met.'

'Oh my God…' Amy gaped. 'Was that – *Trudy Pankhurst?*'

Mendoza clicked his fingers and snapped out of it, pointing sharply at her with sudden accusation.

'There! There it is, Pyne! What did I tell you?'

'What? You haven't told me anything!'

Xylata tried to prop herself up a bit. 'Mendoza; I see it.'

Mendoza glanced at her. 'This place is a hot spot now, nothing's going to seal that properly other than the universe itself; it'll take a century.'

Amy clicked her fingers by his nose three times. 'Mendoza!'

He swung back at her. 'I know I haven't told you anything! But you need to listen to your Anunnaki buddy here; anything could come through that hole you made, and more likely than not it's gonna be slimy and earthy, and weird with sharp teeth, following the scent of something that's made it hungry, and super-pissed off that it's had to come all the way here to find it!'

'Stop trying to distract me with more of you bullshit, Mendoza!'

'I can't tell you, Pyne! I was there, watching – from the grassy Sirian knoll – for a reason! Because – *it was the moment,* the *very moment* where something happened, *something pivotal,* and I tracked it down through the spirals, to here; to then, *here and now, just then, up there;* here and now and then – a nexus, *a true pivot* – but – !'

He moved right into her eyeline, looked right up, almost nose to nose.

' – that is not what happened when I foresaw it! And that is not what happened – *when Misha foresaw it!*'

'*Misha?*'

'We need to get out of here…' Xylata muttered. '…that hole is still open!'

'Wrap this up, sorcerers!' Harding snapped, staring up at Amy.

She looked down at him; feeling his intensity, and seeing Xylata's silky-white dress was fully soaked in blood, something in her broke.

Tears formed in her eyes.

'Amy…' Harding uttered, '… your *actual friend* here is *real-time dying*. Her people are not coming. We are wounded, ill-equipped to defend ourselves, and need to move her, with or without her phantom rescue squad, before anything comes through!'

She looked back.

'Mendoza, *please.*'

'Pyne-Kid…!' Mendoza implored, never having taken his eyes from her. 'You would not be ready for my theory, for my best guess; it would change everything. *It would destroy you before you even got going!*'

'No!' Amy cried out. 'Oh my good God, Mendoza – you can't do this! Now you *have to tell me!*'

Mendoza shook his head.

'See?'

And in a blue flash, he was gone.

CHAPTER 80

'*No!*' Amy shrieked. '*Fuck you!*'

Tarni came up to her. 'He's gone! Snap out of it!'

'*What?*' Her huge brown eyes were so arrogant. 'Who the fuck are you to –'

'I lied! I am here to clean things up! Listen to your friends!'

'What the fuck do you know about my friends or what I just went through?'

'Your friend is bleeding out! And you're just standing here, bleating like a – *a stupid old woman!*'

Amy nearly slapped her. *What?* Nobody had ever called her that, in that tone, like that – ! Her arm tensed, her elbow flexed as her fingers stretched down; she was going to.

Old woman?

She was only – nine – twent – *she didn't know how old she was!*

It was Harding who actually snapped her out of it, speaking sharply; but not to her.

'Xylata; waiting for your people might take too long.'

Tarni Lavé stared down at Xylata. 'Who are *her people* exactly? Why has no-one called an ambulance?'

Harding helped Xylata unsteadily to her feet.

She stood, but she was weak, unstable.

For a second she looked disorientated, uncomprehending, then she managed to steady herself with Harding's help.

Amy caught her heart in the throat – to see her friend in this state was unbearable.

'You should all get out of here, leave me.'

'What?' Amy was appalled.

'Thys Pyne, if I weaken, if I were to accidentally manifest here in my actual fourth density body, I would detonate; kill you all and be sentenced to the Karma Forge.'

'Detonate?' Tarni demanded.

'The flesh of Anunnaki bodies are made of astral matter that, when they come into contact with Earth's atmosphere, without an FIV suit, or a strong, sustained act of will –'

'You explode?' Even Harding seemed a tad disconcerted now.

'Quite violently sometimes.'

'How violently?' Tarni demanded. 'And what if there were two of you? Willing yourselves to explode? In an office block on Circular Quay?'

'What?' Amy stared at her, astonished.

Then it clicked.

'You said you name was – Tarni Lavé? You're Miss Lavé? Uncle Bo's assistant? That my Dad saved that day from the elevator?'

'Yes.' Tarni raised her chin and her posture tensed. 'To all of that. My grandmother, Yelina, sent me here –'

'Yes! She brought you to the Port, you and five others, and made you an intern at...'

'The Port?'

'You were asleep...' Amy's eyes narrowed. *Why are you here?*

'I told you, Yelina sent me.'

'None of this is helping,' Harding decided squarely. 'Xylata, can you walk? Lavé; help how?'

'Can she walk?' Tarni was aghast as she whipped a smartphone from her back pocket. 'Seriously; for a start, I'm calling a God-damned ambulance!'

'Don't do that!' Amy ordered, contemptuously. 'Conventional authorities will get in the way!'

Amy stared down at three rapid tap-tappings of blood, maybe more, that were hitting the floor and pooling at Xylata's feet.

'Conventional authorities?' Tarni scoffed. 'As opposed to what? The Superfriends? I'm afraid I am going to have to ask you all to leave, right now, and never speak of this to anyone. Someone from Yelina's office will be in touch.'

'Yelina's office?' Amy fumed. 'We *are* Yelina's office!'

But she was right. Her friend was stooping now, unable to stand on her own. There was no way she could walk.

'Harding, let me carry her. I can focus my healing abil –'

'No!' Xylata snapped. 'The strength it would take for you to carry me would completely neutralize your meagre healing powers, Thys Pyne. I do not understand why Tzaebi and her people are not here!'

Amy whispered sharply. *Again with the Thys Pyne...*'

'You have been on the astral plane years now, Thys Pyne. Almost three, although I confess, I am not counting; that is your name there. You must try and focus, remember this past year especially. You came back for a reason, but the factors which determined that decision have changed. You must recall the dream, the dream of reality, that is your life!'

Suddenly everything seemed distant, yet tightly focussed and intense.

'Merrily, merrily...' Amy whispered, recalling something far off.

A party, a diamond; stars behind a glass wall, a doorway held open for her...

'*...life is but a dream...*'

Then it hit.

'Xylata – The Intersection...!'

Mystified, Tarni slowly lowered her phone, and spoke softly. 'I do not understand. Why are you all behaving like this...? I don't think you realise the danger you are in; there is a very, very dangerous anomaly occurring right above us, right there, right now, and unless I close this door and seal this room in the correct fashion, people... *more people,* could get hurt!'

Xylata sighed and rolled her eyes as Harding lifted her, up into his arms, as easily as a boy would lift a puppy.

Harding nodded sharply. 'She's right.'

But Amy was distant, barely paying attention, caught by astral memories.

'I was coming back home; I was worn out... the fighting was

just endless; disorientating, dispiriting. I needed to go home...'

Xylata hooked an elbow around Harding's thick neck, as his giant hand came up under the royal robe, under her legs and raised her. Now her bloody, dripping feet were dangling over his arms from her knees, like a ventriloquist's dummy.

'I must have homed in... on this place! My first real home – as me!'

He carried Xylata toward the door as his other arm came up, under her shoulder blades, but as they moved, she drew in a sharp breath. He secured her fully with one last heft and then, as she winced once more, the purple robe seemed to tighten itself independently about her, cocooning her like an Egyptian mummy.

Amy was still trying to concentrate, trying to remember.

'Xylata – something happened. Something – *important!* Somebody stole – !'

'You were defeated, Thys Pyne!' Xylata snapped. 'You retreated, and with good reason!'

'I – *what?*'

Xylata groaned. 'Ohhh; Thys Pyne! I want to get you a tee shirt –'

'*What?*'

Xylata winced. 'With the word *WHAT?* printed in huge, bold, neon letters!'

'Wha – !'

Xylata squeezed her eyes tightly shut as she once more telekinetically tightened the purple robe. Then she met Harding's eyes.

'That should buy some time, plug all the bits that want to fall out... until Tzaebi gets here...'

'Let's hope...' Harding nodded. Suddenly her whole back flinched and she curled, pushing her head into Harding's shoulder like a tired, unwell child, growling in pain.

'You were wrong, Thys Pyne, to despair, but it could not be helped – but your absence had a side-effect; and so, when I die, you must go back without me. You must go back and see, see what –'

But her pain was too great to finish the sentence.

'We need to make a decision!' Harding barked. 'Before it is too late to move you!'

'I told you! Tarni insisted. 'You all need to leave!'

Xylata spoke through gritted teeth. 'Very well… there is another way. I need to get to Ymira Station. It is a secret safe house, there is one in the centre of the city, where I can jump into a new body.'

'You can't just do that from here? I thought –'

'Don't you think I would have by now?!' Xylata snapped, then sagged again. 'No. There is tech involved.'

'Ymira Station is where you keep them? You need a… what was it? A – starcophagus?'

'I am sorry for my manner, Harding. You are helping me with no real cause. It will be noted. Yes, it is where we store emergency starcophaguses – you know of such things?'

Harding glanced at Amy. She shrugged.

'I have heard…' He looked toward the door again. '…tales.'

'If I can get there – before this… F-I-V… completely gives out; and if my… focussed will… to remain within it… does not bleed out… and diminish, along with it…' She shook her head as though this were increasingly highly unlikely. 'These… bodies are fitted with transmitters…'

Amy tried to think. '…Tzaebi – she must have been ambushed, detoured… like you were, getting here?'

'Xylata; I mean to help you, but…' Harding frowned. 'Do you intend to hijack another human body? Like you did with Sapphire Edge?'

'No; no, things have changed with the coming of Thys Pyne. We have exploited Cleverco's bio-technology to make neutral FIV body suits; new, blank bodies…' She sighed. 'Hot celebrity bodies, yes; but there are rules we have agreed to…' Xylata looked over to Amy. 'Are you remembering yet Thys Pyne?'

'No! Yes! I don't know! Xylata; I can't gap out of here!'

Xylata turned back up to Harding. 'She is often like this. Conflicted. It is very...'

'Human?'

'Annoying. Although we Ymira have begun to find it – 'endearing'. So we tell her anyway.'

'Oh!' Amy's eyes widened. 'How gracious of you, *Your Majesty!*'

'It was you, Thys Pyne, who insisted the Ymira no longer piggyback and manipulate the minds and bodies of free-roaming humans. Now we call it; Pyne-backing.'

'You do not!'

'Yes... we do now.'

'Uh.'

'We found her; I mean, the idea, extremely annoying at first, as you can tell; but she is noble, and she persisted.'

'Xylata; you are rambling! *Why can't I gap out of here?*'

'We soon saw the benefits; the Ymira and our allies now accept a new and more structured code of morality toward humans.'

Harding nodded, and grinned tightly. 'Xylata that is all very interesting; but Amy has a point. Why can she not...?'

His eyes narrowed, then he looked around as though something had occurred to him.

'Where is...?'

Xylata continued. 'The new bodies are 'just the flesh and bone', just FIVs, as Thys Pyne insisted – and things on our plane of existence... are beginning to change.'

'F – I – V?' Tarni frowned.

'Flesh Immersion Vehicles. Spirits born into third density FIVs, normal human bodies, are more dense; more physical than spirits born into bodies on the astral plane. My normal body, an AIF, is in here, within this FIV body.'

'Aye-eye-eff. Astral Immersion...Force?'

'Field.' She smiled. 'Nice try though. However, because of that, while I am in this body, my Anunnaki consciousness is tethered to the reincarnation cycle of this planet.'

'And will be for the next five hundred astral years!' Amy snapped. 'If we just stand around waiting for Tzaebi to show up!'

'She will come!' Xylata gasped. 'You know her! She is – one of our –'

'Best?'

'– our gang, Thys Pyne! Our cool gang of Field Marshalls and their best friends! Try and make sense!'

Tarni remained infuriatingly on-point. 'So, if you die in this body, the planet will not be able to tell the difference between an Anunnaki AIF and a true Earthling AIF?'

'Yes.'

'I can't believe I'm asking this...' Tarni uttered to herself, shaking her head. 'But; you call bodies Immersion Vehicles? Because you believe yourselves to be spiritual beings immersed in a physical density, via a physical body?'

'Yes.' She looked to Amy. 'This new one asks almost as many annoying questions as you –'

'Then stop talking to her!'

'A – flesh vehicle?' Tarni made a pfft. 'If you mean *spirit*, why don't you just say 'spirit'?'

Xylata rolled her bloodshot eyes. 'Truly? Some people in our world find the religious connotations too complicated. Like your new age hipster clan, using the term 'Universe', instead of the word 'God'. The words do not matter; to a planet, an AIF is and AIF; an ego is an ego; a spirit is a spirit; a soul is a soul. The planet's recycling system simply takes the spirit in any given deactivated and untethered third density FIV into the astral for recycling; there is no stopping this, any more than you can stop physical death. It is part of the process we could not avoid. It is the greatest risk that this new, Pyne-backing process involves to us.'

'That tracks...' Tarni smiled slyly, nodding to herself as she turned away. 'Yes, that tracks with everything she said.'

Amy snapped again. 'Tracks with everything who said?'

Tarni's eyes narrowed as she glanced at Amy.

'Yelina said you could be difficult.'

'Fuck you! She did not! We're trying to save our friend!'

'Then take her to a hospital and leave me here to do my job!'

Harding looked down at Xylata, and once again she stared up at him.

But this time, she rolled her eyes.

Harding nodded, almost imperceptibly, like, *I know, right?*

Then he looked around.

'Where is Pod-boy!?'

Terry came forward; Amy looked to him, barely recalling his presence in the room. He had been standing far enough back from the group to go essentially un-noticed, well behind Harding and Xylata, staring at them all like they were in turns crazy, fascinating and terrifying. It seemed clear he did not believe himself to be anywhere near out of danger.

'Boy; check the corridor outside. She is losing too much blood. I have to risk carrying her to the carpark.'

Terry had been standing near the skull-staff, the one that Harding had used to incapacitate the Anunnaki during the parlay. Amy only saw it now, propped up against the wall behind him, as Terry summoning his courage, walked cautiously past Tarni, and went to the apartment doorway.

'That!' Xylata pointed, suddenly seeing it too. 'The artefact!' Her finger hovered, shaking. 'Yes! It is the Cook-Skull Staff!'

'The what?' Tarni demanded.

Terry opened the door quickly, looked left and right and closed it.

'Clear.'

'Harding; tell me, how did it get here?'

Harding grit his teeth and spoke quickly as they moved toward the door.

'Pod; hold it open, then – '

'Terry.'

'What?'

'My name is Terry.'

Harding sighed. 'Okay. Sorry. Terry. Open, then follow.' He turned back to Amy and Tarni. 'Deal with your shit, then follow.'

Both the women recoiled.

'Harding!'

'How dare you!'

Terry's hand went to the door again.

'Wait.' Xylata ordered. 'Harding; you must tell me! Where did it come from?'

Harding rolled his eyes.

Are you determined to die and detonate yourself in this room, woman?

Xylata huffed. 'It could be very important!'

'One of Everett's people turned up at my door with it yesterday; he said Amethyst Pyne would be here today, and she would require it.'

Upstairs, or perhaps not actually upstairs, something groaned.

'Listen to me; that sound did not come from upstairs…' Tarni uttered. 'You all need to get out of here, *now*…'

'Harding, do not listen to her; tell me!'

'Can we walk and talk? You might be slight, but you are hardly –'

'Harding.'

'Okay; the courier said it was a profane object; that it would work against the power of other profane objects that work to block the powers you people have…'

'I can feel that it is…' Tarni frowned, shifting uncomfortably. '…profane.'

'When I arrived here and saw what was happening, I gained entrance through the side balcony – as soon as I did, the totem started up, on its own…' Harding looked to Amy. '– it spiked. My instinct was to get it into your hands as soon as possible. There were some of Yelina's people; at least they looked like hers –'

'You?' Tarni was stunned. '…know my grandmother?!'

Harding ignored her.

'They summoned that wilder-storm; their words, without me

even asking, as cover.' He looked to Tarni. 'Good people; good instincts; not pompous at all.'

Tarni squirmed.

'The case that the staff came in is still on the balcony – what is it? Even walking through the airport, at the cab rank, people seemed to – step away?'

Amy looked at Harding.

She had the same feeling she'd had, waking up beside him on the boat, years ago.

She liked Harding.

Just, plain, liked him.

'It is a very powerful totem,' Xylata stated sharply. 'Before we do anything else…'

The groan came again; then another.

Louder.

'…we need to get rid of it. Quickly.'

'What does it do exactly?' Terry enquired.

'Long story short; when it comes into contact with astral energy, it automatically generates a field that disperses it.'

'That's what that other thing was doing…!' Amy realised. 'I could see it, even when they had me blindfolded… it was hoovering in the opal dust and churning it out like ash!'

'Yes, Thys Pyne – in my mind it was like… a spear of light?'

'Exactly!'

'That is not good. The Ymira have exploited and deployed many of the sources of symbolic power that Eissley and Kyvza and the Draco were wielding to gain power, and the Ymira have gained traction on the Trade Diamond because of it, but we still do not understand the significance of many, particularly those to do with popular culture on Earth; not as Thys Pyne does.'

Amy huffed. 'Okay, okay…'

'Many of the powerful ones cross over with the historical totems, with people's fantasy perception of history…' Her voice was becoming dry. '…but the ones that interact with the astral, and the dreaming, and this reality; direct, hardcore three-dee reality, and the terrible or tragic acts or bizarre acts that have been performed here, within third density – these totems are even more rare, and more powerful to wield. These two, here today, were such as they.'

Tarni seemed queasy. 'That was one of them? And this is, too? Did they have anything to do with opening that portal?'

'It is impossible to tell. The meeting here was insane; so many different energies...' Xylata winced. '...in such proximity, with so much distrust and anger and hubris? When they went off, something was bound to happen.'

Tarni looked up. 'Where the hell am I going to even start...?'

'One item neutralises the astral matter, that other totem disperses. They are connected, if they are what I believe them to be, they are connected in a very terrible way.'

'Some of those beings seemed immune...?' Terry offered.

She winced again. '...that would only speak to how powerful those beings are.'

Terry looked at Amy.

'They were all here, just to see you...?'

She didn't even want to think about it.

'No...' Amy protested. 'They can't have bee –'

There was a flash of light; discordantly, the room seemed to grow darker. Everyone backed away from the hole, towards the door.

'Residues of all that conflicting energy remain...' Xylata coughed. 'Truly, this body will not last very much longer.' She shook her head slowly. 'We need to be rid of the Cook-staff – I am not thinking clearly; in conjunction with the cloapals –'

'The what?'

'The opals you were given – the cloaking opals, opals that contain disguised astral matter; the Cook-staff will increase their powers, their range and the density of the cloaking aura – I see it now; one or the other has to go. It is the reason...'

'Tzaebi can't find you!' Amy cried out. 'Yes!'

Terry turned to them. 'I know what to do!'

He turned and ran back inside the room, collected the staff, looked around quickly, then raced halfway up the stairs with it. He placed the staff upright, against the wall, about half way up, then looked around again, up and down, before turning back and jumping back down the stairs and back across to them, his hand outstretched.

'Quickly, one of you, I need one of those stones!'

'I'm sorry!' Tarni stepped back, hands raised. 'After what I've seen, no way! If this is really real, I'm gonna need protection from this madness!'

Amy fetched hers from her pocket and held it out to him.

'You'd better know what you're doing, Terry!'

'Believe me, this is going to work!' He closed his fist on it. 'You won't regret this!'

Terry turned and ran back up the steps, picking up the staff on the way. He turned left, to the exterior balcony door, and tried the handle. When it turned out to be locked, he raised the staff and cracked the tip sharply onto the glass, shattering the entire frame in one hit. Then he quickly ran the tip around the edges to clear the largest of the shards, allowing him to squat through. With a quick and terrified glance back across at the open portal, Terry was through the broken balcony door to the outside, and was out of sight. They heard him run across the balcony, then clanging footsteps as he descended the fire escape.

'He's going down the fire escape…' Amy uttered.

There was silence for a few seconds more as they listened to his footfalls recede.

Amy's next question was essentially rhetorical.

'He's not coming back is he?'

CHAPTER 81

'No...'

Tarni muttered this so knowingly, so earnestly, that she once again gave Amy the complete shits.

'...he is not coming back.'

Before she could tell this irritating interloper once again where to fuck off to, Tarni walked toward the portal, looking up.

'Is this really it?' She seemed to be asking herself. 'Through there? The Inner Earth?'

'Yes...' Xylata whispered, even more hoarse. 'At least, it is where you will end up when you go through, once it has fully stabilized. Right now it is still mostly a hole between floors. I still cannot pinpoint my people; something may have happened; the Draco dare not directly fight or hurt unpossessed humans, but they can fight other Anunnaki. Perhaps in the aftermath of DeVora's stupidity, our Ymira rescue squad has fallen to them?'

Harding did not hesitate now as he moved toward the door; Amy opened and held it wide as Harding and Xylata went through and moved swiftly down the corridor.

She looked back.

Tarni was still looking up.

'Odd – to be looking up at it. I always thought it would be a hole in the ground.'

'It is, from up there.'

Amy felt a power rise in her; but she had forgotten something.

Needed something.

Lost or forgotten everything, but...

She was remembering some things.

She summoned the things from the kitchen and brought them to her, raising her hand and drawing them telekinetically through the ordinary hole in between floors. She felt the energy there as they heard the kitchen cupboard door burst open, and the towel containing the passport, the cards, the money… the *everythingelse*, whip down, through the hole, and into her physical space; into her pockets, into the outfit she was now wearing; the catsuit, and the white bath robe, and the Ymira uniform as well, she suspected, somehow merged and transformed by her, unconsciously, using skerricks of the opal-astral energy that had remained within her body after years of coming and going, into something that had made her seem powerful, as she had been standing before the powerful, by protecting her modesty as though it had been nothing.

And her modesty had been nothing; flesh upon which they projected whatever they wanted.

Now, around her and over her and into her possession, her hidden possessions came, reclaimed.

She was remembering.

'Somebody stole my gun.'

Tarni's eyes were wide with Amy's magic trick; impressed, but not blown away.

Good; she was stable.

She might still be helpful.

'Get a grip and move it, or we'll leave you behind.'

With that, Amy turned her back and was out the door.

CHAPTER 82

She heard the door click shut behind her, heard the heavy footfalls on the hallway carpet as she saw Harding's mighty back and shoulders and buzz-cut carrying Xylata toward the elevator.

Ymira Station?

Had she just shown off to Tarni?

No; she needed those things.

But – had she?

Why had she done that?

She took a breath, looked, assessed.

Fire escape door behind her, sealed. No sanse of danger coming through. The room she'd left behind; a great sanse of every kind of danger.

Was Tarni coming?

Harding was moving quickly. Apartment room doors all the way down either side. Her friends and allies; gone now, she supposed. People who had come to The Pan later than her; they were another clique, the third floor down. Got to know each other when The Pan had already been a thing.

'Great Goddess have mercy it's true!'

There was a woman's voice, crying out from down the hall. Amy could see her, coming up toward the giant form of Harding, as he clutched the bloody Queen look-alike in his arms – completely ignoring that alarming sight and moving straight past them.

'Amethyst Pyne! Great and powerful Goddess! Amy – is that you?'

Amy blinked.

'Lorena?'

Lorena had been on the mission with her yesterday; no, *last...*

...three years ago?

Five?

– on the chopper that time, out to rescue Everett's boat.

'Amy? Amy! Jesus! Oh my God! Amy! Oh my Goddess! You're alive! You have returned! *You have returned!* Where have you been?'

Lorena was an attractive girl, Amy had always thought, from British producer mother and a Spanish actor father, with big black hair, big brown eyes, big gold glasses, a tiny nose and pursed resting-lips, which lent her something of an cute, owlish aspect, accentuated now with those brown eyes as wide as she had ever seen them.

'Where have you been?' Lorena demanded as she closed in. 'We thought you were dead!'

'Dead?'

'All of you!'

'All of – ?'

'You and your father and Bo Everett and all those people who never came out of Oliver Hines' mansion!'

'You… know about that?'

'Oh yes! You were all in the Hines mansion! When the Miracle Quake hit! They said you were dead – your friends returned, but you did not come back to us!'

The door clicked and Tarni came out.

'She means the Los Angeles quake in twenty-twelve.'

She closed the door behind her.

'I know what she means!' Amy snapped.

'They call it Miracle Quake because the city was levelled but hardly anyone was killed.'

There was a crackling from inside the room. Something sparked, then something crashed.

The power went out, leaving the corridor dark.

'Great.'

There was scrambling behind the apartment door.

It sounded big.

'Was it angels, like they say?' Lorena demanded, as though

nothing else were occurring round them, just their conversation. 'Did you offer yourself, for us all? So that we all could live?'

'Wh...?'

'Your friend's tee shirt idea is sounding pretty good about now, isn't it Amy?'

Amy turned to Tarni. 'You know about this?'

Tarni shrugged. 'You've only been seen publicly once or twice since then; and people seem to think it's not you.'

'Not me?'

'They say that the paparazzi pics on the red carpet from that Achilleios film premiere aren't you, that you're dead because of something Satanic your father did at the Hines mansion and now he's hired an actress, a Regene look-alike, to play you in public.'

Amy looked at Tarni.

'Why wouldn't Dad say something...?'

Harding was almost at the lift with Xylata; but there was no power.

'I mean; he knows I've been out in –' She saw that Lorena was listening keenly. ' – *on* the boat, out at sea all this time!'

Tarni leaned forward and spoke softly.

'I called Yelina. I don't believe there's any cause for concern so long as this room and the one above it are kept sealed for the time being, and the apartments are shut down for a while...'

'A lot of info for one short call...' Amy frowned at Tarni.

Tarni shrugged, again. 'We have a shorthand.'

She took out a magic marker and drew a large red circle on the apartment door. Then she took out another marker, this one green, and drew eight symbols, perhaps runic, within the red circle, in a long, diagonal-diamond pattern.

'Yelina will be here soon to deal with it.'

Smiling smoothly at Lorena, she capped both pens, put them back in her pocket, then took out a bag of dried herbs and scattered them all around the doorway.

'Nothing to see here, Lorena!'

Lorena didn't even acknowledge Tarni, just Amy, somewhat

adoringly.

'I'm sorry, Ames. We waited as long as we could, we kept your apartment just as you left it...'

It suddenly struck Amy:

That's why I homed in...

They made it a shrine!

What happened was blown out of proportion by rumours...

(Although - what had happened - had, actually been...)

Never mind -

'The Pan... made my room into a shrine?'

...and I homed in:

Literally and figuratively!

The power sprang back on.

'Kind of...' Lorena gave a cute shrug. 'More like... a memorial space.'

A furious metal tapping started coming from the end of the corridor; Harding had swung Xylata so she could start hitting the elevator call button with an irritating firmness and regularity.

'...but once we got word that The Pan was being moved to a new location...' She winced. 'It was just as it was, for ever so long!' Her shoulders sagged. '...until we had to go –'

'Moved by who?' Amy demanded.

'Whom by?' Tarni corrected.

'*Whom by* – has all my shit?'

'Don't worry.' Tarni smiled tightly, ever so slightly smug. 'Yelina says it's safe.'

Amy returned the smile. 'I have heard many definitions of the word safe and virtually all have singularly failed to impress when applied to real world testing.'

Lorena reached out and touched Amy's arm, the snatched it back, with a little giggle.

'They did take good care of it, Amy! Trudy wanted the location moved after the handover. After Everett's *vanishing stunt*. She said that The Pan was at risk of becoming less of an "active urban myth" than a...' Lorena frowned. '...a "publicly-confirmed corporate paramilitary wing", I think? So she thought a more covert base of operations was called for.'

Tarni confirmed it. 'Mister Everett asked me to find somewhere new; your father and Heather helped.'

Lorena was still staring at Amy.

The scrambling from behind the door had now become scratching. It sounded like the large claws of a huge animal, asking to be let out.

Amy moved toward it.

Tarni stepped in her way.

'It's trying to trick you. It can't be let out.'

Amy shook her head. 'Of course...'

But; she had so badly wanted to let it out.

She still did...

Why?

Lorena kept adoring her. 'They said you'd be back. They told us, told me, it would be a sign, when you came back; a good sign, that things were going to change for the better. That things were going to start to get better, and then, the world would see!'

'The world would… see?'

'I must tell them – tell The Pan! Our Amy is back!'

Suddenly the lights came back on.

Lorena raised her hands and closed her eyes and declared in a tone altogether too Evangelical for Amy's liking:

'Power has been restored!'

The elevator at the end of the hall dinged.

Just in time, Amy sighed to herself.

'Move it!' Harding shouted. 'We're not waiting!'

Amy ran.

Just as she did, she thought she heard something behind the door... whimper?

As though; it had been genuinely sad for her to go.

'Oh!' Lorena squealed, distracting her yet again.

Harding turned as Xylata reached out and hit the button for the carpark. Her hand was limp, almost directionless, but she made it.

Tarni kept pace with Amy, just at her side, with Lorena behind them. As the doors closed, Tarni slammed her arm in and held them back as the three of them slipped through.

'Who's this?' Harding demanded.

'Friend from The Pan...' Amy told him, her tone of voice making it clear that she could be ditched at the first opportunity.

Lorena was a little breathless, but kept talking.

'There were all sorts of famous people that the press said were treated for injuries after the Oliver Hines Mansion collapsed; nobody's seen some of them since, either. But I knew you would be back, Amy! People still go there, looking...'

'Stay away from that place,' Harding commanded.

'Satan lives there!' The Queen informed Lorena quietly, her head leaning heavily on Harding's shoulder now.

She was white as a ghost.

Already the elevator floor was being splashed with droplets of blood.

'The cat suit...' Amy recalled. 'Hines had all the waiting staff in cat suits! He said that, with Regene, everyone would have nine lives...!'

Xylata coughed blood.

'Was...?' Lorena stepped forward, concerned for nobody but Amy. '...was there an accident, Amy? Has your memory been affected? Did something fall on your head in the earthquake...? Is that where you've been? In hospital? In a coma?'

'No!' Amy turned to Xylata. '...unless...?'

The bloody Queen quite tightly shook her head.

Lorena was becoming increasingly more anxious. 'You're not going to... disappear again, are you? Go back to... wherever it is you've been?'

Amy and Xylata exchanged another look.

  ❰ *That's exactly what is going to happen. You and me are getting the fuck off this plane and back to the Port and -* ❱

  ◊ *Something tells me that will not play well with Lorena's new*

Amy turned back to Lorena.

'Frankie and DJ. They're dead, right? They haven't come back as well, have they?'

The power cut out again.

The elevator stopped, there was a collective groan, and the cage went pitch black. Then something kicked in and a low red glow illuminated them all.

'No...' Lorena breathed. 'Don't you remember, Amy?'

There was something terrible in her voice; a very tightly bottled anger.

'They were shot right in front of us!'

'No, no, Lorena, I do remember!'

'On that...' Lorena glanced to the side, and all of a sudden Amy recognised the fire of her old friend. '...that *fucking boat* that Trudy sent us to reclaim. Could have been any one of us!'

Lorena looked back to Amy; a different light in her eyes now.

'They say that's why Trudy vanished!'

'Who do?' Amy asked, cautiously.

'Huh! Our first paramilitary mission, and three of us – well, two of us now; got killed! There was never supposed to be any killing – not even the pirates! We rehearsed and rehearsed every scenario over and over for like three months back there in that old ball room. Then we discovered it hadn't been stolen, that it was your Dad, and he'd been through some kind of "Bermuda Triangle Situation" where he went through a storm and came out the other end three months later! Bizarre shit; and it keeps coming, all the bizarre shit!'

Her eyes seemed brighter.

A real angry-fire in her eyes now.

Their cage seemed darker.

'You liked DJ, right? Well, I liked Frankie and he died right there, right in front of me! Pissing himself! When I got the helmet off, half his neck was missing, and his eyes looked shocked. They looked – *heartbroken!*'

Amy remembered.

She had been in the back of the chopper with everyone, heading back to Sydney when they'd done that, taken the helmet off.

'And then we get back, and where's our glorious leader? Trudy Pankhurst? Gone! Six months she's gone and none of us have any clue what to do about it! April off working for Everett; who else was I supposed to…?'

'Where are they, Lorena?' Amy asked in a deliberate tone, as softly as she could. 'Are they… remembered?'

'Oh, Amy. How angelic of you. I knew you would ask. They were cremated. There's a plaque.' Then, as though switching personalities, the adoring light was fully switched back on in her eyes. 'It's glorious that you have returned, Ames! I'll text you the address. Do you still have the same number?'

She was phishing.

'Yes, I…' Amy shrugged. '…I think? As soon as find my –'

'Your phone is in storage with everything else.' Tarni sounded quite sympathetic now. All the talk of murdered boyfriends, probably. 'Nobody touched you things, Amy. Other than Heather.'

'Heather?'

'Yes.' Tarni was a little stunned. 'Is that – a problem too?'

'*Too?*'

'You're friends now, remember…?' Xylata croaked. '…we… all are.'

'No, of course not; I just… thinking back about that awful day, seeing Heather with Dad for the first time… I remember now, it's all…'

The lift dinged and opened to the hotel's basement carpark. They piled out, looking around, but Harding was striding his way toward a large white SUV, the largest in the near-empty bay.

'I'm going to put you in the back, with…' Harding turned back and shouted 'Amy!'

'Head to the Bridge…' Xylata ordered. '…if Tzaebi and her medics are coming, they will intercept us there.'

Amy and Tarni caught up with them as Tarni's phone rang. She looked at the caller ID and answered straight away.

'Yes – the basement carpark!'

Harding glared. 'Who is that?'

Tarni looked Harding in the eyes.

'Caller ID was Tee-zed-aye...'

'Tzaebi...' Xylata sighed.

'Tzaebi has anticipated the situation...' Tarni kept looking at Harding. 'She needs to ditch the body. They'll be here in a few minutes.'

'How...?'

'Yelina has advised them of the Cook-staff problem. They're not equipped to deal with a human body this badly wounded; there is no effective way to get her to Ymira Station without critically injuring the body; it's safer if Xylata exits on her own – directly to the astral.'

'If I could have done that, I would!'

'They say there is another way....'

Tyres shrieked and they all looked toward the down-ramp as a plain white van stopped at the gateway. A hand reached out for the ticket, even as a woman leaped out of the passenger side door and sprinted toward them; a lean woman with pale skin and flowing blonde hair. Xylata caught sight of her though droopy eyes.

'Tzacbi!'

As she drew closer it became apparent that the Ymira's Chief Medic had chosen the twenty-seven-year-old Gwyneth Paltrow for the novelty shell of her human FIV armour.

Harding had already placed Xylata on the back seat. They watched as Tzaebi moved her hands over her leader's face.

'She will not make it.' Tzaebi turned to Amy. 'Thys Pyne; you will need to open an astral gateway and take her astral body through to Ymira Station. She cannot do it alone; in its current state, the FIV will cease to function at more than eighty zees – she will be lost in the Karma Forge. We cannot lose our leader, not ever, but especially not now.'

'Especially?'

Tzaebi shook her head. 'The human propensity to forget astral experiences upon returning to the Earth Plane is part of this experiment, but – '

'Experiment?'

'The Siren Experiment – it has succeeded – but now you must remember, Thys Pyne. Xylata's life, the life of your ally, your friend, depends on it; the fate of your world may turn upon it. You must remember who you are, what you have become, and you must remember – right now!'

CHAPTER 83

Xylata was moaning, delirious.

Another medic was looking her over; she looked like Julianna Margulies, back when she had started out in *E.R.*

But Xylata wasn't having it.

'This is too dangerous, Tzaebi! I am done for! I have come this far, now I must accept the karmic burden I have wrought – I will be born into the Earthling cycle and –'

'No, Field Marshall!' Tzaebi was furious with her. 'Absolutely no! I will not allow this disaster to unfold!'

The Margulies medic spoke. 'Tzaebi – we can still keep this body alive here for a few minutes; maybe ten. That will be enough time for her to get to Ymira Station if she leaves now, but she must be tethered to a human guide.' The medic looked to Amy. 'Thys Pyne, as a Pandoran, you are her only hope.'

'I remember…'

'How could you forget? I only just told you…?'

'That's okay... Exyli?'

She was Thys again.

'Yes Field Marshall.'

Thys nodded.

'What do I do?'

Exyli smiled, relieved.

'Just hold her hand, pull her out - and gap!'

CHAPTER 84

They were walking along, on The Moon, holding hands.

'I mean, you saw what happened when Kyvza manifested, in his vault, out on the Mojave – the more worked up he got, the worse the desert storm outside became.'

'How many times do I have to remind you – I wasn't there!'

'Well, go and look at your father's memory. Go and look at Heather's, or mine if you will, like you go and look at that time when he was almost flattened by the flying subway engine.'

'She says something to him.'

'Who?'

'Cricket Wilde. They make a deal.'

Xylata looked around. 'Well this doesn't happen very often.'

'What's that?'

'This is The Moon.'

'The Moon?'

'Yes. The Moon.'

They both looked around.

'Yes…' Thys nodded. 'It certainly is.'

'What is this?' Xylata raised the bonded hands between them and stared at it. 'What are you doing? This is most unusual!' She looked Thys in the eyes. 'Why are you crying?'

'You are my friend, and I almost lost you.'

'Is that all? Really Thys Pyne, you are truly set off by her most obvious of things. Besides, Anunnaki do not have friends. We have…'

Thys stared at her expectantly.

'Very well, Anunnaki do not have friends, except one, and that one is me, and that friend is you. Satisfied?'

Thys shrugged. 'I guess.'

They kept looking around.

'This is the Moon Portal. Usually, people come through in the hyper-millisecond gaps, or fall asleep so quickly, in the blink of an eye, that they never see this; especially since the real lunar surface has been landed on and photographed; they don't want to see this 'The Moon' anymore.'

'So what's this one?'

'Well, obviously not the real one or you would be dead.'

'Obviously, thank you, Edgar Mitchell.'

'This is the idea of The Moon; the story-book The Moon, the Sandy Lunar Plane that leads into the Sleepy Dream Realm.'

Thys looked around at the expanse of the lunar surface; it was exactly as you would imagine it.

'Don't let go of my hand, Thys Pyne.'

'I won't, Field Marshall.'

They stood a while, then kept walking.

Then Xylata started talking again.

'The Moon is the doorway to The Astral Realm. They call them planes and densities, dimensions and realms, but it's all the astral plane really. The Astral Realm is like saying The Terrastral Territories.'

'The ocean is the ocean. It doesn't care how we divide it, or what we name it.'

'Yes. That is true. You are not as stupid as everybody thinks.'

'Thank you so much.'

'Some of us think it's a massive star-gate.'

'The astral plane?'

'No; The Moon. We think – maybe, it's the remnants of a gate humanity built millions of years ago. Your second or third major evolution, or 'Iteration' as the Orions say. And the thing that was pitched at this planet, that wiped out the reptiles, the dinosaurs and such, that would have led to a species like mine developing here for the first time, was a measured attempt to prevent that happening. By the remnants of a past human civilization, evolved to who-knows what plane?'

'Oh dear.'

'The Draco use that in their Anti-Apey Recruitment Propaganda.'

'I bet they do.'

They stopped as Xylata paused for more reflection.

'The old human stargate. Exactly in position to provide mammalian life, exactly in position to unconsciously remind humanity of their legacy, and destiny; their impossible ancestor's giant stargate staring down at them in the sky, most nights, some days; always there, unconsciously pulling you all out into the galaxy again.'

'A meteor that hit Earth, exactly so; so that a buried astral stargate could be flung back out into orbit, placed in the sky, exactly in alignment for eclipses and things? And just so; so that it prevents the planet peopling with reptilian people? That's what you're saying? That would have to be –'

'Nonsense, you think?'

'Who knows?'

'Norionsense?'

Thys shook her head. '…it's just nice up here, walking. Things have been so stressful.'

'Well, that won't stop.'

Thys shrugged. 'I suppose I could try meditating every now and then.'

Xylata sighed. 'You could try masturbating, or getting laid. Exercising, or binge-watching entertainment. Temporary solutions. Won't stop the stress.'

They kept walking a while.

Then Thys made a declaration.

'I seem to have sex with somebody incredibly bad for me, every time I go back.'

'Not this time you didn't.'

'Well, I didn't have time, did I? And besides; I was in the Inner Earth for…'

Thys drifted.

'What?' Xylata demanded, after a short silence.

'Nothing. I don't think I should try and remember it.'

'Very well. So, The Dark Thing that burned its way down to control Hines…'

'The thing behind the door…'

'Behind the door?'

'I think it…' Thys gulped.

'You think what? Why are you squeezing tighter?'

'I think… it was my dog.'

'Your…?'

'I don't know. Maybe I'm just…' Thys had tears in her eyes. 'I think I had a dog I left behind. I think I had a whole life. But, my dog came to…'

Xylata squeezed her hand back, hard.

'Listen to me. If there is something from the Inner Earth that wants to find you enough that it crosses over the density barrier from there to here; it will find you eventually.'

'You think?'

'That is a certainty. Just like this Great Evil Thing. The Dark Thing they won't call Satan. But I will. Not 'The Devil', not 'Lucifer', 'Beelzebub', whatever. I've studied my Gnosticism, I know. Your father knew. It's the real thing and it's as Dangerous As Hell. More dangerous. And it's taken an interest here again; in the whole paradigm of reality.'

'Paradigm of Reality!!!'

They stopped a few seconds and listened to those word echo.

'Wow.'

They walked on.

'Hines got its attention – your father pissed it off; and now he is scared of it. And rightfully so; his theory is correct. You've seen what the Sirians can do. That God Map that fool Gordian made. These kind of cosmic – who is that man in your memes who designed the crazy moving puzzles?'

'Rube Goldberg.'

'Yes. Look at the things he did; look at what your domino

people can do with some thought and skill and imagination and wit and willingness, and physics and some time. Imagine what a race who lives their lives not measured by tens, or fifties, or one-hundreds being special markers for a lifetime, but by one thousand years as being 'a good run'. Imagine billions of them, like there are billions of Humans, their accumulated science and culture and spiritual power – imagine the smartest and worthiest of them. Deciding to kick-start mammalian humanity one last time. Because ten thousand years ago, you used to be allies, because you've fallen on hard times. Because the Universe missed you.'

'Maybe they will protect us from The Dark Thing?'

'They? Maybe they already are. But until we can ascertain that fact, we can but persevere, and seek.'

They walked on.

Thys couldn't think of anything to say.

She didn't feel like saying anything.

'The reason you're not talking is that your whole mind is being used as a conduit to replenish my astral blood.'

'Okay.'

'The reason I am doing all the talking is because that makes me very agitated, and aware.'

'That's fine.'

'I think that was the reason Kyvza had the vault out there in Mojave the first place.'

'Kyvza again?'

' – it could just as easily have been under the actual house on Mullholland, with all the Sirian security systems he had set up there. But he wanted to be able to go out there and blow off steam – to make an actual storm.'

'And the Sirians cause earth tremors...?'

'They do appear to disturb the earth itself when they arrive. Likewise, when the Pleiadeans appear, which they hardly ever do – there was a lot of rain at Pan's wake. For just a few minutes, the Pleiadeans manifested, and protected your father and Heather from the Orion Renegades, and it did not stop raining for a whole day over that part of the coastline. Yes, maybe somehow they do correspond with water.'

'They're called Norions now.'

'Who?'

'The Orion Renegades.'

'Really?'

'Apparently. And remember; the ones who worked with Gordian; they called themselves O'Renegades.'

'The No-Orions and the O - Renegades. I like the first one. Because they are so negative, and say 'no' all the time. That is very funny, Thys Pyne, you are learning humour. The No-Orions and the Yes-Orions.'

'Norions and Yorions?'

'The Yorions; the ones who don't want to kill us, like Obsidian.'

'I will think on that. Your humour still needs work. Perhaps an improve class.'

'Do you mean improv?'

'Improv? Why must you Australian Humans contract every word? You take the classes to *improve*. That is what they are call improve-ization classes.'

'Then, I might be working with not only Yorions but also Yes-and-rions…?'

Xylata stopped walking and stared blankly at Thys for a second or two.

Then they kept walking.

'Regardless, during these storms that were caused by the alien presence in the world, Suzie Saturn was able to make contact in the astral with your father at several different points, and arrange to have herself freed from the Draco Sirian-starcophagus.'

'Like the one Pan is in, still?'

'And I need not remind you, we still do not know who provided those advanced, black starcophagi to my former clan.'

'I thought maybe… Orions? Yay or Nay?'

'No proof. Not of anything. It is a matter we should look into, when we return.'

'I told you, I have no current plans to return. I want to stay here, in the astral, fighting Draco and hanging with Ymira clan.'

'You can do that, yes, you must do that; but you must also return to your third density family periodically. Or you will become lost here, and fall out of touch; eventually you will be more astral than earthly and that is not good for you. Perhaps when there are more of your own kind, who can travel here as you do, in a real body.'

'But – why not? I don't mind that I get more used to it here.'

'You should not lose touch with your own world. The reason we created these starcophagi devices was to walk amongst you. One must do that – or one can lose track of what is happening on Earth, in third density. Time works differently here, as you know. You can sometimes be here for what seems like weeks, when really, it is months. Or you can return to Earth for a day, and when you arrive back in fourth density, many things have occurred, that make it seem like much more time has passed. But it is the moving back and forth that prevents this. The moving back and forth creates a pattern, a web, a bridge; and both densities attune to that and intuit a navigable path; a relatable context; a narrative that holds together for you.'

'We could do with one of those now.'

'We keep walking, one will show up.'

'If we think about your starcophagi?'

'That's where we're going. Ymira Station.'

'But…'

'Have patience, Thys Pyne. The Universe wants us to succeed. It wants us to learn and progress. Sometimes, we do not listen to its advice; our intuitions. Sometimes we wish for things, when our actions prevent those eventualities from manifesting. But, The Universe, if you ask nicely, will always place you in, or send you to, or direct you to, the closest place from which it is possible for you to reach your highest destiny. All you need to do… is be open, and aware.'

'Well, I feel like I have been, but, what can happen in a landscape that is almost completely sand?'

'We have been walking in quicksand for the last minute, Thys Pyne.'

'Oh.'

'Hold your breath.'

'Yep –'

CHAPTER 85

The sand enveloped them, then fell away, leaving them prone, on their backs.

Amy was still holding Xylata's hand.

They were on a beach.

Sunbaking.

'Who has my other hand?'

'It's Heather,' said Heather.

They were silent a while.

The sun was glorious, they could hear the ocean lapping, not too far away, past their feet.

There was a huge storm, much further out.

'There is a tipping point.'

'There is?' Heather asked.

'You were made as the planet made you and modified by the original Anunnaki colonists. We did this on many worlds. There are other species in the fourth density, on the astral plane, who do otherwise – they alter species to be more aggressive, less aggressive, more in tune with the astral plane, more in tune with their own versions of second density; of the Inner Earth. All the combinations of the above. It's what apex astral species do.'

Heather raised her other hand as a shield to the sun.

'Out there in space?'

'Yes. Or they, or we, will arrive and announce ourselves formally. One or the other is inevitable.'

'Will we live amongst them?'

'Yes. You might die and reincarnate to do it, but you will. And by the time humanity is doing that, you will remember that you were once Thys Pyne and Heather Everett, just as you now remember within this life, and this field of consciousness, that you were once children, but are no longer children.'

'Cool.'

'I am very far gone, am I not?'

'I think so, Xylata.' Heather squeezed her hand. 'They said it would help if I came here too, as a second conduit. Amy and I are the best at being here for now. You are on a very low level of the astral plane and we are keeping you there, away from nightmares and fever dreams, while Tzaebi monitors you in a starcophagus.'

'The nightmare realm is the storm…' Amy heard herself speak. '…we are the sunlight.'

'Hmmm…' Xylata closed her eyes. 'Poetic.'

Amy watched herself walk past, naked.

She could see herself; her stronger jawline, her bigger eyes, her fuller lips, her curvier breasts, her more pronounced bottom, her longer body, her fuller hair. The Pandora Sequence had not added anything to her, but in combination with the power of astral matter and her own culturally-manufactured dream idyll of herself, had reformed the combination that her father and mother, and their ancestors had concocted for her in a normal birth, and somehow accentuated all the aspects of those possibilities to their greatest aesthetic effect.

She saw herself look at the storm, shielding her eyes, then take the catsuit out of the car boot and put it on, leaving the ears and tail behind.

Something made her want to tell herself; no, take them, they will come in usef…

But she had made her choice in the moment.

She saw herself on the prow of the ship, the first moments within the astral; saw the catsuit morph into a wetsuit.

Saw herself coordinating a defence of the boat, weeks later, and the wetsuit beginning to develop the crocodile pattern as she began to trust and come to admire the Ymira, her new, rebellious reptilian allies; and as they began to appear in the pattern also, as a sign of camaraderie.

She saw herself walk down to the water, toward the storm, as she had walked down the stairs in her apartment to face DeVora and her cabal, with the catsuit, and the wetsuit forming about her; swirling astral matter, shimmering opal, without her even knowing. Pulling in the black coat; Everett's coat that had been bequeathed to him, which Mitch had bequeathed to her, in front of him that day in what was now the Cleverco building; the bathrobe, all that was left of the comfort of her stripped homestead, forming a white fur-trim around the coat, adding a white-trim hood; not even knowing that she had done it, and that she had been dressed like that the whole time since, until she had fallen:

And come out now with the same clothes, but leather, and home-made. Real, dark green and deep olive patterned reptilian leather, real hide from a real, giant creature; real fur, dark brown lace-up leather boots, tight, with a matching lace-up vest... an outfit that a costume department would have created, but real.

And then, finally, as it had all morphed back into:

A version of the Field Marshall uniform, with the new-coloured stripes, but somehow fusing it all together, keeping everything but simplifying it; layers of texture and symbol and memory and such a strong, beautiful costume with her flowing blonde hair, full and down around her shoulders and chest and then then she leaped, and flew off into the storm at ferocious speed, and exploded in a ball of white sunlight.

Still on the beach, still holding Xylata's hand, she sighed.

'That felt good.'

Xylata grumbled a little.

'You never said why you changed the human colour from pink.'

'Not all humans are pink.'

'We chose it because you are a vibrant race; filled with engaging enegries.'

Thys looked across at her, a few seconds without blinking.

'And because you are pink.'

'I knew it.'

'You, Thys Pyne. You are pink. Not all of them, not every human. That is not possible for just one colour. Pink; for just you.'

Thys sighed. 'I changed it to bright orange because it's the colour of sunsets and deserts, something none of us live far from and we can all see just about every day. And... look, it can symbolize a mixture of skin tones. I could have gone mocha or caramel, or whatever, but quite frankly none of those colours pop. I thought; red, for red blood, which all humans share, but red on black was too stark. Too... war-y. Bright blue? The sky, water? Almost. But then we're back with the good ol' "blue-eyed white people" again, and; well, bright orange was...'

'You overthought it...' Xylata smiled.

'It's a bright compromise!'

Heather looked over at her. 'You overthought it.'

Thys let out a breath. 'I overthought it.'

Heather smiled. 'You do that. It's okay. You're going to have to use every colour in the rainbow eventually, when more people start turning up.'

Thys let out a long, long breath, then Heather waved her hand, like a fairy godmother. Where she shoulders and insignias had been bright orange, they were now burnt-orange chrome. Still bright, just...

'Oh...!' Amy gasped.

'Not so pop. You're Field Marshalls, not flight attendants.'

Then Xylata started talking again.

'If I might resume?'

Thys and Heather looked at each other, like *resume?*

'Your species may or may not have responded; they may or may not have responded in the way we desired, but they did respond and we were able to exploit that response as the species spread. But there is always a tipping point.'

'Oh right.' Thys remembered now. 'So you were saying.'

'A tipping point of karmic virtue. Your species does not have to enter into appalling mass slaughters, or genocides. It does not have to listen to the psychopaths, the fanatics and zealots

– but most species at this point of development inevitably do. Sometimes within the astral, sometimes within the Inner Earth, sometimes overlapping – it is a cosmos, after all, and there are many variants of any number of overlapping worlds and species who would look at this world and see it so, too; as an overlap that is different to their own 'real' baseline overlap. But once that tipping point is tripped, and that group – a family or tribe or clan or city or city-state; nation or country; fascist dictatorship or enlightened democracy – chooses – to disembark the karmic wheel for a station somewhere between love and hate and all stops in between, then the energy of the culture that forms – *can be harnessed.* Then, we move in. We do not care what the energy is – on Earth it is almost all what you would call negative, when your people act in unison. It is, sometimes, love. But ever so rarely. That, in itself, is a magnificent harvest for its very rarity. But across the galaxy, the Anunnaki have other worlds, where all we harvest is love – and the value of the energy from the rare, hateful outbursts are just as incalculably valuable as true love is here.'

Heather turned to look at her.

'Don't look at me like that – every empire on your world has operated in exactly the same way. Some without any semblance or cosmic law or self-restraint.'

Heather looked away again and smiled.

'I just wanted you to know what you have let go of my hand.'

'Oh.'

Xylata reached over and took it again.

'I think the point…' Heather smiled. '…is that you might not need to anymore.'

Xylata hummed. 'We'll see.'

The water was lapping up to their feet.

'We'll see.'

Up to their knees, their bellies…

'Hold your breath again!' Thys warned.

And the water was there.

And then so were they.

CHAPTER 86

Thys was right there, watching the lowered starcophagus case that contained the Anunnaki body of her friend Xylata drain of a bright blue liquid. She could see the beauty in her passive features as she slept; her mostly deep-lime scales were covered in a pale-blue astral glow, lending her the aquamarine aura of the Ymira. The bright lime streak of scales down the middle of her crown, her Mohawk, was striking, but spread out in a subtle way that Amy hadn't ever really noticed, across Xylata's cheeks, with the sprinkling of slightly darker lime there, over the deeper lime of her major complexion, seeming like... well, freckles, she supposed. She'd really never seen it because Xylata's lime-yellow irises, when open, were so arresting that they almost always drew complete focus.

'They are, of course, designed as cages...'

'Bodies?'

She hadn't asked, but she had wondered.

She didn't remember reaching Ymira Station; but this was it. And this was herself; she was Thys, in her own physical, human, astral-morphed body.

'...traps, really, to catch and contain the human astral form, the human AIFs, as they return from astral slumber.'

The operating Anunnaki smiled at her. He was older than most.

'We would not do that with you of course, Field Marshall. Even if we so desired, it would be incalculably dishonourable to ourselves and ever so rude to you. Still; we did believe that our Anunnaki AIFs were uniquely bonded to our physical astral bodies and that was that; until we needed to decide otherwise. Then there was a way found.' He smiled at her. The elder

Anunnaki seemed to smile more. 'I am sure you are uniquely bonded; material and astral, inseparable, Field Marshall. Nothing to concern yourself over.'

'That's nice to know.' She didn't believe it. Maybe he did. She didn't know. 'Eyotzaf?'

Eyotzaf nodded, pleased she had remembered. 'The cases; starcophagi, as they have been coined, each contain a generated astral field – technology that was pioneered by the Sirians, but that we have reverse-engineered to our own purposes. We program the artificial field with a human's DNA and spirit pattern; essentially their FIV signature, so that instead of the human returning to their body after sleep, they are tricked, and diverted to the starcophagus. The sleeping body is then left vacant of its AIF, and any old Anunnaki can then jump in, 'hijack', as you say, or 'piggyback' as you say moe politely, wake the FIV, and pilot it around as third density armour.'

There was a swirl and a flash, and Heather arrived. She and Thys exchanged smiles, then Heather examined Xylata, up and down, concerned. Eyotzaf had draped her body from neck to knee with a long white towel, and Thys recalled two things upon seeing this; first that Ymira women, while apparently brusque in manner, were actually notoriously coy, and chaste; and second that Xylata was considered to have been hatched with an almost supermodel-level physical attractiveness which she pretended to find a burden. Thys was beginning to understand that this, too, was Anunnaki etiquette.

'But you don't do that anymore.'

'We Ymira do not, no.'

Eyotzaf was a male Ymira elder with seven letters to his name, the 'Ey' vowel at the start denoting a skilled scientific mind. There weren't many male Ymira that she'd seen; she did not really know why. He did not have the squarish head of the Draco and Chenek Anunnaki she'd run across, although he did have the common, pronounced central snout and low lips. The thing that made him stand out was his more downturned-triangular face; essentially he had an extremely wide cranium and forehead. The few male Ymira she had seen appeared the same; it was almost like the Anunnaki version of the classic 'alien grey'; something in itself that she had yet to behold.

'We bargain now, if we must inhabit an active human. Pyne-backing, I believe is the Ymira slang?' He smiled again, with quite a wily look in his eye for an Anunnaki. 'The process is the same, but the targets are chosen more wisely, an approach is made, discussions undergone and bargains achieved with the human in question. The first approach is made in the astral, of course – should they decline, or become distressed, they remember nothing when they wake other than a soon-forgotten nightmare.'

'You bargain?' Heather asked.

'We never used to, when we were allied with the Draco. But, this is what you have taught us; you, Thys Pyne, along with Xylata herself. After her experience with Sapphire Edge, who recognised and acknowledged her, but only sought to communicate, she was changed. Then you appeared, Thys Pyne, to show her the way. Changing our ways, we discovered the advantages of bargaining; to grease the wheels rather than to threaten and force. It is much easier, and humans respond so much more easily, and gracefully; beneficially, primarily – and the Ymira clan are pleased to be the forerunners with this new technique.'

Xylata blinked, then opened her eyes.

Immediately, her uniform; the crocodile-print, military-style leather suit with the lime arm-bands and chest stripes, reappeared to replace the towel. It was an unconscious, automatic; perhaps even ingrained, modesty-based etiquette.

'I remain?'

'Field Marshall Thys Pyne and her attendant were able to hold you and protect you in lower dream levels, Field Marshall Xylata. From there we were able to transfuse your astral body with dreama, and plasma; your body is healthy and resumed with the rest.'

Xylata raised her head a little to look down at herself.

'Huh.' Her head dropped back. 'I remain.'

Her face was impassive.

'Is that…' Thys began. '…okay with you, Field Marshall?'

Xylata looked to Heather.

'Would you mind?' She glanced at the lime shoulder pads.

'Of course.'

Heather waved her hand. The pads and stripes changed, becomin a shining, pine-green chrome.

'Most distinguished, Field Marshall.' Eyotzaf looked to Thys. 'Field Marshalls.'

The Field Marshalls both nodded in approval.

Xylata suddenly rolled her lime-yellow eyes and looked to Eyotzaf.

'Oh! Of course! You modified the starcophagus so that it would attract an Anunnaki AIF to an Anunnaki FIV?'

'Indeed, Field Marshall Xylata.'

Xylata closed her eyes again and nodded. 'That is good. You have done well. I and my allies thank you, Eyotzaf.'

'Ymira always, Field Marshall.'

'Always…' Xylata sighed.

One of her hands spread out and relaxed.

The other tensed into a fist.

'…always.'

CHAPTER 87

There were times, with anyone doing anything, anywhere, or anytime, that you needed a break. When you couldn't see the wood for the trees, the trees for the forest, the forest for the canyon, the canyon for the continent, or the continent for the planet.

Or, see the dream for the plane.

'The plane for the dimension, the dimension for the…'

'That's not right, Thys Pyne…' Xylata smirked. 'We are putt-putting across the dream plane right now and you can clearly see that we are in the astral dimension; there is astral matter; dreama and opal and –'

'Aren't they the same thing?' Heather asked.

'No, no, no; dreama is astral matter affected by Anunnaki; opal is astral matter effected by humans. By you, mostly.'

'When did that happen?' Thys recoiled, frowning. Then she sighed and went back to watching it all, the dreama and the opal, glittering on the water, in the moonlight, in the daytime. 'Anyway; I am not sure the analogy goes on.'

'Oh, it goes on Thys Pyne. Ever on. Just like your questions.'

Thys shook her head. She was Amy again; at least, in appearance. She was dressed again in the black dress and the diamond necklace from the movie premiere.

'This astral amnesia is doing my head in. But I remember now. I remember, I just needed a break. I mean; I know, in war movies, they send the guys back from the front, once in a while. Just for a week or two. But, nothing seemed to be working. This ocean, this "Sea of Humanity", was getting bigger and bigger, but things down on Earth just seemed to be getting worse and worse.'

Xylata was guiding the rudder at the back of the small

motorboat… although there was nowhere to go. Just the vast expanse of purple-lavender and cobalt-pink water.

'You would not stop; you would not listen. You created a drama for yourself because you were exhausted that allowed you to leave in an energetic huff without feeling guilty. And now you are back – again – after; what? Half a day? Is that what you think?'

'Back saving your life, you mean…?'

'Very well. Extenuating circumstances.'

Heather looked at them, smiling happily.

She was at the front, staring out at the pure whiteness of The Moon above.

She spoke softly.

'You have each other's backs.'

'And now, I suppose…' Xylata growled, strangely. '…we have you, and yours.'

'I suppose you do.' She looked at Thys, dressed as Amy. 'But you are driven, aren't you Ames? I see that now.'

'You must see that…' Xylata insisted. '…and that is not what happened. Like a normal human, you create a scenario from the parts you most want to keep, and call that the truth. Sometimes it is. Sometimes it is only part. Do you remember what happened, Thys Pyne, the last time you left and came back?'

'I went to a movie premiere…?'

'And when you returned, Yelina built the port. And Jason Axelrod found us. And soon after that, more enlightened, creative, open, searching humans found us.'

'I left for a reason.'

'I have had some time to piece this together, Thys Pyne; and this is what I believe to have happened. We fought a long time, and the ocean expanded; but nothing happened. You said, you wanted to return to Earth, to see who it was that was causing the Draco City to expand, to see who it was, that was making it happen; to see who your enemies were. But you were distracted; you were called to the Intersection. The higher planes beings knew you were important, and planning something; they wanted to see you, sense you; feel you, approve and sanction or disapprove and prevent you; one last time before your first big move. And there, your plan, to reappear on Earth and wait, to find out who your enemies were, was blasted with an enormous burst of conscious, cosmic energy and approval. Misha showed you her creation, her Arcana; Norions and O'Renegades, whichever is which now; they tried to kill you before you could return to Earth. Other Anunnaki came for you, and someone was so terrified of what you would do if Misha offered you the Arcana that they stole it. From a Sirian!' She shook her head. 'Someone will pay for that one! Then, you returned to Earth, and the conscious energy from your approval by the higher planes beings at the Intersection came with you, again. It drew all of your enemies to you in one place; it executed your plan… what did you call it?'

'The Siren Experiment.'

'Yes; yes, the deceptively powerful woman who draws her enemies to her, by coming out into the open. Yes. That was a good plan.'

'It nearly got you killed!'

'But it did not. And now we know; we can identify them; the Australian media barons, the European woman, DeVora; Oliver Hines' sister; many Black Ops; many countries; many corporations; several independent operatives. Various races from outer and inner space. And many others besides. Some friendly. We can revisit and unpack that scenario as we wish.'

'Yes…'

'But the other part of the plan was to see what else would happen. It is a basic rule of cosmic manifestation that once the spell has been cast; once the wish is fully visualised and formed, worked upon and… whatever method one chooses to use for whatever manifestation they desire or require; they must then let it go. They must then release it into the winds and the wilds and the tides and the times of the astral, and allow it to have its own life, create its own form, and then return; as the best and closest possible manifestation for your karma, your dharma; for the benefit of the cosmic scheme of things.'

They were getting closer now, to it.

'And this…' Xylata stared out, into the horizon. 'This, Thys Pyne, is what manifested, when you left the battle; the war, and forgot about it for a day.'

Thys kept staring.

Heather turned from it, closer on the horizon now, and looked down at Thys.

There were tears in her eyes.

'You really did look absolutely stunning in that dress, Ames.'

Thys looked down. She was in the middle, between them, as though she were being transported somewhere. She could see the diamonds, resting above her pushed-up, squished-in cleavage, pale and white but reflecting the colours of the water off the diamonds.

'But…' Heather sniffed, lightly. 'You are Thys now. Thys Pyne.'

Heather smiled.

'I will still call you Ames…' Heather looked away. '…but Xylata is correct, you are Thys now.'

There was silence.

They were getting closer, but it still seemed so far away.

'I think this dress helped me find myself a lover that night.'

Suddenly, the whole mood on the little putt-putt motorboat changed.

'Really?' Heather glanced back. '*Do tell!*'

Thys frowned, trying to remember. 'Have I been back three times? Like properly back, now? Not just hops home and back; but, stayed home a while? And it's been roughly five years, since the Quake?'

Heather frowned. She didn't seem certain. 'You two were walking across The Moon for weeks. Then we three were sunbaking on that beach for… I don't know how long. It felt like a proper holiday to me, anyway. I feel like I haven't seen your father for – ages!'

'I do feel better. I'm almost twenty-one, aren't I?'

'No…' Xylata shook her head. 'You were almost twenty-one when you wore that dress to the movie premiere. Then, you went back to have your party, a few months later.'

'But I…?'

'You feel safe there; now. Now, where you have settled in your consciousness, you have not turned twenty-one yet. But, soon. Soon, we have a nice gathering on that boat we keep coming back to – the one Everett gave you. Everyone is there; your human friends meet Gexvi and Vlynk, and Tzaebi and Lyveq and the others. Everyone gets along. Suzie brings her guitar. Everyone sings along. It all… goes along.'

Thys nodded. 'I'll look forward to that.'

Heather remained curious. 'So, can I ask, Ames; was it anyone we know?'

'Who?'

'You know!' She blushed a bit. 'The lover! After the movie premiere? Will he be at your twenty-first gathering?'

Thys looked out, then back at Xylata.

Xylata was staring past her, ahead; at something only she could see.

'No, he wasn't.'

'Oh.'

Thys started talking. 'When it happened, though. After the preview? I mean, it had been a while, since DJ, and there have been a few… fumbles, and quickies, and – mistakes, here and there. But, I'd never had anything like this man.'

'Really?'

'He was a real, experienced, generous lover. Someone who just – attended me, sought out; *knew,* my every sexual need. And, it seemed like, it meant something to him; meant – a lot to him. Meant *everything to him,* maybe; but the fact that it meant *so much to him,* made me feel – adored. And that made me feel – everything. It was simply –'

She gushed.

' – incredible!'

The motorboat putt-putted on; the astral water lapped and splashed.

'Wow.' Heather gulped.

'It didn't happen again, sex I mean, until I went back the second time; I mean, I didn't think you could replicate that night, the first time. And I had been away, a while. Then, my phone rang, and; it was… *very unexpected.*'

Thys shook her head, with a sideways smile.

'And, we talked. We talked for hours. Then, finally, when I thought; yeah, okay, I'm ready again, I got in a cab and we met at a bar, at the bar where he was staying. We theorized, on and on…'

'About what?'

'Everything. He knows about – all this. The corporate occult, he calls it. But that's just one name for – all this? Right?'

'One aspect…' Xylata uttered. 'One lens.'

' – anyway, we went to his room and started making love almost as an extension of the talking, without trying. We went on and on and it became – well; occult, I suppose. The things we were talking about, we sort of did, but *as sex.* It was so sensual, and mystical, and rhythmic and heart-pounding – but then pure, and technical, and… yogic, I suppose? Tantric? At times, it was as though there were people watching, from somewhere else, whispering, telling us things; we knew so much at the end of the night that we hadn't before we started.'

Heather was getting a slight contact high, and spoke in a very dreamy voice.

'Ooh. That's… *amazing!*'

'Too amazing, Heather. For the second time, I decided; it was something that could not, should not be replicated.'

'Oh, Ames!'

'And, the third time…'

'Oh, good! Good for you!'

'…in a way, that was the weirdest of all! He just… I mean, I've never experienced anything like it. It was nothing like that second time. We hardly even *talked.* He just, I mean, we started and he just kept going and going; just pure, hot and sweaty fucking, *like; fucking,* like, you *wouldn't believe.* He just – I mean, like a machine; *like an animal.* I was just *slaughtered,* like *gutted;* wide open! I mean, the next day, I could hardly walk, or talk! I could hardly think! I was floating, but clear-headed. It was like being here, in the clouds or on the ocean, just floating in – *powerful, primal ecstasy!* Then I was just weak, like a baby deer. But, seriously; man! Woman! It blew the cobwebs right out of my soul! I mean; phew!'

'Oh, *goodness...*'

'But; then I went home.'

Again, there was silence a while.

'Jeez, Ames.' Heather laughed, shaking her head. 'Looks like you found the total package!'

'Oh yeah!' Thys laughed. 'Yeah; in there somewhere between them all.'

Heather laughed again, very floury.

The she jolted.

'Wait; what?'

'So, the only thing now is – which one do I – you know, keep seeing?'

Xylata looked at her and scowled.

'Thys Pyne; you are mixing things up. You do not see the second boy until you go back this time, after you see what you are about to see. Then the third boy is not for six months after that.'

Thys stopped.

'What?'

Something shifted and she looked down.

She was naked, with wild bed-hair, except for a long tee-shirt with one word printed on it.

WHAT?

'Very funny, Xylata!'

Xylata grinned. 'It wasn't me! That is your own self-awareness manifesting unconsciously!'

Heather stared at her.

'So; Hearty, Talky and Fucky? Three different men?'

She was quite flushed.

'It just happens, Heather; and they are always – terrible choices for me! I don't really understand why!'

Heather made a face. 'Huh. Yeah, well I know that one.' She laughed some more, huffingly. 'And, I know one other thing that has changed today, other than one of my more innocent perspectives.'

Thys smirked. 'What's that?'

'I am going to have to start keeping secrets from your father!'

Thys rolled her eyes. 'He knows!'

'No really, Ames. He doesn't.'

'Oh.' Now Thys was blushing.

Xylata had released the rudder and was standing now, with her hands on her hips, looking down at them.

'I have said that you need to start building a structure here, Thys Pyne! I have told you that most humans who come here build a dream house, or houses, and keep many rooms in these houses. And each room is a different time, a different important memory, a different event, a different aspect of who they are in their lives. They might have a mansion for each of their incarnations; a room in a mansion for each; a house for each; it is fractal and individual and it goes on and on. This framework seems to be included in the human package, this basic infrastructure of dream navigation; it is how the Draco and Chenek built that enormous, black, ugly city of smoke and waste, by exploiting that basic infrastructure!'

'Glitchy… very glitchy.' Thys frowned. 'Now, who told me that?'

'Nobody, it's obvious!'

'Is it?'

'Yes. Terribly.'

'The Queen of England isn't dead, by the way.'

'No? Well, it can't be too long though, can it? What year was it there, where we were? Twenty-seventeen, I believe? June again? And also, we agreed to a fifty-year limit; if they are still alive but aged, then we can appear as their younger selves, then it can't possibly be them and confuse or frighten anyone. Anyone stupid, really. They would have to be – so stupid.'

'You just made that up.'

'I did make it up, then I did ask you if it could be real, and you did say yes. That is how things work almost everywhere. You agreed; we use the recreated DNA of the deceased, just like Regene say they don't, but do…'

'What?'

Heather leaned forward and waved her hand over Thys' chest.

Now the tee read:

"What!?"

'It's really much more like that, don't you think?'

'Yes, very good Heather Everett.'

Heather looked at Thys.

'We still have a lot of work to do, Ames. Everco and Olivera didn't change, just because we mashed them together and changed the name. There are still lots of guardians and gatekeepers from the previous incarnation. The war isn't just up here.'

'Up here, down here, around here somewhere; out here, in here…' Xylata muttered. 'Humans and their crossed-words…'

'What!?' Heather asked, winking at Thys.

Xylata looked out again. 'The modified version of Holland Pankhurst's genetic cocktail is already available on the black market; you would be naïve to think otherwise. Just think of that Hollywood party you were at before the Quake. Now it is five years later! Or two, here and now, where Thys Pyne believes she is still twenty years old, and still wearing that dress. We are in between because we are so far out on the ocean.'

'And why is that?' Thys asked.

'You have become distracted again; and now we are here.'

Thys turned around.

'Why is that, Thys?' Xylata raised an eyebrow. 'Well, there's that.'

They all saw it.

They all stared.
They all stared a long time.
Finally, Thys spoke.
'What?!'

CHAPTER 88

'We don't know…'

The little putt-putt motorboat pulled up beside the main boat.

Then, they were back on the prow of the main boat, gapping unconsciously for a better view.

'But it's something to do with you, Thys Pyne.'

Thys Pyne reached over and took Xylata by the hand. She grasped her hand, fingers between fingers, and held tight.

'We made that together, whatever it is.'

Xylata squirmed.

'I am squirming, but I understand.'

'Good.'

'But you are wrong. You made it. That is the point. I helped you create the space; this ocean. Me, and the Ymira. You are counted amongst the Ymira, we co-lead the armies of the Ymira, but you are not Anunnaki. That – is not Anunnaki. That is pure Human, absolute Earthen. And the only Human here on the astral Plane, whose presence could possibly have generated something like that – is you. There is no other.'

Thys stared at it.

'What do we do?'

'I do not know.'

She was back now, back in uniform, slightly modified to accommodate her adventures in other densities, on other planes… and all that jazz, but back to being Thys Pyne, where she had left off.

'Are they our ships?'

'Yes. Ymira ships. But once they come within its vicinity, they change.'

'They're beautiful now.'

'Yes.'

Heather was crying again. 'What is happening? What am I seeing?'

Xylata continued. 'And over there; up there; base of operations, and outposts. As before, it is taking a kind of human military shape – because this is who you are, and how you fight. But the war will also be fought like an Anunnaki war – an astral war. With deception and imagination. Everything will be important. Your body, your clothes, your possessions; you cannot leave anything anywhere now. If it has been here with you, if it has been used by you on the Earth Plane, it has been transformed, and then retransformed, like you, to become iconic. Like you father will become – is becoming. Like you too, Heather Everett, are becoming. Like Bo, and all the Everetts. The Pynes and the Everetts; The Pandorans. The Hines. The Wildes; others, with us and against us.'

'So what do I do?'

'You have to go there.'

'I do? Why?!'

Heather walked forward, staring out.

'But… what is it?

'It's a new star.'

'A new star?'

'Yes.'

'Why?'

'We don't know. But it's something to do with your Amethyst Pyne. My Thys Pyne. Our Amy. And if you don't go, we will never know what it is.'

'But...?'

'Because nobody can get near it. But we think you can.'

'Why?'

'Will you try?'

'How?'

'Just think yourself –'

Amy went.

CHAPTER 89

And was there.

'Oh. Kay.'

'So... this is...'

'Oh!'

CHAPTER 90

Thys gapped back to the boat.

It was night now; at least, it was dark.

She went downstairs.

Xylata was at the bar, Heather was asleep on a couch.

She woke as Xylata turned to see that Thys was back.

'You were right – I do have to go back home. Go back. Then come back here again. Then again. And probably again.'

'I am right? But; of course I am! Only – why, this time? What is it?'

'I think it started as an island. But – now it's a mountain. But, I think it's becoming a castle.'

'You shall rule the astral! It shall be your Palace!'

'No – that's the last thing I want. It can't be just for me, or I am no better than the Draco! I need to channel energy here that corresponds with the vessel – we need a power structure as free of Anunnaki and psychopathic corporate interest as we can get; make something here that is nothing to do with them, and draw people away from their toxic astral temples, unholy astral high-rises and pitiless astral skyscrapers.'

'But – you have your own company now. You are an heiress!'

'Cleverco!' Heather cried out.

'Yes!' Thys nodded. 'Nobody knows what it is, so everybody is waiting for it to all apart! No human psychopaths, and no Anunnaki clan has come anywhere near it; they're just waiting for it to fail and fall, like vultures in the trees!'

'Really?' Heather sounded disappointed. 'I really thought we had started to… pull it together?'

'But now, after what happened with DeVora, and Styger; clearly, this is the time that attention will turn to it. We must be extremely cautious, and stunningly cunning in order to maintain control of it. Heather, I have a plan. Some time, it might take a while, it might be years, but I have been to my palace and I have walked the corridors and I have thought and thought and thought, and now I know. I know what to do; I know where the path is, I know where it leads, I know how to get there. Sometime in the future I am going to come home and tell you the war is over. But it will be just like it always is; I won't remember, and it will take a while for it all to come back. When that happens, I need you to pull a trigger. We'll set it up, and put things into play, but the whole plan, the whole execution – will all rest on you doing this thing.

'I… I'm honoured! But – are you sure? I mean; don't you think you should tell us what it is, this plan?'

'There's no need to be honoured. You're okay. You make my Dad happier than I've ever seen him.'

'He does the same for me.'

'Okay, then, we have a deal. We're friends.'

Thys held out her hands.

'Come with me.'

CHAPTER 91

They stared out a while, again, from the windows of the highest level of the Palace.

Xylata raised their conjoined hands.

'Are we done with this?'

Thys was startled. 'Oh! Yes! Of course, I had forgotten! Sorry!'

'That is alright. What are you thinking?'

'That I know what to do.'

'And what is that?'

'I need to go and back and find out what it happening.'

'I will stay here. What then?'

'We need to find a way of getting sleeping Earthlings to come here, to the Palace.'

'How?'

'We do this again. We run the Siren Experiment mission again, only this time, on a much larger scale.'

'How big?'

'I dunno.' She looked out, across the astral, at the Ymira State in the Terrastral Territory.

'How big can we go?'

She shrugged. 'Cosmic. I guess?'

Heather nodded to herself.

'They were right; Mitch and Bo. When they told you to keep going.'

'When was that...?' Thys scratched her head and pulled her fingers through her hair air. 'I need a bath.'

'Time is all screwed up again, but I think I need to talk to Suzie Saturn – I don't think I've slept for a year.'

'Talk about what?'

'What else? About finding a place to sleep!'

'You already had that conversation. Five years ago. I think. Maybe you haven't. But I think you have; I think that you learning to sleep properly here was what started all this.'

'I can feel the conversation about sleep that I have with Suzie Saturn either coming or going or being; but I know I have to have it, and then I need an actual, *actual* sleep.'

'Maybe we all need some sleep.'

'We do. Can we all sleep here?'

'I think you need to go and find that talky corporate occult boy and have your human needs quenched. Learn whatever it is you said you learn from him. Then walk the Earth a while and come back. This place will still be here.'

Thys turned from the balcony and looked back.

'I've already done all that; but I still need to do it all. Perhaps, remembering, here, is like... doing it all over again? Am I just finding this place, this Palace, now? Five years after I first arrived? Or am I remembering that I found it, two or three astral years ago, five Earthling years later?'

Xylata nodded. 'That ponderance possesses an absolutely-possibly higher-than-low likelihood of being headed toward an almost-entirely convincing percentage of truthfulness.'

Thys nodded. 'Xy; if I go back to Earth now, and be normal, am I going to be twenty-three years old?'

'Yes?'

'Huh.'

Thys let thank sink in.

'You'll remember it all...' Heather comforted her. 'You kept dropping by. Never for long; but you have been in our lives. Let's just hang here a little while and see what we remember.'

The pink and purple and fuscia and violet and lavender and indigo and... the walls; had many doors, leading to many places.

'Or...' Thys proposed very suddenly. '...am I just realising now that I sowed the seeds of it... several astral and Earthling years ago; but I am only now *consciously* finding it, even though it has been here the whole time?'

She looked at Heather.

She looked at Xylata.

She looked up the giant staircase behind them.

'A Palace this size has to have a bath, surely.'

'You'd think.'

'You would.'

'But wait; before we all go our separate ways again, there's one last thing. It won't take long. I need to tell you the plan. Because – things are going to get weird from here; weirder than before.'

CHAPTER 92

Five hours later, a stone-walled banquet hall had manifested around them; along with a sturdy wooden dining table, lined with high-backed chairs, and a roaring fire in an enormous hearth with a huge dog sleeping in front of it.

'Whose dog is that?' Heather asked.

Thys shrugged. 'I think it's mine.'

'Big.'

'Yep. Loyal too.'

The enormous canine grumbled as he adjusted his back to the fire. They watched to see what he would do next.

There had been a gap in conversation; they were near the end.

'But anyway... that's basically it. That's... 'The Plan'. That's "Amy's Plan".'

It was coming close to sinking in.

'But wait...' Heather frowned. 'You haven't told me what the thing is I have to do at the end, to make it all work.'

Thys told her what it was – the last thing in her plan; the most important piece of the puzzle that would make everything else work.

'Oh...'

Heather suddenly saw it; saw the whole thing and her part in it.

'...kay.'

EPILOGUE

Heather sat at her desk in Mitch's old apartment, which was Pan's old apartment, which she now used as her own private office.

In the end, there had been simply too many rogue cosmic and mischievous mystical forces remaining from Pan's long-term storage of so many powerful occult items here that it just made sense to have someone stay around.

Just in case.

It was classy now; Heather had redecorated and restored it herself, keeping only the old couch, which had never left, and the matching single lounge-chairs, which had been brought back.

There was a white flash in the room before her and she spoke without looking up.

'Been wondering what time you'd turn up.'

Ames made a face. 'What *time*...? Very funny.'

Heather handed her a large white envelope.

'Save the day. We're doing it. On the *Lady Ann*, next Feb. You're a bridesmaid, but I know what you're like so just show up and I'll do everything.'

'So... is that... this...; no, next...?' Heather could see Ames struggling with the notion of time having passed; of connecting that passage with needing to be somewhere, sometime, in the future. '...actually, Heth; let's start with; what year is this?'

Heather nodded. She'd been expecting this. 'We should do the Everett Protocol. But I've done a spreadsheet based on everything you told me. I asked Uncle Bo to ask *Lady Ann* to scan your history of astral travel.'

'And?'

Heather shrugged. 'Nothing.'

'Nothing?'

'Nothing. You were gone longer than you thought, but *Lady Ann* says you were there the right amount of "astral time". However *that* works. There's nothing you can do about it, Ames. It's October, twenty-seventeen, and in a few days, you will be twenty-four years old. Body and soul.'

'Huh.'

Ames flung herself down to sit in a single couch.

'You've made that work...'

Heather indicated her outfit; it was more refined now. Still commanding, but more fashionable.

There was now a burnt-orange chrome buckle.

'...very stylish.'

Ames waved her hand absently.

'Uh. I've learned to adjust it. For here and there, you know. Added things.'

'You can do that?'

'Sure, why not? If you have it in the astral, you can manifest it here. Mix and match. Merge and morph. It's a thing.'

'It is?'

Ames didn't answer; she just huffed.

'Okay; out with it.'

Ames huffed again, reclining even more forcefully and more agitatedly into the old black couch, as her waving hand played about her face.

'The three men I told you about. There's complications.'

'Complications?'

'I've been sleeping with the enemy!'

'The enemy?' Heather was stunned. '...which one?'

Ames' restless hand finally came to rest, slapping across her tightly-shut eyes.

'All of them, Heather! All of them!'

THERE ENDS

The Pandorans
Book Two
"The Pandora Inheritance"

Next in the series is:

The Pandorans
Book Three
"The Omega Sequence"

For further exciting titles in this series visit...

www.GalexyTales.com

THE PANDORANS:

Book One: The Pandora Sequence
Book Two: The Pandora Inheritance
Book Three: The Omega Sequence
Book Four: The Pandora Arcana
Book Five: The Sirens Sequence
Book Six: The Daughters of Pandora
Book Seven: The Lucifer Sequence

(and keep searching

"Galexy Tales"

at Amazon!)

ACKNOWLEDGEMENTS

MANY, MANY THANKS TO:

Melissa Sheldrick,
Stan & Gennie James,
Lily McDonnell, Gretel Newman-Sugrue
Pat McNamara, Gary Turner
Travis Pollard, Adam Dutkiewicz,
Kay Leanne, Julie Dinsdale and Michael Aspden,
Chris & Ange Collings, Adam Vale
Greg C. Grace

Gallifrey Stands!

Alex James,
June 2019

About the Author

Alex James is a writer who lives in and is inspired by Adelaide, South Australia.

Alex studied European History, Classical Mythology, Film Studies and Screenwriting under the Communications and Liberal Studies banners at the University of South Australia.

Between 1992 and 2005 he wrote many, many, many outlines, treatments, concept documents, bibles, pilots and screenplays, for just about every active Australian production company there was.

From 2008-2014 he was an in-house writer for Angel-Phoenix Media, who published his first two e-book novels, *The Pandora Sequence* and *Venus AI*, both of which were launched at the 2013 San Diego Comic-Con.

Alex's most recent works are ongoing epic novel sagas which include *The Saga of The Urban Sorcerers*, *Amazon Seven*, *Dark Streets*, *The Chronicles of The Terraguard*, and *The Pandorans*.

He publishes via his own independent imprint, Galexy Tales.

www.GalexyTales.com

(OR SEARCH "GALEXY TALES"
AT AMAZON!)

'It's Amy… *not Amy!*

Amy… not Amy?'